it's
not
never

Louise Gregory

n.g.k

FIRST EDITION

www.ngkmedia.com

LG - To my daughters, the sky's the limit.

n.g.k. – To my family.

Acknowledgements

L.G.- Thank you to the people who read this book before it was fully formed, and to friends who have cheered me on from the side lines or from Instagram and Twitter.

Thanks to our lovely editor Holly McCulloch. The people have spoken. It was an ice cream, not a lolly.

I'm grateful to Kavisha Mandalia who kindly advised me on medical procedures.

Thank you to Commander Chris Hadfield, a long-time hero of mine, for kindly granting permission to use his quote.

Thanks to my mum, another formidable Elizabeth, for her packages of chocolate and postcards, and my dad, Greg, for many nights of virtual drinks, and to both my parents, and James and Sophie, for unswerving and unconditional support.

To my amazing writing partner, N. Genuinely, this book wouldn't have happened without him. He has taught me so much about storytelling, publishing, and about working in a partnership. Thanks buddy, can't wait for the next one.

Finally, huge thanks to my husband and children, who have supported me with patience and interest; to my lovely, funny, stubborn girls, who had opinions on everything as I was writing; and to F, who gave me all the time I needed as he always does when I have a new scheme, and who this time built me a cabin to write in. Thank you, my gorgeous family.

Glossary of Terms

Aneris - Sister to the Aries capsule. Multi-functional, this small capsule takes the crew of the Harmonia into space to become part of the Harmonia, down to Mars from orbit, and back to Earth. In between is docked to the Harmonia and becomes the bridge of the craft.

Aries - Sister capsule to Aneris, different only in it doesn't land on Mars. It docks with and becomes part of Concordia.

Bridge - The control area of the spacecraft.

CAPCOM - Capsule Communicator. The one person entrusted with being the single director communicator with space crews.

Concordia - Sister spacecraft to the Harmonia. The Concordia is the first spacecraft to launch to Mars and orbit around it.

EVA - Extra Vehicular Activity, a spacewalk. Astronauts on the walk may be referred to collectively as EVA, or individually as EVA1, EVA2 while outside.

Harmonia - Sister spacecraft to the Concordia. The Harmonia is taking the crew to land on Mars

NARESA - North American, Russian, and European Space Agency. A multi-national agency, Headquartered in Cologne, Germany, dedicated to the mission to Mars.

NARESA does not replace NASA or the other National Space Agency but works alongside them.

Pegasus - The rocket that takes the Aries and Aneris capsules into orbit.

SAMSON - Semi-autonomous Mars Surface Navigator, the Mars rover used by the astronauts to travel on Mars.

*"To some this may look like a sunset.
But it's a new dawn."*
– Commander Chris Hadfield

Chapter One
Countdown to first Mars walk: 9 years.

Jessica

The only sounds that broke the still morning air were the beat of her trainers hitting the path and the birds twittering their dawn chorus from the trees. Jessica barely noticed her surroundings, she fixed her eyes on the path ahead, her arms pumping, her breathing heavy. She tilted her wrist to check her sports watch, frowned, and sped up. Her lungs burned, her legs ached, but still, she didn't stop running.

The path steepened into a hill. Sweat dripped into her eyes, blurring her vision, but she pressed on, willing her legs to take her just a bit further. She wouldn't let herself stop. Her feet pounded rhythmically on the ground. The steep path peaked and plateaued; only then did she slow down to a walk. She checked her watch again and clicked to stop recording her progress, allowing herself a slight smile of satisfaction. She paced the ground, wiping the sweat from her face on her sleeve, then paused, breathing in big lungfuls of air, clear and crisp this high above the city of Cologne, away from the traffic.

Now that she'd reached the top of the hill, Jessica could see across the entire city, the Rhine snaking through the landscape, pale blue in the early morning light. When the sun was fully up and the sky was clear it would sparkle green and turquoise. The streets of the Cologne would be quiet today. It was Sunday, the day of ruhezeit in Germany; quiet time. There would be no sound of lawnmowers or hedge trimmers, no loud gatherings outside in the spring weather. Most of the shops were closed, but the parks would fill with young families and the cafes with couples drinking coffee and eating cake.

Jessica had left a sleepy university city in the north of England. Cologne was a vast metropolis with enormous buildings sprawling below her. But already she loved Germany and the

Germans. She liked their efficiency and fondness for the rules. They were her sort of people, though with her dark brown hair and olive skin, she shared none of the classic Germanic physical traits.

Still pacing on the brow of the hill, Jessica turned to look towards the south. There it was, on the outskirts of the city, a grey steel and glass building stood surrounded by flags of different nations, flanked by smaller satellite buildings. It was the European Headquarters of the North American Russian and European Space Agency, NARESA. The nations had joined together, in a rare show of unity, for a long-term collaboration which aimed to put humans on Mars. In one week, she would be walking through the glass front doors as a trainee astronaut.

A cool shiver of anticipation went through her body. It had taken ten years of hard work, of tenacious studying and determination to make it here, and still, this was only the beginning of the next chapter. Before her stretched another two years of training, and yet more studying, and even then, she might never get her space wings. The chances of her travelling to Mars were even smaller. She would do everything in her power to be the best candidate. 'Go and wake up your luck' her grandmother used to say to her in Persian. 'You get what you work for in life, Jessie *Joon*, you can only be the best if you do the best.'

For now, that meant keeping her body in shape, strong and fit, running four times a week, no matter the weather. As time progressed the job would require more sacrifices; this was all or nothing.

Jessica took one last look at the stark, utilitarian NARESA building before breaking into a run again, nodding at another runner who passed her. She had only been in this city for a few days, and her German was still conversational at best, but she already felt more at home here than she had anywhere in a long time. The long hours spent in her lab back at the university had left little time for a social life. Any free time had been spent collecting skills she thought would help her get to here. With no family in the UK but her grandmother, she had been successful but lonely. *Stop dwelling on the past*, she admonished herself.

Focus. Mars is the goal now. Gritting her teeth, she sped up again, trying to ignore the complaints from her muscles.

She only stopped running when she made it back to her new neighbourhood. Jessica permitted herself a pit stop in an early-opening café where she ordered a drink and a cake before taking a seat outside in the morning sun. She smiled warmly at the waitress as she came out with a coffee, a tall glass of water, and a pastry, delicately sprinkled with icing sugar.

'*Danke schön.*'

The sweet warm pastry with its buttery layers melted in her mouth. Jessica had few vices in life, but she would do anything for something sweet, even if that meant running twenty kilometres on a Sunday morning. She watched the few early risers come and go from her table on the street, mostly runners, young people off to their jobs in coffee shops, and a harassed looking dad frantically pushing a crying baby in a pram. A young couple walked by, arms entwined, laughing at a private joke. The pang of loneliness returned.

Apart from the odd friend, she hadn't left anyone special back in her old city. There hadn't been anyone special for a long time. *You're about to embark on your dream, you don't need anyone or anything else*, she thought to herself. *Well, apart from strudel,* she polished off the final crumbs, *you always need strudel.* She left a few Euro notes on the table, enough for a decent tip, she remembered what it was like to be working for minimum wage, and set off back to her new apartment to unpack the last of her boxes.

Her new life was about to begin and she couldn't wait to start.

Chapter Two

Countdown to first Mars walk: 9 years.

John

The taxi pulled up outside a nondescript block of flats. John gazed up at the identical windows with identical balconies, new but familiar. They could have been in any city.

The driver prattled away incomprehensibly.

'Er...' John offered up his open palms in the universally Western gesture of 'I don't have a clue,' cursing himself not only for not attempting to learn more German before his move but also for seemingly picking the only taxi driver in Cologne who didn't speak English.

The driver pointed at the meter and John counted out an extortionate number of Euro notes.

'*Danke schön.*' He knew enough to be polite, he wasn't that bad a traveller. Though there was little attempt at pronunciation, he hoped the driver would appreciate the effort.

The small apartment had blank white walls and a few functional pieces of furniture. There was a comforting familiarity to the impermanence of the place. He had long ago learned not to become attached to things. The kitchen had everything he needed for now, but as he went into the bedroom he realised that in his quest for minimalism he hadn't thought about bringing bedding. That was ok, it would give him a reason to go out and check out the city and pick up some essential supplies. And some food. Definitely some food.

He lay down on the bare mattress, trying not to think about the many people who had slept on it before, though the apartment was spotlessly clean. The thing about having moved around a lot your whole life was that people thought you got exceedingly good at it, well-practised. That it got easier each time, instead of harder, as the prospect of setting up another new life dawned on you. The time you would have to spend investing in relationships that you knew were short term. The exhaustion of learning the layout of a new place, new customs, new food, and sometimes a new language. And this time a new career.

He had left the States, not home, but the closest thing he could call that. In three days, he would be starting as a rookie astronaut on the NARESA training programme. His whole life had been leading up to this moment. Space travel was in his blood. He hadn't chosen it as a career, spaceflight had chosen his family. The path had seemed inevitable. Especially after - no he didn't want to think about that.

Whatever the reason, it seemed like doors had opened for him, but he was never quite sure who was holding the key. Was it his dad? Even though he had died before seeing his son join the multinational agency he had helped to create. Or perhaps it was his grandmother, famous and formidable?

He was good at what he did, he knew that. There were satellites thousands of miles above that contained parts he'd worked on, bolts he'd tightened with his own hands. But he wanted to be up there too. Some force that even his engineer's brain couldn't explain was drawing him into the vacuum of space. There was an inevitability about it for him. He couldn't imagine it not happening. At the same time, there was a quiet voice, only audible when he stopped to listen, that whispered, 'It wasn't meant to be you. Perhaps you're not good enough'. The rest of the trainees would be among the brightest and best in their fields, selected for their intellect, their skills, their experience, and most importantly their attitudes and behaviours. He knew he possessed the necessary qualifications, but had he been chosen because he fit the bill, or because of who his family were?

The question made him feel acutely aware of his idleness, reminding him why he never usually stopped, was never usually still or quiet. Soon his sparse apartment would be full of projects, pieces of machinery in various states of construction – or destruction.

He got up and opened his suitcase, riffled through the clothes and found a large, worn leather rolled pouch. It was heavy. It had taken him well over the weight limit for the flight, but he hadn't cared. He unrolled the tan leather. Nestled in the suede interior were a dozen or so tools. He picked one out: a cast-iron wrench, mottled with age. His grandfather had given it to him when he was fifteen and starting to mess around with old motorbikes. It had been handmade here in Germany over fifty years ago.

It was cool and familiar in his hand. When he held it, he could solve any problem. Engineering required logic and patience. There were universal rules, things were predictable. Things only went wrong when people got involved.

He replaced the wrench and put the tool pouch on the chest of drawers. The clothes would remain in their case for weeks, mundane domestic activities always low on his priority list. In the quiet of the apartment, the voice in his head returned 'Do you think you are good enough?' He didn't know the answer and wasn't sure if he wanted to know. His only option to quiet it down was to go out into the strange new city and get the things he needed to sleep tonight. Perhaps he would stop somewhere for a drink. Wherever he had lived in the world, he'd always been sure to learn how to say 'A beer, please' in the local language, and he had learned to be content with his own company, in fact, that's the way he liked it.

Chapter Three
Countdown to first Mars walk: 9 years.

Jessica

Jessica walked quickly, though she wasn't late, laying a hand on her stomach to quell the butterflies dancing around. She took the steps to the third floor, trying to keep her body language easy and relaxed, wanting to reassure herself that easy and relaxed was how she felt. She was not fooled.

She turned left along a corridor that could have been in any government building, with its tiled floor and off-white walls. Only the photos of rocket launches, spacecraft, and familiar-faced astronauts hung at intervals, gave a clue to what went on in the inner workings of the building. Even though she had never been here before, she knew exactly where she was going; she'd studied the floor plan from the orientation pack until she had the entire building, every twist and turn, memorised. Mostly to eliminate any worry about being late because of getting lost in the winding hallways of an unfamiliar place, but also because she liked to have the answers to questions, and she had already been asked twice by two different people where the cafeteria was.

Level One. East Wing.

And now, there was her destination: room 2810.

She stood in the doorway, getting the measure of this new situation before launching herself into it. Her first encounters always ended up being a slow assessment of people, allowing her to file them under various categories, perfected over years of quiet observation. Her quick mind, and ability to understand something with scant information, so often an asset in the tidy world of science, sometimes failed her in the messy world of human dynamics. Perhaps that was why she had chosen to study neuroscience. What better way to understand people than to know how their brain worked?

A dozen or so people were milling around the room or sat at lecture theatre style desks. They were all wearing identical light blue jumpsuits. Jessica was wearing the exact same outfit and, even though light blue wasn't really her colour, she liked the idea of a uniform. She could just pull on one of the standard issue suits every morning, rather than having to think of a fitting outfit to wear, it was one less thing to waste time on. The efficiency of it was gratifying.

She could hear several different languages being spoken by the dozen or so new recruits. Though English was the universal language of NARESA, they would be given intensive courses in Russian to aid communication.

Settling in her seat, she pulled out a notebook and a pencil case. They all had tablets uploaded with their course material, but Jessica still liked to write most of her notes by hand, she found she remembered things better that way. She loved a fresh notebook, and any excuse to buy new pens. The blue and white stripes of the same pens she had used since university were comforting in their uniformity, spilling out indigo ink onto the page, as she wrote the date in the corner and underlined it.

'Do you have a pen I could borrow?'

The voice was familiar; the half British accent tinged with an American twang. She was transported back to a lecture theatre with graffitied desks, a musty odour, and an unlikely seatmate. She turned around, unable to suppress a smile at the familiar face, the warm hazel eyes and sandy brown hair.

'John Eden, did you really start your first day of astronaut school without a pen?'

'Of course I didn't,' he held up a silver pen from his desk behind her. 'Look, it's a fancy one. It even writes in zero gravity. Think that might be useful one day?' He raised an eyebrow at her.

She hadn't seen him since her second year of university. He had disappeared suddenly halfway through the semester. A family bereavement she had heard.

'I didn't know you'd be here,' she said, still reeling from the shock of seeing her former classmate.

'I knew you would be,' he said sincerely.

She smiled at him, feeling suddenly as if a warm blanket had been placed around her shoulders. The glimmer of familiarity was welcome in a place that was entirely new. New city, new country, new career.

'Good morning everyone. Welcome to your first day of Basic Astronaut Training.'

Everyone immediately settled down as their instructor, a short, bald headed military-looking man with a German accent, started the class.

She cast another look back at John, who winked at her, and the tingle of excitement that she always felt at the start of a new adventure ran through her. She was going to be an astronaut.

***

There was a clank of beer bottles as the twelve trainees toasted the end of their first week of astronaut training. They were in a dimly lit bar on the outskirts of Cologne near campus. It was a dive of a joint, with sticky tables, greasy food, and the cheapest beer in the area. Modern Europop played in the background.

Jessica gazed around at the group, picking absently at a fry from one of the bowls that littered the table. Though diverse in nationality and discipline, each person was at the top of their respective profession, with a shared sense of drive and determination. People had broken off into smaller conversations. A week of intensive training had begun to forge friendships, but it would be a while before they all had the measure of each other. Jessica sensed they had all been on their best behaviour all week.

'You're not about to bail on us already are you?' asked May Wu, a petite Chinese-American woman, clearly noticing her reflective silence.

'No, of course not,' though even as she said it she had to stifle a yawn. 'Sorry!' she laughed 'But it's been a long week, don't you think?'

May shrugged her tiny shoulders, 'I did two years in a Brooklyn ER, I'm used to getting about four hours sleep.' In the short time since she had known her, Jessica had immediately warmed to the straight-talking May. She was dressed in a black

Star Wars t-shirt, black leggings, and chunky black boots. It was odd seeing all the group in their own clothes instead of the regulation flight suits they had worn for training all week. Jessica's taste in clothes hadn't changed much since University. She wore black trousers and a patterned shirt; smart but unfussy.

'Come to the bar with me,' May stood up, 'I'll buy you another beer.'

They stood waiting at the bar while the barman served another customer. He was tall, pale and skinny, with shoulder-length dyed black hair and several piercings. May eyed him with a grin.

'What are you smiling at?' Jessica asked.

'He's cute,' May whispered.

As the barman served them another two bottles of German beer, May beckoned to him and whispered something in his ear. Jessica waited patiently, sipping her drink as the two of them laughed together.

'May!' Jessica exclaimed as they walked back to the table 'You're terrible.'

'What? Nothing wrong with making friends.'

'The half a dozen men over there not enough for you?'

May made a dismissive noise, as they reclaimed their seats. May next to Jessica and Jessica opposite John, who was laughing at something with two of the other male trainees.

'That over-achieving all-American Joe schtick gets a bit boring after a while.' May muttered to Jessica. 'Besides, this lot are out of bounds, even if I wanted to date someone who enjoyed debating the relative merits of liquid versus solid fuel propulsion. Which I don't.'

'Out of bounds?'

'Yeah, you know we can't date another potential crew member. Causes all kinds of problematic group dynamics.'

'Oh, yes of course. I know it would be a terrible idea, I just hadn't realised it was an explicit rule.'

'What hadn't you realised?' Mike Sanders was listening to their conversation. He was an African American former Navy test pilot.

'I was just saying to Jessica how it's completely verboten for potential crew members to date.'

'Yeah, I heard a couple of the last intake got thrown off the programme because they refused to separate,' said Tom Wilson, a Canadian physicist. He had wavy black hair that Jessica noted had a habit of falling forward into his blue eyes, making him blink and gently brush at it with his long fingers.

'I can't imagine doing all that work, spending all those years training, getting so close to being an astronaut then giving it all up for another person.' Jessica shook her head. 'Besides, who even has the time?' She grinned and took a swig of her beer.

This past week had been so intense that Jessica had been too exhausted to do more than go back and crash at her apartment. She had no idea how someone could do this job and start a relationship at the same time.

'Ah, all work and no play, Jessica...' John said. She just smiled at him. They'd had very little time to catch up this week. Everyone had been tired and he had kept his distance.

'We were telling our stories before you sat down.' Tom said, 'Why did you want to become an astronaut?'

Jessica laughed 'What's this, the assessment centre all over again?'

'No,' he said with a smile, 'Just curious. John here tells us it's because he likes the flight suits. Women can't resist them apparently.' He slapped him genially on the back.

Jessica looked at John carefully. She knew there was more to his story than that. The space programme was in John's DNA, but he rarely told people about his family connections. She wondered how long he was planning on keeping it quiet.

'And Mike here was headhunted from the Navy.' Tom continued.

'You're a test pilot, aren't you?' Jessica asked.

'Yep, I've been flying planes since I was seventeen.' Mike leaned back in his chair. From what Jessica had seen of him so far, he was talented, but with a self-belief that was bordering on arrogance.

'Amazing.' She said, 'I had flying lessons a few years ago, being a test pilot is on another level. What about you May?'

May leaned back in her chair. 'I watched a lot of space movies and played space video games when I was a kid,' she said. 'I fell in love with it then. But my parents wanted me to be a doctor, so that's what I did. I never stopped hoping though. My dad's still pretty mad I gave that up to come here.' She laughed lightly but her smile didn't quite reach her eyes.

There was a small sympathetic pain in Jessica's chest at May's words. Her own grandmother could not be more proud of her. Every graduation photo was framed on her walls, every piece of school art work carefully stored away. The team photo they were due to have taken next week would be released to the press and the cuttings would go into a file her grandmother kept.

'What about you, Jessica?' May asked, brightening again.

'It wasn't something I was into as a kid. I didn't know what I wanted to be really, I wanted to try everything. But then I fell in love with space at university.'

'Where you met John?' May asked. The group had noticed their familiarity.

John turned to her, his face impassive but his eyes looking deep into hers. A jolt ran through her body. *Just nostalgia*, she thought, her mind wandering back to the night when everything changed for her.

Chapter Four
Six Years Earlier

Jessica

The lecture theatre buzzed with the chatter of the hundred or so students waiting for class to start. Jessica noticed that most students sat in the same seats for all their classes. The mature students sat in the front rows. The ones who had yet to shake off their too-cool-for-school demeanour sat in the back rows. Glassy eyed and hungover, they might as well have not been there. Jessica sat in a row halfway down the room, a couple of seats in from the edge.

She took out her notebooks and pencil case, filled with multiple versions of her favourite pen, blue and white striped, filled with deep indigo ink.

A middle-aged man took to the stage and cleared his throat in front of the microphones. He was exactly how an astronomy professor should look; tall, wiry, with tufty grey hair and wire-rimmed glasses. The hum of noise ceased abruptly.

'Welcome to AST102: Planetary Science,' the lecturer began. 'If you are here to learn about star signs, little green men, or other little green things - you'd be surprised how many people misread planets for plants - you will be sorely disappointed and might want to leave now.'

The students laughed.

'I'm Professor Richard Godfrey, but you may call me "Professor G", or just God for short.' More laughter. 'Now, let me tell you what delights I'm going to introduce you to in this module...'

Ten minutes into the talk on the material structure of the planet Mercury, the lecture theatre door creaked open. Almost everyone's head automatically turned to see who the latecomer was. He was a tall, slim, brown haired man, in the classic student uniform of jeans and a hoodie.

'Come in, come in,' the Professor welcomed him warmly, with no hint of a reprimand. The latecomer grinned, gave a quick scan of the room and selected the seat next to Jessica. She shifted as he spread himself out, and tried to concentrate on the lecture. He pulled out an A4 notebook with the name John Eden scrawled on the front, then continued to rummage around in his bag. After a minute or so of watching him search fruitlessly, she slipped a pen out of her pencil case and put it in front of him.

With a flash of a smile he whispered 'Thank you.' But after writing the date at the top of a page in his notebook he didn't pick up the pen again for the rest of the lecture.

Jessica tried to concentrate on what the Professor was saying, but was distracted by the movement of her seat mate. When his knee bumped into hers as he shifted in his seat she ignored it. It happened again. The third time he brushed against her she turned and raised her eyebrows at him. He really was rather annoying. He mouthed 'Sorry' at her, and she turned back to focus on the lecture.

As she was noting down the exospheric properties of Mercury, there was a mild vibration in the wooden desk that ran the width of the hall. She glanced down to see John Eden's leg jiggling, shaking the row of chairs and desks. Without thinking about it, she put her hand on his knee to hold it still. He stopped, gave her an apologetic grin, and the last ten minutes passed in relative peace.

There was a flurry of movement when the lecture came to a close, and most of the students hurried to leave to another class, or more likely to the local coffee shop, but John Eden turned to her.

'Sorry, didn't mean to get on your nerves,' he said, not looking apologetic at all, 'I'm John,' he offered his hand. He had an accent that she could only describe as half American, half British.

'Jessica,' she took his hand and smiled despite her annoyance. There was an easy charm in his manner, his hazel eyes danced impishly. 'Nice pen.' He handed it back to her.

'You keep it,' she said, 'for the next class. I've got plenty.' He laughed as she showed him the case full of identical pens.

'Thanks.' That smile again. She didn't have time to be distracted by it though, with a class starting in twenty minutes on the other side of the campus. Jessica stood impatiently waiting for him to move out of the way so she could leave the hall.

'I'll see you next time,' he said, slinging his bag over his shoulder and wandering out of the hall.

***

Three days later she sat in the same spot waiting for the next class to begin. There was no sign yet of her previous neighbour. She opened her notebook to a fresh page, but the page wasn't blank. Scribbled in the corner was a message: 'Thanks for the pen, J'. Jessica smiled to herself. When on earth had her fidgety seatmate had time to write that without her noticing?

Just as the Professor was shutting the door to start the lecture, John Eden darted in, muttering an apology. He caught her eye and slid into the seat next to her again. 'If I promise to keep still can I sit here?' His warm breath tickled her ear as he spoke quietly into it.

'Yes, but I've brought a straitjacket today in case you don't,' she whispered back.

He chuckled, pulling out his notebook and the pen she had given him. She raised her eyebrows, surprised to see he still had in his possession. 'I'm going to treasure it forever,' he said, eyes twinkling.

'And are you going to actually write some lecture notes with it, or just leave messages in my notebook?'

He just responded with a wink.

True to his word he remained still for almost all the lecture, and even took a few notes, but she was conscious of his presence the whole time, his knee occasionally brushing hers. She focused as hard as she could on studying the pictures of Venus displayed on the screen in front of her. As they packed their things away at the end of the class, John turned to face her 'So are you enjoying this class so far?'

'Yes, it's not my usual subject, but it's interesting. What do you think of it?'

'I think... I think that you won't learn about this sort of stuff in a dusty lecture hall.'

'What do you mean? I've learned loads today. Look at all these notes.' She brandished her notebook.

'That's just facts and figures. It's not very inspiring, is it?' He gathered up his bag and moved aside for her to get out of the row of seats.

'Inspiring? What are we supposed to be inspired to do?' Jessica asked as they left the lecture hall.

'Anything. You think that Holst guy composed The Planets after listening to a lecture on them?'

'Holst wrote The Planets after reading a book about astrology.'

He stopped in his tracks and turned to her in surprise. 'Really?' his eyebrows raised almost comically 'That's some very random trivia there. I bet you're great in a pub quiz'.

He kept looking sideways at her as they carried on walking, 'Anyway, there's stuff you never get from a crusty old Professor. Let me show you the real deal.'

'What do you mean?'

'What are you doing tonight?'

'Nothing, I've got an essay to write –'

'Meet me later then,' he started to walk off in the opposite direction to where she was going, 'Ten o'clock, outside the main library.'

'Wait, what? What do you mean?'

'Just meet me later. Trust me.' He called the last words over his shoulder and walked off before she could protest.

Ridiculous, she thought. *I'm not going to meet a virtual stranger late at night, without any explanation.*

***

It was the first really cold night of the autumn. Jessica hurried towards the library building, red and yellow leaves swirling on the ground around her. She was early as usual, and she expected John to be late, just as he had been to class. That's if he even turned up at all. Why had she agreed to this? Although she hadn't actually agreed, she had just been ordered. Would he even turn up, or was it all some joke? What had even compelled her to come? This guy could be a serial killer. But somehow there was an irresistible charm about him. *Well, of course there is,* she told herself, *that's probably what attracts people to serial killers too.* Wait, was that someone whistling? She turned a corner and there he was, shifting from one foot to the other in what she was starting to realise was characteristic restlessness.

He was wearing a thin jacket open over a brown jumper. He didn't look cold. Jessica had already switched to a proper coat and even a scarf.

'So where are we going then?' she said, skipping any pleasantries.

'Yes, it is a wonderful evening, delighted you could join me.'

Jessica just rolled her eyes.

'Follow me,' he said, 'and you'll see where we're going.'

They walked in silence for a few minutes. It should have felt awkward but somehow it didn't. They walked companionably until Jessica's curiosity got the better of her.

'So, what are you studying, obviously apart from Planetary Science?' she asked.

'Aerospace Engineering.'

'Wow, so you're an actual rocket scientist?' she said, genuinely impressed.

'I'd like to tell you we don't call ourselves that. But...' He grinned. 'What about you?'

'Neuroscience.'

'Learning to read minds?'

'Not quite, but I could cut your brain open and label all the parts and what they do.'

'Maybe later,' he grinned at her again. 'Come on, we're nearly there.'

His hand slipped into hers and pulled her along. It was warm and strong. They sped up and passed the increasingly elegant buildings of the old part of the city, heading up a hill.

'This way,' he said, and turned left onto another road.

They stopped in front of a large redbrick Victorian building. It was surrounded by black iron railings, and dozens of tall, ornate windows. Built to the right of the building was a wide circular tower, topped by a weathered green copper dome. A modern sign in the University colours read 'Eden Observatory'.

'I didn't even know this was here,' Jessica said.

'Well, sometimes you have to get out of the lecture hall and into the real world.' He headed towards the entrance before she had a chance to reply. There was a high security, modern glass door that appeared out of place in its old brickwork surrounding. Inside a uniformed guard sat behind a desk.

'Are we allowed to be here?' She sensed that John didn't have the same regard that she did for rules.

'It's fine. They know me here.' He pushed open the door, gave a thumbs up to the security guard, who just waved in return, and led the way up a set of old stone steps that curled around the centre of the tower.

At the top of the stairs was a nondescript door that creaked as John opened it. Jessica had never been in an observatory before and didn't know what to expect, but it wasn't what she saw. There were no banks of computers with flashing lights, spewing out data. In fact, the only nod to modernity was the long narrow telescope peeping out of a hole in the dome. The rest of the room looked more like the inner workings of a ship, large exposed metal struts creating the dome. A metal gangway ran around the circumference of the tower, and everything was slightly damp and tinged with rust. The telescope was clearly far more well cared for. It was sleek and modern. Jessica stared through the gap in the dome to the black night, while John fiddled with the telescope. It was a clear night, and already she could see stars twinkling against the dark velvet sky.

'Are you ready?' He beckoned her over.

'Yes, but I'm not sure how impressed you think I'm going to be. We've all seen the Hubble photos. I know what planets look like.'

He just smiled enigmatically and directed her to the eyepiece. 'Do you need a step?' he indicated a set of spindly metal steps, mounted on castors. The telescope was mounted on a tall pedestal.

'No, I'll be ok, thank you,' Jessica said curtly, drawing herself up to her full five foot four inches of height and moving to the telescope. She pressed one eye against the eyepiece and squeezed the other shut. It took her a few seconds to focus. At first, all she could see was black, then in the top corner she saw it, slightly more blurred than if she was looking at it in a book, but clearly and unmistakably 'Saturn!' she said, looking back at John.

She turned back quickly and looked again. This was nothing like looking at the photos in a book or on a screen. The image was hazier than the textbook images, but she was seeing this with her own eyes, and it was just like Saturn should be; tilted at a slight angle, showing off its rings to full effect. She felt the smallness of her height as she tried to imagine the magnitude of the distant planet. Her skin prickled with excitement.

'Well?' John's voice drifted in from behind her.

'It's so surreal.' She couldn't take her eye away from the view finder.

'Ready for the next one?' he said, tapping coordinates into the digital positioner.

'Ok.' She tore herself away and watched as he typed in more figures.

'This one's my favourite.' He said.

She peered through the telescope again. A dark orange orb, about an inch in diameter, filled the view. 'Mars?' she whispered softly.

'Yep. The red planet. Looks a bit like Venus, but if you look closely you can see the ice caps on Mars. They look slightly blue. Astronomers in the nineteenth century thought Mars was probably covered in red vegetation, red trees, red fields of grass, they thought it was a red Earth... But it's mostly just rusty rocks and dust.'

His words echoed around the room behind her, but she was focused on the view in front of her. It wasn't as clear as the pictures she'd seen, but it was somehow more real.

'It's like something you see in a book but I'm seeing it in real life right now.' She couldn't hide the excitement in her voice. She felt that familiar feeling of pleasure running through her at discovering something new.

'Yes, well, you're seeing it about fourteen minutes ago. If you were looking at a star, it might be dozens of light years away. It might even have died in the time it's taken for you to see it.'

'It's so beautiful. Imagine being on a planet that far away. I wonder what Earth would look like if we were looking at it from a telescope on Mars?' Jessica turned to look at John.

'Well, it would be a bit clearer, because Mars has a much thinner atmosphere. But the Earth would appear in phases like the moon, depending on where it was in relation to the sun.' He stood tall and upright. He had lost the languidness of the lecture theatre. He was engaged and eager to share.

'Isn't it amazing that we can see something so far away with just a few bits of glass?'

'I can't believe you've never used a telescope before. Why did you pick an astronomy module?'

Jessica shrugged, one hand still resting on the telescope. 'Just curious really. My degree topic is so narrow, I don't want to miss out on other things. I want to know everything about everything.'

'Well I think understanding our universe is as close as you'll get to knowing everything.'

He tapped another coordinate into the machine, peered into the telescope and said, 'Take a look.'

The viewfinder had exploded into a riot of colour and light, an orange hue, speckled with flashes of white and blue light. It was as though someone had pierced a hole the black sky and glowing embers of stars and stardust had spiralled out. She let out a gentle gasp.

'It's so beautiful. What is it?'

'That is M31, the Andromeda galaxy. The nearest major galaxy to our own.'

'Andromeda galaxy,' Jessica repeated in a reverent whisper. How could something so beautiful be real?

'The word galaxy actually means milky. Our galaxy is called the Milky Way, because of the bright whiteness, and it was the first one we could see. But now we know there are, like, two trillion galaxies in the universe.' Jessica noted the sense of pride in his voice, like a kid showing off his work. She had an inexplicable feeling that he was trying to impress her. She tried to suppress a smile.

'Sorry,' he looked sheepish as she turned to face him. 'I'm boring you, aren't I?'

She shook her head, 'You're really not.' And he wasn't. Far from being awkward, the last hour had felt comfortable and natural, as if they had known each other for much longer than two lectures. 'This was a brilliant idea, I love hearing all about it. And seeing it is on another level.'

She studied him thoughtfully. 'You know a lot about this stuff for an engineer.'

He shrugged. 'It's sort of a family hobby. My dad basically built his own observatory in the garden. And my grandparents were really into this stuff.'

'That sounds cool.'

'I'm not sure if 'cool' is really the word for it,' he replied with a wry smile. 'What about you? Didn't your parents make you do any nerdy things?'

'Nah.' Now it was her turn to shrug. 'My dad wasn't around and my mum worked all the time till she died when I was sixteen.' Her voice remained steady, but the familiar weight descended on her chest, even though it had been nearly four years. 'My grandma looked after me, and I mostly studied and learned how to cook Persian food. She came over from Iran in the seventies.'

'Well, that's a lot less nerdy and far more practical than looking at the night sky,' he said gently.

'Show me Mars again,' Jessica said urgently. They would have to leave soon and she wanted to soak up as much as she could. There was something compelling about the planet. It was their closest neighbour; so near yet so far. Her mind dizzied thinking about the vastness of the universe. There was something bigger out there than them. The sensation was new to her. She studied the human brain. People had always been at the centre of her universe. She'd thought that nothing could be as important as human interaction. Perhaps there was something more. John had been right. Looking at pictures in a lecture theatre would never have made her feel like this.

She turned back to the telescope, drinking in the view, imprinting the image of the planet in her mind. An orange mass in the indigo sky. 'How far away is it?' she asked.

'Average of about 140 million miles. It depends on the time of year.'

She turned away from the telescope and chuckled at him. 'You're such a nerd.'

'Takes one to know one. Anyway, you'll know all about this after studying Mars next week.'

She returned to the telescope, unable to take her eyes off it for long. 'It looks so near, like you could just fly there.'

'You could.' John's voice was suddenly serious. She looked up at him. 'And one day we will.' In that instant the circular room seemed infinitely smaller.

'It'll take nearly a year to get there though.' he continued.

'That's not such a long time in the grand scheme of things.' Jessica said quietly. The grand scheme of things suddenly seemed a lot grander.

She glanced at her watch. 'It's getting late. Should we be going soon?' She didn't want to, but she didn't want John to get bored with her. He was so engaging and he must think her so serious. She wanted to come back here to see more of what was out there.

'Yeah, better had I suppose.' He reached for the power button on the telescope.

Wait,' she said loudly, 'one last look...' She tried to commit the view to memory. The orange glow, the blue tinge of the ice caps. The sense of the unexplored land that felt almost within travelling distance.

John said a warm goodbye to the security guard on the way out. How many other women had he brought here to show off his telescope skills? They passed the sign at the entrance, and Jessica read it again. Eden Observatory.

'Wait,' she said again, stopping in her tracks and staring at John. 'Eden. John Eden. That's your name. Is... do you... Is that some relation?'

John stopped too and turned around to face her. He didn't say anything for a moment and Jessica worried that she had said something wrong. His eyes seemed to search her face.

'Yes,' he seemed to hesitate. 'My family... my grandmother. She was a Shuttle astronaut, Elizabeth Eden. My grandfather worked at NASA too. And my dad... He works for NARESA now. My grandmother donated the money for the telescope a few years ago. She studied and taught here at this Uni before she left for the States to join NASA.'

'Oh.' She studied his face for signs of familiarity. She had learned about Elizabeth Eden in school, the first British astronaut to go into space and the first female Shuttle Commander. It had been well before she was born, but there had been controversy at the time because she was leaving two teenage boys, a situation that had clearly not been as important for all the men that had left children behind on Earth. It wasn't that space was a family hobby, his family was a space travel dynasty. She now realised why the security guard had waved them through without question; John practically owned the place.

'Growing up must have been pretty exciting for you,' she said as they started walking back down the hill.

He shrugged, 'We moved around a lot. My dad had various positions in NASA, and we followed him until he got the NARESA job and we came back to Europe. We lived in various places, but I wanted to come to England to study.' He was silent for a minute as if deciding whether to continue. 'It's hard always being the new kid, never quite fitting in.' In that moment he was like a child. He'd lost the self-assuredness she'd seen in the observatory talking about space, and now looked a little lost. 'But, you know there were some benefits to being an international man of mystery.' He winked at her, and the moment of vulnerability was gone. Jessica just rolled her eyes.

He insisted on walking her home, against her strong protestations. He hovered at the bottom of the steps to her flat as she turned to go inside.

'Don't worry, I'm not waiting for an invitation inside.' He held his hands up. 'I just want to wait till I know you're in safely.'

Jessica rolled her eyes at him again, but there was something quite reassuring about it.

'You want to come and check inside for intruders too?' Her tone made it clear that there was only one acceptable answer.

'Nope, you're on your own once you're over the threshold. I will have discharged my duty.'

'Thank you for tonight.' She looked at him from the top of the steps. She felt relaxed and warm despite the cool night. 'That was amazing.'

'Really.' The lost boy look flashed momentarily across his face once more. 'I didn't bore you?'

'Not for one minute,' she smiled. 'Thank you.'

'You're very welcome. Anytime. I mean it.' She sensed it was a genuine offer.

'I hope you're not right though,' she said over her shoulder as she unlocked her front door, not quite ready to let him leave.

'About what?'

'About not learning anything in a lecture theatre. It'll make for a very boring class this semester.'

'Don't worry,' he still hadn't turned to leave, 'I'll keep it interesting for you.' She believed he would.

She smiled, 'Night John.'

'Goodnight Jessica.'

She let herself into the flat. As she closed the door she peeked through the spy hole, true to his word he hung around for a minute before walking off along the road, resuming his whistling. He cast a quick glance back at her door before disappearing out of sight. Damn it. She liked him. That was inconvenient.

Chapter Five
Countdown to first Mars walk: Eight years

John

The cavernous cafeteria of NARESA HQ was noisy as hundreds of space programme workers stopped for lunch. Astronauts and trainees were conspicuous by their blue flight suits, though they made up a tiny proportion of the workforce. Around them scientists, engineers, administrators, and other people in myriad fields of work chatted away while eating their lunches. Over a year into the programme and the place felt like a second home.

'I love wiener schnitzel Tuesday.' Jessica announced putting her tray down at a table where John, May, and an Italian geologist called Lucca Costa were already sitting. John moved his chair over so she could sit next to him and snickered at her.

'What?' She asked, laughing at his response. 'I do love it.'

Over the past year John and Jessica had fallen into an easy friendship. Seeing her in the classroom on that first day, he had been paradoxically surprised to see her, but also left with a sense that she would be there all along.

The long hours left little time for socialising, but to John's own surprise he enjoyed spending time with the group of friends he had made in the trainee programme. As a natural introvert, he liked to retreat to the solitude of his apartment at the end of the day, but he had learned the art of being good company.

May eyed Jessica's plate of food with distaste. 'Urgh, how can you eat that? More importantly, how can you eat that and still stay so slim?'

'I run fifty kilometres a week,' she replied through a mouthful of food.

'Well, maybe you should spend less time running and more time cooking real food.' Lucca interjected. John liked Lucca. They shared the same easy sense of humour, and there weren't many other people who would challenge Jessica like that.

'Hey, we don't all have lovely wives at home making us fresh pasta to bring into work.' Jessica shot back.

'How do you know I didn't make it myself?'

Jessica just raised her eyebrows.

'Ok, yes, Giovanna makes my pasta.' Lucca admitted.

'In between raising two gorgeous boys? Jeez, I'd marry her. Anyway, John's with me on this, aren't you?' She nudged him in the ribs.

'What? Marry Giovanna? Damn right I would.'

'No!' She elbowed him again as Lucca pretended to glare at him. 'You like wiener schnitzel too, don't you?'

'John would eat roadkill if you breaded it and fried it.' May said, rolling her eyes.

'You can mock,' John pointed his fork at May, 'But next desert expedition, we might actually have to eat roadkill.'

'How much roadkill do you think there'll be on Mars?' May countered.

'Hmm, you could be right. But the point is, you can't be fussy in space.' He waved his fork around again. 'There'll be no miso soup,' he pointed at May's flask, 'or fresh pasta,' he pointed at Lucca. 'Jessica and I will be ahead of the game with our immunity to junk food.'

Jessica slid her ultra slim NARESA issue tablet out of its case and propped it up at the table.

'Jessica,' May moaned, 'do you have to work through lunch? Put it away.'

'I'm just catching up on messages,' Jessica replied distractedly. Suddenly she let out a gentle, 'Oh.'

'What? Everything ok?' John looked up from his lunch.

Jessica slid the tablet over to him, and he read the message.

'27th September 1400 – Talk with Elizabeth Eden, first female Shuttle commander.'

'Oh,' was all John could say. Well, it had to happen sooner rather than later. He was grateful that it had been this long. Eighteen months without them all knowing. At least he assumed they didn't know, no one had mentioned anything. And he was sure Jessica wouldn't have told anyone, not without checking with him first.

'Looks like a good talk coming up,' Lucca was looking at his tablet now. 'Elizabeth Eden. She sounds pretty awesome. Hey, wait a minute...' John was almost amused watching Lucca process the information, seeing the light shine in his eyes as he made the connection. 'Eden? John, is she a relative of yours?'

'Yeah,' he said with a sigh. 'She's my grandmother.' If Lucca had figured it out it was only a matter of time before everyone else getting the same message made the connection.

'*Che bello*, John! Your *nonna* is an astronaut?' He looked at May and Jessica. 'Hey, why is no one else surprised?' He turned back to John. 'And why didn't you tell us?'

'Well, I've known for years.' Jessica said. 'But I didn't say anything to anyone,' she said earnestly to John.

'I know.' He put a hand on her arm gratefully.

'I guessed.' May said. 'And that means your dad...'

'Yeah, basically helped start this place.' John's voice was flat. He looked down at his lunch and pushed it away. He'd lost his appetite now. Why hadn't his grandmother warned him she was coming? He presumed she'd be flying out from England, where she had retired to a village near where she had grown up. It was typical of Elizabeth not to mention it. No doubt she would contact him the night before, imperiously demanding his presence at dinner.

'Why didn't you say anything?' May asked. 'Your grandmother is awesome; I'd be so proud.'

'I am proud of her,' he knew they wouldn't understand, having that following you around. They couldn't understand what it would be like telling colleagues that the Board of Directors meets in a room named after your dad. He needed some headspace. It was clear that not only would he have the challenge of everyone now knowing who his family were, but there would also be the added question of why he never told them. He pushed back his chair and picked up his bag.

'John, are you okay?' Jessica looked up at him, her eyes full of concern.

'Yeah, I'm fine.' He gave a brief smile. 'I've just got to do something before we go back for the afternoon. I'll see you in a little bit.' And he walked away without waiting for a reply.

***

'Oh my gosh, John, I love her.'

The day of his grandmother's visit had arrived and Jessica was hanging onto his arm excitedly. Several of the trainees were already chatting with his grandmother at the front of the lecture theatre, a ninety-minute talk clearly not having sated their appetite for conversation with a legend of their profession. John could see why Jessica liked her so much. They shared a no-nonsense attitude and an impatience; they were both highly driven. It was hard to find female icons as revered in the world of space exploration as much as the traditional males, even now, but Elizabeth Eden was the closest thing that came to one.

'Come on I'll introduce you.' He grabbed her hand and pulled her over to where his grandmother still stood at the front of the lecture theatre. The hundreds of seats had been filled with NARESA employees from astronauts to HR. They all wanted to hear what she had to say.

'Hello, John.' His grandmother greeted him as cordially as though she were greeting a neighbour on the street, not the grandson she hadn't seen for at least six months. She had flown in that morning and they were meeting for dinner that night. John hadn't had a choice in the matter. The crowd of people parted to let him through.

It was now common knowledge that Elizabeth was his grandmother. There had been curiosity, with people asking him what it was like to grow up so close to the space programme. He didn't tell them it was lonely. There had been no comments yet about the link to his family and being on the trainee programme. But it was only a matter of time before it would start.

'Hey, Grandma,' he leaned in and gave her a peck on the cheek, mainly just to annoy her with overfamiliarity in a professional context. 'This is Dr. Jessica Gabriel.'

'Dr. Gabriel.' Elizabeth Eden held out her hand to Jessica. 'I've heard a lot about you from my grandson of course. You're a neuroscientist?' She didn't pause for a response. 'Now I don't keep up with the latest neuroscience as I used to. Tell me, what is the biggest risk to the brain in long duration space flight?'

'Oh, please, it's Jessica...' John zoned out as Jessica launched into a description of changes in ventricular fluid and the parietal lobes. He hoped she hadn't noticed his grandmother's pointed mention of hearing a lot about her. Elizabeth was deliberate about everything she said; she must have known how that might be interpreted. Thankfully Jessica appeared too star-struck to notice the comment. It wasn't that he talked about her a lot, but she was so smart and engaging, he knew his grandmother would like her. He might not understand half the stuff Jessica was talking about sometimes, but he loved to listen to her. She was so passionate when she talked about something she loved, whether it was the brain, space, or simply food. They both wanted to understand how things worked, but for John it was machines, and for Jessica it was people.

The crowd of trainees finally dispersed, and only Jessica was left still animatedly talking to his grandmother. 'John, I've asked Jessica to come out for dinner with us, I hope you don't mind.'

'Of course not, it'll be fun.' He smiled at Jessica. An evening with his grandmother was many things, but it wasn't usually 'fun'.

'Yes, I want to talk to her about group dynamics in a remote setting. There's an ongoing experiment in Finland at the moment, with some very interesting initial findings that we want to discuss.'

'Sounds fascinating, Grandma.' John sighed.

'Don't be sarcastic dear, it doesn't become you.' said Elizabeth with a slight frown.

He was going to need a large drink to get through the evening.

It turned out he had needed several, the last few of which he was now severely regretting. Morning light shone blindingly through the gap in his curtains. He squinted at his watch. Shit, he was late for a 9 a.m. Russian class. Well, there was no point in him going now, the class had already started. John rolled over and buried his face in his pillow. His mouth felt like cotton wool, and his head was pounding.

Elizabeth and Jessica hadn't noticed him getting steadily more drunk while they talked about biosphere experiments and fMRIs. Despite her stiff manners and emotional detachedness, he loved his grandmother dearly. She was one of the few family members he had left, the only person he had looking out for him. Jessica was one of his friends. So why had he found the evening so uncomfortable? He wasn't intimidated by intelligent women, his grandmother had been an influential force in his life, and his mother may not have had the reputation that his father had, but she had been a NASA data scientist until her husband's job had brought them to Europe to set up NARESA. John loved smart women. He had loved watching Jessica debate with his grandmother last night and they had talked and late into the night.

But he couldn't shake the nagging feeling that he hadn't been able to keep up. With Jessica. With his Grandmother. And he was worried he couldn't keep up with the rest of the programme. He struggled with sitting in classrooms, trying to absorb reams of information. The Russian language class was one of the ones he could ill afford to miss. He had no natural ear for languages, and passing the class was a core requirement for the programme. He'd rather be in the lab doing real work.

He'd had to pass rigorous selection tests to get here, only the best were supposed to be selected, people who could keep up with the intense training regime. And if he couldn't keep up, that must have meant they lowered the bar for him, that they let him in because of who he was. Had someone pulled strings? Is that something his grandmother would do? He didn't know. His head pounded.

The thoughts didn't go away. Over the next few weeks, John found himself drinking more and more and missing more briefing sessions. When he was training, he struggled to focus. Three weeks after his Grandmother had visited he was in the simulation suite, a windowless room full of monitors, with a cramped replica of the inside of a launch capsule. John looked blankly at the dashboard. Alarms sounded, red lights flashed in front of him.

'For fuck's sake – now we're dead.' Mike slammed his hand on the dash next to John.

The simulated launch vehicle was a replica of the craft that took astronauts into low Earth orbit. The spacecraft that would take the first crews to Mars would be constructed in space and crews would hitch a ride on a rocket carrying a vehicle that would dock with the Mars-bound craft. Astronauts trained in identical simulations of the vehicle so they could practice responding to every eventuality. It wasn't uncommon for the astronauts to fail the sim if they were testing a new procedure, or they needed more training. It shouldn't be because he had made a mistake.

'That was a simple readjustment John. How could you screw it up?' Mike slammed down his headset and left the cabin. John climbed out behind him.

'Look, I'm sorry,' he held out his hands in a placatory gesture. 'I wasn't focused, I-'

'Damn right you weren't focused. Some of us are trying to train here. Some of us need to work on our careers. We didn't all get a family ticket here.' Mike's dark eyes flashed angrily.

'What the hell is that supposed to mean?' Heat rose in John's face, and his ears started to ring.

'Nothing.' Mike began to walk away.

'No, come on, finish what you started, Mike. "Some of us need to work on our careers." And I don't, I suppose?' John was as squared up to Mike as he could be.

'You're not acting like it at the moment. But I guess you don't need to try so hard when your family's an industry dynasty.' His eyes were icy as they bored into John's. 'They really do like to keep it in the family here.'

The movement was almost involuntary. John didn't realise his fist was flying through the air until it was too close to its target to stop. Everything seemed to slow down. His knuckles landed with a smack on Mike's chin. He let out a groan as John's arm reverberated backwards. Suddenly everything sped up again. Mike lunged towards John. A few of the other astronauts grabbed him and held his arms down.

The anger drained away from John immediately and was replaced by regret. 'Mike, I'm sorry –' He held up his hands in a conciliatory manner.

'Fuck you, John.' Mike spat, blood-flecked spittle flying through the air, and walked out. John sank down onto a chair, his head in his hands.

'What a bloody idiot.' John said into his hands.

'You mean Mike?' John lifted his head in surprise. It was Lucca. He'd sat down opposite John, who hadn't noticed he was still there.

'I meant me.' John replied with a grimace.

'Everyone's wanted to punch Mike at some point.' Lucca reassured him.

They both sat quietly for a few minutes. John's knuckles were throbbing. A young man appeared at the door and coughed nervously. John recognised him from the administration team.

'Erm, Mr Eden, Mr Vogel wants to see you in his office.'

'That was quick. As usual, news travels at light speed in these offices.' John sighed.

This was it. Hans Vogel, the flight director for the Mars programme, had been waiting for a reason to kick him off the programme, and John had just given him one. He felt numb. He was no longer angry, just ready to apologise and take the consequences, whatever they might be.

John stood up to leave. 'It's James isn't it?' he asked the young man, who nodded in return.

'Call me John,' he said as he walked past him. 'Mr Eden was my dad, and he's causing me enough trouble at the moment for a man who's been dead five years.'

A few moments later John knocked tentatively on Hans Vogel's imposing wooden door.

'Enter.'

Hans Vogel was responsible for the entire astronaut and training crews. He had the last word in all mission selections. The first German Commander of ISS1, his cool demeanour belied a fierce protectiveness of his crews. He'd moved up through the ranks of the European Space Agency, and had been one of the key figures in the inception of NARESA's international consortium of government bodies along with John's father.

His office was sparse and utilitarian. There were no plants or personal effects on his desk. The only thing that gave it away as belonging to Hans was the framed official astronaut photo of a much younger Hans on the wall to the right.

'Sit down John.'

John sat head bowed, waiting for the inevitable lecture.

'Tell me what happened.' Hans said. John's head snapped up in surprise. What happened was indisputable.

'I punched Mike Sanders.'

'So I hear. Why?'

'Because I'm an idiot.' He wasn't being flippant.

'Well, that may be true,' Hans gave him a wry smile, 'but what provoked you?'

'No good reason, Sir.'

Hans was silent for a few minutes. John looked up to see him staring contemplatively at him.

'John, I've been hearing reports over the last few weeks.'

'I know.'

'You've been missing training sessions. When you are in them you are not focused. I'm even hearing of excessive alcohol use.' Hans gave a slight shake of his head.

John simply nodded. Everything he said was true.

'I assumed it was a temporary crisis of confidence. It's not uncommon for highly intelligent people such as you and your colleagues. And what we ask of you is difficult and intense. Others in your group, and your colleagues who came before you, went through the same thing.' said Hans.

John was briefly distracted wondering who in the group had been in a similar situation.

'These things usually pass. Sometimes they don't and we need to make an intervention.'

Kick people out, you mean.

'When things come to a head and someone assaults a colleague, I cannot ignore it.'

'I know. I'm so sorry.'

'What did Mike say that provoked you, John?'

'It was nothing. He didn't deserve to be punched whatever he said.' John wanted this conversation to end as quickly as possible.

'I can't help you unless you are honest with me.'

'Help me?' John's eyebrows furrowed.

'This behaviour is out of character for you John. It's my job to understand what is going on for everyone in the team.' He leaned forward, his hands steepled and pressed against his mouth, 'Tell me what he said.'

John hesitated. As much as he believed Mike's accusations to be true the thought of saying them out loud, or revealing his true fears, made him wince with embarrassment. Or maybe it was just that he was afraid they would be confirmed.

'He said... he implied that the reason I was here was because of my family connections.'

There was a faint look of satisfaction in Han's eyes as John admitted this.

'I thought that might be it,' he said gently.

'You did?'

'Yes. These problems all started when Elizabeth visited. I assume this was the first time that some people had made the connection?'

'Yes.' He paused and took a deep breath. 'Well, is it?'

'Is what?' Hans frowned at him.

'Is it the reason why I am here on the programme? Is it the reason why we are here having this cosy chat instead of you kicking me out the door like you should be doing?'

'Is that what you really believe?' Hans' clear blue eyes stared appraisingly at him.

'Well, I'm clearly not here because I'm doing a great job. You said yourself you've been getting reports about me.' said John.

'You've got this idea in your head that you are here through some misguided nepotism, instead of because you are a gifted engineer with a mind that can tackle problems calmly and methodically. You are a steady, considered member of a team, and get on with everyone. When you aren't punching them of course.' He raised his eyebrows at John, who returned his gaze with a sheepish look.

Hans continued in his patient manner.

'You have an immense passion for the programme. Now whether that passion is innate, or something that has been instilled into you by your family, I don't know and I don't care. You have insecurities, I know. And instead of rising up and proving people wrong, you fed into the insecurities by sabotaging yourself. If I kick you off the programme now you will say "See, I was right, I wasn't good enough through my own merit."'

John silently digested everything that Hans was saying.

'I blame myself in some way, I should have seen it coming. It was mentioned as a potential risk factor in your assessment. I should have kept a closer eye out. However, you do have to take some of the blame for being, as you said, "an idiot". I can't condone that sort of behaviour in my crew, especially not in the building.'

John closed his eyes waiting for the inevitable.

'You're suspended for a week. Without pay.'

'What?' John's eyes snapped open.

'John, I can't let this incident go unpunished, no matter how much I understand the reasoning behind it.' Hans knew that John would understand.

'No, I mean, I'm still on the programme?' John couldn't hide his surprise.

'Do you know how much it costs to train an astronaut, John?'

'No.'

'Well, if you did you would know that there is no way we would recruit anyone into the programme who didn't meet the standard. I don't care who your grandmother was. I meant what I said, John. You have a gifted mind combined with a sense of pragmatism. You are exactly the person we need on this programme.'

'Sir, I don't know what to say. Thank you for giving me another chance.' The tension John had been feeling seeped away from his body. He looked down and realised he had been clenching his fists for the entire meeting.

'And you will arrange to see the staff psychologist.'

'Really?' John grimaced.

'I insist upon it.' Hans said with a smile. 'And you will apologise to Mr Sanders.'

'I tried already. But I'll do it properly when he is a bit calmer.'

'John, you and some of your colleagues will be going to the US for three months soon. Make it count, and we will review your progress on your return.'

'Thank you, Sir.'

'Don't screw this up, John. You're better than that.'

'Yes, Sir.' John awkwardly stood up and walked towards the door.

As soon as John left the office he leaned against the wall, and let out an enormous exhale. His legs were shaky. He had been close to losing everything he had been working towards. He knew he'd have to face the rest of the team, but as uncomfortable as that would be, it was nothing compared to how he would have felt if he had been walking out of the building for good.

***

He had to admire German craftsmanship. A cheap apartment like his and the work was still flawless. John lay on his sofa later that evening, inspecting the ceiling and not finding a single crack. He craved the metallic taste of a cold beer but had so far resisted. What would he do for an entire week off? *It's not a holiday,* he reminded himself, and he wasn't getting paid. Not that he ever spent much money, and certainly not on his spartan apartment. It might do him good to go away and get some headspace.

A sharp knock at the door jolted him out of his reverie. He pushed himself reluctantly off the sofa.

'I'm coming, I'm coming,' he muttered as the knocking grew insistent. Jessica stood stiffly in the doorway. She had changed out of her flight suit and was wearing jeans, low heeled boots and a brown jumper. A long scarf trailed over her coat. A bag hung from the crook of her folded arms, and she wore a thunderous look.

'You idiot,' she said flatly.

'Why good evening to you too. Please do come in.' He said as she stalked past him into the apartment. He followed her into the living room.

'Here, take these.' She shoved the bag at him roughly, almost winding him.

'Ow.' He opened the bag. Inside was a metal tin. 'What's this?'

'Pistachio cookies.'

'What? Why?'

'I bake when I'm angry.'

'Firstly, that's really weird. Secondly, why are you angry at me?' John tilted his head waiting for a response.

She whirled around to face him. 'You punched Mike!'

'Yes, I did. And while I share your assessment of me as an idiot, I don't get why you are mad at me.'

'It was just such a stupid thing to do. You're risking everything, John.' Jessica put both hands on her head.

'Yes, but I still don't understand why that would make you so mad at me.' John looked confused.

'Because... because we are all part of a team. And even though we may not all get on all the time, we have to be there for each other, because sometimes it might be life or death. And because we need you on that team, John. I need you.' Her words got quieter as she spoke.

She looked so disappointed in him. He didn't know how to respond. They were both silent for a few minutes, Jessica breathing heavily with indignation.

'Can I have one of these cookies?' He asked hesitantly, unable to stand the hostile silence.

'Yes. Although you don't deserve them.' She sighed and sank down onto his sofa. John tentatively sat down next to her.

He peeled off the lid of the box of cookies and was immediately hit by the sweet, nutty smell. They were small and golden, with flecks of green pistachio nuts sprinkled on top. He bit into one. It was crisp and buttery, not too sweet, with a nutty crunch.

'How are the cookies?' Jessica asked.

'They taste of anger, although very delicious anger,' he said through his mouthful. Jessica burst into laughter, her face, previously taut and serious, now light. He loved making her laugh, her face changed in an instant.

'Alright,' she said. 'Tell me what happened.'

'Oh, I am allowed a side in the story then?' He grinned at her.

'Shut up or I'll take my cookies back. Just tell me why you punched him.'

'Oh,' he waved a hand vaguely, 'you know how it is.'

'No, John, I don't. How is it?'

He wanted to tell her, to explain that he wasn't just some Neanderthal who couldn't control himself. He wanted to tell her that what Mike had said had played on one of his biggest insecurities. He wanted to tell her everything. But then she would realise how pathetic he was; the thought of telling her made him cringe.

'These cookies are really good,' he said, taking another, playing for time. She didn't reply. He knew Jessica could wait him out.

'Look, it was just he said... he implied... he said something about me not having to try because of my family name.'

'And?' She demanded.

'And, well...' He hesitated. 'I'm worried that he's right.'

'Firstly, Mike was a dick.' John was taken by surprise. He had never heard Jessica describe anyone in that way before, let alone one of their colleagues. 'Secondly, do you know how much it costs to recruit and train us? Do you think for one minute they are going to bring someone onto the programme because of their family connections?'

John chuckled at the familiarity of her words.

'What are you laughing at?' She glared at him.

'You. You'll make a great NARESA Director one day.'

'What do you mean?' Her forehead creased in a frown.

'That's pretty much exactly what Hans said to me.'

'Well, that just proves I'm right.' Jessica said, folding her arms again.

'But what if it wasn't conscious? What if just knowing what my dad and grandma did makes them expect more of me than I'm capable of?'

'John...'

'Jessica, I was never meant to be here.' said John.

'What do you mean? Of course you're meant to be here.' Jessica looked genuinely confused.

'I mean, it wasn't supposed to be me.' A crease appeared in Jessica's forehead as she looked at him in confusion. 'It was supposed to be Charlie here. Not me.' It was the first time he had spoken his name aloud since he had got here. It felt strange to wrap his mouth around the name, like a once fluent language not spoken in years.

'Who's Charlie?' Jessica asked gently, almost as if she knew what he was about to say.

'Charlie is... was... my older brother.' He was quiet for a minute and she didn't press him. Memories flashed in front of his eyes; ten year old Charlie racing ahead on his bike while John, two years younger, struggled to keep up; Charlie teaching John to surf; his stomach aching with laughter at something Charlie had said.

'He was going to be an astronaut. He had wanted to for as long as I had known him. Boxes, closets, trees, everything was a spaceship to him. He was Commander, of course, I was always the second in command. He went to MIT to study astrophysics.' He had loved it so much. John had gone to visit him one weekend. Charlie had shown off of course; he was the Big Man on Campus. John didn't need to be impressed. He thought the world of Charlie. Everyone did, especially their parents. Charlie was their favourite. John didn't mind; Charlie was his favourite person too, he was just happy to be brought along for the ride.

'Two months into his final year he died. It was an aneurysm. The irony was, he would never have been able to go into space even if he hadn't died. He wouldn't have passed the physical.'

Jessica was still quiet, looking at him intently. He rarely shared this with anyone. There was something about her that compelled him to keep talking.

'After Charlie's death, the baton just seemed to pass to me. It was up to me to keep on the family name. I liked engineering. I was always taking stuff apart and putting it back together. I had never yearned to go to space the way Charlie had. I just sort of found myself following his path. It seemed to make my parents feel better.' He fell silent, the weight of the day pressing on him.

Jessica seemed to sense that he had finished. She spoke more softly than usual. 'I'm so sorry to hear about Charlie. Losing someone you love is a lot to bear at that age, I know.' She smiled sympathetically.

'But John,' she continued, 'you are meant to be here, I just know you are. I've seen you; I've seen nothing you can't solve. You're smart, and you're fearless, and you make a great team member. You know, when you're not punching people.' She smiled wryly.

He grinned back, grateful that she had stopped being angry at him. He still felt like an idiot after everything that had happened today, embarrassed, and mad at himself for losing control, for nearly jeopardising everything.

'Just promise me you won't do anything else stupid enough to get yourself kicked off.' She gave him a stern smile, then her face softened again. 'I need you around.'

His heart gave a little leap at her words. The feeling took him by surprise, but he dismissed it as soon as it came. He was feeling emotional talking about Charlie; it was making him sensitive.

Jessica slid along the sofa closer to him and gave him a hug. She was warm and smelled sweet like her cookies.

She stepped back and looked him in the eyes. 'You ok?'

'I'm fine. Thank you.' John smiled.

'Do you feel better?'

'Yeah.' And he did. 'But I'm just thinking...'

'What?' she still looked concerned.

'I'm just thinking,' he grinned at her, 'what do I have to do wrong to get you to make me an angry cheesecake?'

Chapter Six
Countdown to first Mars walk: seven years

John

The twist of each chrome bolt into its exact position made John truly relax. He sat cross legged, the bolts that he was working just above shoulder height. He shifted along the concrete floor as he worked his way around the section, replacing and tightening bolts. It was 8.45 p.m., and he was the only person in the vast hangar. It wasn't part of his job to be here but he had quickly made friends with a few of the engineers here at the Johnson Space Center in Texas, and had got to know the whereabouts of the practicing kit. It didn't matter where he was in the world, he felt at home with the familiar smell of oil and the echo of tools in the cavernous space.

He was halfway through putting together an O ring section of a rocket booster that had taken him over an hour to take apart in the first place. The repetitive movements were meditative, and there was an immense satisfaction as each piece slotted perfectly into the space it was designed for. Even one bolt not aligning with the hole it was intended for by one millimetre was enough for him to take everything apart and start again. Though bigger in size and complexity, he marvelled at the fact that the mechanics were little different from the motorcycles, mowers, and then the cars he fixed as a teenager. It amazed him that it was the 2030s and things were still held together with nuts and bolts, which had been around in some form or another for hundreds of years. He flashbacked to his grandfather telling him about screws being used in Pompeii to extract oil from olives, and here he was, tightening nuts and bolts together on a copy of a piece of engineering that would fly to Mars. It was the precision that John loved, how the nuts and bolts fit perfectly together, the sheer solid steel of the discs that he was bolting together; it was beautiful.

'Hey you, I thought I was the only one left here.' Jessica's voice broke through his daydream, echoing around the hangar. John hated to be interrupted whilst he worked, but her voice was one he welcomed.

She stood there in her blue flight suit, the one she always wore, the one they all wore. She looked different somehow. John glanced between her and the bolt he was tightening, not wanting it to appear like he was staring.

'Hey, late night?' John asked, knowing there were a thousand better things he could have said or asked. Even after nearly two years of working together he still wanted to impress her.

'You know we were working through those rendezvous equations that we were going through today? Well, I didn't totally get it. Can I sit here?' Jessica gestured towards John's tool chest which was about waist height.

'Sure, take a seat.'

'Thanks.'

'But you did get it today Jessica, you got your equations right, I remember them telling the rest of us.' said John with a smile.

'Well, yes, but it wasn't natural John, I had to work at it, it didn't flow. So, I've just been going over them for a bit.'

'You haven't been back to the apartments? You haven't eaten?'

Their cohort of trainees were posted in Texas for three months, and NASA was housing them in small military-style apartments near the Space Center.

'No,' she replied. 'Have you?'

'No, not yet.'

John was kneeling in front of the sections of the booster he was now working on. He glanced in Jessica's direction as she stared in awe at the assembled sections of the spacecraft. They were illuminated right to the top against the darkness of the hanger.

'Can you believe these very spaceships will be travelling away from here, all the way to Mars?' Jessica gazed up at the craft. 'Do you think we'll ever be on one?'

He considered their chances. Currently only two Mars missions were planned, the first just circumnavigating the planet and depositing supplies for the subsequent mission. The crew of the second would be the first people to land on another planet. Each mission would have a crew of five, with a backup crew for each. There were twenty-five active members of the astronaut pool, each coveting a spot on one of the missions.

John tried to figure out what was different about Jessica. Her hair, she had let it down which was unusual for her. He then noticed that her flight suit was slightly unzipped at the top, and her collar was pointing up. These tiny things made her look completely different.

'What are you doing there?' said Jessica.

'Oh, it's just the practice rig,' said John. 'I just like to know how these things are put together.'

Jessica raised her eyebrows at him.

'This helps me relax, Jessica,' he said.

'So that's not even going into space? You're here at nine at night basically working on a Lego spacecraft?'

John laughed and threw a small washer towards Jessica. It tinged off the floor way before getting to her. She looked up smiling.

'Oh, it's like that is it?' She looked around for something to throw back in John's direction, grabbed a large roll of tissue paper, and hurled it towards John, missing him and hitting the rocket booster.

'Jessica! This thing is worth a fortune, that's why they don't let you in here!'

'You started it.' said Jessica, her face flushed.

'Anyway, I refuse to be judged by the girl who's still here at nine at night doing extra homework.'

'How long until you leave?' she asked, clearly ignoring his jibe.

'I've just got to put the tools away. Are you walking back?'

'Yes, I can wait, let's walk back together.'

As John and Jessica left the main operations building they talked, about the next day's events, and their microgravity training in the

Neutral Buoyancy Lab. It was one of the main reasons for their trip out here.

It was a still Texan night as they walked through the site towards the apartment complex. The chirp of cicadas rang from the nearby trees. They chatted about inconsequential things on the way home, things that had happened during the day, May's latest disastrous date. She was easy company. He had grown adept at reading her. He could sense the quiet pride she felt at work, but could also see when her need for perfection was getting the better of her. He got swept up in her energy when something excited her. And he was himself with her too. He found himself sharing things with her he had never shared with anyone else. She alone knew about his family, and the impact they had on him. He hated showing any kind of weakness, but something about her compelled him to talk deeply with her. Tonight though, it was a light conversation.

'Hey, I'm going to invite a few people over for dinner on Friday. You want to come?' said Jessica as they stood outside the apartment blocks.

'Sure, that will be nice.' He said it to make her happy, but suppressed a slight sigh. He didn't look forward to group social activities. He was a team player, but work was work, and he liked his own company. But he knew he would have to get used to it if he wanted to be on a crew to Mars. The selected crew would be housed together in a space barely bigger than his apartment for two years. But Jessica loved being part of a group and he enjoyed seeing her in her element.

'It'll be lovely, plus, you get to sample my cooking,' said Jessica, giving John a playful punch.

'I can't wait,' he teased. 'Although, I'm also a pretty good cook.'

'Oh really?' said Jessica, 'Well, we'll have to put that to the test. Fancy being my sous chef?'

John grinned, 'Do you always have to be in charge?'

'Not always.' said Jessica. 'But definitely in my kitchen.'

They'd been standing outside the apartment block for a few minutes. Never normally one for long conversations he found he could happily just keep on talking to her, and even when they parted company he could still think of a thousand things he wanted to tell her.

'Okay,' said Jessica, 'I'll see you tomorrow? I think we have a few things together.'

'Do we?' said John. He knew they did. He'd compared their schedules to see where they crossed over. He berated himself even as he feigned nonchalance. It was pathetic, but he just enjoyed her company.

They both stood smiling at each other companionably. John wondered whether she was as reluctant as he was to end the conversation.

'I'd better go and get something to eat.' Jessica reached out and touched his arm as she turned to leave.

John laughed, 'You're always thinking about food.'

'Not always,' she said, putting her hands on her hips, 'Only about seventy five percent of the time.' She laughed and walked to her stairwell, leaving John watching her shiny hair swinging across her back. There was a lightness in his body as he turned towards his own apartment. *You never know*, he told himself, *Friday might even be fun.*

***

Friday evening came around before he knew it after an intense week of training. John stood waiting at the door to Jessica's apartment block with a carrier bag. She had called him in a panic, a mild one, but still something he had never heard in Jessica before. She had forgotten an essential ingredient. He liked that she had asked him for help. It wasn't something she did very often.

'Hello?' Jessica's voice crackled in the intercom.

'It's me, John.'

'Hey, come right up.' The security door clicked and he entered the hallway identical to the entrance to his apartment. Before he had even got to her front door it flew open.

'Did you get them?' She said impatiently.

'Er, hello?' He laughed.

'Sorry! Hello.' She leaned in and gave him a peck on the cheek before inspecting the bag he'd been carrying.

'Yes, I got them.'

'Thank you, thank you, thank you! I can't believe I forgot pomegranates. Come in, come in.' She disappeared off with the bag. There was an excitable, nervous energy around her that he'd never seen before.

'What else have you got in here?' he heard her call.

He followed her into the apartment. It was identical to his own, but Jessica's just felt different. They had only been here for three weeks of their three month stay, but already Jessica's place felt homely and welcoming. There were throws and cushions on the ancient sofa, and pictures on the wall, which he was sure Jessica must have put up herself. They were bold colourful art reproductions. He recognised Matisse and Hockney; cheap prints from a homeware store, but they lifted the plain white walls. There were books on a bookshelf that he wondered how she found the time to read. He wanted to spend time here, something he didn't feel in his own bare apartment. The kitchen was a tiny space connected to the living room and in it Jessica was unpacking the bag that he had brought.

'John, you didn't have to bring these.' She pulled out a bottle of prosecco, beers, and some chocolates. She beamed at him in surprise.

'Oh, well,' a heat rose in his cheeks, 'I know you have a sweet tooth. And my grandmother taught me never to go anywhere empty handed. So,' he said, changing the subject, 'What's on the menu?'

'We're having tabbouleh, lamb kofka, rice, and flatbread.'

'Sounds amazing. What time will everyone else be here?' John leaned against the sideboard.

'In about two hours. We'd better get cracking.'

'Yes, boss! Ok, what do you want me to do?' John clapped his hands together in a motion of action.

'Right, here's everything you need for the tabbouleh.' She pushed a pile of ingredients, including the pomegranates he'd bought along, along the counter towards him. 'There's a pan for the bulgur wheat...' she dived into a cupboard beside the oven, 'here.' She brandished a saucepan at him. 'Is that ok? Do you know what you're doing? Just cook the bulgur wheat and chop everything else up and chuck it in.'

He grinned. 'I'll be fine, and I'm sure you'll tell me if I'm doing anything wrong. What are you going to do?'

'I'm going to do the rice.'

'Hey, you got the easy job.' John smiled.

Jessica shook her head, 'Have you ever tasted Persian tahdig, John? It's divine. And a skill that takes years to perfect. Then I'll get the kofka ready for cooking, and when you've done the tabbouleh you can help me with the flatbread.'

They both set to work, stepping around each other in the small kitchen space, filling up pans of water, chopping herbs and other ingredients. John eyed the cast iron pan Jessica was using for the rice, one that he suspected didn't come with the apartment. She took this stuff seriously. John liked to cook, and clearly, Jessica did too. Despite never having been here before he didn't feel like a stranger in her kitchen. He barely needed to ask where anything was as it all just seemed to be where it should be, in typical Jessica efficiency. With music playing gently through a speaker in the corner, they chatted about their training and their colleagues.

'Do you want a beer?' she asked him after they had been working for a while.

'That'd be great.'

They continued pottering companionably, moving around each other with a sort of sixth sense that they had developed through endless training simulations together. Jessica was more relaxed than he'd ever seen her. Though she plainly cared passionately about cooking and wanted to make a good impression on their friends, on her own, outside of a group situation she was more at ease.

John chopped herbs and vegetables, and then made a dressing for the salad. He was a good cook, borne more out of a desire to eat good food than the love for it that Jessica seemed to have developed from cooking with her family. He felt a need to impress her that he couldn't explain. She always seemed so capable at everything, and he wanted her to think he was too.

'How's it going?' she asked, her hands knuckle deep in minced lamb.

'Good, I'm done. Want to try it?'

'Yeah, and if I'm still alive when the guests come it's fine to serve it to them.' Jessica's eyes were alive with mischief.

'You're hilarious,' he said. She grinned back at him. 'Here you go.'

He loaded a spoon with the tabbouleh, rich green with herbs, and pomegranate seeds glistening like rubies. Her hands were dirty so he fed her straight off the spoon himself. It was a strangely intimate act, and he watched her with her eyes closed as she savoured the mouthful.

'That's perfect. Did you put garlic in it?'

'Yes, I know it wasn't in my "designated ingredients",' he put air quotes around the phrase, 'but I found it in your fridge. Is that ok?'

'It's unorthodox. But it passes the test. I'm not voting you out yet.' She smiled.

'Gee, thanks.' John said sardonically.

'Right, these can be cooked later.' She put a tray of meatballs to the side and washed her hands.

As he watched her move around the kitchen familiar strains came through the speaker. Jessica reached out and turned up the speaker as ABBA began to loudly sing *Take a Chance On Me*.

'ABBA?' He raised his eyebrows at her. He'd had no idea what sort of music she liked, but never in a million years would he have put money on her loving a pop band from the 1970s.

She didn't respond. She turned around for a second, and the next thing he knew she had spun back round brandishing a wooden spoon as a microphone. John burst into laughter. He had never seen her like this before. He bit his lip and shook his head at her in wonderment as she shimmied around the tiny kitchen, singing into the wooden spoon.

'Alright, you asked for it.' He opened her drawer and pulled out a whisk. He had never let himself go with someone like this before, but there was something so compelling about her.

'Honey, I'm still free, take a chance on me,' he crooned into the whisk.

Jessica's eyes widened in delight, and they danced around each other, singing at the top of their voices. John couldn't remember the last time he felt so light, so carefree. His worries about the programme, about his grandmother, all left him in that moment. He didn't even care that he was murdering a classic pop song in front of a woman he wanted to impress so much, and for once Jessica didn't seem to care either.

As the clipped tones of Agnetha and Frida launched the 'Ba ba bas' John put down his whisk, took Jessica's spoon out of her hands and before she could protest he took one hand, and put the other on her waist and spun her around the kitchen. She threw her head back with laughter, strands of hair falling out of her messy ponytail.

As the song ended they both tried to catch their breath.

'ABBA, Jessica?' John looked at her once again, trying to cover the return of his awkwardness.

'I make no apologies,' she was still gasping for breath. 'My grandma loved them, and then when the musical came out she made my mother go with her. They both made me watch the film when I was old enough. Now what's your excuse?'

'My grandma loved them too.'

'Yeah, right. I already used that excuse.'

'I swear it's true,' he laughed again, holding up his hands. 'When my grandmother was Commander of the Shuttle, ABBA was one of her requests. You can ask her. Don't take my word for it, it'll be on a NASA record somewhere.'

'Ok, ok, I believe you. Right,' she straightened her ponytail, 'break time's over. Time to get back to work.'

'Yes, Chef.' He gave her a mock salute.

'We're making barbari, a Persian flatbread.'

She grabbed a large bowl covered in clingfilm that he hadn't noticed sitting in the corner and removed the cover. A warm, yeasty smell filled the kitchen.

'We'll do half each.' She sprinkled some flour over the counter and scooped out the sticky, airy dough.

'Did you bring all this stuff over with you?' John rolled up his sleeves ready for kneading.

'What?' Jessica carried on with her task, with a small smile.

'The dough scraper, the cast iron pan... I don't have any of this stuff in my apartment. You know we're only here three months, right?'

'I know, but there are some essentials I just can't live without. And fortunately, there's a cheap homeware store not far from here.'

'I'm impressed with your commitment.' He honestly was.

'Well, I don't do things by halves.' Jessica smiled.

'You definitely don't,' he said, looking at her in awe. There had been an incident during training last week. Jessica had made a mistake while training in the buoyancy lab, at the end of a gruelling five-hour session. Her face had retained its usual stoicism as she had been bawled out by the instructor. Later that evening, when she hadn't turned up to a night out with the rest of the trainees, he'd tracked her down to the training lab where he'd found her watching the video of where she went wrong. It was ten o' clock at night and he'd had to drag her away. He realised then all the hard work that went into her seeming so capable.

'Right, you just want to knead this for a bit and then shape it into two ovals.' Jessica gazed over John's work.

'Yes, Chef.' John snickered.

She elbowed him playfully. He liked this side of her. He didn't often see it in the stresses and strains of their training programme. They kneaded the dough side by side. It was warm and sticky, covering his hands. He reached for the jar of flour.

'What are you doing?' Jessica said, grabbing his hand.

'It needs a little more flour.'

'Uh uh. No more flour.' She pulled his hand away.

'It's really wet.' He held up hands covered in sticky dough.

'It's supposed to be. Just be patient with it.'

'You're so bossy,' he complained.

'This surely isn't news to you.' She looked at him smiling.

'You're right, I don't know what I was thinking.' He laughed at her.

'Look, just keep going with it, like this.' She reached over and put her hands over his. She guided them over the dough, pushing it and stretching it. The movement was hypnotic; the warm pressure of her hands made the muscles in his arms relax.

She was so close that he could inhale the scent of her hair, lemon and peppermint, mingled with the strong smell of the bread dough, which had now become silky and pliable in her expert hands. He watched as she rolled and stretched it. She turned to look at him, and there was a flash in her eyes; a look he had never seen before. It passed in an instant and she straightened up, releasing his hands.

'I think you've got it.' She smiled at him. John didn't say anything. The atmosphere in the tiny kitchen felt suddenly fragile.

'Come on you, let's get these finished,' she continued. Whatever the moment had been, it had passed. Perhaps he had imagined it. He tried to forget about it as Jessica returned to instructing him on how to make the barbari. She showed him how to shape the flatbread and make indentations along its length.

'It stops the bread from puffing up,' she told him. They covered it with a flour paste glaze and scattered black and white sesame seeds over it before putting it in a hot oven.

'I'd better get changed before everyone arrives.' Jessica wiped her hands on a towel.

'But you look great already.' John tried to not sound too odd.

'Really?' she raised an eyebrow at him. He gave her an appraising look. Her long brown hair was falling around her face, and she was covered in flour. She looked amazing.

'Well, yeah, maybe some clean clothes. But don't forget this...' He reached up and brushed her face tenderly. She put her hand to her cheek.

'Hey, you put that there!' She wiped flour from her face. 'This means war.' She scooped up a handful of flour and threw it at him. Within minutes there was a cloud of flour in the air of the kitchen and they were both laughing so hard they were clutching their stomachs. He couldn't remember feeling this light in a long time. It had just been so easy being around Jessica this evening. With a jolt of disappointment, he remembered that their friends would be joining them soon.

He held up his hands. 'Truce, truce. You really had better go and get changed now.' A sprinkling of flour dusted almost every surface and misty puffs still hung in the air.

'Yeah.' She looked back at him. 'What about you?'

'Oh, don't worry about me. I'll just brush myself off. Can I use your bathroom?'

Of course. You know where it is?'

'Yep.' It was in the same place as in his apartment but, just like the living area, Jessica had made it feel more homely. There were plants on the windowsill, and candles on every surface. A heady familiar smell hung in the air from the shower she'd had before he'd arrived. She had somehow made the tiny, generic apartment like a haven.

He took off his t-shirt and shook it out over the bath then splashed his face and hair with water. He wanted to clean up the kitchen for Jessica before she came back out.

By the time she emerged from her bedroom he'd swept up all the flour, and set the small table in the living room ready for dinner, repurposing a couple of the candles from the bathroom for the centre.

'John,' she exclaimed. 'You didn't have to do all this.'

'Well, I did start the fight, so it was the least I could do.' He rubbed the back of his head absently. It wasn't that he was trying to impress her, he just wanted to please her, to make her happy. There was something so energetic and captivating about her. He could already tell that she was going to be an important person in his life. He didn't know how. It wasn't that he wanted anything more from the relationship. That was impossible anyway, they all knew that. He just wanted her to want him around.

John enjoyed the evening much more than he expected. He wasn't a natural people person but he had learned to work a crowd. His parents and grandparents had always been big hosts, having people around for potluck dinners that were the fashion in the US. He'd been included from a young age and expected to engage with the grownups, and consequently was a good conversationalist. Tonight, he'd return to his apartment exhausted from it all, but he was having fun nonetheless. Jessica had a knack for bringing people together and engaging them in discussions. He looked at her; she was sparkling with joy. He loved seeing her like this.

'So, did you hear we're getting a new instructor in the buoyancy lab?' May asked the group.

'They're replacing Commander Daniels?' Jessica replied.

'Your favourite person,' John nudged her.

'Don't,' Jessica groaned, covering her face with her hand. 'He hates me.'

'He does not hate you,' Valentina interjected. 'He just tries to push you because you are very capable and he knows you can be even better.'

Valentina Kareva was a former pilot in the Russian Air Force. She had once fought against the West in the Middle East. But politics and nationalities were almost forgotten in the federated agency of NARESA. At five foot ten, with ice blonde hair and a steely demeanour, she terrified the junior engineers at NARESA. But John enjoyed her very dry sense of humour.

'Oh.' Valentina's analysis appeared to take Jessica by surprise. John has seen how she had taken the instructor's behaviour personally. But he also knew Valentina was right. Jessica was highly capable, and the instructors could see that and pushed her hard. Not that they needed to. John had never seen anyone as driven as Jessica.

'Anyway,' Jessica leapt up from her seat, 'I'm going to get us more wine and then May can tell us about her latest date with that cute lab assistant.'

They continued talking late into the evening. John realised how little he knew about most of his colleagues. Suddenly he was seeing a window into their lives.

May had them all enthralled with her tales of her many dates... 'So, we're on our way back from an early dinner and he says, "Can I introduce you to my mom?"' John and Lucca both let out groans.

'What?' Jessica said, 'It's quite sweet.'

'Jessica,' Lucca said, 'even Italian mama's boys would not do that on a first date.'

'Wait, you haven't heard the worst of it,' May interjected.

'It is worse?' Valentina had been characteristically quiet throughout the evening. People often thought she was shy, but John recognised that she was just a woman of few words. She spoke when she had something useful to say, which wasn't the same as shyness at all.

'He drives me to his mom's, it's dark, and we pull in.' She paused, evidently enjoying the drama. 'It was the cemetery. He wanted to take me to his mom's grave to "meet" her.'

John, Lucca, and Valentina fell about laughing. Only Jessica remained astounded.

'May! What did you do? That's terrifying.' Jessica blurted out.

John smiled indulgently at her. She was so serious, it made him laugh even more.

'I went along with it of course. He was driving, what else could I do?' May shrugged.

'But he could've been a serial killer?' Jessica said, open mouthed.

'Jessica, if he was a serial killer you think I'd want to piss him off by saying "no, sorry I don't want to see your dead momma, you freaky weirdo"?' Even Jessica laughed this time.

'I'm sorry it didn't work out,' Jessica said, putting her hand on May's arm.

'What do you mean not work out? I'm seeing him again tomorrow. He's cute!'

John caught Jessica's eye as they all laughed. There was no sign of the look from earlier, but her smile was warm and familiar.

They finished the evening with sticky baklava that Valentina had bought, along with John's chocolates, and coffee.

'And then Matteo, he run across the garden, no clothes on, *cacca* in his hands, Giovanna chasing him.' Lucca was regaling them with horror stories of parenting young children, his Italian accent thicker after a couple of glasses of wine. May and John were laughing mainly at Valentina's horrified look.

Lucca's wife and two young boys had joined him for the stay out here in Texas. Few of the astronaut trainees had children, and those that did had older children. The long hours, and slavish dedication that the job required meant many of them didn't even have serious relationships. John certainly hadn't had any since he'd joined the programme, just several flings, usually women he'd met in a bar, or the occasional contact from one of the other government agencies based in Cologne. He liked to keep his work life separate. But Lucca was a family man, who'd married his childhood sweetheart Giovanna, from Genoa where they had grown up, and who had moved with him to Milan where he went to University and then worked as a geology researcher, and then to Cologne with their young family when he was accepted as an astronaut trainee.

John had a lot of time for Lucca. In the weeks since being at the buoyancy lab, they had been regularly paired up for simulations. They shared a practical approach to problem solving, and a relaxed, easy manner.

'Can we talk about something else?' Jessica said, wrinkling her nose. 'Does anyone want another coffee?'

John excused himself to go to the bathroom. As he returned through the hallway he saw a small table with a notebook and pen on it, next to a bowl containing keys and her NASA pass. He smiled to himself, *could this woman be any more efficient?* In that brief moment, he had an idea. He flipped to a blank page in the notebook, trying not to snoop at what might be written in there. He scrawled a note on a clean sheet and tore it out. Glancing around, he saw her jacket hanging in the hall. It was Jessica's, wasn't it? It didn't look like something May or Val would wear. Yes, he'd definitely seen her wearing it. He took one last look at the note. *Don't forget you're amazing, J.* Because he knew she did forget sometimes, and if she just remembered, he thought she could take over the world. He folded it up and slipped it in the pocket of her jacket.

Chapter Seven

Countdown to first Mars Walk: seven years

Jessica

Rust coloured earth stretched as far as the eye could see. Tall, angular buttes, striated stacks of rock, rose incongruously out of the Arizona desert plain, looking like they had been chiselled out of thin air. Mountain peaks and plateaus ascended from the horizon.

The NARESA trainees were still on their training mission in the US. The arid desert stretching across the southwestern states of Arizona and Utah had long been used as a Mars analogue, an environment akin to the red planet, where they could test equipment and procedures.

'How long till we reach our target?' Jessica looked up from the mission checklist that she was reading on a tablet computer.

Red dust was kicked up by the giant wheels of the buggy that carried John, Jessica, and May, as it rolled over the rocky terrain. John was driving the buggy, as far as the Semi-Autonomous Mars Surface Navigator, affectionately known as SAMSON, needed driving. It was manoeuvring itself, following coordinates to a site where they were to collect geological samples in a simulated exercise.

'About twenty minutes,' John said, glancing at the navigation panel. They had already been travelling through the unchanging terrain for forty minutes.

'Next leg it's one of your two's turn to sit in the back,' May grumbled from the cramped space in the back of the buggy.

She was wedged between helmets for their Mars Surface Suits, food, water and camping gear. The Mars Surface Suits were lighter and more flexible than the traditional EVA suits; the thinking being that, unlike in space, they would be spending the majority of their time outside exploring the planet. NARESA also considered there to be fewer risks on the surface than in the vacuum of space. Not that Mars was without risks, and none of them would survive being on the surface without the lifesaving suits. SAMSON was sealed and self-supporting, enabling them to travel without their bulky helmets on.

'What is on the list to do at the next test site?' John peered over at Jessica's tablet.

'Hang on, let me check.' She swiped at the tablet screen, looking for the checklist. Something out of the corner of her eye made her jerk her head up.

'John, look out!'

A large red rock loomed into view. John reached for the autopilot override but he was seconds too late, and Jessica's body pitched to the left as the buggy tried to mount the rock. Her insides fluttered as they teetered in mid-air, balancing on two wheels like the tense pause at the top of a rollercoaster. Her stomach lurched and she screwed her eyes shut, bracing for impact with the ground. The thump came sooner than she expected her body juddered; her eyes snapped open and she was momentarily confused. The horizon in front of them was at a 45-degree angle, and to her side she could see the red ground still a couple of feet below. She looked around, and only then noticed the weight of John pressed against her right arm, though his harness stopped him from crushing her.

'Are you ok?' he turned to her, his face creased with concern.

'Yeah, I'm fine. May?' Jessica strained to turn her head to the back of the buggy. 'May, are you ok?'

'I'm not sure. Something fell on me.'

May's tiny frame was crushed among various pieces of equipment that had come loose in the crash.

'John, we've got to get her out.' Jessica scrambled for her harness with shaking hands.

May looked unusually pale in the warm desert light. Was she seriously injured? Jessica's stomach gripped with fear. She was leading this training mission. It was her job to keep everyone safe.

John grasped at his seat to stop himself from falling onto Jessica as he unbuckled his own harness. He reached through the gap between their seats to try and release May's harness.

'Wait,' he said. 'Does anything hurt May?'

'Yeah, my right leg.'

'Ok. If I unbuckle you, you're going to fall to the side, and probably be in even more pain. If you've broken something I don't want to make it worse.' He turned to Jessica. 'We're going to have to set the buggy upright.'

Jessica tried to assess the situation from her position pressed against the passenger window. It seemed like after attempting to mount the rock on the right SAMSON had overbalanced, but instead of hitting the ground, it had fallen against another boulder. John was right, the only way to safely get May out was to set the buggy upright again. But even with NARESA's lightweight design it weighed nearly three tonnes; it wasn't going to be easy.

John pressed a few buttons on the dashboard, but there was no response.

'The electronics are off. There must be something wrong with the battery.' He started to wrench the door open with his hands.

'John, wait!' Jessica grabbed his arm. 'None of us are wearing helmets!'

'Is that really important right now?' John said with a noise of impatience.

'Of course it's important,' she replied evenly.

'Jessica, we're in the middle of bloody Arizona. May is injured and we need to fix this damn rover.'

'It's a simulation exercise. What if this happened while we were on Mars?' The whole point of these exercises was to test them under Mars-like conditions. That's why they had been bought out to this godforsaken desert, which was the closest environment they would get to Mars on Earth.

'Yeah, but we're not on Mars.' John replied.

'But Mitch-' Jessica started. Mitchell Emery was the project director for the Desert Research and Technology Unit of NARESA. He'd expect them to follow strict protocol.

'Mitch can kiss my ass. I'm getting us out of here.'

The door opened with a crunch as he pulled himself out.

'John!' she yelled. 'Oh, you just like to play the maverick, don't you?' She muttered to herself. There was no point. He wouldn't listen. She worried that his refusal to play by the rules would get him into trouble. Protocol was everything in NARESA, that's what kept them safe. On the other hand, if anyone could fix SAMSON and get them back on track it was John. She had never seen him face a mechanical problem he couldn't solve. But at what cost?

She was just up to climb out of John's door when the buggy started rocking. May moaned in pain.

'John, what the hell are you doing?'

'Trying to see if I can tip it back,' he shouted from outside.

It rocked again, and May grimaced.

He came back to the door.

'It's no good, it's too far over its centre of gravity. I need your help.'

'Fine, but we need to get some of this stuff off May. Plus, it'll be less weight for us to move.'

Jessica handed John various pieces of equipment that he set on the desert surface until all that was left in the back was May.

'How are you doing?'

'I'm ok,' May said, even though she looked like she might faint.

'Ok, we're going to try and right the buggy, but it's going to hurt when it hits the ground. Are you going to be ok?' Jessica couldn't hide her concern.

'Yeah.'

Jessica squeezed May's small hand. 'We'll get you out of here in a minute.'

She pulled herself out of the rover, stood on the edge of the door frame and looked around. She could see for miles. There was nothing but desert, rusty rocks, and mountains. The simulation base was thirty miles to the north.

'Do you want a hand down?' John reached up to her.

'No,' she replied shortly.

'Fine,' he retorted. 'I see you're not wearing your helmet,' he said as she sat on the edge of the door and lowered herself to the ground.

'Well, there wasn't much point since you decided unilaterally to abandon the experiment.' She landed deftly on her feet.

'Let's just get this thing up. We can get May out and check her over. Then I'm going to have to look at the battery. Be prepared for us to call this in if I can't fix it.'

The parameters of the simulation meant they weren't supposed to be in synchronous contact with Mission Control, as would be the case on Mars. They had the means to contact them in an emergency, but that would feel like a defeat for all of them.

'You'll fix it.'

'I know,' he said with the briefest hint of a smile. 'But just on the minuscule chance I can't, we might have to be rescued.'

'We might have to anyway, depending on how May is.'

'I can hear you,' May called from inside the vehicle, 'and I don't need rescuing. You're not calling it in. John, just fix the goddamn rover.'

Jessica and John exchanged relieved smiles. At least May was well enough to protest.

'We'll discuss it when I've checked you over.' Jessica called back. 'She so stubborn,' she muttered to John.

'Pot and kettle spring to mind,' he muttered back. She ignored his comment. It was the only way when he was in this sort of mood.

While they had been talking he had wrapped some rope around a bar on the rover.

'I'll pull, and I need you to push,' he instructed Jessica.

The rover looked almost comical leaning against the rock, like a remote-control car, abandoned by a child. Jessica braced herself against the side, ready to push.

'On my count,' came John's voice, 'three, two, one, push.'

Planting her feet firmly on the ground, she heaved her weight against the rover. Her slender body belied a strength, built from years of training. Her arm muscles burned as she pushed. She could hear the groans of strain from John as he pulled on the rope. It didn't budge.

'Ok, stop a minute. Stop!' John called.

Jessica stopped pushing. She walked back round to John. He had let go of the rope and was flexing his fingers.

'This isn't working,' she said.

'This isn't working yet,' he replied with emphasis on the 'yet'. 'We have to do this. If we were on Mars we would have no choice.'

'Oh, so now we're back on Mars? I just hope that if any of us is on Mars this thing has improved navigation systems.'

'Right, we're going to try again. We can't get May out till we get this thing upright. You've gotta push like your life depends on it.'

'Ok.' She wiped her forehead with the sleeve of her suit.

'Jessica, don't stop pushing when it starts to move, even when you think it's hit its centre of gravity, keep pushing. I'll have to drop the rope because there's a risk I could pull it right over the other way. But there's no way you can push it over, so just keep going, okay?'

'Is this actually going to work?'

'Trust me, Jessica. We can do it.'

They resumed positions and John counted them in again. Jessica thought of May, in pain inside the rover. She gritted her teeth and a guttural moan rose from the back of her throat. The rover lifted off the rock with a creak.

'It's moving!' she yelled.

'Don't stop pushing!'

She willed the energy into her arms, muscles screaming, she pushed with all her might. As the rover lifted further and further she involuntarily stopped. Sensing her pause John yelled again.

'Don't stop. Keep going!'

With a final burst she heaved the machine, and the two wheels bounced back onto the earth, sending up a cloud of desert dust. Unable to hold herself up any longer Jessica fell against the rover and let herself collapse to the floor where she lay for a moment catching her breath. Through the space underneath the chassis she saw John in the same supine position, the rope abandoned on the ground.

'Hey, you ok?'

'Yeah, you?' he peered at her through the gap.

'Yeah. We did it.'

There was a knock on the window of the rover.

'May!' Jessica scrambled up and wrenched open the door. She and John carefully helped May out. The two of them carried her away from the rover and sat her against a nearby boulder.

'Tell me where it hurts?' Jessica ran her hands along May's left leg. As she reached her calf May let out a cry of pain.

'Ok, ok, sorry.' She moved further down the leg and held May's foot. 'Can you press your foot down onto my hand?'

May screwed up her eyes and shook her head.

'Ok, it feels like the fibula. I can't tell if it's broken or just fractured, but you're not going to be able to walk on it.' Jessica looked at her colleague and friend wincing in pain and made a decision.

'I'm going to call it in.'

'No! I'm fine. John will fix SAMSON and we can finish the experiment. Don't call it in. I'll be fine.'

'May, you've probably broken your leg. We need to get you to a doctor.'

'I am a doctor, and I am telling you, I'll be fine. We're only a few hours away from base camp. John, how long is it going to take to fix that thing?'

'There's a problem with the electrics. If it's a simple fix it'll be under an hour.'

'And if it's not?' Jessica asked.

'I'll make you a deal May,' John crouched down beside her. 'We'll give it an hour for me to get the rover done. If I can't get it done within that time Jessica's going to call into base and get them to pick us up. Ok?'

'John...' Jessica interrupted.

'Jessica, she says she's fine.'

'Will you stop talking about me as if I'm not here?' May interjected.

Jessica smiled despite herself. At least May was being her usual veracious self.

'Alright.' She turned back to John. 'We'll go with your plan. You need a hand?'

'I'll tell you if I do. You keep May company.'

'Ok. There's morphine in the first aid kit. I'm going to give you a shot. This I absolutely do insist on.' Jessica said, seeing May's look of protest. 'There are no medals for suffering through the pain.'

After administering the jab, Jessica settled herself next to May. Jessica handed May a bottle and a silver foil packet.

'Here, eat, drink.'

'I'm not hungry,' May said, taking the water.

'It's a brownie. You need some sugar.' Jessica held the packet out insistently until May relented.

They sat in silence for a while Jessica considered their situation. The air was humid, and they were wearing thick suits which May and Jessica had both unzipped. The ground was hard and dusty. Jessica couldn't help feeling disappointed in herself. Her job was to complete the mission successfully and keep everyone safe, and she had failed at that so far.

She tried to reassure herself that she had made the right decision. They were meant to be on a training exercise to test the rover and the equipment. She wanted to follow the experiment protocols, which they had already broken by not wearing helmets and oxygen. But she also didn't want to unnecessarily risk a member of her team. It was one thing being in space or on Mars with no choice, but they weren't on Mars. They were in the Arizona desert and within an hour May could be airlifted to the nearest ER. But May wanted to prove herself. They all did. They weren't just testing equipment out here in the sweltering desert, they themselves were being tested. In a few months, they would hopefully graduate from the AsTra programme and would join the roster of fully-fledged astronauts, all waiting for a flight. The places were coveted, but they all had to work as a team, Jessica couldn't let her need to prove herself as a leader override May's need to prove her resilience. She would hold off calling for help unless it became absolutely urgent.

John had taken a panel off the back of the rover and was busy poking around with various tools. Jessica looked at May, a little more colour had come back into her cheeks after eating, but she was still wincing in pain. Jessica had to take her mind off it.

'May, tell me the weirdest thing you ever saw in your time in the ER?'

'You sure you got the stomach for it? You couldn't even cope with a conversation about Lucca's kid's poop.' May winced as she shifted slightly.

'Try me.' Jessica said.

With the morphine clearly kicking in May launched into several anecdotes mostly involving things that men had shoved up their backsides.

'A curtain rod? Seriously?' Jessica grimaced.

'Uh huh. Poor guy was only seventeen. His mum brought him in, he asked her for help. It's quite sweet actually.'

'Sweet isn't exactly the word I'd use.'

'There was a lot of grim stuff,' May said.

'Why did you decide to become a doctor?'

May sighed. 'I don't remember ever deciding. It was just the plan. When your parents tell you something from a young age you just believe it. Like the tooth fairy. But unlike when I was twelve and they no longer wanted to leave a dollar under my pillow, they forgot to tell me the truth, that I didn't have to become a doctor. So, I went to med school, just like my parents wanted.'

'Then what happened?'

'I was a resident for two years in an ER Brooklyn.'

'What made you finally leave?'

May was quiet.

'Sorry, I shouldn't have asked.' Jessica rested her hand on May's. 'I was trying to take your mind off that leg—'

'There was a shootout. In a school. Brooklyn High School.' May's voice was flat.

'Oh God, I remember it.' Jessica pressed her hand to her mouth. It had been all over the news, even in the UK. Her blood ran cold just thinking about it.

'These kids just poured in, one after the other. We got so full we had to reroute the non-life-threatening cases to different hospitals. But the worst ones came to us. We lost nineteen kids that day.'

She paused. Neither of them spoke for a few minutes. Jessica looked up and saw John had stopped what he was doing, though he didn't turn around.

'These kids, they were sixteen, seventeen. They were supposed to have had their whole lives ahead of them. They could have been whatever they wanted. That was when I decided I needed to be what I wanted. I couldn't do it anymore. I switched my residency and spent a year preparing for a NARESA application in my spare time.'

Jessica couldn't even imagine the horror of seeing all those children dead and injured that day. And a small part of her was grateful that she couldn't. She grabbed May's hand and squeezed it. 'We're so glad you did.'

'What about you? I know you have John to thank for your love of space.' They both glanced over a John who had resumed his attempts to fix the rover's battery. 'But what got you here?'

'Well, unlike you, my family told me I could be whatever I wanted. But they also told me I had to work hard to get it. '"Go and wake up your luck" my grandmother would tell me. She came over to the UK from Iran in the 1970s. And my mum, she wanted to do so much with life, she was so smart.'

She saw her mother now, always well-dressed though they had little money. She bought clothes second hand, good quality, and altered them to fit perfectly. She always had a book in her hand; she read to Jessica every night. Even up to her early teens, they would snuggle up together and her mother would read her grown up book, classics like Austen and the Brontës, or even more modern novels. But they all had strong women in them.

'My grandmother put a lot of pressure on her. When your family leaves their home country for a better life they expect a lot, they want their children to do better. I expect you know what that is like.' She glanced over at May, who nodded. 'But then my mother had me. She was young and at university. I wasn't planned. She dropped out to have me. My grandmother was so disappointed. She was meant to do all the things my grandmother didn't have the opportunity to do. That was part of the reason for emigrating to England. I mean, she worked, she worked her whole life, my grandmother looked after me while she was at work. But she never had the life she was supposed to have. Neither of them did. And that's why it was important that I did.'

'Did she ever get to finish her university degree?'

'There wasn't the time or money when I was younger. But when I was a teenager she started studying again. She was doing English Literature. That's where I got my love of books, from her. She loved them so much. There were books on every surface in our house. It was small and we never had enough bookshelves.'

'What happened to your mother?'

Jessica swallowed. 'She died when I was sixteen.'

'I remember you saying. What happened? If you don't mind me asking?'

Jessica was quiet for a minute as they both sat uncomfortably on the desert floor, watching as John poked around the rover.

No one else, apart from her grandmother, knew the story. But with these two people she trusted with her life, stuck in the middle of the desert, she felt compelled to share it. She swallowed hard.

'There was a party, to celebrate finishing our exams. My mum didn't want me to go. She was worried there would be alcohol, she was really overprotective. I think she worried the same thing that happened to her would happen to me. But I honestly wasn't interested in that sort of thing when I was that age. I just wanted to be around people, around my friends. My grandmother persuaded my mum to let me go. "She's worked so hard, Rosana. Let her have a night with her friends." It was so rare for me to go out like that. I was a good girl. I studied a lot. So, I went, on the proviso that my mum would pick me up at eleven p.m. I argued for midnight, but she was adamant.'

Half the year group had been at the party that night. It was at Alice's, one of the cool girls. Her parents had a lot of money and an enormous house. They stayed out of the way that night. They didn't hover over their daughter like her mother would have done. Jessica remembered the music. No one danced. It wasn't what you did at that sort of party. You just talked and laughed.

After months of hard study under the watchful eyes of her mother and grandmother she felt carefree. Exam results wouldn't come out for six weeks. Other than a Saturday job in a local cafe, she had nothing else to worry about until then. Before she knew it, it was 11 p.m. She checked her phone. Yes, there it was. A text from her mum letting her know she was leaving. She knew better than to keep her waiting. She grabbed her jacket, said goodbye to her hostess and went outside. Her mum was likely to already be out there.

She wasn't there yet. Jessica sat on the doorstep. The early summer air was already balmy even that late at night. She would be here any minute, in her blue car, old and temperamental, but immaculate inside. By quarter past eleven there was still no sign of her. Jessica checked her phone again. The last message sent thirty minutes ago.

Just leaving. Mama x

Should she call? She didn't want to disturb her mother while she was driving. Perhaps there was traffic. No, not at eleven at night. Maybe she had got lost. But it was only ten minutes' drive from their own house. Her grandmother would be asleep by now and she didn't want to wake her. She tried calling her mother. The phone rang and rang with no answer. Eleven thirty. She called again. It rang a few times then suddenly picked up.

'Mama, where are you?'

It wasn't her mother who answered. It was a man. A stranger. He was a paramedic.

'A drunk driver had driven into her while she was on her way to pick me up.' Jessica told May, coming back to the hot dusty present. 'They said she would have died on impact so at least she wasn't in any pain. She wouldn't have had time to think about anything.'

Jessica felt May's hand squeeze hers.

'It was my fault she was out that night. If I hadn't insisted on going to that party she wouldn't have had to collect me. She wouldn't have died.'

She had never told the story before. Her classmates knew. They had watched silently as the police came to pick her up and take her home to her grandmother. She didn't go back to that school after the summer. She couldn't bear them all knowing, looking at her, feeling sorry for her, when it was her fault. She transferred to a different sixth form where she worked and worked and she hadn't stopped since.

'Jessica...'

'It's fine. I'm fine.' She wiped her eyes, and turned to May, pasting a smile on her face. 'I'm fine. I'm going to see how John's getting on.'

She looked over at the rover. John was leaning against it looking at her, his expression unreadable. She wondered if he was thinking about his brother. They had both lost someone before they should. Was it still having such an impact on them both all these years later?

'Hey, how are you getting on?' She called out to him. 'Your hour's up you know?' She leapt up and went to inspect the rover.

'Jessica...' he said quietly as she drew near.

'You think you can get this thing going?' She looked at him purposefully, willing him not to mention it any further.

'I think I might be done. Let's give it a go.' He got into the driver's seat and pressed the power button, Jessica leaning against the door. There was a gentle purr and the rover began to vibrate. They both whooped with delight.

'You did it, John! Oh, you're so clever I could kiss you.' She took his head between her hands, kissed him firmly on the forehead then leaned back and smiled at him. She had trusted his judgement and he had come through for her. The tension she had been feeling dissipated, the self-doubt temporarily ebbed away.

'Right,' she was back in action mode now, 'we need to get May and all this stuff back in. Have we got anything we can use to make a splint for her?'

***

Thirty minutes later, with May laid up on the back seat of the rover, and all the other equipment shifted around to make room for her, they were heading back to the base. John kept his hands firmly on the wheel and his eyes focused on the landscape. They were all quiet. Jessica imagined John and May to be hot and thirsty like she was. She was sweaty, and her whole body itched with red dust.

She still wasn't sure if she'd done the right thing today, letting May stop her from calling for help. Jessica looked back at her. She was still pale; her eyes had a glazed look. But they would be back soon. May was strong and stoical and hadn't complained about the pain once.

'Look, there's the base,' John pointed towards some shapes emerging on the hazy horizon.

John pulled the rover in front of a cluster of aluminium buildings, where they were met by a committee of scientists and engineers who would spend the next few hours grilling them and making them write reports. Jessica fired off an order for emergency support for May. She and John followed behind the base staff, as May was stretchered inside, protesting loudly that she could actually walk.

Tired and stiff from their journey and the accident Jessica and John walked slowly towards the door. As they reached the entrance Jessica felt John's hand on her arm.

'Jessica,' he squeezed her arm, 'It wasn't your fault, you know that?'

'You mean May? Well, we're going to have to answer some questions about how it happened-'

'I mean your mom. It wasn't your fault. You do know that?'

Jessica tried to swallow the lump that had risen in her throat. She'd do anything, anything to take back that night. She'd insisted, insisted on going out. Her mum had been trying to protect her, and in doing so she had lost her life, and Jessica had lost the most important person in the world. How could it not be her fault?

'It's that or I'm just really unlucky. All the people I love leave me.

'It wasn't your fault, Jessica.'

She tried to reply but all the air had left her lungs. She just looked at John's kind face, full of concern; his hazel eyes boring into hers as if he were trying to read her mind. Somehow, he always made her feel better.

'Come on,' she said. 'I don't know about you but I need a shower.' She carried on walking towards the door.

'You mean together, right?' he called from behind her.

She turned around, laughing now. He always made her laugh. 'There's literally no moment too serious for you to make a joke is there?'

Oh, you thought I was joking. Er, yeah sure, ok.' But his smile was wide and he put his arm around her shoulder as they walked into the base. She felt a warmth that had nothing to do with the desert air. When John started to joke about serious things she felt as if it might all be ok.

Chapter Eight
Countdown until first Mars walk: four years

Jessica

Rachel Goldman wanted to make the most of the last of the warm weather and decided to hold a party late September that year.

An astronaut of seven years, Rachel was a good friend of Jessica's and something of a mentor. The American woman shared a large house on the outskirts of Cologne with her husband Max, a German high school teacher ('Well, one of us has to have a normal job'), and their three year old daughter Lilli.

It had been three years since Jessica had graduated from the training programme, and two years since she had got her wings. She had flown to the International Space Station Two, successor to the original International Space station, and the national Skylab and Mir crafts that had preceded it.

Her training in the US had been exciting and challenging but Jessica had been grateful to return to the comforting familiarity of Cologne. The astronauts still returned to the US for flights. Cape Canaveral in Florida remained one of the most conveniently located launch pads.

Almost the entire astronaut pool and various other members of the teams they worked alongside were spilling out into Rachel's garden. Music was playing through a speaker, and people were chatting and laughing. The late September air was still warm.

Jessica was making her way through the garden back to the house. The Riesling she'd been drinking had gone straight to her head and she was in search of something to eat. She was filling a plate when the front door opened and footsteps came along the hall.

'Do you ever stop thinking about food, Gabriel?' John stood in the doorway to the dining room, holding some beers and a bottle of sparkling wine.

'I was going to ask if you ever stop being anti-social, but it turns out you do.' She grinned at John and gave him a hug. 'I'm glad you came. It's not the same without you.' John took a lot of persuasion to come to big social events, but he was always good company when he did.

'Where's Rachel, I want to give her this.' He indicated the bottle he was holding.

'Well trained as ever.'

'I've told you before,' John said, 'my grandmother was a stickler for manners.'

'She's in the garden, I'll come out with you.'

They wandered through the house and into the garden, John nodding at people who greeted him as they walked past.

'Hey, look who I found,' she announced to the small group sitting on a random selection of borrowed patio chairs at the end of the garden.

'John!' There were genuine smiles as he approached the group, and Rachel stood up to give him a hug. Jessica knew now how difficult John found this sort of thing, but he never betrayed it. He appeared to make friends so effortlessly; he was well-practised at making conversation and a good listener.

John kissed Rachel on the cheek and handed her the wine. 'Thanks for having us over Rachel.'

'It's my pleasure.'

'Where's the lovely Lilli?' he asked.

'With Max's parents for two whole nights.' She sighed contentedly. 'I love her to bits, but she's a handful. Two nights off will be lovely.'

'Hey,' Max, Rachel's husband elbowed her in the ribs. 'You'll have about three weeks off next year when you do your moon flight.'

'That's your first flight since Lilli, isn't it?' Jessica asked. 'How are you feeling? First crew to go back to the moon in sixty-five years.'

Rachel had two flights into space to Jessica's one. Currently the only missions were to ISS2, but flights around the moon to test the technology for the Mars mission were about to begin. The missions would be shorter than the long stays on the space station but would venture much further than crewed ships had been since the Apollo programme.

'Well, if anyone else asks, I'm totally cool about it. But since it's you guys, totally fricking excited.'

They all laughed.

'She was bouncing around the house the day they told her,' Max confirmed.

'Lilli keeps drawing pictures of mommy in her spaceship, it's so cute,' Rachel said.

Jessica looked at Rachel and Max. Rachel had her legs looped over Max's. They were so at ease with one another, so affectionate. Rachel was only a couple of years older than her, but she was a world away from Jessica, with her husband, calm, quiet Max, mischievous and precocious Lilli, and their family home, which wanted only a dog to complete the cliché. They were her 'grown up' friends. Jessica would come over for grown up dinners, and then she and Rachel would sit on the sofa and talk and giggle, while Max put Lilli to bed and quietly topped up their wine glasses. Jessica was staying here tonight, as she sometimes did when she came over. Rachel was the big sister she had never had and had taken Jessica under her wing.

Looking around at all the people at the party Jessica had to remind herself that she was living through a moment in history. Everyone here was part of the mission to put humans on Mars. There had been countless interviews, documentaries, films, and books documenting the Apollo programme and the people involved. Would there be the same interest in this group? Would there be photos from this party in books on the Mars programme?

The party went on late into the evening and Jessica, never one to stay still for very long, moved around different groups. She found herself perched on the edge of a table in the middle of a conversation between Tom, Mike, and Lucca talking sports. The varied nationalities all still supported their own national sports: Tom as a Canadian was a die-hard ice hockey fan; Mike worshipped the New York Knicks basketball team, and Lucca was football obsessed. But it was traditional for all the sports fans at NARESA HQ to put their differences aside and pledge their allegiance towards the local Bundesliga football team FC Köln. They were arguing the merits of the most recent signing.

'They paid way too much for him.' Mike was arguing.

'They had to, players that good hardly ever come on the transfer market.' Tom countered.

'Yeah, but he spent half of last season with Bayern injured.'

'But look at how many goals he scored when he did play; he could be the new Messi!' Lucca interjected.

'You are joking? Messi was the GOAT. This guy's not fit to clean his boots.' Mike was getting animated, his hands waving around.

'Goat?' Jessica whispered to Tom with raised her eyebrows.

'Greatest of All Time,' he whispered back with a grin.

'Oh.' She rolled her eyes.

Jessica wasn't particularly interested in football and let the conversation drift over her as she looked around the garden. May and Rachel were dancing with a small group on the patio. Max was talking to some of the few people who weren't astronauts or NARESA employees, partners of some of her colleagues. It was such a close-knit community, Jessica thought it must be tough to be on the outside.

She looked through the open patio doors into the dining room. John was chatting closely with Ingrid, a tall blonde Swedish woman who was an engineer working on a robotics project that John had been helping with. *They look pretty cosy.* She studied their body language. They sat at an angle to each other, knees almost touching. John had his arm draped casually across the back of his chair, resting lightly on Ingrid's chair. Jessica smiled to herself. She knew John had dated several women since they had begun their training, but Jessica had never seen him in action before because they were usually part of their small crowd of trainees. There was a pang in her chest. It was just loneliness. When was the last time she'd had a date? How long since she'd been physically close to someone? Too long. There just didn't seem to be the time. She wrapped her arms around herself as she noticed the temperature had dropped.

'Hey, are you cold?' It was Tom, his blue eyes looking at her with concern.

'I'm ok.'

'Here, have my jacket.' He took it off and placed it around her shoulders.

'You don't have to do that.'

'Hey, this is practically tropical where I come from.' His face dimpled as he smiled.

No, not him Jessica. He's a crewmate, she told herself sternly. *Shame though*, she smiled to herself and pulled his jacket tight around her, breathing in the masculine scent that radiated from it.

The party quietened down around a little after midnight. Jessica hadn't seen John for a few hours. She wandered into the house to look for him, collecting empty glasses as she went. He wasn't in the house, and none of the guests still around had seen him recently. Jessica began to tidy the kitchen before settling down in Rachel's spare room. It was unlike John to leave without saying goodbye. Parties like this were rarely his thing. She hoped he was ok. For a moment it occurred to her that he might have not gone home alone and the pang in her chest returned.

***

Jessica emerged puffy-eyed and tousle-haired from Rachel and Max's spare room. She followed the smell of coffee to the kitchen where Rachel was sitting at the table reading the news on a tablet.

'How are you up so early?' Jessica said.

'This is a lie-in compared to normal. Coffee?'

'Please.' She sank onto a chair opposite Rachel.

Rachel slid a mug of steaming coffee under Jessica's nose. As she breathed in the intoxicating smell the haze of sleep left her body.

'Where's Max?' she asked with a yawn.

'He's gone out for a run. He's going to make us pancakes when he gets back.'

'Is there anything wrong with that man or is he just perfect?' Jessica said with a groan.

'He colour sorts his wardrobe,' Rachel said in a mock whisper.

'Does he?'

'Even his pants and socks.' They both giggled.

'I'd take colour sorted pants if it meant pancakes for breakfast.'

'It's definitely worth it.' Rachel sipped her coffee and looked at Jessica thoughtfully. 'Isn't there anyone out there you're interested in? You know, sometimes, Jessica, you just have to accept colour sorted pants.'

'It's not even that there is no-one suitable, I just don't meet anyone who isn't at work.'

'Well, the crew are off limits, which is probably a good thing, because astronauts are all workaholic space bores,' Rachel smiled, 'but there are cute guys in engineering or R&D if smart and nerdy is your thing. And hundreds of men in the rest of HQ. Want me to find someone to set you up with? I could see if Max knows anyone suitable.' She grinned devilishly.

'No! Absolutely not.' Jessica put her mug firmly on the table. 'Seriously though, when would I even find the time?'

'Jessica, I manage to raise a three year old child while doing our job. I think you could meet a guy.'

'I'm sorry, I know.' She bit her lip. 'You're doing an amazing job. Look at everything you do, and here I am complaining about not having time.'

'That's not what I meant,' she smiled and stroked Jessica's hand. 'I'm not telling you off because you're not doing enough. Quite the opposite. I'm telling you it doesn't have to be that way. You make choices. How often are you in the lab late? How many times do you run "just one more sim"?'

'I just want to do a good job.'

'Oh, we all do, honey,' Rachel's voice was warm and gentle, it made her feel like someone was looking out for her. 'You work harder than anyone I know. But there's more to life than work.'

'It's not just a job though is it? It's more than that. It's a life choice.' She ran her hand through her hair absently. Was Rachel right? Was she just making excuses?

'I know that. I know that more than you think. Don't you think it's going to be excruciating for me to be so far away from Lilli? And for so long if I'm on a long duration mission. I know what it's like to make sacrifices. But Jessica,' she looked earnestly at her, 'it's about balance. And as much as NARESA wants dedicated astronauts they also want well rounded, balanced people. This lifestyle only works when you have the support you need around you. I know you don't have your mom or your dad, and your grandmother is back in England...'

Jessica looked down at her hands. Hearing it like that made her sound pretty tragic. She suddenly felt a longing for more in her life.

'Oh, I didn't mean to make you sad, sweetie. You've got me,' Rachel grabbed her hand again. 'And Lilli adores you.' Jessica smiled at the thought of the little curly haired blonde girl who liked to be pushed as high as possible on the swings and go down the slide backwards. 'And you've got May, and John, and your other friends.'

'I know. Thank you. You're so lovely.'

'Don't be silly, I'm your friend, that's my job. But think about what I've said, ok?'

'I will, I promise.'

'Speaking of John,' Rachel grinned over the rim of her coffee cup, 'I do believe he left with Ingrid last night.'

Jessica felt a jolt of surprise. 'Oh, I did see them talking. They've been working together haven't they?'

'Yes. Ingrid's gorgeous, and so nice. Do you know her?'

'Only to say hello to.' She had met Ingrid a couple of times and spoke to her briefly at the party last night. She was tall, Scandinavian, with hair like corn silk. She looked like she should be a model in a catalogue for overpriced outdoor clothes. She hadn't pegged her as John's type, but she was smart and very pretty.

'See, John can find someone at work. There's no reason you can't too.' Rachel said.

Jessica just pulled a face and drank some more coffee without saying anything.

'Jessica?' Rachel looked curiously at her.

'What?'

'It doesn't bother you that John went home with Ingrid does it?'

'What? No, of course it doesn't. Why would it?' *Oh god, please don't answer that Rachel.*

'It's just-' Rachel started to speak.

'No, don't be silly.' Jessica interrupted her before she could continue. 'You're right, there aren't any excuses. If John can find someone, then I should be able to too.'

She looked up at Rachel who raised her eyebrows.

'Stop it,' Jessica said firmly. 'Whatever you're thinking, you're wrong.'

'Alright, alright.' Rachel held up her hands in mock surrender.

'So, is there any more coffee?' Jessica changed the subject, quashing the memory of John with his arm across the back of Ingrid's chair flashed into her mind. It was fine. She was fine.

The front door opened and slammed shut and Max called out from the hallway 'You girls up?'

Rachel rolled her eyes at Jessica, 'We are now, honey, with all that noise.

'Sorry!' he poked his head around the door. 'I'll just take a shower then make us breakfast.'

Jessica turned to Rachel with an 'isn't he sweet?' face. Rachel just mouthed 'Colour sorted pants,' and Jessica spluttered into her coffee. But even though she was laughing she couldn't quite ignore the feelings floating around her body, feelings that she couldn't quite put her finger on. Feelings that she didn't quite trust herself with.

Chapter Nine
Countdown to first Mars walk: three years

John

The room was like any other that they had sat in for dozens of crew briefings. Every briefing room in the NARESA building looked the same. However, since the meeting appointment had gone out everyone knew that room A741 would be a room that changed the lives, one way or another, of every astronaut that walked through its door on this particular morning.

The previous day the entire pool of astronauts had received an appointment instructing them to be in A741 at nine a.m. The meeting appointment was titled 'Crew Selection'. They hadn't expected to find out like that. John tried to keep his expression neutral. He was above all a quiet optimist, but it would be difficult to put a positive slant on not being selected for the Mars mission. John couldn't think of another situation in his life where there would either be complete elation or complete dejection. There was nothing in between. The hopefuls stood in the room, and a small amount of nervous chatter could be heard above the noise coming from the room's air conditioning vents. John glanced around the room, wondering which of them would be selected.

Through various rounds of selections that had gone on over years of training, it had come down to the twenty people in this room. They were all going to be selected for something, but the vast difference between being on the first mission to land on Mars, and being on the backup crew of Concordia, was too huge to contemplate.

Of the two Mars missions, the Concordia would set off first, orbit Mars and deliver supplies to the surface with a crew of five, but it wouldn't land. Harmonia would follow the same mission plan, but a separate craft, the Aneris, would take five astronauts down to the surface. John looked around; five people in this room would walk on the surface of another planet for the first time in human history. Another five would be the first humans to orbit the planet. Then there would be ten who would act as the backup for those missions, and the likelihood was that they would not be going anywhere. Nothing would have made any difference now but there was still an amount of bravado going on in the room. Even when he caught Lucca's eye, one of his closest friends, the pair of them puffed out their chests in an involuntary show of domination.

John's thoughts were confused. Everyone wanted to be on the Harmonia crew, but then there was a slight consolation of being on the Concordia crew, not landing on Mars, but at least travelling to it. John's mind drifted to Apollo 8, and the first crew to orbit another astronomical object. They didn't land, but their achievement still contained lots of firsts. Would that be enough? Everyone in the room had a one in two chance of being on a mission. John then started to contemplate something that had been tucked away at the back of his mind. If in the unlikely chance Jessica wasn't on the mission to land on Mars, would he rather be one of the first people on another planet, or would he rather be on Jessica's crew, even if that meant not being on a prime mission?

For just a fleeting moment John thought about his brother Charlie, how he should be here in this room, certain that if his health had allowed, he would have been on one of the prime crews.

'John!' Jessica's excited whisper jolted him from his thoughts, and at the same time calmed his nerves.

'Hey you,' his face broke into a smile as he saw Jessica, 'how are you feeling'?

'Terrified' said Jessica, biting at a fingernail.

'You'll be fine.' He was convinced she would be.

A door at the back of the room opened and in walked Hans Vogel. They all knew this was the time.

'Please take a seat, everyone,' Hans said as he placed some papers onto the simple podium on the raised stage at the front of the room. His voice was amplified by a microphone that was on the podium; hardly necessary to brief fewer than two dozen people. John was pleased to see that Jessica had taken the seat next to him. This would be such a huge moment for both of them; she was the one he wanted to share it with.

'Ok.' the authoritative message from Hans cut the chatter and movement in the room to complete silence.

'I'm looking out at the most capable and dedicated ladies and gentlemen that I have ever known. Everyone in this room has the skills and expertise to be on these crews. Unfortunately, only ten of you will be making the journey and only five setting foot on Mars. But I know that everyone in this room will remain committed to the Mars programme.'

Come on Hans, get on with it. John felt something at his ankle. Jessica had hooked her foot around his.

'Stop jiggling,' she whispered, but she was smiling, eyes focused on the podium, and she didn't remove her foot even once he had stopped.

'This will be the running order,' Hans announced in a loud voice.

'I'm going to announce the two backup crews, then Concordia, then Harmonia.' It would be clear by the pace of those words that this was going to be fast, and there would be no pause for dramatic effect.

As the names for the Concordia backup crew were read out it was silent. This was the worst list to be on; this group of five would just be reserves for the astronauts who were going to fly around Mars. No mention of John or Jessica. He allowed himself a moment of satisfaction.

'Harmonia backup,' continued Hans.

John clenched his teeth. *Just survive this group and you're going to Mars.*

'Harmonia backup Engineer - John Eden.'

Everything else fell away into nothing. The room closed in on him. He wasn't going to Mars. A jolt on his ankle brought him back into the room. Jessica was squeezing his leg with hers. He felt her sympathy but remained numb. He hadn't even heard the other names on the backup list, but he knew none of them had been Jessica.

'Concordia Prime Crew.' Hans's voice was calm and methodical.

John glanced at Jessica whose gaze was transfixed on the podium. It dawned on him. She was going to Mars.

His mind was still a blur as Hans read out the first four names on the Concordia crew, still no mention of Jessica.

'Commander of the Concordia-' Hans paused, the first so far, as if he was still assessing a decision that had taken a while to make.

'Rachel Goldman.'

A hushed gasp went around the room, many had expected Rachel to be the Commander of Harmonia, and she had always been the favourite for the first person to walk on Mars, that was no longer going to be the case.

Only five names hadn't been read out, and Jessica was one of them.

Jessica straightened her back. They all knew she was going to walk on Mars.

'Commander of Harmonia - Jessica Gabriel. Ok thank you everyone, that's it.' And without further discussion he left them all to it.

'Are you ok?' Jessica whispered.

'I'm fine. Congratulations, Commander. You're going to Mars.' He tried with every part of his face to give Jessica a genuine smile.

'We need some great people on backup John,' she said, clearly struggling to find something comforting to say.

John looked again at her and smiled. Everyone had left their seats and he and Jessica were the only two people still sitting. Everyone else moved around the room and hugged.

'Jessica, you need to go and enjoy this.' John reached down to hold Jessica's hand, knowing that he wouldn't be able to do it for long, so wanting to make the most of every second.

'Are you going to be ok?' asked Jessica.

'I won't see you for years.' The words slipped out of his mouth before he could stop them.

Jessica looked to the floor.

'Is Ingrid around today? Will she make sure you're ok?' She didn't respond to his comment. Yes, Ingrid would be waiting for him, waiting to hear what his fate was. They had been together for a year now. She was kind and loving. She wouldn't quite understand the scale of his disappointment, but she would try and make him feel better.

'Yeah, I'm sure she is,' said John. Ingrid couldn't be further from his thoughts. 'Go on, enjoy this moment.'

Jessica's expression slowly shifted. Her eyebrows relaxed and a faint smile appeared on her face.

'John!' She half groaned, half laughed. 'Oh God, I can't believe this is happening.'

'Look,' he pointed. 'May wants you. You're proper crewmates now. Go and see her. I'll catch up with you soon.' His show of cheerfulness was unconvincing.

She looked reluctant. 'I'll be fine. Trust me.' He pasted on a smile.

She squeezed his hand and he gripped hers back, then reluctantly letting go. 'Go on.' He said ushering her away. She didn't need him burdening her. This was her moment.

Jessica stood up and walked towards the closest group of people and was hugged three times in quick succession.

John felt a strong hand on his shoulder.

'I'm sorry buddy.' said Mike, he had been selected as engineer in Jessica's crew, the role that John would have had. John bristled at being called "buddy" by Mike. They rubbed along together as colleagues but they had never been buddies.

'Thanks,' said John, swallowing his bitterness. 'I'm really happy for you.' He hoped he sounded more sincere than he felt.

Mike looked over his shoulder to see what John was looking at. John's eyes were still fixed on Jessica, taking her hugs and congratulations.

'Anyway, I'll catch you soon,' said Mike, turning straight into an embrace from another of the successful crew members.

For the first time since the announcement John found himself alone, watching everyone else in the room.

He looked towards the door. Hans had made it clear that everyone was free to go afterwards, and could take the rest of the day. John just wanted to leave. The room was closing in on him again. Setting the door at the back of the room in his sights, he plotted a way out through the messy labyrinth of chairs which had been pushed aside and jumbled in the excitement. Through the morass of bodies, John picked out Jessica's hair and shoulders through a gap. None of the other astronauts had left the room yet, and although he didn't want to be the first to leave, he also knew things couldn't get any worse for him right now and that people would understand if he just left. Not that he cared what anyone thought at this moment.

He headed for the door giving one last backward glance before leaving. He caught Jessica's eye. She mouthed 'Where are you going?' and held both hands in the air. John turned, without saying anything in return and walked into the quiet, sterile hallway that led to the meeting rooms.

Each step he took away from the room helped the excited chatter disappear into a memory that he wanted to forget.

He took the stairs to give himself more time to think about where he was going. He hadn't planned to be leaving early and on his own. It struck him that he hadn't climbed up or down these stairs alone before, he was always with other people from the crew, but that was exactly the way he wanted it. He should go and find Ingrid, but he just couldn't face her at the moment. He would message her. He had only allowed himself to contemplate making the call to her saying 'I'm on the main crew!' He hadn't rehearsed this version of events at all. Was that what was bothering him the most? Letting everyone down? Ingrid. His grandmother. Charlie. His face involuntarily screwed up at the thought of his larger than life big brother. Charlie would never have let everyone down.

Without knowing how he got there, he was in his apartment. He slumped back into his sofa and put both hands on his forehead, to try and come to terms with what had happened that afternoon. Cruel thoughts ran through his head where he would see visions of the Harmonia crew celebrating as they landed on the surface of Mars. He didn't know how long he'd been lying there, and he didn't care. This was one of those days that just needed to end. He felt strangely optimistic that every minute away from that day would feel better. Then the crushing blow of not being on the crew would hit him like a hammer in the chest.

For the first time since being home, John glanced at his phone. Three messages from Ingrid and a missed call. Nothing from anyone else. Nothing from Jessica. He fired off a reply to Ingrid to discourage her from coming over. He didn't want her to see him like this. John put his phone down to his side and turned away.

Why hadn't Jessica messaged him? She would know he wasn't fine, no matter what he told her. She would understand what this meant to him. Then came a thought that hadn't hit him yet. *Jessica is the commander of Harmonia, she's probably going to be the first human to walk on another planet.* John smiled to himself; for a moment his happiness for her overshadowed his own disappointment. No sooner had that thought arrived, it was replaced by the realisation that he wouldn't be there with her. She was someone different now. It felt like a fissure had occurred between them; a crack that would get wider with time till he was too far away to reach her.

Daylight faded, yet John did not move, except to occasionally get a beer from the fridge. The room grew dark. The lights from street lamps glared through the still open blinds and made patterns on his ceiling. An occasional car headlight illuminated the detritus of the day. Still John did not move. The ding of his phone broke the silence. He knew without looking that it was Jessica. Only two people had a different message tone to the default: Jessica and his grandmother, though they each provoked very different thoughts when he heard them. Every time Jessica's tone went off he made a mental note to create a special tone for Ingrid, but for some reason he never got around to it.

John resisted looking at the message, telling himself that he didn't care. He lasted twenty seconds.

Jessica:
Hey, Are you ok? X

John read the message over again, happy to have it, but wishing it had come earlier.

He again tried to leave it as long as possible, not wanting to seem desperate, but within five minutes he replied.

John:
Yes, Commander, I'm fine. :-)

Jessica:
I've been so worried about you. Are you ok? I'm so sorry John x

John wanted to believe Jessica, but the elapsed hours detracted from Jessica's apparent concern.

For the first time in hours, John pulled himself up from the sofa and walked to the fridge to get a beer. At eye height was a note from Jessica that he had pinned to his fridge, it read "To Mars and back, J x". Jessica had written it, although with his head full of the day's events he couldn't remember when or why. He took out a beer, closed the door and stared at the note. Removing the top and downing half the bottle he kept eyes still fixed on the note. "To Mars and back". It still hadn't sunk in that he wasn't going to Mars, that Jessica was and he wasn't.

John picked up his phone and stared at it before typing his message.

John:
I'm fine. Have you enjoyed your day?

Jessica:
I just can't believe it. I couldn't have done it without you John x

John:
Yes, you could, you know you could.

Jessica:
I couldn't. John, I wish you were coming.

John:
I know.

Jessica:
I have to go, we're all having a drink together. Want to join us? X

He couldn't think of anything worse. Not even one percent of him wanted to. She should know that.

He typed out a response.

John:
I really don't feel like it. I'll leave you all to be happy with yourselves. It's a night for winners.

His thumb hovered over the send button. No, delete, she didn't need to see his bitterness. He wouldn't bother replying.

Jessica:
I know you're disappointed. I'm sorry. I'll see you tomorrow at the press conference? X

The press conference. It had completely slipped his mind. Placeholders had been put in all astronauts' agendas. Officially, they had been told that only the successful crews would be required; the backup crews could attend if they wanted to. John knew that meant they were expected to as a member of the backup crew, but he had no intention of going. To have to stare at the ten successful candidates smiling under the bright glare of the media lights? To see Mike sitting next to Jessica? There wasn't one part of him that wanted to see that. He should be there, if not for anyone else then for Jessica. But he just couldn't bring himself to do it. He should be the one sitting next to Jessica tomorrow.

The empty beer bottles stacked up on the coffee table. Although astronauts were allowed to drink, it was an unwritten rule that they shouldn't drink 'too much' and as the astronaut group had matured it had become socially unacceptable to have more than a couple of drinks. *One, two, three, four...* He lost count of the empties. NARESA and its rules could go to hell. All the constraints on his life for the past few years now seemed pointless.

He got himself ready for bed so he could just fall asleep where he was. He wanted to banish the day's events from his mind for long enough to drift off or get drunk enough that it wouldn't matter.

Jessica:
Hey, you didn't reply, are you ok?

John glanced at the message but was way beyond caring about replying. He thought not replying would have more of the desired effect. Whatever that effect was. He no longer knew how he felt, but in the back of his mind he sensed he was trying to punish her for some reason.

Jessica:
I'm back home, I missed you there tonight. You know if I could change it I would?

John watched as the clock in his room ticked over midnight. It was as if the second hand meeting the twelve had a cleansing effect. It was a new day, and he would never again have to spend time in the previous one.

Jessica:
I'm going to sleep. Hopefully you had an early night, I'll see you tomorrow x

The sun shone in a narrow, intense band across John's face. A shrill noise rang through his pounding head. By the time he worked out it was his phone ringing the noise had stopped. Three missed calls from his grandmother.

For a few beautiful moments John imagined that it had all been a dream, maybe today was the day they would find out about the Mars crew selection. He gazed around the room where there were reminders of the day before, his crumpled clothes, the empty beer bottles. The realisation creeped through him all over again.

John hadn't even thought about what he was going to say to his grandmother. How should he play it? Try and sound like he was unaffected? Or admit to her how disappointed he was? Before his foggy brain could complete this thought process, the phone rang again.

'Hi, Grandma. Sorry, I must have been in a really deep sleep,' said John, deciding on the spur of the moment to take the cheerful route.

'Hello John. Yes, I always sleep well after drinking that much.'

Damn. Was it his hoarse voice that gave him away? Or did his grandmother just know him better than he thought?

'I thought I would leave it until this morning to call you. I just want you to know how sorry we all are, I know you would have wanted to have been on a prime crew,' said Elizabeth.

John wasn't surprised with her cutting straight to the purpose of the call without small talk. Years of being in the space programme had moulded her in that way. Astronauts didn't have time for verbosity or prevarication.

'I'm fine, Grandma, really, I'm fine,' said John, trying to sound convincing.

'I'm aware that I am not always the most emotionally astute, but I have learned in my long years that how fine someone is, is usually inversely proportional to the number of times they declare they are fine.'

John smiled in spite of himself. His grandmother was really something else.

'I am, I really am.' Why couldn't he just tell her how he felt. Of course she'd understand, she'd understand more than anyone. But they didn't have that sort of relationship.

'Ok,' Elizabeth continued. 'You'll pretend you're ok, and I'll pretend to believe you.' He could hear her wry smile down the phone line. 'I'll see you later? At the press conference?'.

'No, you won't,' said John, 'I don't need to go to that, Prime Crews only.'

'John, you need to support your team mates.'

'I'm sure they'll be fine,' John continued 'They're all so happy with themselves right now.'

He was so thirsty but he couldn't move from the sofa. He reached for a nearly empty bottle of beer on the table and swigged down the dregs, silently gagging as the warm, flat liquid ran down his throat.

'John, you know how proud I am of you, you know that pride didn't change one bit yesterday, but it will today if you don't go along to support your crewmates, your friends. How do you think Jessica will feel if you're not there?'

That was a cheap shot bringing up Jessica. He wouldn't be guilted by his grandmother.

'You know John, it's up to you, but I think you will go, that's the man you are. You won't let them down, you won't let Jessica down on her big day.' Her conviction in the face of opposition impressed him.

He had a flashback to his childhood, learning how to ride a bike aged about four years old. A fall had left him with skinned knees and gravel in his palms. Embarrassed and in pain he had thrown the bike into the driveway and declared that he was never going to learn and riding a bike was stupid anyway. His grandmother had come to find him with a wet cloth and some plasters.

'I know you're going to keep trying John,' she said firmly. 'That's the sort of boy you are. Brave and determined. I wouldn't be surprised if you were riding that bike by the end of tomorrow.'

He was jolted back to the present having only just processed his grandmother's words. 'Wait, you're going to the press conference?'

'Of course I'm going, they're announcing the first team to attempt to land on Mars. It's historic, John.'

As his grandmother finished that sentence it hit him all over again, a team was going to travel to Mars, and he wouldn't be on it.

'Well, I hope you enjoy it, Grandma, let me know how it goes.' said John, the emotion of the day making him feel braver than usual.

'You wouldn't disappoint me, John, you always do the right thing. We'll speak later.' That was clearly a command.

John didn't think for a second about going to the press conference, the only thought that crossed his mind was how mad his grandmother would be and how long it would take her to get over it.

The phone line went dead, Elizabeth rarely waited for John to say goodbye.

He briefly scanned through Jessica's unanswered messages from last night. A knot formed in his stomach, and he rubbed the back of his neck squeezing his eyes shut. She didn't deserve to be ignored. He threw his phone down beside him. He couldn't yet articulate himself properly. He'd message her later.

John squinted into the sunlight bursting in through the window. Imagine if he had been picked for prime crew. Today would have been the perfect day, he would have walked to that press conference feeling like a million dollars, sharing the admiration and smiles with Jessica and the rest of the crew.

That wasn't the day that John was going to experience, but he thought to himself that he should at least try to make the best of things. He hated to admit it but Elizabeth was right, he wasn't that guy. He thought back to that day with his bike when his grandmother had tended to his wounds. The next morning, without telling anyone and wincing at the stinging in his knees, he had climbed back on the bike and practised and practised till by the end of the day he was confidently riding up and down the street.

***

There was a palpable sense of excitement in the crowded outer room of the press area. The air hummed with chatter. Journalists fiddled with equipment. Suited NARESA officials gripped and grinned with politicians and the press.

Even though he wasn't one of the prime crew, there was an interest in John as he passed through the crowd identified by his blue flight suit. He stood taller, his posture confident as he navigated his way through the room. The hubbub reminded him that he was part of something huge, even if he wasn't a main player, he was working towards a goal that the entire world would take an interest in.

He spotted the telltale flight suits of some of the rest of the backup crew. Their faces didn't betray whether they too had spent the night wallowing in self-pity like he had. But like John, they appeared to be appreciating still being at the heart of something big.

'John, good to see you here,' out of nowhere Hans Vogel had appeared, the man who had decided against John, and the man who had made the announcement the day before.

'I wouldn't miss it, it's important that we support each other,' he said with a crooked smile. *A little too much, John. He'll never swallow that.*

'Well,' said Hans, taking him at his word 'I wish the other members of the backup crews felt the same, there's only a few of you here. Bravo John. For me, this says more about you than any of the tests we put you through.'

Hans squeezed his shoulder and moved away. John breathed deeply and tried to quell the feeling of hatred that rose in his chest. He knew Hans had just been doing his job, but he could spare him no concessionary thoughts right now.

'One minute until we start everyone.' A voice boomed from the speakers that were in the outer room. The buzz in the room increased, and everyone flocked like birds into the press room.

The room wasn't large, but John's view from the back was partially obscured by the morass of people scrambling for space. It was busier than he'd ever seen it. It would be busy again at various key points, but with two years until mission launch, then an eighteen month round trip, interest would soon wane. The NARESA press office would be working hard to make sure they stayed relevant during that time.

A bright light shone in the corner of the room. John looked over to see his grandmother, very smartly dressed, finishing an interview on live TV. As she exchanged pleasantries with the interviewer she locked eyes with John and just looked at him with a satisfied smile.

John shifted to get a better view as the prime crews were led out to the waiting seats on a raised platform. They walked in with their heads held high, strong but not stiff. They exuded professionalism and self-control.

The gulf between John and the prime crews felt wider than this briefing room. They sat elevated and illuminated under spotlights. He lurked at the back of the room, unseen in the dark. It was funny, he mused to himself, he had spent so long hiding his connection, worried about how people would feel about him when they knew his family connections. Today, for the first time ever, he just wanted to yell 'Don't you know who I am?'

John looked at Jessica, eyes wide under the glare of the lights. Her lips were pressed together, but slightly curled at the edges. He could tell she was happy, but there was an edge of nerves, given away only by the way she grasped her hands. He couldn't help but smile to himself as she took her seat. She had come so far, beaten all the odds. Selected as Commander for the most historic mission in generations.

Jessica was first in line for press questions. John didn't pay attention to her answers, he was just captivated by the sight of her. Soon she would be away for nearly two years. He wanted to commit her to memory. John's feelings were still a mix of feeling sorry for himself, but he knew a large part of it was not seeing her for such a long time.

When the press moved on to questioning the next crew member, Jessica started to squint and look through the audience. She raised her hand above her eyes to shield against the lights. She was looking for someone.

She looked in John's direction and seemed to stare, as if trying to see him through the dazzle of lights. She broke into a relieved smile. John knew she had seen him. His body relaxed and all the bitter thoughts left his head. He knew the smile was for him.

Chapter Ten
Countdown until first Mars walk: three years

Jessica

The NARESA press room was packed full of journalists. There weren't just the regular science writers in the crowded audience, looking up at the stage where Jessica sat. It was standing room only today, with news editors from all over the world. Through the glare of the studio lights Jessica could just make out some of the NARESA astronauts and other staff at the back of the room.

She sat at the end of a table with the four other members of the crew seated next to her. The crew for The Concordia, the spacecraft that would travel ahead of The Harmonia, around Mars, sat at an adjacent table. Three microphones were stationed on the table in front of them, in between glasses of water. Jessica took a sip and peered over her glass at the people waiting to hear her speak. *This is just the beginning,* she reminded herself. *This is part of your job now.*

Jessica blinked several times as flashes exploded in her face. All this publicity after less than twenty-four hours to get used to the idea. People in the astronaut pool had told her it was a foregone conclusion that she would command the crew, but nothing would make her believe it till the Flight Director announced it.

'Dr Gabriel, are you worried about the safety of this trip? It's a long time to be in space, and so far away.'

She paused before answering. There wasn't time to be worried. This was her job, and her responsibility now was to make sure everyone was as prepared as they could be for the coming mission. She couldn't pretend it was risk free, but for her, the risks were worth it. She leaned into the microphone.

'Well, no journey into space is without risk.' Oh crap, a stern look from George the NARESA press officer. Cameras continued to flash as she tried to figure out the appropriate answer. 'But, uh, everyone in the Mars programme is highly skilled, and safety is always at the forefront of everyone's mind. I am confident in the scientists and engineers across the globe who are contributing to the design and build of the Harmonia spacecraft, and I have complete faith in my crew to get us to Mars and back safely.' Her words became more fluid as she warmed up to the media circus.

'Dr Gabriel, you're the youngest person to command a mission since NARESA was established. Do you think you are experienced enough to lead this, such an important mission?'

She resisted the urge to roll her eyes at the grey-haired male reporter who stood in an ill-fitting suit, and simply said 'Yes' into the microphone.

The rest of the press corps laughed. She glanced sideways at George. He wasn't laughing, and she knew he'd give her a lecture for that answer. But really, how else was she supposed to respond to such an inane question. Sure, she was young, but she had successfully completed two flights to the ISS2. She had built up a reputation for assertive leadership, her directness and impatience softened by a warmth and charm, and an ability to motivate people.

'Dr Gabriel, NARESA hasn't announced who will be the first person to set foot on Mars. But as the Commander it is most likely to be you, can you confirm that?'

'With such a long time until we land, NARESA has decided to delay the decision. It will be made while The Harmonia is en route to allow the crew to focus on the vital work we need to do to maintain a safe mission. All the crew are highly skilled and any one of us would be honoured to be the first person to set foot on another planet.' She was in her stride now, 'But the Mars mission is about more than whoever is the first person to step on the planet. It's about the crew, everyone at NARESA, and all the people and organisations working across the world to make this mission a success. The Harmonia crew are simply the ambassadors for humankind on this momentous mission.'

Was that too much? The room was silent except for the click of cameras and the scratch of pens from the old school reporters making their notes in shorthand. George gave her a barely perceptible nod of satisfaction. She could do this.

'Captain Kareva, can you tell us how flying Harmonia will differ from the Soyuz spacecraft?'

The rest of the crew's turn to answer questions now. Valentina launched into a detailed description of the recent advancements in manoeuvrability of spacecraft and Jessica relaxed for a few minutes. She didn't mind being in front of the cameras, and enjoyed the almost adversarial nature of the press room, but it was so easy to say the wrong thing. This conference was being broadcast on the NARESA TV channel, all the major news outlets. Within minutes, whatever she said could be on social media for scrutiny. She knew this mission was about more than their capability as astronauts and scientists. As the first people to land on another planet they would be paraded in front of the cameras not just before and after the mission, but during the mission too. There would be cameras in parts of the spaceship, a portion of NARESA's funding came from media revenue. They were public property in almost every way.

John would be good at this, she thought, much better than her. He had a charm and ease about him that she could never achieve. Her eyes searched the edges of the room hoping to see him. Several other NARESA astronauts were standing around the room, offering the crew moral support. They weren't resentful, the ones who weren't picked. At least not openly. They all knew that being a working astronaut was no guarantee of getting a flight in your career, let alone on the most momentous mission in recent history. There was disappointment in not being selected, of course, but you picked yourself up and carried on supporting the prime crew, hoping your time would come.

Everyone was surprised when John wasn't selected for prime. Of course, some had assumed his name that made him a shoo-in. But Jessica knew there was far more to John than the legacy of his family. He had worked on the design of the launch and re-entry vehicle, and she couldn't understand why he was only on backup crew.

Her eyes scanned the room till she found him, standing stiffly at the back. She couldn't see his face in the glare of the lights, and in his NARESA jumpsuit he could have been any one of the dozens of astronauts in the agency pool, but she recognised the set of his shoulders and lean torso. She smiled; she knew he'd be there to support them.

Jessica turned her attention back to the press conference, comforted by his presence. She had missed the last question, but Lucca was animatedly describing what they expected to find on the surface of Mars. Jessica surveyed her crew mates for the next few years.

Lucca, a geological Mission Specialist, was the only one of the crew with children. Would anyone ask him what it would be like to leave young children at home like they did to the female astronauts? Rachel Goldman had been made Commander of The Concordia, Jessica would put money on the first question to her being about leaving Lilli. Everyone knew it was a tough decision for the parents among the crew, it was a long time to be away from your family. But this was the dream mission, the one you couldn't turn down.

Valentina had been selected as her pilot. She sat stiffly, her back poker straight, her face surveying the audience sternly. The quiet, stoical Russian couldn't have been more different to Jessica. But she knew they would make a formidable team, and her years of flight experience would be invaluable.

The crew aboard The Harmonia would be ably cared for by May, who was supplementing her physician qualifications with dental skills for the mission. May was also an amazing computer coder, in fact Jessica had found nothing May couldn't turn her hand to.

Finally, there was Mike Sanders, their engineer. Though they all had basic engineering training, Mike, with his military experience, would be the one responsible for keeping their vehicle and their home for the eighteen months of their mission space-worthy.

And she, Jessica, was responsible for the whole crew and the mission. She had armed herself with every skill she thought she might need in her journey to become an astronaut, and even more since she'd been selected to work for NARESA. But despite her dedication to collecting skills and knowledge she knew she'd never be an expert in any of them. Her expertise lay in people and how they worked, and she had known early on that her best opportunity would come from leading a team. She studied leadership books, took courses in group dynamics, and tried to be a source of support for everyone on the team. Her dedication had paid off, and yesterday as news of her selection was announced at the crew briefing she had to stifle the cry of delight that threatened to escape.

The only thing that dimmed her happiness was John not being selected. In the last few years since working on the Mars project together he had become her best friend; they saw each other almost every day. Even when they weren't working together, they ran together, cooked together. He managed to draw out the fun part out of her serious personality, he was light relief in the sometimes oppressive and overwhelming atmosphere of the space programme.

Why hadn't John been picked for a prime crew? It wasn't in Jessica's nature to question authority, and she trusted the judgement of Hans. But why Mike over John? John was a more skilled engineer and knew the spacecraft better than anyone. But John wasn't like the others; he didn't have the same deference for authority. Maybe it came from growing up so close to the programme. Jessica had always admired the way he didn't seem to care what other people thought of him, but had that cost him a place on the crew?

At least him being part of the backup crew meant they would still work together over the next year. That was consolation for her, if not for him. But then how would it feel when she was hundreds of thousands of miles away from him, for eighteen months? She hated to admit it, but she had come to rely on his presence in her life.

Jessica hadn't seen him since the announcement. After Hans Vogel had briefed the astronaut pool John had disappeared. His pride would be wounded and he needed to process the news alone before having to put on a brave face. She knew how he worked.

It seemed like the crew had answered every question possible about the impending mission, though Jessica knew the press were just getting started and this would be part of her life now. George called an end to the conference and photographers and journalists filed out of the room. Jessica stepped off the small stage and headed to the back of the room. She needed to catch John. Who knew when this media circus would be over?

'Jessica!' George called 'You need to stay here. Time Magazine has an exclusive interview.'

'Two minutes,' she called over her shoulder, hurrying away before he could stop her. From now on so little of her time would be her own, she was going to maintain as much control as she could, while she could.

'John,' he was about to leave on the tail of the journalists. He stopped and turned to her. The smile he gave her didn't quite reach the corners of his eyes, but she could see that he was trying.

'Hey, Commander,' he said softly. The emphasis on the word 'commander' was congratulatory, without a trace of bitterness. They both just stood for a moment, looking at each other, then John stepped forwards, wrapped his arms around her, and kissed the top of her head. 'I'm so proud of you.' His voice was warm and sincere, his arms familiar and comforting.

'John, I'm sorry –' Jessica leaned back to look at him.

'Don't. It's fine, really.' His expression was suddenly closed and she knew not to press him.

They locked eyes, each trying to silently communicate what they were feeling without having to say it out loud. 'I'm sorry it's not you,' she wanted to tell him.

As they stood in silence Ingrid approached them and slipped a hand into John's. 'You ok, honey?' she said to him, looking at him with concern.

'I'm fine.' He slipped his hand out and ran it through his hair. He turned to Ingrid. 'I'll be out in a minute.'

She took the hint and turned on her heel, squeezing John's arm as she left. 'Well done Commander Gabriel,' Ingrid called over her shoulder, but her congratulations lacked the warmth of John's.

'Thanks,' Jessica called after Ingrid's retreating back. 'Is Ingrid ok?'

'I think so, why?'

'She just seems a little off with me.' Was she mad at Jessica on John's behalf?

'Oh, she's just, you know...'

'No, I don't know. What?'

'She's just a little jealous of you. Everyone knows you're my best bud.' He punched her playfully on the shoulder, but there was a tension in the air. They didn't talk about their friendship or what it meant to each of them, there was a tacit agreement that they didn't need to. Or was it just avoidance?

'John, you do tell her she has nothing to worry about, don't you?'

'Yeah, of course. But you know... it's you. You're pretty amazing.' Jessica snorted at this.

'Well, make sure you reassure her. I promise I won't get in your way. Anyway, I'll barely have any time from now on. Speaking of Time,' she looked over her shoulder 'I'd really better go. I'll catch you later ok?'

'Sure.' John stuck his hands in his pocket. In that brief moment he looked to Jessica like a lost little boy.

Reluctant to leave him like this she reached out and touched his arm before heading back towards the rest of the crew.

'Jessica?' She turned around as John called her name. He was still standing there. He looked rooted to the spot.

She tried to read his expression. She knew he was devastated at not being chosen for prime crew. She would have to be sensitive about it over the next few months, not make things worse for him with her success.

'Jessica, we really need to go.' George's voice was insistent.

'Sorry John, I'd better go back before George spontaneously combusts. I'll catch up with you later, I promise.'

'Sure, no problem. Good luck with the interview.'

He'll be fine. Trying to blank out John's dejected face, she hurried to join the departing crew. It wasn't her job to act like John's girlfriend. Of course Ingrid was being cool with Jessica, why hadn't she seen it before? Jessica would stay out of their way for a while. That would be easy with the packed media schedule for the next few weeks. The sooner she could get back to some real work the better.

Chapter Eleven
Countdown until first Mars walk: three years

John

John was becoming well acquainted with the ceiling of his apartment. The sofa had moulded to his prone body, the comforting bottle of beer on the floor beside him. The press conference had been excruciating enough, but his lingering thoughts were of Jessica being swept away for the first of many rounds of interviews. Where they had once been on the same track, he sensed their paths diverging. *This train will divide at the next station. Jessica: destination Mars.*

And why had he told her about Ingrid? She didn't need to know that. He didn't want her doing anything differently. His relationship with Ingrid was completely separate.

Tomorrow was the weekend; two more days before he had to face everyone again. It had hit him harder than he had expected. They all knew this was how it was. Ninety eight percent of an astronaut's career was spent on the ground. A hundred percent for the ones in the wrong place at the wrong time. They were recruited knowing this, and it was drilled into them from day one.

He was lucky. He'd been into space twice. Two flights to the ISS2. The memory of the first launch would never leave him; the anticipation, a lot of waiting around, going through flight checklists, then the unforgettable noise of the engines firing, the G force that pressed on every part of your body. The simulations they repeated over and over again were good, preparing them well for the flights. But there was nothing like the real thing. It was unmistakable.

The buzzer to his apartment sounded, disturbing him from his reverie. He screwed up his eyes and ignored it, hoping whoever it was would go away. Only two people in his world would visit him unannounced, and if he was honest, he wasn't sure which of them he wanted to see.

The buzzer growled harshly twice more and John peeled himself up off the sofa.

'Who is it?' he asked into the intercom.

'It's me,' came the female voice.

John paused. He definitely didn't want to do this tonight. He had avoided leaving the press conference with her.

'Are you going to let me in?'

He pushed the door release button, unlatched his apartment door and went back to the sofa.

'John?' Ingrid entered, her blonde hair as perfect as ever, her blue eyes wide with concern. They had been dating for over a year, since working on a robotic arm project together that would help construct the two Mars bound spacecraft in low Earth orbit. Her intelligence and pragmatism stretched across both work and their relationship. Always knowing just what John needed, she was uncomplicated in return, just kind and easy company. They sometimes spent the night at each other's apartments, but he had never brought up the topic of them living together, though he was sure she wanted to.

When he examined his feelings, he knew his heart wasn't in it. Ingrid was a good person. She deserved more of him than he could give. Work dominated his life in a way that it didn't for her, even as someone within NARESA. It wasn't all consuming for her the way it was for the astronauts.

He knew his friendship with Jessica bothered her too. She rarely said anything, it wasn't her style, but he knew. And he also knew that if he had to give up one of the two, it would be Ingrid without question. Jessica's impending absence was playing on his mind, and making him realise how integral to his life she was.

And now Ingrid was here to see if he was ok. Of course she was, that's what she did. But tonight, he just wanted to lick his wounds on his own.

'Hey, *sotnos*,' she crooned at him. Normally he loved the Swedish term of endearment, but today it just made him wince. 'How are you feeling?' She swooped in and engulfed him.

'I'm fine,' he said, extricating himself from her grasp.

'There'll be other opportunities. You are so talented.' she said.

She didn't understand just how important this opportunity was.

'And you're on the backup crew, that means that they value you.'

That meant that he had to train alongside his colleagues for a mission he would likely not be going on. Watching the others train to go into space and trying to maintain enthusiasm was going to be tough.

'I'm fine, don't worry.'

'Oh *sotnos.*' She kissed him and stroked his cheek, then sat down beside him. 'Of course I am worried. I just don't want to see you like this. It's not like you.'

Turns out it's exactly like me. He was so disappointed with himself.

Not just at not getting on the crew, but at his reaction to it.

'You don't have to stay,' he told Ingrid. 'I'm terrible company right now.'

'I don't mind,' she said patiently.

'I've got to go out and meet my grandma later anyway.'

'Shall I come? I like your grandmother.'

John wasn't sure that Elizabeth felt the same. When she described Ingrid as 'nice' it never sounded like a compliment.

'No, thanks for offering, but it's going to be an awkward enough evening with her. You don't want to sit through that.'

She sat down next to him and stroked his face. She was so affectionate and lovely. Why couldn't that be enough for him?

The ping of his phone interrupted them. Knowing at once it was the wrong thing to do, he looked down towards it. It was an involuntary response. He already knew from the tone who it was.

'Jessica.' Ingrid's voice was quiet. The name hung in the air between them.

'Yeah, she's just checking up on me too, I expect.' He replied quickly, hoping to move the conversation in a different direction.

'I bet she's pretty happy,' Ingrid said neutrally, so John couldn't detect her meaning.

'Being made Commander? Yes, she's over the moon.' He grinned at his own pun, and how inappropriate that was.

'She got what she wanted then. Somehow she always seems to.' She said it lightly and anyone else might not have noticed the uncharacteristic meanness.

'I don't know what you mean.' He was being disingenuous.

'I think you do.' Ingrid replied simply.

'Look, Ingrid, Jessica is one of my best friends -'

'Just friends? Of course you are.'

'Ingrid. There is nothing going on with Jessica. You know that. Of course there isn't. And even if I wanted anything to happen - which I don't,' he added quickly, as her face turned thunderous, 'You know it wouldn't anyway. It's not allowed. And I care about my career far too much for that.' His career. What was left of it.

'It doesn't matter John. It doesn't matter what I do. I'll never be her. I'll never be enough for you.' Ingrid looked away at a blank patch of wall.

She was wrong. This wasn't about Jessica. It had nothing to do with her. It was about him. He was the one who could never be enough.

'I take it from your lack of response that I'm right.' It wasn't a question.

'No, Ingrid, look, I'm sorry.' The weak protest spoke volumes. His heart wasn't in it. Ingrid knew that. She probably had done for a while.

'It's too late. I can't do this anymore. I can't be second best.' Ingrid seemed resigned.

'It's nothing to do with you. Or Jessica. It's just me. I'm not good enough for you. You deserve more.' John looked Ingrid in the eyes.

'You're right, maybe I do.' Ingrid shook her head, and gracefully left the room. There was the sound of a zip, the clanking of plastic bottles, and the squeak of hangers. She was packing her things. Would a better man have followed her? Convinced her to stay? No, he was doing the right thing letting her go. Who was he kidding? Not even bothering to get up from the sofa to properly break up with your girlfriend was nothing to do with "doing the right thing" and everything to do with being an absolute idiot.

It was a testament to her integrity that she faced him one last time before she left.

'Goodbye, John.'

'Bye Ingrid.' John stood in an attempt to show his sincerity. His voice was as small as hers was calm and dignified. How ironic that the sweetness and calmness that had made it so easy to be with her also made it so easy to break up with her.

He knew he should feel sad, and he would; tomorrow when he caught the jasmine scent of her perfume still lingering in his room. But right now, there was nothing, a numb emptiness in his body. *Hello ceiling, old friend,* he stared upwards at the now familiar sight, *it's just you and me now.*

He downed the rest of his beer and wondered what the chances were that he could put off dinner with his grandmother. *Slim to absolute fucking zero.*

An hour and a half, and a cold shower and a shave later he opened his apartment door to Elizabeth.

'Hello sweetheart.' Only his formidable grandmother could use such a term of endearment without a hint of warmth.

'Hi Grandma.' He pecked her politely on the cheek.

She surveyed him appraisingly, and then gazed over his shoulder at the beer bottles that he'd forgotten to clear off the living room floor. Damn, so close. She fixed her steely grey eyes on his.

'Let's go and get you something stronger to drink.'

It took a glass of Chardonnay and two whiskies for his grandmother to relax a little, but John found he had a surprisingly enjoyable evening with her. He loved her dearly, but she had a briskness and reserve that despite, or perhaps because of, her decades spent living in the US, she had never shaken off. He had found her quite intimidating as a child, and even now he tried to be on his best behaviour around her.

'Tell me some more about this young lady of yours. Ingrid is it?' Elizabeth had already picked up a feeling in the room.

'Yes, and she's not my "young lady" any more.'

'Oh?' Elizabeth said simply.

Yeah. We've split up.' He swilled the whisky around in his glass. This was the last conversation he wanted to be having with his grandmother. 'Just this evening actually, before you came over.'

'By mutual consent?' She arched a single eyebrow.

'Fairly mutual. Well, in the end.' He grinned ruefully.

'And how is Jessica?' she asked.

Why did she have to make that connection? Was she psychic or something?

'Jessica's fine. Great, obviously, really happy. She's going to do such a great job. I hope they pick her to walk on Mars first. She totally deserves it.'

'It's probably a good thing you're not on the same crew together. It's wise to spend less time with her.'

'What?' He frowned at her. 'Why would you say that? I thought you liked her?'

'My dear, I think she's absolutely delightful. The problem is, so do you.'

'What?' he spluttered, drops of whisky scattering the table. 'I don't know what you're talking about.'

'Of course you do dear, you're a smart boy.' She patted his hand. 'I presume Jessica is the reason you and Ingrid have gone your separate ways?'

'No, that's not why. I mean, she was mentioned, but that's not why... There were other reasons.'

John's mind was racing now, the blood pumping round his body making his cheeks warm. What was she saying? How could she think that? How often had she even seen him with Jessica? Hardly at all. She didn't know what she was talking about. It was always the way when you were close friends with someone of the opposite sex. Everyone always assumed... but no, he had always been clear, they were friends. They couldn't be any more than that, not while they did the jobs they did. They both knew that, so it never even entered his mind to think about her that way.

Of course he thought she was pretty, but anyone would think that about her. She had those warm brown eyes that crinkled when she laughed, and a smile that lit up her usually serious face. But he didn't even care about how she looked. She was clever, and caring, and engaging, all the things he wanted in a best friend. But that was all, right? Yes, she was the person he thought about when he went to sleep at night. And when something really great happened he wanted to share it with her. And when he'd had a bad day he just wanted to sit quietly in her company. But that was all completely normal for a best friend.

'John,' his grandmother said gently. 'How long has it been?'

'How long has what been?' said John, though he thought he knew the answer.

'How long have you been in love with Jessica?'

He was silent for a moment, and took a deep breath. 'Since the day I met her.'

Chapter Twelve
Twelve Years Earlier

John

John ran the final hundred metres to the physics building. That was the last time he stopped to give someone directions. One of the two elderly ladies who had intercepted him had been partially deaf, forcing John to repeat himself several times. The other had insisted on taking him through their holiday itinerary and asking his opinion on the arboretum at this time of year, and didn't the leaves look beautiful in their autumn colours? Only a sternly drilled sense of politeness stopped him walking away before they had finished.

John paused outside the lecture theatre door to catch his breath. He hated being late; it was so rude. Something else drilled in him from a young age. He contemplated skipping the lecture rather than disrupt it, but sometimes they checked attendance and included it as part of the grade. The door creaked as he opened it. To his surprise the lecturer welcomed him warmly rather than admonishing him. John relaxed, and smiled gratefully back, sliding into the nearest half empty row next to a woman furiously handwriting notes. Someone else was old school like him.

She was hunched over her notes, long brown hair hiding her face. He pulled out his own notebook, and felt around the bottom of his bag for a pen. Shit, he didn't even have one. What was wrong with him? He was never without a pen or a pencil. No matter where he was or what sort of conversation he had, he always had cause to scribble on a napkin or a scrap of paper some sort of diagram to illustrate what he was talking about. Today was just going to be one of those days. One more check in the depths of his rucksack; definitely no pen. Looking up he saw that a pen had appeared on top of his notebook. It was an unusual blue and white striped pen. He looked at the woman next to him; she was using an identical one to take her own copious notes.

She sat back in her seat and he could finally see her face. Warm brown eyes, framed with long dark lashes, her nose turned up slightly at the end, and nostrils flared with obvious irritation at his intrusion. He mouthed a hurried 'thank you' at her, and her expression softened a little. Her hair fell back over her face again as she returned to her note taking, and he resisted the urge to tuck it behind her ear. *Focus, John, focus,* he chided himself.

He picked up the pen to give himself something to focus on. Indigo ink poured out of it as it moved across the page. He was unlikely to write much more than the date. This class was basic for him but was a prerequisite for a module he wanted to take next semester, so he had to force himself to sit through it. It might be more interesting if his seatmate relaxed a little. Every time he shuffled in his seat he could hear her sigh of annoyance. At one point she put her hand on his leg, and he raised his eyebrows in surprise, until he realised he had probably been jiggling like he always did when he was bored. Trying hard to keep still and not annoy her, he tuned in and out of the lecture on the physics of Mercury. Such a boring planet, too close to the Sun for anything of interest to thrive there. There were so many more interesting planets to study.

The lecture finished and all the students started packing up their things. He turned to the woman, suddenly able to take all of her in. Man, she was pretty. He tried to think of something impressive to say. 'Sorry, didn't mean to get on your nerves.' *Excellent, really impressive.* 'I'm John,' he held out his hand.

'Jessica.'

'Nice pen.' He handed it back to her.

'You keep it.' Her smile came out of nowhere, and every part of her face looked happy. 'For your next class. I've got plenty.' She showed him her pencil case full of identical pens. He laughed at the idiosyncrasy. He couldn't explain it, but he wanted to get to know this woman better.

'I'll see you next time.' What was wrong with him? It wasn't like him to be tongue tied, even around pretty women.

***

Three days later, heading back to the Planetary Science class he forced himself to hang back before entering the lecture theatre, not long enough that he'd be late, but he wanted to sit next to Jessica again, which meant he had to be sure she was there first. Given her annoyance at his behaviour during the last lecture he couldn't guarantee she wouldn't avoid him if he was already seated. This time he would make a better impression. She was seated exactly where she was last time, as he was sure she would be. Sliding into the seat next to her he whispered 'If I promise to keep still can I sit here?'

'Yes, but I've brought a straitjacket today in case you don't,' she whispered back, but she was smiling.

She was funny. And he couldn't have annoyed her that much. Result. And now to deploy his next move. He took out the pen she had given him in the last lecture. She raised her eyebrows in surprise. 'I'm going to treasure it forever,' he said with a grin.

The lecture, on Venus, was slightly more interesting, and Jessica continued to take reams of notes. But John was distracted again. He wanted to get to know Jessica a bit more. He just had to figure out how. He was convinced that asking her out for a drink wasn't going to cut it. He needed to be a bit more creative. As the professor droned on about atmospheric pressure he had an idea.

They chatted briefly about the class as they were packing up. 'Listen,' said, taking his chance, 'there's stuff you never get from a crusty old Professor. Let me show you the real deal.'

'What do you mean?'

'What are you doing tonight?' *Don't say a date, don't say a date.*

'Nothing, I've got an essay to write, why?' said Jessica quizzically.

'Meet me later then,' he started to walk off, 'ten o'clock, outside the main library.' John was relieved that Jessica hadn't mentioned a 'date'.

'Wait, what? What do you mean?'

'Just meet me later. Trust me,' he called over his shoulder, and forced himself to walk away before she could say no.

That evening he got to the library early. He didn't want her to think he was late to everything, and he didn't want to leave her hanging around on her own. That's if she even turned up, which given that he hadn't even given her a chance to agree he wasn't sure she would. To be fair he hadn't given her a chance to disagree either.

He shifted his weight from side to side. It was a cool evening, but the cold didn't bother him. He found it impossible to keep still, his lean body a testament to a nervous energy rather than any dedication to keeping fit.

Footsteps came around the corner and Jessica suddenly appeared, five minutes early and clearly surprised to find him already there. He smiled involuntarily at the sight of her, reminded of just how attractive she was. But something told him there was much more to her than that, something drew him to her. He wasn't sure what it was yet but he hoped to be proved right this evening.

She still didn't know where he was taking her, and he was determined to surprise her. Was it a lame idea? Oh well, too late to worry about that now. They chatted a little as they walked. She told him she was studying neuroscience, and he realised then that she was really smart. He liked to think he was too, but half the time he felt like he was blagging it. Jessica seemed like someone who never had to blag anything.

Feeling impulsive he grabbed her hand and pulled her faster. 'Come on, we're nearly there,'. She laughed as they kicked their way through autumn leaves, her emerald green scarf trailing behind her. They stopped in front of a large redbrick Victorian building. He keyed in the code for the door. Alex the night security guard was behind his desk and nodded to John who gave him a thumbs up. John led Jessica through another door and up some stairs.

'Are we allowed to be here?' she whispered.

'It's fine. They know me here.'

She appeared unconvinced, and he would put money on her not liking to break any rules. Well, he wasn't. Not technically. Ok, he should have booked a slot, but given that his family had basically refurbished the place, he figured it wouldn't hurt every now and again. He loved it here, and knew from numerous visits when it would be busy, and tonight he knew it would be quiet.

He could tell when they walked into the observatory that she had never been in one before. He tried to see it through her eyes; damp and slightly rusty in places, chilly from the big hole in the roof. But to John it was a second home, familiar and welcoming. He thought of all the hours he had spent with his dad in the observatory he had built in their garden. They hadn't talked much at any other time, but they bonded over planets and stars. He played around with the settings on the sleek modern telescope that his grandmother had donated.

'Are you ready?' He beckoned her over.

'Yes, but I'm not sure how impressed you think I'm going to be. We've all seen the Hubble photos. I know what planets look like.'

She'd change her mind. You could see all the pictures you wanted on the front pages of newspapers or on websites, but there was absolutely nothing like seeing the real thing with your own eyes.

Jessica was small, and John wondered if she would be able to reach the eye piece as the scope was configured. 'Do need a step?'

'No,' she said defensively, drawing herself as tall as she could, which still wasn't very tall. She looked into the eye piece and a few seconds later she turned to him.

'It's Saturn!' she exclaimed. Her eyes were wide and sparkly, and he recognised the face of someone who had just seen a close look of their first planet. She turned back to the telescope. 'That's amazing. It looks just like you expect it to.'

He let her stare at it for a minute. 'Ready for the next one?'

'Of course,' said Jessica.

John moved over to a tablet mounted on a stand nearby. The equipment around them looked older than the tablet John was using.

John pressed the screen a final few times and a second later the whirring of electric motors filled the silence. Although the sound gave the impression that the motors were moving quickly, the telescope hardly looked like it was moving at all. After a few seconds the sound stopped and silence once again fell.

John gestured towards the eye piece and Jessica put her eye back to the telescope.

'Mars.' The word came out almost as a breath. He knew with this scope she'd be seeing a clear view of the planet, the different shades of orange, the tinge of white-blue at the polar ice caps. It would look tantalisingly close.

'Astronomers in the nineteenth century thought Mars was probably covered in red vegetation, red trees, red fields of grass, they thought it was a red Earth... But it's mostly just rusty rocks and dust.' *Oh shut the hell up John, you want to bore her to death?* But she was too focused on what she was seeing to hear his trivia.

'It's like something you see in a book but I am seeing it in real life, right now.'

'Yes, well, you're seeing it about fourteen minutes ago. If you were looking at a star, it might be dozens of light years away. It might even have died in the time it's taken for you to see it.' *That's right, give her an eighth grade science lesson.*

But she didn't seem bothered by his explanations. It was like she was drinking up all the information she could.

'I can't believe you've never used a telescope before. Why did you pick an astronomy module?' The randomness amused him.

Jessica shrugged, 'Just curious really. My degree topic is so narrow, I don't want to miss out on other things. I want to know everything about everything.'

'Well I think understanding our universe is as close as you'll get to knowing everything.'

He tapped another coordinate into the machine, peered into the telescope. She let out a gentle gasp.

'It's so beautiful. What is it?'

'It's M31, the Andromeda galaxy. The nearest major galaxy to our own.'

She would be seeing flashes of pink, blue, orange, and white light, surrounded by clusters of stars.

'The word galaxy actually means milky. Our galaxy is called the Milky Way, because of the bright whiteness. But now we know there are, like, two trillion galaxies in the universe.' What was it about her that made him try so hard to prove how much he knew?

She smiled, and a shiver ran through his body that had nothing to do with the cold night.

'Sorry, I'm not boring you, am I?'

She shook her head, 'You're really not.' She sounded genuine as she said it. It had been a gamble thinking this trip might impress her, but he thought it might have paid off.

'This was a brilliant idea, I love hearing all about it.' She studied him, and he got a sense that hers was a mind that never stopped whirring, never stopped trying to figure out the world. 'You know a lot about this stuff for an engineer.'

He paused. Did she not know about his grandmother? He knew he was something of a small town legend on campus, not because of anything he'd done, but just by being the grandson of the first female Shuttle commander. He decided to play it safe.

'It's sort of a family hobby. My dad basically built his own observatory in the garden. And my grandparents were really into this stuff.'

'That sounds cool.'

He laughed, 'I'm not sure if "cool" is really the word for it. What about you? Didn't your parents make you do any nerdy things?'

She shrugged, and her face which had been lit up like a child at Christmas when she looked through the telescope suddenly closed up. 'Nah, my dad wasn't around and my mum worked till she died when I was sixteen. My grandma looked after me, and I mostly learned how to cook Persian food. She came over from Iran in the seventies'

He didn't know what to say. Had he touched a nerve with his question? He wanted to know more about this woman.

'Well, that's a lot less nerdy, and far more practical than looking at the night sky,' he said, unsure how else to break the sudden tension.

'Show me Mars again,' Jessica said, the smile returning.

Enjoying her eagerness, he moved the viewfinder back to Mars and smiled indulgently as she tried to drink in the view.

'It looks so near like you could just fly there.'

'You could fly there. We will one day.' *I wonder if it will be Charlie?* His big brother was following in their grandmother's footsteps.

'It'll take nearly a year to get there though.'

'That's not such a long time in the grand scheme of things.'

She took one last look at Mars before they left. They stepped out into the cold night and as they were leaving the observatory she stopped. She was looking at the sign that heralded the Eden Observatory.

'Eden. John Eden. That's your name. Is... do you... Is that some relation?'

So, she really didn't know. If only she hadn't made the connection. He was captivated by her, and he wanted her to like him for himself, not for something his grandmother had done, or because of his family. But he couldn't keep it from her now.

'Didn't you know?' he asked slowly.

'Know what?'

'My family... my grandmother. She was a Shuttle astronaut, Elizabeth Eden. The first female Commander.' However annoying it was people talking about his grandmother, he was fiercely proud of her. She had succeeded in a man's world, bringing up a family at the same time. 'My grandfather worked at NASA too. And my dad... He works for NARESA now, helped set it up. My grandmother donated the money for the telescope a few years ago. She studied and taught here at this university before she left for the States to join NASA.'

'Wow, growing up must have been pretty exciting for you.' They carried on walking back down the hill.

He shrugged, 'We moved around a lot. My dad had various positions in NASA, and we followed him until he got the NARESA job and we came back to England.'

He paused. There was something about her that made him want to keep talking. 'It's hard always being the new kid, never quite fitting in.' He'd never said that to anyone before. Suddenly he felt a little exposed. He didn't want her feeling sorry for him.

'But, you know there were some benefits to being an international man of mystery.' He winked at her and she just rolled her eyes at him. Well, at least she wasn't pitying him.

'Where do you live, then?' he asked. He wanted to walk her home, though he sensed already she would be affronted at his gallantry.

She stopped and stared hard at him. *Or maybe she'll interpret it as a come on.* He wasn't that bad.

'Hey, I didn't mean it like that.' He raised his hands in mock protest, 'I want to make sure you get home safely.

'I don't need to be looked after, John.' Jessica said defensively.

'I know you don't, but it's nearly midnight, and I want to make sure you get home safely.'

She breathed in irritably through her nostrils.

'Sorry, Jessica, this one's a non-negotiable. I don't want some creep following you home.'

'So, you're going to follow me home instead?' Jessica smiled.

He laughed, 'Yeah, basically. Pick your lesser of two evils.'

She pretended to seriously contemplate this. 'Oh, alright then, I live down near the river.'

They chatted as they walked, sharing stories about the courses they were studying. Too quickly it seemed, they stopped in front of a row of tall student flats. He insisted on waiting till she was inside the door.

She stopped on the top step, 'Thank you for tonight. That was amazing. Really.'

He glowed at her words. 'You're very welcome. Anytime. I mean it.'

'I hope you're not right though,' she said over her shoulder as she unlocked her front door.

'About what?'

'About not learning anything in a lecture theatre. It'll make for a very boring class this semester.'

'Don't worry, I'll keep it interesting for you,' he called up to her.

She smiled, 'Night, John.'

'Goodnight, Jessica.'

He waited a minute until he saw her door was properly closed, and then turned to walk to his own flat. Despite the late hour, he couldn't stop the cheerful whistle as he walked down the street. He wasn't sure what was happening but he knew this woman was something special. He couldn't wait to see her again.

Chapter Thirteen
Countdown to first Mars walk: eleven months

John

'Aries, we are at T minus thirty-five minutes. Just waiting on a weather report. How are you guys doing up there?'

'We're peachy, Control.' The voice crackled over the radio. 'Ready whenever you are.'

John grinned into the headset as he stood looking at the crew on a video feed to a large screen. 'Don't worry, Goldman, as soon as we are good to go you'll know it.'

Rachel Goldman was the redoubtable Commander of the Concordia crew. It was launch day. The Aries capsule containing the crew was stationed atop the enormous Pegasus rocket. The Pegasus would launch the Aries into space, then each stage would separate, finally leaving the Aries capsule to make its way to the enormous Concordia spacecraft waiting in low Earth orbit. The Aries would dock with The Concordia in nineteen hours, then twenty-four hours later Concordia would fire its own rockets that would send it on its trajectory to Mars to deliver its payload, everything that the Harmonia, which would launch four months behind it, would need for its crew to spend thirty days on Mars.

Rachel was the best person for the role. After Jessica, she was the person in the astronaut pool he most admired. He had seen her in action, and she was a self-assured, experienced leader. If she was disappointed not to be commanding the mission that was to land on Mars she didn't display it for a minute. She had been incredibly supportive to Jessica as she navigated the role as her counterpart.

It was a privilege to be CAPCOM for the Aries launch mission; Rachel had requested him. As the crew's conduit for information for the next twelve hours, his live feed with them would be broadcast all over the world throughout the launch. The Launch Control Center in Cape Kennedy was a hive of activity, and there were hubs all over the world working to support the launch, but John was the only person permitted to talk directly to the crew, relaying essential information. After his first twelve hour shift he would hand over to Mission Control in Houston who would be responsible for the craft for the duration of the journey.

John loved the CAPCOM role. It required an ability to quickly assimilate data, and sift through the important information to relay to the crew. This needed to be balanced with empathy and humour, all of which John knew he was good at. NARESA preferred to assign astronauts and former astronauts to the CAPCOM role; they had the most empathy for what it was like being on the receiving end of the radio, and knew what they needed to hear to do their job effectively. With the long-duration missions to Mars it was impossible to have astronauts from the backup crews assigned to CAPCOM full time, but they used them for critical points like launch and re-entry.

The Launch Control Center was a windowless room, with scientists, engineers, and other ground support crew stationed at rows of consoles. John listened to the chatter of the different streams doing pre-flight checks.

The Concordia launchpad was just a few miles away along the coast but John's only view of the enormous rocket was on one of the multiple large screens stationed along the front wall. Vapour was billowing out of the rocket as the freezing liquid rocket fuel was being pumped into it. External cameras from three other angles showed the Aries capsule stationed on top of the two-stage rocket, named Pegasus, that would blast it into orbit on its way to dock with The Concordia. The final image showed the inside of the Aries capsule where the five crew members were strapped in, Commander Goldman and her Russian Pilot Josef Lisitsyn both in front, watching monitors in front of them. Behind them were Kaspar Beck, a German engineer, Paloma Navarro, a Spanish physicist, and Olivia Kelty, a Scottish geologist.

Though John was backup crew for Harmonia, the four crews had been training together specifically for the two missions for over a year. They were his colleagues and friends, and though he felt more than a pang of jealousy at their being in the exact place he wanted to be right now, he was also proud of them. These people were about to embark on the longest crewed mission to date. Though they wouldn't land they would be in close orbit and be the first humans to see another planet close up.

'Aries, we are at T minus seventeen minutes. The weather is clear, and in five minutes we will commence go-no-go pre-flight checks.' John loved the cadence of the launch comms, the way the inflections on the words rose and fell like poetry.

'Copy that Control. Hey, Eden, you sticking with us for the entire ride?'

'Yep, I'm here for the whole night. Bet my coffee is no better than yours on board though.'

'Don't joke, we've got eighteen months of it.'

'I'd say rather you than me, Goldman, but I'd be lying.' John stood looking at the screen. He could see the crew clearly but they could only hear his voice.

'Well, there's a bit of space between me and Joe here, I'm sure we can squeeze you in if you hurry.'

John laughed looking up at the five of them in their bulky pressurised flight suits, and helmets with oxygen supplies. The launch was one of the most dangerous parts of space flight, along with re-entry, and they wore these as a precaution.

Commander Goldman sounded confident as she spoke, and John doubted there was even a hint of nerves for her. Astronaut selection procedures ensured that as a profession they were innately calm under pressure. They were also highly trained at their jobs, repeating the launch sequence in the simulator hundreds of times, with different outcomes, so they all knew exactly what to do, even in an emergency. And they had the confidence of knowing that they had the best minds across the globe working to support their mission.

'This is Flight, we are at T minus nine minutes and holding. Commencing launch status check, verify ready to go for launch.'

John was stationed next to the Flight Director, Matias Garcia, whose job it was to oversee the launch. While John had the freedom to walk around, Matias was rooted to his console, concentrating on the multiple screens in front of him. Each of the major flight controllers would be polled for readiness to launch.

'Telemetry? Matias said.

'Telemetry is go.' The response came from the flight controller.

'Recovery?'

'Recovery is go'

A dozen controllers reported in until finally Matias called 'Mission Commander?'

There was a brief pause and the entire room held its breath for Rachel to respond.

'Mission Commander is go.' The crackly voice of Commander Goldman came through the radio from the launch pad.

'Thank you, everyone. Aries is go for launch.'

'Copy that.' John said, 'Aries, you are go for launch in T minus two minutes forty-five seconds. Crew please close and lock your visors'

'Copy that Control. All visors down'

'Aries, from all of us here across the globe we wish you good luck and Godspeed.' John's comment was for the listening media. The crew had already done their goodbyes with their colleagues.

'Copy that Control.' Rachel replied. 'From all of us on board Aries, we thank all of the amazing people who have worked to get us here, as we embark on this pioneering journey.'

It was time for John to start counting down to launch. He steeled himself for the intensity of the coming hours.

'Ten, nine...' Even as he said the words they felt surreal, like he and Charlie were playing make believe.

He kept his eye on the screen where he could see the entire rocket about to launch.

'Five, four...' He continued to count.

The engines ignited; plumes of smoke billowed across the launch pad.

'Two, one...'

The supporting arms fell away as white-hot flames shot from the engines.

'Zero, ignition, lift off...'

It seemed to barely move at first, as three thousand tonnes of rocket and fuel lifted from the ground. John marvelled at the extraordinary magic of physics that defied the laws of gravity as it rose towards the sky. Hundreds of years of thinking, experimenting, and creating had led to this point in time where five humans were on their way to circumnavigate another planet.

'Throttle down.' Rachel's voice came over the radio as she travelled at ten kilometres per second. As the rocket reached maximum air pressure it momentarily slowed to stop it breaking up under the pressure.

'Aries, you're looking good from down here.' John said to the crew.

'Looking good from here too, Control. Everything looking and feeling just as expected.'

Millions of people across the globe would be watching the launch and listening to his feed live with the crew. He put that out of his mind. His sole focus had to be the crew.

A small boom could be heard from the live feed 'Vehicle is supersonic,' John said, more for the benefit of the live feed than the crew. They were now flying faster than the speed of sound.

'Throttle up.'

'Copy that,' John replied to the crew. They were back up to full power.

Two minutes forty seconds into the flight and the first stage engine was about to separate from the rocket.

'Pegasus stage one separation confirmed,' Rachel said.

There was a gentle cheer in the control room. There were so many crucial points to the launch.

'Copy that Aries.'

'Control we're seeing a warning light on the B84 panel.' Rachel's voice was calm but immediate.

John looked up and he could see a red flashing light on one of the large screens overhead. He was immediately alert.

'Copy that Aries, are you experiencing any other problems?'

'The G's feel a little sharper than expected Control' The crew were trained to anticipate every sound and move of the spacecraft. It sounded like the force of gravity on the crew was stronger than expected.

John turned towards the Media Relations Director and mimed cutting his neck to get her to cut the live feed. It could be something or it could be nothing. But if something was wrong he didn't want fifty million people witnessing it live.

'Oh, I think you all just needed to spend more time in the practice sims rather than at the bar drinking beer. Perhaps you guys just can't hack it.' John tried to inject some levity into his voice to maintain calm and buy some time. 'Stand by, Aries. We're looking into it.'

Adrenaline coursed through his body. His arms grew heavy as all the different scenarios played themselves out in his head. He took a deep breath. He needed his mind to be crystal clear.

He listened to the concerned chatter of the technicians as they discussed the problem. He searched his brain methodically. He knew he had seen this error before. The backup crew had been in a simulator with the Harmonia prime crew observing. Jessica had been CAPCOM for the crew that day when they had reported the error. It was a simulation, not a live event but they still took it seriously, and time had been of the essence. He combed his memory for the sequence of actions they had taken to correct it. Finally, he remembered it.

He muted the CAPCOM feed to the crew and spoke to Matias, the flight director.

'Matias, I know what this is.'

'John, I'm not even hearing from the technicians what this is.'

'Mat, I've seen this error and worked it. They have to shut down the horizontal adjustment tank before the burn has finished, it's a jammed gimbal.' He knew that's what they needed to do. He was sure with every cell in his body. He just wanted to get this crew into orbit safely.

'John, if they do that then we will lose the arc we need.' Matias concentrated on his screen.

'They can correct it with standard air thrusters when they have the craft under control.'

Matias called into his headset 'Do we have any idea what the hell is going on?'

'Negative, Flight, we're still looking.'

John locked eyes with him. 'Trust me Mat, they have to shut it down and they have to do it right now.'

'Control, the error's still flashing and we're just sitting here, please advise.' Rachel's voice interrupted them.

'Trust me Mat.' John looked him squarely in the eye.

Matias pulled at his face with his hand, then nodded. 'Alright, do it.'

John unmuted the channel to the capsule forcing his voice to remain even, 'Aries, this is Control, that error is a go, please shut down R21, the horizontal adjustment tank, we have a jammed gimbal, confirm?'

'Copy that. Confirming shutdown of R21.' Rachel said.

'Shutdown.' She affirmed a moment later.

A few seconds of silence passed.

'That's burn end control.' Rachel continued her reporting.

A voice came over the ground control radio 'Flight, this is SSP. They need to shut down R21, we think it's a jammed gimbal.'

'Already done.' Matias looked at John and sighed.

John just sat down in his chair and closed his eyes, the adrenaline still pumping around his body. He took a deep breath and ran his hands through his hair. He gathered himself before switching back to the capsule.

'Aries, how are you doing up there?'

'We're looking good. We no longer have the error and the G force has lessened.'

'Copy that Aries, looks like we have you back on track.' He could feel his heart rate slowing. He looked up at the video of the crew in their capsule, relieved that they were still there.

The rest of the launch continued without a problem. The two-stage rocket successfully detached, leaving the Aries capsule on a trajectory to dock with the Concordia spacecraft in 18 hours.

John was surprised by a hand on his shoulder. He turned around and was face to face with Hans Vogel.

'Excellent job, John. Your quick thinking might have saved the launch, and their lives.'

'I got lucky, I had the same error on a sim a while back. That's why we do the work, right?'

'But you kept calm under pressure.' He looked at John like he was studying his face. 'I know you would rather be up there than down here.'

'I don't care about that right now.' And for the first time, in that moment, he really meant it. 'My priority is the crew, and I'll do whatever it takes to keep them safe.'

Hans clapped him on the shoulder. As John watched him walk away he caught sight of the Harmonia crew and backup crews in the observation area of Mission Control. John had forgotten they were there. How had they felt watching this? Thinking it could be them?

John fleetingly wondered how they thought he'd done. For a moment he felt vindicated, like he had finally proved himself worthy of his role.

He caught Jessica's eye. Her face was pale and she stood stiffly. She would be in Rachel Goldman's place in four months' time.

She didn't move from her position, presumably not wanting to get in the way of the job the Control team was doing. He just saw her mouth 'Well done,' with a slight nod of her head. John nodded back in acknowledgement and turned back towards the screens.

The remaining hours of the shift passed without incident. The crew were on scheduled sleep time, as the Aries orbited towards the Concordia. The room was stale with cold coffee and adrenaline. John was grateful Mission Control was no longer the smoke-filled room of the sixties and seventies, when middle aged men chain smoked their way through launches.

John didn't hang around when his CAPCOM shift was over, and he had handed over to Mission Control in Houston. The roads home were empty as he drove glassy-eyed on autopilot. His head was full, his ears were ringing, and he was worn out. He squinted out of the windscreen through his tired daze. There would be no better feeling than crawling into bed for a deep sleep after a shift, a sleep where nothing would occupy his mind.

Chapter Fourteen

Countdown until first Mars walk: eleven months

Jessica

Clear blue skies stretched as far as the eye could see. The air was scented with the heat of the ground, sea salt, and the faint smell of orange groves.

Jessica savoured the warmth of the day as she stood at the entrance to John's apartment block and rang the buzzer.

There was a pause and she imagined him dragging himself out of bed. It was 11 a.m. He'd had a late night on shift but something made her think he'd need someone around today.

'Hello?' His voice was heavy with sleep.

'It's me,' she said.

'Oh hey. Come up.' There was a buzz and the outer door clicked.

He was standing in the open doorway as she reached his apartment, tousle haired and squinting into the light. He was wearing shorts and a rumpled green t-shirt.

'To what do I owe the pleasure?' he said. His voice was still husky and his accent had grown stronger in the short time they had been back out in the US.

She handed him a cardboard tray with two reusable coffee cups and a paper bag.

'Breakfast.' She replied.

'Jessica!' He said in surprise. 'That's so sweet.'

'It's breakfast for two. Are you going to invite me in?' She wondered for a moment if she'd done the right thing imposing on him. Yesterday had been an intense day, especially for John. Would he have preferred to be alone to process it all?

'Of course. Yeah, sorry. I'm still half asleep.' He shook his head as if trying to wake himself up.

'Sorry for waking you.'

'You never have to say sorry for that if you bring me breakfast,' he said, his eyes creasing in a smile.

They sat down at his table and John opened the bag, pulling out bagels and freshly squeezed orange juice.

'Florida's finest of course,' Jessica said.

'Oh man, this is just what I need. Thank you.'

'And after we've finished I'm taking you to the beach. You don't need to pack anything. I've got towels and sun lotion in the car.' She helped herself to a smoked salmon and cream cheese bagel.

'What did I do to deserve this?' He asked through a mouthful of food.

'It was a tough day yesterday. I just thought you might need to get out of your head a bit.' And she wanted to see him, to make sure he was ok.

'Thank you.' His face was thoughtful for a moment as he chewed on his bagel. 'I'm fine though.' He flashed her a smile.

They were both quiet for a few minutes as they finished their breakfast.

'Come on then, you. Get ready. Let's make the most of the beach and glorious weather before we have to go back home to cloudy, dull Cologne.'

Thirty minutes later they were coasting along the causeway towards the Cape, where to the north lay Cape Canaveral Air Force Station, and to the south, Cocoa Beach stretched along the Atlantic. The window blew in Jessica's hair through the open windows as she drove. Even in Florida she preferred the fresh warm air to the air conditioning, which she and John had squabbled over.

'It's boiling Jessica.' He had complained.

'I'm driving, I'm in charge of the controls.'

'So much for my day to make me feel better.' He had folded his arms feigning indignation.

Cocoa Beach was a small city and a popular tourist spot. The sand dunes of the eponymous beach stretched for miles against the turquoise sea. Jessica and John walked barefoot along the warm sand, shoes in their hands, watching surfers catching the crest of waves and families paddling in the shallows.

They ambled along the shore unusually slowly for them. When they saw each other it was usually to do something, go for a run, make dinner, or meet friends for a drink. It was rare for them to wander without a clear purpose. Jessica's body felt light and she could feel her breathing slow to match the lap of the waves.

She deliberately avoided talking to John about work. Instead they talked about everything and nothing. About Cocoa Beach and the area where they were staying, about things they'd seen in the news, about the American foods they loved and what delicacies they were going to fill their suitcases with to take back home. Twinkies and Red Vines for John. Hershey's Kisses for Jessica.

'Every variant I can find.' She told him. 'Oh, and maybe a box of macaroni and cheese. How can something so terrible taste so good?'

'So many childhood memories of that,' he said. 'With a glass of grape juice. Why does nowhere else have the same affection for grape juice as America?'

'Oh, I'm pretty sure most of that stuff you drink has never even seen a grape.'

John stopped and bent down to pick up a stone.

'Look,' he showed her. 'Perfect for skimming.' Putting down his shoes he launched the stone towards the water. It skipped across the water with four hops before dropping into the sea.

'Oh my god, that's amazing. How did you learn how to do that?'

'I had a lot of time on my hands as a kid,' he grinned sheepishly. 'Don't you know how to skim a stone?'

Jessica shook her head. It felt like the sort of thing a dad would teach you how to do. She tried not to imagine all the other rites of passage she might have missed.

'I'll teach you,' he said.

They deposited their shoes and bags on a dry patch of sand and John showed Jessica the sort of stones to look for. There weren't many on the sandy beach, but after a while they had a small collection of smooth, flat stones.

John showed her how to flick the stones level with the water. Again and again Jessica tried. Each time the stone broke the surface with an unsatisfactory plunk.

'Thank god,' John called out to her, as Jessica scoured the beach for more pebbles. 'I've finally found something you can't do.'

'It's not that I can't do it,' she replied through clenched teeth, flicking another stone into the water. 'I just can't do it yet.'

'Give it up, Jessica.' He walked towards her. 'You can't be good at everything.'

'Why not?' She stood with her hands on her hips. 'Wait, what are you doing?'

Before she had time to protest John had picked her up and thrown her over his shoulder.

'John, John!' She shrieked with laughter. 'What are you doing?'

'Time to cool off.' He carried her effortlessly towards the water.

'No, not the sea. Put me down! I'm still wearing my clothes!' She was yelling and laughing at the same time, barely able to catch her breath from her prone position.

John splashed into the surf still holding Jessica. The spray hit her legs and she squealed. As the water rose beyond his waist he lowered her down into the sea. It was warmer than she had expected but she still gasped as the water enveloped her. Her clothes felt heavy but her body felt light in the water. The waves gently lifted them both deeper until she could no longer touch the sandy floor. She kicked her legs, treading water, her strong body at ease in the swell.

She looked at John, his face dripping, his hair plastered to his head. He returned her gaze looking inquiringly at her, as if unsure quite how much trouble he was in.

'Right, you're going to pay for that, Eden.' And she dived towards him with a splash. They were both strong swimmers, and he swam away from her as she chased after him. Catching him up she attempted to pull him under the water but she was laughing too much. She bobbed up and down on the surface, barely able to stay afloat, trying to catch her breath.

'Hey, come here you.' John reached out for her and steadied her.

'No, you'll make me laugh again and I'll drown.' She hiccupped.

'I promise not to make you laugh.' He said gently, pulling her towards him. 'I mean, I'll try really hard but sometimes I just can't help it.'

'Stop it!' She gasped again, swallowing a mouthful of water as she laughed.

'I'll stop, I'll stop.' He smiled and held her round the waist. 'Go on, hold on to me till you get your breath back.'

She reached around his shoulders, feeling his legs kick beneath her. They floated in each other's arms for a few minutes, not speaking, just looking at each other. Jessica looked at him as she steadied her breath. His face was tanned, his long eyelashes glistened with drops of water. It was a face that was comforting in its familiarity. Over the years of close working she had got to know the micro expressions, spotting when no one else did flashes of impatience, when he was plagued with insecurity, and when he was content. His face then took on a softness, his features expanded, his eyebrows relaxed. Despite the ocean lapping around them, and the high stakes events of yesterday his face had that look now. And even though her clothes hung heavily around her, and her eyes stung with salt water, she felt a weightlessness that had nothing to do with the buoyancy of the water.

She suddenly remembered that in a few months she would be separated from him for nearly two years, and she shivered involuntarily.

'Are you cold?' John looked at her with concern, then continued without waiting for a reply. 'Come on, let's get you back and dry.'

They swam back towards the shore, Jessica in front, John hanging back. She knew he was doing that deliberately so he could make sure she was ok. She didn't have the energy to protest his gallantry, so she let him do it without putting up a fight.

Back on the beach they wrapped themselves in towels and perched next to one another on a slightly raised sand dune, both of them looking out at the ocean.

For a few minutes they simply listened to the sound of crashing waves, and seabirds cruising the surface of the water for food. Jessica heard John take a deep breath, and finally he spoke. 'So, that was pretty scary yesterday.'

It was the first time he had mentioned his CAPCOM shift since she had woken him up that morning.

'It was a scary situation.' She said, wanted to reassure him.

'But *I* was scared, Jessica. I've never felt scared like that before.' He spoke quietly.

She looked at him, his head bent towards the floor, as if something fascinating was happening on the surface of the sand. She couldn't remember ever seeing him scared, in all of the training situations and launch preparations she had shared with him. Jessica had learned over the years the power of silence. If she just gave him space he would say what he needed. He seemed to be chewing on the silence, his jaw twitching with unspoken words.

'I wanted to be up there so much, you know?' The words seemed to tumble out, taking him by surprise. 'But in that moment, I was glad it wasn't me there. That's terrible isn't it?' He brushed at the drying sand on his shorts, unable to look Jessica in the eye.

'No, I think that's completely normal. It could have been any of us up there.'

'Do you think about when it's you?'

Jessica paused. She did think about it, in fleeting thoughts that she deliberately didn't dwell on, because if she stopped and thought about the magnitude of what they were doing she might be crushed by the weight of it.

'Yes, I think about it. And yes, yesterday scared me a little too. We all know what the risks are. But we do it anyway. Because the risks are small, and the gains are so big, so important. This is bigger than us, John.'

She really believed that it was. She had to believe it was all worth it. She studied his profile, and as if sensing her stare, he looked up at her.

'But you know what, John?' She continued. You didn't look scared for one moment. You looked calm and considered. You thought on your feet and you made the right call.'

'What if it hadn't been the right call?'

'Then you wouldn't have made it.' She trusted him beyond doubt.

He paused taking this in.

'Don't tell anyone I said this stuff, Jessica, will you?' This time the micro expression was that of a young boy, an expression she had only ever seen when it was just the two of them.

'John...' she admonished.

'I know, I know you wouldn't.' He nudged her. 'Thanks for today. Breakfast. The beach. It's my idea of a perfect day.'

'It's mine too.' She smiled at him.

'I really needed this,' he said with a serious look.

'I know,' was all she said in return.

After a few minutes of silence she nudged John back. 'Hey, shall I get us something to eat?' She nodded towards the strip of shops and restaurants along the promenade.

'Do you ever stop thinking about food?' He laughed.

'Nope,' she replied with a smile. 'Back in a bit.'

She headed up the beach towards the strip. There were bars, take away restaurants, a frozen yogurt shop, gift shops selling typical tourist wares, postcards, bumper stickers, straw hats and purses, and space paraphernalia. The space programme was one of the biggest employers in the area, and the Cocoa Beach Floridians were proud of their long heritage of supporting space travel.

Jessica selected a small seafood take away restaurant and ordered fried shrimp and French fries. Wandering along the strip while their food was cooked to order she paused outside one of the gift shops.

Ten minutes later, brandishing her second brown bag full of food of the day, she sat back down next to John.

'A beautiful woman who keeps bringing me food, what more could a guy want?' He grinned then his face froze as if he had suddenly realised what he'd said and regretted saying it.

Jessica looked back at him. She knew he was just joking.

'Stop it.' She elbowed him with a smile, reaching for some food.

'By the way, I got you a little present.' She said to him, handing him a small gift bag.

He took it looking quizzically at her. 'What for?'

'Does a girl need a reason to buy a present for her best friend?' She asked lightly. 'Don't get excited, it's only small.'

He pulled out a small plastic model of a Space Shuttle and smiled widely.

'I love it. Thank you.'

'Look,' she pointed at it. 'It's Discovery.'

'That's my favourite Shuttle.'

'You know it's weird to have a favourite Shuttle, right?' Discovery was her favourite too. It wouldn't do to admit that to him, she smiled to herself.

'Jessica, you have a favourite pen. You use them exclusively and you import them from France. Don't talk to me about being weird.'

'Yeah, well...' She sniffed indignantly. 'Anyway, I did buy you it for a reason.'

'Why?' He raised his eyebrows at her.

'Will you CAPCOM for me when I launch?' She asked the question quickly, unsure how he would feel about it after yesterday. Was it too soon to ask him?

'Jessica...' John looked lost for words.

'You don't have to answer, now-'

'Of course I'll CAPCOM for you.' He suddenly glowed, then his face fell slightly.

'What?'

'Oh nothing, it's just,' he hesitated. 'I'm going to miss you when you're gone.'

Jessica felt the warmth in her body again. She was going to miss him too. She couldn't imagine going so long without seeing him. But right now, in this moment, she was happier than she could remember being in a long time.

She leaned her head on his shoulder. 'I'm going to miss you too.'

Chapter Fifteen
Countdown until first Mars walk: ten months

Jessica

Jessica was in the office of Hans Vogel. Hans always exuded a contagious sort of calmness. He had an air of having things under control at all times. He rarely betrayed a hint of emotion which made him, at times, appear intimidating. His ice blue eyes focused on Jessica, who sat to the side of his polished wooden desk.

'Are you satisfied that it's the right decision?' he asked in his slightly accented English.

'Absolutely. You know he was my first choice.'

'It was a difficult decision Jessica, but I agree with you it was the right one.'

'There may be other people more experienced, I know. But he'll be a good fit for the team and more than capable.'

'I trust your judgement.' That was high praise from Hans indeed.

'Thanks for letting me sit in on the conversation.'

'It is only natural, as Commander, that you should.'

Jessica couldn't pinpoint the reason for the butterflies in her stomach. Perhaps it was the presence of Hans, who even after eight years under his care of the astronaut office, she still regarded with paternalistic admiration, someone she was always eager to impress. Perhaps it was just anticipation at the good news they were about to impart.

There was a knock at the office door. 'Come,' Hans's clear voice rang out.

John entered, and seeing Jessica a puzzled look appeared on his face. She gave him a reassuring smile. She had said nothing to him about the possibility of this meeting, not wanting to give anything away until it was certain.

'John,' Hans leaned forward, his hands steepled together. 'You know why you are here?'

'Er, no, not really.' He looked from Hans to Jessica and back again.

'I will cut to the point, John. Mike Sanders has been grounded. He has been sadly diagnosed with a heart problem. It is not serious, and he is not in any imminent danger, however he has been assessed as unfit to fly and relieved from the Harmonia crew.' Hans leaned back in his chair. 'John, we would like you to take his place. It is short notice, with only three months left till launch, but as backup, you have had the same training as the rest of the crew, and I think you will do an excellent job.'

Jessica watched his face as he took all this in. She could see the moment the news hit him. She saw his suppressed smile, the shift of his body.

'Assuming you agree you will report for duty tomorrow. Nadia Dubois will be taking your place on the backup crew.' Hans paused, allowing John to respond.

'How's Mike?' he asked.

Jessica felt a rush of pride. She knew he must have a thousand questions going through his head, but she was glad that his colleague was his first thought.

Jessica spoke, 'He's devastated, John, obviously. But he knows we're talking to you and he thinks you'll do a great job. As do we all.' She beamed at him. 'I'm going to speak to the rest of the crew as soon as you've agreed.'

She knew they'd be disappointed for Mike, and it would disrupt the carefully developed dynamic they had built over the last year or so. But the backup crew had been working closely with the prime crew and they'd quickly adapt.

'So, John,' Hans pressed on, 'You will agree?'

'Of course I'll agree. It'll be an honour.' Hans held out his hand and John seized it, 'Thank you for the opportunity.'

'John,' Hans continued in his serious manner, 'I have no doubt you are the right person for the job.' This was high praise from the indomitable Hans. 'Come back and see me in the morning, Mr Eden. Nine a.m. sharp.'

John gave a mock salute and turned to Jessica. 'I'll talk to you later?'

'Wait, I'll walk you out.' She gathered up her bag and notebook. 'I'll see you tomorrow Hans.'

'Make sure you do Commander Gabriel.' He bestowed a smile on them both. 'Off you go. You have some celebrating to do no doubt.'

John opened the door and allowed Jessica to pass before following her out. By mutual silent consent, they said nothing until they had walked down the corridor and turned the corner. Jessica stopped and turned towards John.

'Hello shipmate,' her voice was quiet, almost a whisper, 'Ready to spend the next two years with me?'

'Of all the spaceships in all the towns and I get selected for yours.' He could no longer suppress the wide smile that broke across his face. He shook his head. 'I just can't believe it.'

'Come here, you.' She pulled him into a hug. His familiar smell enveloped her like a warm blanket. He squeezed her tightly. His strong arms made her feel secure. After a hug from John she felt like she could take on the world. He released her and contemplated her with a serious expression on his face.

'Is this going to be weird for you?' he asked.

'Of course not. I'm so pleased. Why would it be weird?'

'Well, you're my Commander now. You're in charge.'

'Hey, I've always been the one in charge in this friendship, you know that.' She grinned but stopped seeing the serious look on his face. 'John don't worry, it won't be weird.' She hesitated. Would it? How would this shift the dynamic between them? 'We'll make sure it's not. Deal?' she held out her hand.

'Deal. *Commander.*' He beamed at her.

'Alright,' she put her hands on her hips. 'You can stop saying that like it's some kind of joke. I really am your boss now.'

'Like you said, no difference there. Hey,' he reached out and touched her arm, 'do you still want to run tomorrow? We can grab some lunch after.'

'Yep. Let's make the most of real food while we can.'

They both stood for a minute, smiling at each other. Then the serious look returned to John's face.

'Are you sure it's the right decision?' His brow furrowed. 'Are you happy with it?'

She held his gaze, no longer smiling, 'John,' her voice was lower now, 'I'd trust you with my life.'

John looked straight back at her.

'And I trust you with mine.'

***

Saturday was one of those unexpectedly sunny late March days. Jessica's windows were wide open, framed by freshly washed curtains. She had spent the previous weekend spring cleaning the house in time for Nowruz, the Iranian New Year. As she had scrubbed her apartment from floor to ceiling she had thought of her mother and the years they had spent doing the same before every spring equinox, at her grandmother's insistence.

Her body felt like it woke up during the spring. The clear sunny days were like the fresh new pages of a notebook. Jessica hummed to herself as she put on her running gear ready for John to call for her. He buzzed as she still was getting her trainers on so she let him up.

'Jeez, Jessica, it's freezing in here,' he exclaimed as he stepped into the apartment.

'It's fresh,' she said, closing the windows.

'What's this?' John asked. He was looking at a cloth spread over one end of her breakfast bar. On it were various items, an apple, a bottle of vinegar, a dish of spice, some gold wrapped chocolate coins, a bulb of garlic, some dried fruits and a pot of hyacinths.

'Oh, that,' she hesitated, wondering what he would think. 'It's a *Haft-sin* table.'

'Haft-sin?' He repeated.

'Yes. It's to celebrate the Iranian New Year, *Norwruz*. Seven things each starting with S. In Persian anyway.'

He stroked a delicately patterned egg. 'This is beautiful.'

'The eggs are to symbolise fertility. Like at Easter.'

'You do surprise me sometimes.' He looked at her, smiling through half closed eyes.

'What do you mean?' she said, straightening her back and frowning.

'I just never had you down as the type for traditions.'

'Oh,' she wasn't sure if he was mocking her or not. 'Well, my grandmother sent me most of it in a care package. It's always been a big deal for her. And you know, it reminds me of my mum.' She said these last words more quietly.

'Well, I think it's gorgeous.' He ran his fingers over the beautiful turquoise silk cloth, embroidered by her grandmother. 'So, do I say Happy Nowruz?'

'You can. Or you can say *Nowruz Pirouz*.'

'*Nowruz Pirouz*,' he repeated slowly. 'Nowruz Pirouz Jessica,' he said again, and leaned forward and kissed her forehead.

His lips felt warm on her skin. She looked up at him, his hazel eyes were flecked with gold in the sunlight streaming through the window. A wave of contentment washed over her. Spring always made her happy.

Outside it was cool in the shade and warm in the sun. Small fluffy clouds hung in the bright blue sky, a backdrop to the blossoming trees and colourful spring flowers that dotted the Beethoven park in the centre of Cologne.

The warm weather had brought out families, cyclists, and other joggers. Their usual quiet route was crowded and they dodged toddling children and dogs straining against leads. They often didn't talk much while they were running. Jessica was fit and loved to run, but John was practically a foot taller than her with long rangy legs and it took two of her strides to keep up with every one of his. She would never admit that he was too fast for her. She just focused on keeping up, trying not to betray how heavily she was breathing. After a relentless forty-five minutes they saw a kiosk on the path ahead of them.

'Want a drink?' John asked.

She nodded breathlessly and they both slowed down.

'I'll get them, you go and stretch.' He wiped his brow on his forearm and turned towards the kiosk.

Jessica found a clear patch of grass half bathed in sunlight, and half shaded by a tall sycamore tree. She adored the sun, something she put down to her Middle Eastern genes. John hated it and complained when he got too hot. She stretched her legs and arms then collapsed exhausted onto the grass. The ground was warm and the grass tickled at the bare bits of her skin. She closed her eyes to the warmth of the sun on her face.

'Here you go, one water...' He handed her a bottle.

Jessica leaned up on her elbows and took it from him. It was ice cold.

'...And one ice cream.' He handed a packet to her with a flourish.

'Oh my god, I love you.' She exclaimed. He sat down next to her in the shade of the tree, just as she had known he would.

'Mmm, my favourite,' she said, unwrapping the ice cream. Chocolate and vanilla flavoured ice cream covered in crunchy chocolate.

'How 'bout that?' he said with a smile. 'Good run, don't you think?'

'Mmm hmm.' She was busy biting the chocolate from the edges of the ice cream.

'I'm going to miss it when we're on mission.'

'Yeah, the treadmill won't be quite the same.' She picked a shard of chocolate off and put it onto her tongue where she let it melt. She looked up to see John watching her. He smiled and shook his head.

'What? Are you judging my lolly consumption?' she raised an eyebrow at him.

'Not at all,' he said with a laugh.

She poked her chocolatey tongue out at him.

'Nice. It's good to see they put someone so mature in charge of the most important space mission of this generation.'

'What else do you think you will miss?' Jessica asked, ignoring his teasing.

'Hmm, perhaps the solitude.'

'Solitude? We're going to be millions of miles away from life in all directions. How much more alone do you need to be?'

'Yeah, but I'll be trapped in a tin can with four other people.'

'True. On paper, it's a recipe for disaster. But luckily for you we're all trained astronauts. And lovely too.' She licked the last of the ice cream from its stick and grinned at John.

'What about you? What will you miss?' he asked her.

Jessica lay back on the grass and thought for a minute. She had done other space missions. Two visits to the ISS2. But they had been just for a few months, not long enough for the novelty to wear off, too short to make the loss of anything unbearable. She would miss nice food and good wine. She would miss her grandmother and all the different people in her life. She considered the question some more, closing her eyes as the sun warmed her skin, inhaling the fresh smell of warmed earth.

'The weather.'

'The weather?' John's question rang through her ears.

'Yes,' she replied, her eyes still closed, her face turned towards the sun. 'When it's warm like this and you can just feel your body waking up from the cold winter. When you get caught in an unexpected rain shower and get drenched. Even when it's grey and grim outside and you can sit by the window in a blanket with a cup of tea all cosy and warm. Every day the view will be almost the same for us for years. No fresh air. No change of seasons. Everything just the same.'

There was no response from John. 'Are you even listening to me?' She smiled with her eyes still shut. He was probably distracted by someone's dog, or an attractive woman walking past. When she opened her eyes, he was just looking at her like she was a puzzle he was trying to solve, a smile playing at his lips.

'What?' she asked.

'Nothing,' he said.

'What? You're laughing at me again. Do I have chocolate on my face or something?'

'No, not at all. It's just... you just surprise me sometimes.'

'Oh.' He had said the same thing earlier. How did she surprise him? What did he think of her? She wanted to ask but something stopped her from probing any further. It felt like a thread she shouldn't pull at, for fear of it unravelling.

'Isn't this glorious?' she said with a sigh. She inhaled the scent of spring flowers that were heavy on the warm air.

'I don't think I've ever seen you this relaxed,' John said.

She was laying on her back, legs crossed at the ankle, arms above her head. She was relaxed. Her limbs were warm and loose from the run. Her mind was unusually clear. The last few months had been non-stop, with so much to absorb, so much pressure, and constant media interest. She had to be on her best behaviour the entire time. Not that it was a problem, she always wanted to do the right thing. But she was even more nervous about putting a foot wrong, damaging the reputation of NARESA and the crew, having her coveted position taken away.

When she was with John she was never on edge. It was just easy, he was easy. He brought out the best in her, stopped her from taking everything too seriously, stopped her from being too hard on herself. It felt right, him being on the crew. The five of them would be a tight unit, they knew each other well, how to get the best from each other, and occasionally, how to press each other's buttons. It was all part of creating a great team, Jessica knew that. She wasn't afraid of conflict among them, it was fine - even productive – in a team that trusted one another. If they had differences they talked about them. Jessica loved the straightforwardness of it, there were no games.

'You look like you could do with more relaxation too,' she said looking up at him from her supine position. He was still sitting up, his arms resting on his bent legs.

He stretched out next to her, tucked his arms under his head, and they lay in companionable silence for a while. She felt more comfortable with John than with anyone else. Jessica had a wide circle of friends at NARESA, not just in the astronaut pool, in the scientist, the engineers, and other support teams. She particularly missed Rachel, who was en route to Mars.

But John had been a steady presence since they had joined together. At first, it was a familiarity, a shared connection when they were so far from home and everything was unfamiliar. It had developed into a solid friendship. She needed someone like him. If it weren't for John she might never leave work. And while she would have run today, she always did, she wouldn't have stopped like this, just taken time to enjoy the moment.

Jessica turned over onto her front. She lay her head on her arms and peered at him sideways out of one eye, squinting into the sun. He was lean and muscular, as they all were. The programme worked them hard, and the weight of the spaceship was calculated down to the kilogram. Being healthy and in good condition was part of the deal for them all, and essential to their survival when in space. John was so familiar to her and would become even more so when they were on the Harmonia together. How would their friendship change when they were on mission together, in each other's company day and night for a year and a half?

'John?'

'Hmmm?' he replied, half asleep.

'Do you think we spend too much time together?'

'What?' his eyes flicked open and he turned to face her.

'I just mean, we're going to be spending so much time together in a few months. Do you worry that we'll get bored of each other?'

'Well, I wasn't worried till now.' He was quiet for a minute. 'Are you bored with me?' His eyes searched her face.

'No, I'm really not.' She wasn't. She didn't know why she'd said it.

'Are you worried about something?'

'No, it's just... everything's going to be different up there isn't it? I want us to still be friends like this when we get back.'

None of them knew how the mission would change them, but she was almost certain that each member of the crew would return a slightly different person. John was a constant in her life. Things were great as they were. She didn't want anything to change.

'Of course we'll still be friends.' He was quiet for a minute, and when he spoke again his words came out in a rush. 'Jessica, I don't have other friends like you. You are so important to me. I promise we'll be just as good friends when we get back.' He paused, then grinned 'I just might need a Jessica holiday when we've returned for a couple of weeks though.'

'Hey!' She reached out and swatted him lazily on the arm. He grasped her hand and squeezed it. Jessica closed her eyes again and they lay in companionable silence for a few minutes, hand in hand. She smiled to herself as his fingers traced hers. Even laying down John couldn't keep still. It was so familiar and safe; she could have stayed there all afternoon.

She thought about his words and a warmth spread along her body. She loved feeling like she was important to him. Somehow, over the past few years the annoying boy from class had become her best friends. Knowing him was like knowing Christmas songs. She couldn't remember how she learned the words or the melodies, they were just ingrained in her, comforting and familiar. And he knew her too, could tell what she was thinking sometimes before she knew herself. It was that which was going to make them a great team on the mission to Mars. Jessica gripped his hand. She heard him sigh. She opened one eye and peered at him sideways.

'Am I boring you?' she said.

'What? No, of course not. Why do you think that?'

'That big sigh. Or are you just restless?'

'Yeah,' he replied distractedly, 'just restless.' He had a look on his face that she couldn't read. He let go of her hand and sat up. 'Come on you, race you back.'

Jessica groaned and got up. As she set off after John, she reminded herself that afternoons like these would just be a distant memory in a few months.

Chapter Sixteen
Countdown until first Mars walk: nine months

Jessica

The Pegasus rocket rose monolithically out of the flat Florida skyline. Even surrounded by the launch tower it seemed impossible that it should stay upright. Jessica looked out of the window of the crew bus, nicknamed the Astrovan. It wasn't the first time she had been driven along this route, kitted out in her space suit, but this time felt different. Once they left the planet it would be over eighteen months before they returned. Across the crystalline blue waters of Cape Canaveral thousands and thousands of people lined the beaches and the roads. Even part of the highway had been closed, allowing cars to stop, sandwiched in long stationary lines, to view history being made.

The Astrovan that was driving the nine miles to their destination, the inauspiciously named Space Launch Complex 41, was in fact an Airstream tourer, plush, and smooth, running silently on an electric battery. It was a far cry from the Astrovan of the 1960s and 1970s that the Shuttle astronauts had railed against replacing. Jessica understood; there was something comforting about following in the history of other great women and men. For all the pragmatism of their profession, astronauts were surprisingly superstitious. At times of high pressure there was comfort and calm in the rituals and routines of decades of space travel.

As they drew closer Jessica lowered her head to try and see the very top of the rocket. The Aneris capsule would not only be their ascent vehicle, taking them into orbit as the first two stages of the rocket dropped away, but would also dock with the Harmonia and serve as the bridge to the vast ship that would carry them to Mars. Once in Martian orbit the Aneris would again be deployed to take them down to the surface of the planet. Much like the Shuttle of the Twentieth Century, the reusable vehicle was the answer to economically sustainable interplanetary travel. The Harmonia spaceship itself, not unlike the modular space stations in design, would be tested and rebuilt on their return and would hopefully be redeployed.

The crew were suited ready for launch. While previous Apollo astronauts making this journey wore bulky suits, wrapped with pipes and tubes, the NARESA launch suits were little more than a large jumpsuit. They would don bigger, sturdier spacesuits for any extra vehicle activities, or EVAs. They needed extra protection on excursions outside of the craft where they would be travelling at speed, exposed to the elements of space, at risk even from tiny but potentially fatal space rocks. But the launch suits were the same ones they would wear on the surface of Mars, lighter weight, and more flexible.

The crew were unusually silent during the drive. Jessica wondered if like her they were trying to take in every detail of the day, a day that they would remember for the rest of their lives. The Apollo astronauts, in old interviews, had described this very journey. The gravity of this situation felt hard to grasp, and taking in every detail, every feeling, took all of her attention.

The five of them looked meaningfully at one another as they took their final steps on Earth into the rickety lift that would take them in stages to the top of the launch tower. Jessica noticed a shift in May's posture.

'You ok, May?' she asked through the radio.

'Yeah, I just don't like heights very much,' she faced straight ahead, clearly avoiding looking down.

'May!' Jessica laughed in disbelief.

'What? I'll be fine when I get in the capsule. I'm better if I can't see the ground.'

'Well I certainly hope they spent more money on the rocket than they did this lift. Shocking engineering.' John said, shaking the bars of the door.

'Cut it out.' May's voice shook as she grabbed his arm. He grinned in response.

Valentina and Lucca were both quiet, which wasn't unusual for Val. But Lucca had lost some of his usual ebullience.

'How're you doing Lucca?' She touched his arm lightly.

'Yeah, fine,' he replied. Jessica let him be. It was a momentous occasion, and they were all going through their own internal processes.

The capsule was relatively spacious compared to launch capsules of the past. Two seats, reclined at ninety degrees for launch and re-entry, were stationed at the front. Three seats, also reclined, were stationed behind. When docked with the Harmonia the seats would turn and face consoles, but for the launch all were fixed in a forward-facing position. Jessica and Valentina were strapped into the front two seats, while John, Lucca, and May climbed into those behind.

The launch pad crew did the last of their checks. The last ground crew member did a final handshake with Jessica before closing the capsule door behind her and giving a last wave through the small window. The handshake had become part of the ceremony, partly as an official hand over, but also in the knowledge that this would be the last contact any of them had outside this group for the entirety of the mission. *This is it.* Jessica steeled herself as the capsule door closed and the locking mechanisms engaged with a loud clunk.

'Ok, Aneris, this is Control. We have the capsule door sealed and we have T-Minus eight minutes and thirty-two seconds until launch.' Tom's calm commanding voice came over the radio. He was CAPCOM for their launch, and Jessica momentarily remembered asking John if he would do it. She smiled to herself, thankful he was instead in the seat behind her.

'Copy that Control, this is Aneris, we are about to commence pre-launch checks.'

In reality, there weren't many checks to carry out. The launch vehicle was monitored from the ground, so pre-launch checks for the crew amounted to physical problems within the capsule itself and any issue they were experiencing that the ground crew wouldn't be aware of.

'Ok crew, this is it, final go/no-go from everyone.' Jessica tried to keep her voice steady, but she couldn't contain her excitement.

'May?'

'Go Commander.'

'Valentina?'

'Go Commander.'

'John?'

'I'm Go.'

Jessica was thrown off for a millisecond. He just had to be different, didn't he?

'Lucca?'

'I'm Go... no wait, wait.' There was an urgency in his voice.

'What's the issue, Lucca?' A chill surged through Jessica's veins. Even a small problem could call the whole mission off.

'I'm so sorry everyone, *mi dispiace*. I can't.'

'Can't what? What's the problem?' Something in the pit of her stomach stirred. 'Launch, I'm going off comms for a minute.'

Going off comms for even one minute this close to launch would signal a problem to launch control, but something told her this wasn't a conversation they wanted to be broadcast.

'Ok, Copy that, Commander. T minus three minutes and forty-five seconds.'

Jessica pressed the screen in front of her which kept communications between the members of the capsule.

'Lucca, we have one minute, I need to know what's happening.'

'My kids, my family, I'm so sorry everyone, I can't leave them.' He was speaking quickly, there was panic in his voice that she had never heard before. 'I thought I could but I can't. I'm sorry, I've been thinking about it for weeks. I should have said something. I want off Jessica.'

'Lucca, calm down it's ok, it's completely normal to feel like this.' Jessica tried to keep calm, tried to keep the irritation out of her voice. What happened in the next sixty seconds would determine whether they would launch in less than four minutes, or all climb out of the capsule.

'No, Jessica, I can't do it.' His voice was firm now. 'I've been thinking about it, I should have said something sooner, I want off, call it in.'

From her fixed seat, tightly strapped in, Jessica couldn't even turn to face her crewmate. She wished she could look him in the eyes, to understand what was going on.

'Lucca, I know I can't see you, but I'm hearing you, and I need you to listen to me. You don't want to do this.' Did he though? She felt blindsided, let down by her instincts. She should have noticed something was wrong. Now she didn't know what to think. She just knew she had to ask fast.

'No, I mean it, Jessica, I just want to be with my boys. I can't be away from them this long. What if something happens? I thought I'd be fine, I thought the feeling would go. I'm sorry everyone, they'll replace me, you'll be off in a few days.'

There was a short window. They could get back up, and be back on the launch pad in a few days. But this was her crew. It was her job to keep them together.

'Make the call Jessica!' The volume startled her. Astronauts rarely raised their voice on the radio. Radio etiquette was part of their basic training. It was essential to communicate calmly and clearly at all times. A raised voice always signified something serious.

'Ok, ok, calm down, Lucca. I can call it in, I can abort the launch and you can be replaced on this crew but I want you to just listen to what I have to say. We have about forty seconds and once your decision is made we can't reverse it.' She spoke clearly and evenly.

Jessica hated not being able to see him, so she just closed her eyes and took a deep breath. She had to get this right. She had to be the Commander Lucca needed right now. What if this was just a blip? They would probably all get them at some point, it just so happened that Lucca's was happening three minutes before launch. *Great timing, Lucca,* Jessica thought to herself as she weighed up the decision. Should she attempt to talk him round? What was best for the mission? She made her choice.

'I want you to fully contemplate what's at stake here. If we abort because you don't want to go, you'll never fly again, they just won't take that chance. Plenty of people can take your place.'

'I don't care, Jessica, call it in.' Lucca's voice was almost a whisper. It had lost some of its conviction. She was doing the right thing.

'Ok, Lucca, but just listen to me. I think you're going to regret this. Just listen to my voice, I'm going to call an abort in thirty seconds, because that's what I have to do. But just listen to me once more. Your boys, they'll miss you of course they will, but don't you think sometimes we need to be the hero that our children want us to be? You know what Lucca? I don't talk about this much, but can't I even tell you how much I would like my father to be down there?' She swallowed.

'It's hard to put into words what this will mean to those boys of yours. For the rest of their lives they will be able to look to the stars and know that their father was one of the greatest explorers in human history, a pioneer, something to be really proud of. You turn back now? Sure, you'll see them for the next couple of months, but you'll spend the rest of your life explaining to yourself and to them why you got off this rocket today.' Jessica paused knowing this was her last shot.

'Be the example they need Lucca. I promise you, if my parents were still around, I know how proud they would be of me today, and there's no way I would let them see me get off this rocket.'

'Harmonia,' Tom's voice crackled on the radio. 'We need a read out on your situation, T minus two minutes."

'Lucca?' Jessica asked, still on crew comms. There was a long pause and she held her breath.

'I'm go Jessica, I'm go.'

Jessica released her breath with a sigh. She had taken a risk. An informed risk, based on her experiences and her instincts. But a risk nonetheless. She had turned Lucca around, convinced it was just a blip, last minute nerves, and in the best case he would thank her for it. If she had made the wrong choice, it would impact all of them for the next eighteen months and beyond.

Jessica pressed the comms button on the screen in front of her.

'Ok Control, we are Go for launch.'

Chapter Seventeen
Countdown until first Mars walk: 9 months

John

The starry black sky through the capsule window was suddenly broken up by the gleaming white body of the Harmonia spacecraft. Though travelling at thirty thousand kilometres per hour it appeared to be stationary, still and perfectly controlled.

As the Aneris capsule rotated for docking the Harmonia disappeared from view. Unlike the Apollo days and early days of the space station, the docking sequence was completely automated. Aneris glided towards Harmonia with absolute precision, and connected with the expected jolt. For the first time on the journey the crew released their harnesses and allowed themselves to feel the full sense of being weightless. Each of the crew was an experienced astronaut with at least two flights under their belts, but it always took some time for their bodies to adjust to the lack of positional cues, and bumps and bruises were par for the course for the first few days. John felt a childlike glee as he skimmed through the air.

It was John's job to open the hatch. Like the other two in the second row of the launch capsule he hadn't had much to do up until this point and he hated feeling like a spectator. Their journey was still being broadcast and he was determined to do this task perfectly.

'Ok, Control, opening the hatch.' Millions of people were watching the feed. After a while he would get used to these broadcasts, but today he just wanted to get the words out in the right order.

He moved the door arm downwards and pulled it towards him. The Aneris and the Harmonia were perfectly pressurised to match each other so there was no rush of air when the door opened. John pushed the door back and looked down the dim corridor of their new home. It felt like opening the door to a hotel room at the start of a visit. Everything ready and waiting, familiar yet unfamiliar.

The Aneris capsule, now connected to the front of the Harmonia, became the bridge for the huge space craft, the control centre for their flight.

'Cabin pressurisation confirmed, removing helmets now safe.' Jessica's voice beamed across the radio.

'Confirming that, Commander, removing helmet.'

John slipped the locking switch to the side and lifted off his helmet before stepping through into their new home for the next eighteen months. He knew Harmonia's every inch, but seeing it in reality was very different to staring at layouts for months on end, and working in sections recreated in the lab. He stood at the head of a long corridor, which ran almost the entire length of Harmonia. Halfway along it forked left and right. The right-hand turn took them to the entrance of the gym and their living quarters, and a left turn took them to the medical room and storage areas. They would almost always turn right.

A blue light on a camera in the corridor suddenly lit up. It was being used for a live feed. The Harmonia was equipped with a few cameras, but not everywhere, they didn't want astronauts feeling like they were being watched every minute of the day. It was bad enough having to wear medical patches every day. Mission control could monitor pretty much anything about them from the ground. The patches were wireless and communicated directly with a hub that sent the measurements back to earth. If for some reason the patches weren't registering a signal for more than four minutes Mission Control would be in contact. John had already decided that he was going to take his off for a series of three minute periods. It was these small rebellions that kept him on message for the bigger things.

Stepping through the connecting corridor he felt the full weight of his body again. The central section of the Harmonia was engineered to spin to create enough centrifugal force to give the astronauts the feeling of gravity. It didn't feel quite the same as the magnetically induced gravity of Earth, but it made daily life easier to navigate, and had less of a detrimental impact on their bodies than microgravity. Their main living and sleeping quarters were in the centre, but the Aneris capsule remained static and gravity free.

The Harmonia felt eerie, like a ghost ship, empty of human life, everything laid out neatly. The craft had been built in orbit, over many months and everything they needed was already there. The H series orbital vehicles (Haulage) had been designed specially to carry large amounts of equipment into orbit, which docked automatically with what had already been built, and was then assembled by a crew that lived aboard for the duration of the build.

John's official instructions had ended with the hatch being successfully opened and Jessica giving the "helmets off" authority. For a few precious minutes John was completely on his own to do whatever he liked. He glanced into the opening on his left which was an open plan galley, a living space with a huge table, and the kitchen, as well as some comfier booth type seats. Opposite this room were two labs, completely equipped to run experiments and grow food for the journey.

John wandered to the end of the corridor. He had an overwhelming urge to look at everything before anyone else did, exploring his surroundings like an animal scoping out a new territory. He turned right at the bottom then a sharp left to another shorter corridor. On the left was the crew gym and shower rooms, and on the right five identical doors. The first door had a sign saying Eden. He quickly looked to the door next to his, with a fleeting pang of disappointment that it didn't have Gabriel on it. He was next door to Valentina. John slid the door open and looked around his personal space for the next eighteen months. It contained a bed, a small desk, and a wardrobe.

'Hey,' said a voice from behind. He was no longer alone on the ship.

'Lucca.' They hadn't properly talked since his distress on the launch pad.

'Listen, *compagno*, buddy, I'm sorry, it just really got to me. I'm so sorry.'

'No need to apologise, but you really need to thank Jessica, you would never have forgiven yourself, Lucca.' said John. He tried to hide the lingering resentment in his voice. Years of preparation and he had nearly sabotaged the whole launch for all of them.

'I will, I'll speak to her later.'

Lucca didn't hang around. John felt a pang of guilt at his lack of sympathy. His anger would wear off and they would patch it up later. They had training in conflict resolution. It would be fine. The stakes had just been high today.

As he looked around his room Jessica appeared in his doorway. Without saying anything she stepped inside and looked around.

'Wow, in my room already, we've only been on board a few minutes.' John chuckled.

'They're not bad, are they?' Jessica ignored his comment, as she often did when he said things like that. It just made him want to do it even more.

'Lucca was just here, he apologised.'

'Oh?' said Jessica.

'Yeah, probably best to get that whole issue cleared away as quickly as possible.' said John.

'I will,' she said shortly. She probably didn't appreciate him telling her what to do.

'Listen,' she continued. 'The others are about to start unloading the empty specimen cases from the Aneris into the labs, want to help?'

'I'll be right there.'

Jessica walked out of the room and John realised he'd been staring at the empty space where she had been. He shook his head to rid himself of the thoughts of her that started to creep in.

All of the lights on Harmonia were on motion sensors, and automatically adjusted their brightness according to the time of day. As John walked towards the main corridor the left turn towards it was illuminated. The turn that led away from the bedrooms to the storage and medical rooms was a blind corner that made John feel inexplicably uneasy. It was very unlikely anyone would be down there, but something about it set his hairs on end. A corridor in his grandmother's huge house that she lived in when he was a boy had made him feel the same. It both beckoned him and repelled him at the same time.

Low murmuring came from the galley as he walked past. Glancing through the door he saw Lucca in deep conversation with May. She had a hand over his. The pain was clear on his expressive face. They didn't notice him pass.

Jessica and Valentina were in Lab Number One on the opposite side of the corridor closet to the Aneris capsule, now the Bridge.

'Commander,' said John, poking his head through the open door, prompting both Jessica and May to look up in a confused manner. He didn't know why he was being so formal. Their new home on the Harmonia had a serious air to it.

'Can I have a quick word?'

'Sure.'

Jessica stepped out into the corridor and John gestured to her to follow him towards the Aneris capsule.

'Have you spoken to Lucca yet?'

'No, Val and I are unpacking the plant samples first, why?' Jessica tilted her head.

'He's in there talking to May. He doesn't look good.'

'Ok, well maybe they can talk it out a bit, then I can give a debrief.' Jessica said, shrugging her shoulders. John knew from months of being led by her that Jessica's preference was to give her team space.

'Jessica, I have an idea...'

Twenty minutes later he returned to the galley.

May was on her own now, looking through the cupboards moving a few things around.

'Hey May, where's Lucca?'

'He's gone back to his room, I think he needed some time alone.' said May.

'Is he ok?' John knew the answer, but wanted to ask anyway.

'He just feels like he's let everyone down, he's embarrassed.'

'Well,' said John, 'Jessica and I have had an idea. Go up to the observation deck now and I'll go and get him.'

The observation deck was a space above the bridge in the Aneris, the entire length of the capsule. Like the bridge, it didn't have simulated gravity. Its only purpose was for the astronauts' relaxation. A strengthened glass dome covered the whole area, offering a hundred and eighty degree view of space and the direction in which they were travelling. The dome was covered by a retractable Kevlar alloy, which protected the glass during lift off and re-entry. It had been the most expensive part of the whole of Harmonia to manufacture, and survived several budget cuts, because the behavioural science department of NARESA had insisted on it. The breakthroughs in the link between good mental health and long-distance space travel had arguably been bigger than any of the scientific discoveries that had been made over the past twenty years. For the crew it would be a place of sanctuary.

'Hey, Lucca,' John lightly tapped the open door of Lucca's room, which was open. 'You ok?'

'Yes, fine.' He was sitting on the edge of his bed.

'Jessica wants to see you on the observation deck.'

'Ok.' Lucca nodded. He looked nervous, as if he were expecting an uncomfortable conversation.

'Just get it over with buddy,' John turned and walked off without making any eye contact.

***

The whole crew, having rehearsed a few times dipped into silence as Lucca, expecting just to see Jessica, entered the room transferring from simulated gravity to weightlessness.

'And here is, the star of our show, Astronaut Costa!' May announced in her most dramatic voice.

The crew pushed against one another, parting theatrically to reveal the large comms screen where, larger than life Lucca's young boys, Matteo and Lucca Junior, appeared on screen, with their mother Giovanna behind them. John watched as Lucca's face changed from surprise, to joy, to his eyes filling with tears.

Papa!' the boys excitedly called from the screen.

'Ok boys,' John shouted at the screen manoeuvring behind Lucca and holding him at the waist. 'Check this out!' John lifted

Lucca and put him into a spin, aiming him towards the screen. The children laughed as their father came right towards the camera.

'John...' Jessica admonished and gave him a look that said 'That's not how we rehearsed it.' She gestured at them to link arms with the others into a skydiving pose in the middle of the observation deck. Lucca joined last, trying to concentrate on completing the circle, and unable to take his eyes off the screen where his children looked happy and proud. As the five of them, each with their arm around the next person's shoulders started to spin faster and faster, they all laughed until the circle was broken and they all flew off in different directions. John somersaulted through the air, waving at the boys on camera.

May had managed to rustle up a bag of M&Ms and proceeded to fire them into the air towards Jessica, who ate them Pacman style. John laughed, and was delighted to see the boys were doing the same. Lucca's face had returned to its easy countenance and John was pleased they had done something to break the tension and make him feel better. They continued in this vein for a few more minutes. In the pressure of the mission it was easy to forget how much fun their job could be.

John saw Jessica glance at the screen where Giovanna was hugging her boys.

'Ok everyone, I think it's time to wrap this up and leave Lucca to it,' she said.

The rest of the crew waved goodbye to the boys.

'Jessica, we still need to talk about what happened. I'm so sorry.' Lucca whispered, away from the screen microphone.

'No, we don't Lucca. Everything is fine. We're a team, we rise, we fall, but most importantly we support each other. The matter is closed.' She smiled reassuringly at him. 'Go and talk to your family.'

Listening to the exchange, John smiled and shook his head. Jessica had handled the situation brilliantly. She had made the right decision, for Lucca and the mission. He was so proud of her. Lucca had gone from despair to looking on top of the world. She had talked him down during the launch, and now she had made him feel like it was going to be ok. It was these small actions as well as the big ones that convinced John that Jessica was the Commander they needed.

Chapter Eighteen
Countdown to first Mars walk: 7 months

Jessica

It was the pounding in her head that woke Jessica up that morning, shortly before Mission Control started playing The Rolling Stones 'Start Me Up' through the speakers. The tradition of waking the astronauts up to music dated from the days of the NASA Apollo programme. Each CAPCOM on shift got to choose what they played; mostly they played music, though some picked readings of books or poetry. Some CAPCOMs picked things tailored to the astronauts on board. Today's choice was not one of those. Mike was on CAPCOM today and this was his idea of a joke.

Two months on board and they were still only a quarter of the way to Mars. There had been relatively little drama since Lucca's launchpad attack of homesickness. There was an invariability to their day to day routine, but far from finding it tedious, the crew were just happy everything was running smoothly.

Jessica pushed her eye mask to the top of her head and squinted painfully into the light. Her wrist comms said 06:15. It had been another bad night's sleep, not unusual for her on this journey. The lack of clear day and night was messing with her circadian rhythms; she still hadn't got used to it. The constant low hum of the ship, like being on an aeroplane, was draining. She laid her head back on her pillow and shifted in her sleeping bag. Thankfully the crew quarters were in the part of the ship with artificial gravity, which at least made it easier to sleep.

Their private rooms were about three metres squared. They had a narrow bed, a small workspace with a detachable tablet computer, and storage space for clothes and a few personal items. There were no windows in this part of the ship. A noticeboard held photos of her mother and grandmother, as well as pictures of beautiful natural landscapes: turquoise seascapes and Japanese cherry blossoms, blooming like clouds of candyfloss. In fact, since research that she had commissioned showed that just looking at pictures of nature could be almost as relaxing as the real thing, Jessica had insisted all the crew have their own specially selected landscape pictures in their quarters.

May had picked lush tropical forests and waterfalls; Lucca, rolling Tuscan hills and the Italian Lakes; Valentina had pictures of the Norwegian fjords, and the Northern Lights; and John had views of mountains surrounding crystal clear lakes, and snow-capped peaks. As well as being relaxing, looking at distance views was good exercise for their eye muscles, which were at risk of degeneration due to lack of long-range use and the effects microgravity. The crew had teased her for suggesting it, but in reality, they all knew that their mental and physical health were essential to their survival on this mission.

In her personal effects' locker were hand and face cream to combat the dry air of the ship, a necklace that had belonged to her mother and a worn copy of her favourite book Great Expectations. Her mother had first read it to her when she was about twelve, and this one had been her copy, with fallen pages taped in. The crew had access to all the books and films they wanted through their tablets, but for Jessica, there was nothing quite like the feel of a book, the smell of the paper, and the way the book fell open at the pages she most lingered on. She also had a small stack of notebooks and a cache of pens.

The privacy of the astronaut's rooms was sacrosanct on board the ship. It was the only space where you could guarantee you wouldn't encounter anyone else, where your possessions remained where you'd left them and not borrowed or tidied away somewhere unknown, and where there was no camera transmitting a feed. There was only a small security camera that was strictly for emergencies.

Forcing herself to get up, Jessica unzipped her sleeping bag, put on her wrist monitor, and made her way to the galley. The crew spent most of their working days in their blue jumpsuits; in some ways, the space programme had never quite shaken its military formalities. But the unwritten rule among the crew of

The Harmonia was that you could go to breakfast in your sleepwear, which for Jessica was currently a pair of shorts and a NARESA sweatshirt.

She padded along the corridor to the galley, passing the rest of the crew rooms. They met there every morning for their daily breakfast meeting known as the "rundown" where they would cover the itinerary for the day, with a pre-recorded video from Mission Control. As she sat down, John slid her cup of strong tea, her usual morning brew. She smiled at him gratefully.

'Thanks.' Jessica said then turned to May. 'I've got a cracking headache, can you hit me up with some drugs in a bit?'

'Sure. Are you ok?'

'Yeah, I'm just tired.' Jessica said with a sigh.

'Maybe some sleeping pills too, then?'

'You're such a pusher,' Jessica grinned at her.

'Hey, whatever you need to get by.'

'Thanks. I'll come to the med room after the rundown.'

Jessica opened a window on her tablet. 'Right crew, today is, for those of us losing track, day fifty-eight. Important things first: on tonight's menu – macaroni cheese.'

'A travesty against Italian food.' Lucca moaned.

'Man, I'd kill for a burger and fries.' John said.

'It's six thirty a.m.' May narrowed her eyes at John.

'Time is all relative in space, May, my friend.'

'Any chance we could get through a rundown without the comedy routine? This is going to be a long eighteen months if we have to do this every morning.'

She was only half serious in her admonishment. The routine chatter and rituals they had developed that kept them going and made them feel like a team.

'The good news is, I believe we will be having our first freshly grown space salad with it. Am I right Lucca?'

'Yes, the first crop of lettuce leaves is ready to harvest.'

The rest of the crew let out a cheer of delight.

'Well done Lucca, that sounds great.' Jessica continued and proceeded to read out the other activities on the list.

Almost all of their time on the ship was accounted for. Even their leisure time was scheduled in. And each of them had to spend at least two hours each day doing physical exercise to protect their bodies against the ravages of microgravity and the confined space. After breakfast the crew pared off to their various activities.

Jessica joined May in the med room. May was personal physician to all the crew members, and each of them had to have monthly check ups with her. May took Jessica's blood pressure and her temperature.

'Nothing that looks worrying. Have you been drinking enough water?'

'Yep, my designated amount.'

'How are you sleeping?'

'Not great. I'm struggling with the noise, and frankly, I just miss my own bed,' she smiled, her cheeks tinged with pink.

She was on the journey of a lifetime. Her whole adult life had been leading up to this point, and she was making a fuss over sleeping arrangements? They had been through rigorous and often repetitive training, simulations, stays in underwater labs, extreme camping trips. Despite this life on the ship, day in day out, took some adjustment.

'Here. Take these now,' May handed Jessica two tablets, and she took a sip of water as she swallowed them. 'And take one of these an hour before bed for the next three days. You look tired.'

'Gee, thanks.' Jessica rolled her eyes at May.

'You need to get some decent sleep. She looked at her computer monitor. 'From the looks of your medical patch, your iron levels are a little low.' The patches, attached to their upper arm, monitored their bloodstream for abnormalities.

'I'm going to give you a vitamin shot that might help you feel less tired.'

'Anything else you want to talk about?'

Jessica rolled her eyes again, 'No, May, I'm fine. Honestly, I'm just sleeping badly. We're all finding it hard to get used to.' She rolled up her sleeve so May could administer the injection.

'Except Valentina.'

'Yeah well, she's like a bat, happy to sleep upside down. That'll be all the hardcore military training.'

'Have you been recording your video diaries?' May looked enquiringly at Jessica.

'I've done a few... I know, I know. I need to do it more regularly.'

'Jessica, you know it's good for your mental health. Don't look at me like that.'

Jessica's face was obviously betraying her impatience.

'You've got to stay on top of this stuff.' May continued' You know that. You've studied it even more than I have. And you would say the same to me if the roles were reversed.'

'My mental health is fine, thank you very much.'

'That may be so, you are terrible at talking about stuff.'

'I'm not!' But it was a weak protest. While she was happy to talk and listen to the crew about their feelings, she was reluctant to share her own with them.

'Ok Jessica, what emotion are you feeling right now?'

'I'm feeling interrogated.'

'Interrogated isn't an emotion.'

'Alright, Dr Freud. Is my therapy session over?'

'Well, just do your diaries. And talk about proper stuff, not just "Dear Diary, today I had macaroni cheese for dinner."'

Jessica laughed. 'Alright, alright. I'll do the diaries. Thanks for the check-up, Doc.' And she left to get back on with her work.

The bright light in the onboard greenhouse made Jessica's head pulse in pain, but she tried to ignore it as she tended to Lucca's plants. Lucca had a headache too and had missed lunch, so she had skipped one of her tasks to do the essential watering. He was experimenting with different growing conditions, from aeroponics, which used no soil and little water, to traditional cultivation methods. They weren't going to be reliant on the food Lucca grew, but if he could maintain growth, it would supplement their meals with much missed fresh produce.

The air was damp and warm. She breathed in the tangy smell of tomato vines that gave off their evocative scent as she brushed past their leaves. This was Lucca's domain, having volunteered to undertake intensive botany training to support the mission, on top of his geology specialism. But in the rare few moments Jessica had free she came in here. She loved the earthy smell of the plants, the moist air. It was the one place in the craft where for a few moments you could forget you were on a spaceship in the middle of nowhere. Her few moments of calm were interrupted by May.

'Jessica,' she was frowning at something on her tablet, 'I'm getting some worrying results in the blood tests I took earlier this week. I'm seeing increased levels of carboxyhaemoglobin...'

'CO in the bloodstream?' Jessica raised her eyebrow, her brain immediately running through possible explanations.

'Looks like it. Everyone's is raised, yours and Lucca's are particularly high.'

'We've both had headaches today. You think it's carbon monoxide poisoning?'

'Could be. Have you had any other symptoms? Nausea? Dizziness? Tiredness?'

'Sounds like a normal day on Harmonia to me...' Jessica puffed her cheeks out and ran her hands through her hair. It could be nothing. Or it could be something serious. 'Come on, we'd better go and talk to Val and John.'

They entered the bridge through the narrow corridor that took them from the artificial gravity area to the zero gravity Aneris capsule at the head of the ship. It was here that Valentina and John were working at the main control panel underneath the large window that wrapped around the front of the spacecraft.

'Guys, look at this. May's reading high CO levels in our bloodstreams. Is there something wrong with the CDRS?'

The Carbon Dioxide Removal System took CO from the air and blew it outside the spacecraft, stopping the astronauts from being poisoned by their own breath in the hermetically sealed spacecraft.

'There shouldn't be,' John said, brow furrowed. 'If there was, a warning should have gone off to alert us.'

He moved over to another control panel and started scrolling through menus.

'Shit. There *is* an error, but I can't tell what it is yet.'

'Why didn't the alarm alert us?' May asked.

'I don't know...' he carried on checking the screen.

'Well, can you see what's wrong?' Jessica demanded. She hovered over his shoulder, trying to see the screen.

'Not yet. I can't tell from the control panel. I'm going to have to look at the filter myself.'

'How long will that take?' she demanded impatiently.

'Depends what I find.'

Jessica raced through some scenarios in her head.

'Ok, here's the plan. John, can you check out the CDRS filter and assess what needs doing to fix it? I want to know how bad the problem is, how long before it gets serious, and what the solution is.' She turned to May. 'Can you check on Lucca again and then I want an update on the impact of the carbon dioxide, and the best course of action for crew safety. Val, you help John. I'm going to contact mission control. I want everyone back in the galley in thirty minutes for a sitrep.'

A situation report in half an hour would hopefully provide more data for her to make a decision. Jessica didn't mind making difficult decisions, that was part of her job. But this was the part that made her feel most uncomfortable, not knowing what was going on.

Half an hour later she sat in front of three grave faces.

'How's Lucca?' Jessica asked May.

'Lethargic and nauseous. Classic carbon monoxide poisoning symptoms. I've made him put an oxygen mask on to get his O2 levels back up.'

'Will he need any further treatment?'

'No, the increased oxygen should be enough. He'll be back to normal in a day or two. But we all should be wearing masks to stop any of us feeling any worse.'

'That's going to make it incredibly difficult to get around,' John protested, shifting in his seat.

'That's what Mission Control have recommended too, John, as soon as possible.' Jessica insisted, pulling herself up and her shoulders back, bracing herself for a debate.

'Let me tell you what's going on with the CDRS then we can discuss it?'

'Ok, go on then.' She struggled to bite back her frustration. There was no use arguing with John. The key was to make him feel like he had some control, but ultimately Jessica's word was final on the ship. If only John would remember that more often.

'I think it's an actual problem with the power supply to the fan. I can patch it up temporarily, but if I have to wear a mask it will get in the way and take me twice as long. Give me an hour, then we can reassess.'

'Ok, but May keep an eye on him.' She turned back to John, her eyes narrowed. 'What exactly do you mean by patch?'

'Exactly that. It'll solve the problem temporarily, a couple of days at most, but it's going to need replacing to be completely safe.'

'Tell me we have the part to replace it?' Jessica pinched the bridge of her nose. Her head was still pounding.'

'Oh yeah, we have the part.' John grimaced.

'But?' Jessica sensed she wasn't going to like the answer.

'It needs replacing from the outside.'

Jessica leaned back in her chair and squeezed her eyes shut. An unscheduled EVA. Mission Control wasn't going to be happy. Under normal circumstances preparation for an EVA took weeks, even when already in space. Mechanical failures were inevitable on an eighteen month journey, but some things were more essential than others, and breathable air, even if it was recycled, was one of them.

'Are you sure?' Jessica asked, knowing already that he was.

'Absolutely.' John leaned back in his chair. 'I don't know what kind of idiot designed it so you couldn't repair it from the inside.'

'When's the earliest you'll have to do it?' she cut in.

He shrugged. 'Like I said, I can patch it for a couple of days, but it needs properly replacing, and you know, oxygen is pretty essential and all.'

'I know John,' she tried to keep the impatience out of her voice. She could do without his flippancy at a time like this. 'How long will the patch last?'

'Forty-eight hours probably.'

'Control are going to have kittens,' she said with a sigh.

Jessica's head continued to pound and she felt nauseous. Inside the spacecraft it was easy to forget they were in a small object hurtling through the solar system. She felt relatively secure. Outside, at the mercy of space the risks were higher, and it was easier to make fatal mistakes.

'Hey, this isn't my fault.' John held up his hands in protest.

'I know, I know, I didn't say it was. Valentina, do you agree with John?'

'You're checking up on me?' John said, the indignation clear in his voice.

Jessica leaned forward in her seat and looked at John squarely.

'No. I just want Val's opinion. I need to make sure I've got all the data I need. Just let me do my thing, John.'

'I agree with John. We can make it work for a few days but it must be repaired completely as soon as possible.'

'And I can't do that with a mask obscuring my vision and mobility.' John interjected.

'Alright, an hour?' Jessica inclined her head at him.

'Yes.' John replied.

'Do it.' She just wanted it fixed as soon as possible so they would all be safer. 'What do you need?' She directed this at John.

'I need an extra pair of hands.'

'Valentina, how are you feeling?' Jessica turned to her pilot.

'I am fine.' Valentina nodded.

'Ok, can you help John? An hour tops. No mask for either of you. May, I want you in a mask, and I need you to keep an eye on John and Val.'

'Ok.' May said.

'I want to know we've got it in hand in an hour, ok? More than an hour and I am going to make you put masks on.'

'Yes, boss.' John said.

She tried to ignore his patronising tone. Why couldn't he take anything seriously?

'I'll get Mission Control off our backs, and explain to them about the EVA.' Jessica said as they dispersed once again. She decided not to tell Control about the lack of mask usage.

Jessica went to check on Lucca in his cabin.

'How are you feeling?' she asked.

'Better,' he replied, his voice weak and muffled by the mask.

'Do you still feel sick?' she asked.

He shook his head.

'Just tired?'

He nodded.

'John's going to fix it, ok? You'll feel better tomorrow.'

He dipped his head again.

'We'll keep checking on you.' She squeezed his hand, and he nodded. She headed off to fetch her own mask and left him to sleep.

***

Two day later John and Valentina were tethered to the outside of The Harmonia making the repairs to the system.

Three different windows on the screen showed three different views of the astronauts working out in the vastness of space. Through John's helmet camera they could see him meticulously screwing bolts into a panel. Valentina's camera showed the wider view of John, in his bulky spacesuit, his movements slow but well-practised. The external spaceship camera showed them both tethered to the ship, framed by the inky blackness of space. Jessica and May sat at consoles on the bridge, watching their progress.

At over a hundred million kilometres away from Earth, they were too far out of range for Mission Control to lead the EVA. Jessica had CAPCOMed an EVA from the ground before, but this was the first time leading one without the support of a ground crew. The Apollo astronauts flying to the moon had suffered a delay of just three seconds, notwithstanding the forty-eight minutes of radio blackout as they orbited the 'dark side' of the moon. The distance they were at on the Harmonia now meant two minutes would elapse between the ground team sending a signal and receiving one in return from the Harmonia crew.

'How are you doing EV1?' Jessica asked John.

'The new filter's in. I'm just replacing the external panel, then we're done.' John's voice crackled through Jessica's earpiece.

'Nice work, both of you.' The tension Jessica had been feeling throughout her started to dissipate. They were nearly finished.

The two of them had been out there for four hours, every movement taking many times longer than it would back on Earth. They wore EMUs, or Extravehicular Mobility Units, bulky white suits, pressurised to protect them from the vacuum of space, not much evolved since the days of the Shuttle Programme.

After a few minutes of silence Jessica spoke again 'Sitrep, EVA1 and 2?' She wanted to know how they were progressing.

'Harmonia, this is EV1,' John's voice sounded strained and Jessica immediately sat up straighter. 'I'm experiencing some water at the back of my neck.'

Jessica's mind raced through scenarios. 'EV1, is your drinking pouch leaking?'

'I don't know. Could be.' He paused. 'We're nearly done with the panel anyway.'

'How long EV1?'

'Ten minutes to finish sealing the panel, then fifteen minutes transition to the airlock.'

'Copy that, EV1.' She tried to ignore the gnawing sensation in her stomach. She had to trust John.

Jessica listened to the back and forth between John and Valentina, as the two of them tightened the bolts on the external panel of the CDRS. An activity that on Earth that would have taken John alone a few minutes took the two of them almost twenty.

'EV1, how's the water situation?'

A pause.

'Uh, I'm getting droplets in my helmet.' said John, his voice still calm but hurried.

'How much water?'

'Hard to say, I'd estimate about two hundred millilitres.'

Jessica bit her lip. 'EV1, keep talking to me.' Even though she was leading the EVA from the ship, she felt out of control. She wanted them both back in safely.

'This is EV1. It's starting to affect visibility.'

Jessica paused for a minute, weighing up the options. Replacing the filter was essential. She could call off the EVA early and they could come back out in the next few days when they had checked the spacesuit out. But planning extravehicular activities was a massive deal, and they needed only a few more minutes to finish. Jessica knew John well, and she suspected the situation was more serious than he was reporting.

'Alright, I'm terminating this. EV1 back to base. EV2, I want you to make the area safe as quickly as you can, then I want you back in too, right away.'

'We're nearly done with these bolts Jessica, we might as well finish.' John was insistent.

'Get back in, John.' She was prepared to take his ire when he got back in safely. 'That's an order. EV2 can you make it safe?' Her heart started to pound.

'Copy that Harmonia. I will make it safe and be right behind EV1.'

'EV1, are you moving?' No answer. Jessica's stomach twisted. 'John?'

'I'm moving, I'm moving. I'm about twenty metres from the airlock.'

'How's the water situation?' Jessica took a deep breath, trying to keep herself calm.

'Uh, getting a bit worse. I'm seeing more water on my visor, and my Snoopy cap is wet.'

The comms cap, affectionately known as the Snoopy cap, because of its black 'ears', was a fabric headpiece that contained earphones and a microphone. It was pretty robust but not designed to be saturated.

'EVA1, can you still see out of your visor?'

Visibility out of my visor is poor, and there's water going in my eyes. But I can feel the handrails with my hands and feet so I'm doing ok.'

'Keep going John. EV2, what's your status?'

'The CDRS panel is secure and I have visual of EV1. I'm a few minutes behind him.'

It was quiet for thirty seconds. That was too long. There should be a constant stream of communication on an EVA. Jessica's hands shook and she clenched them together.

'EV1, this is Harmonia, do you read me?'

'I read... Harmonia... difficult...' The radio crackled.

'What's going on?' Jessica turned to May in frustration.

'The water must be interfering with his comms equipment.' May said. 'It'll be floating around his helmet. If he breathes the water in...'

'He could drown.' Jessica finished her sentence. 'Damn, there's no camera covering him. EV1, do you read me? EV1?'

Silence.

'EV2, is EV1 still moving?'

'Affirmative, Harmonia. He's moving, he's about five metres from the airlock.'

'EV1, do you copy?'

More silence.

'EV1, if you can hear me, proceed to the airlock. EV2 is two minutes behind you. When you get in the airlock stay as still as you can, and when EV2 is in we'll re-pressurise the airlock at a nominal rate.'

'You're not going to do an emergency re-pressurisation?' May asked, not hiding the urgency in her voice.

'I don't know what's going on for him. If we re-pressurise too fast we risk damage to both of them. If he's made it into the airlock under his own steam then the situation is manageable.'

'Jessica...'

'I'm monitoring the situation, May.' Jessica said firmly, but she ran her hands through her hair and paced up and down.

Her mouth was dry and her breathing shallow. The nominal re-pressurisation would take longer. If John couldn't breathe the delay could be disastrous. But emergency re-pressurisation wasn't without risk either. She bit her fingernail listening for progress.

'EV2 what's the sitrep?' Jessica asked.

'EV1 is at the hatch. I'm two minutes away.'

'EV2, when you've closed the hatch commence re-pressurisation immediately, then assess EV1. If absolutely necessary open his helmet, but only if necessary. We don't want him passing out.' She was putting her trust in Valentina to make the right call.

'We also don't want him dead.' May muttered.

'How're his vitals, May?' Jessica asked impatiently, ignoring her comment. She didn't want to even think about that.

May checked her screen. 'Low O2, heart rate, high.'

'Keep monitoring him. Bring your tablet, let's go and wait for them.'

They both unclipped their harnesses and headed from the bridge towards the airlock at the rear of the ship. Jessica spoke into her microphone as she proceeded.

'John, I don't know if you can still hear me, but it's nearly over. Val is coming in now. Just sit tight, and don't panic. What am I saying? I've never seen you panic in all the years I've known you.' She kept talking, barely conscious of what she was saying, but just wanting him to hear her voice. 'You did so well out there, John. We're so proud of you and Val.'

Was he scared? She couldn't imagine him being scared. He was always brimming with confidence, often more than the situation warranted. She had a sudden vision of how empty her life would be without him in it.

'This is EV2,' Valentina's voice rang in her ear as Jessica and May reached the airlock. 'I'm in. The hatch is sealed and commencing re-pressurisation.'

Jessica jumped as the re-pressurisation valve opened with a clunk. She could hear the hiss of air pouring into the airlock.

'Well done EV2. How's EV1?'

There was a pause. Jessica held her breath. Her earpiece crackled.

'EVA2? Val? Damn, I can't hear her over the air pressure.' Jessica pressed her fingers to the earpiece, as if the pressure would clear the noise. A memory flashed into her head, calling her mother on the phone, not knowing she was already dead. *Not John too.*

'Valentina?' Jessica called more urgently. 'How is he?'

There was another crackle and suddenly the radio cleared and Valentina spoke.

'I repeat. EV1 has just given me a thumbs up.'

Jessica released her breath with a sigh and heard May do the same. Her limbs tingles as relief surged through them. He was still alive. But Jessica wouldn't be happy till she had seen him in person. She stood outside the airlock and waited, watching for the numbers on the screen to rise to a safe level. She pressed her forehead against the door, willing them to go up.

'How are you both doing in there?' Jessica spoke into the radio.

'This is EV2, we're doing fine. EV1 is conscious but unable to communicate. I can still see water floating around inside his helmet.'

'Two more minutes John, then we'll get you out of that suit. You did so well out there. You didn't panic and you got back in safely. Sure, I would have preferred it if you responded to my first order to return straight away...' she tried to inject some levity into her voice.

'You had us pretty worried there for a few minutes. Not me obviously, I had total faith in you. But you know May, she gets pretty emotional...' She turned and smiled at May as they waited to open the airlock.

An alarm sounded indicating that the pressure had reached the optimum level and Jessica leapt to pull the lever that opened the airlock. The door creaked as she heaved it open. John stumbled through it, pushed from the other side by Valentina into the arms of Jessica and May. John gasped his first breath of cabin air as Jessica removed his helmet. The sight of his face, dripping with water, made her heart leap. He took several rapid breaths.

'Slow down,' she said, stroking his head. His comms cap was saturated. 'You'll hyperventilate.' She crouched in front of him and breathed deeply in and out, indicating to him to follow her lead. John's breathing slowed and colour started to return to his pale face. Her own heartbeat eased with the realisation he was safe. Her eyes searched his face, his bloodshot eyes and damp skin. She pulled the sleeve of her suit over her hand and wiped the water out of his eyes.

'You ok?' Her voice was barely more than a whisper. Everything around her melted away as she focused on him.

He nodded, not taking his eyes off her. She scanned his face as if trying to commit it to memory. He was still in his suit. She gently unscrewed each of his gloves and took his hands in hers. They were clammy and shaking slightly. She ran her thumbs across the top of his fingers, wanting to feel his warm skin, wanting to feel the life in him, wanting to make sure the blood was still pulsing through his veins.

She couldn't find the right words, didn't know what to say. If only he knew how terrified she had been of losing him. Not just as his Commander, not just losing a member of her crew. Losing him. John. Not being able to speak to him again or hear him laugh at his own stupid jokes. Not being teased by him for being too serious. What if she might never again have felt his strong, protective arms around her? The sense of panic that had flooded her body only moments earlier subsided, and other feelings took over her body, feelings that she didn't want to have to think about right now.

'John...' she closed her eyes for a second and took a deep breath. 'John...' She leaned forward and kissed his damp head, then pressed her forehead against his. She couldn't ignore how she felt any longer.

'Yeah?' he croaked.

'John...' she took another deep breath. 'Only you could nearly drown a million kilometres away from Earth.

Chapter Nineteen
Countdown till first Mars walk: 3 months

Jessica

The days on Harmonia advanced unceasingly and unchangingly. One merged into another as the long journey to Mars continued. The time was regulated not by the usual Earth-bound rhythms of sunrise and sunset, but by the pre-programmed mood lighting of the spacecraft that dimmed during the artificial evenings. Back on Earth their days, activities, what they wore, and even what they ate, might have been determined by weather and seasons: wrapped up warm for the cool German winters, springtime running in the park; summer BBQs at Rachel's house. On the ship the temperature was regulated and unvarying, and their days determined by tightly packed itineraries from Mission Control.

Weekends were a little more lightly scheduled, and demarcated the week. They were usually dedicated to ship housekeeping such as vacuuming air filters and disinfecting surfaces.

Rituals and routines kept the crew going. Tonight was poker night; a once a month opportunity for them to have a proper night off and blow off some steam.

Jessica found comfort in the routine of the ship, comfort she'd clung to since John's near fatal EVA had turned her world upside down. She tried to suppress the flutter she felt each time she saw him, and instead immersed herself in the safety of the relentless daily schedule. She couldn't let herself succumb to those thoughts.

That day began like every other day. Jessica padded to the galley for breakfast in her shorts, sweatshirt and socks. The artificial gravity in this part of the ship made it easier to move around, but the continuous rotation, though imperceptible, made her feel dizzy if she stood still for too long.

Something was different when she entered the galley that morning. A selection of unfamiliar objects had been arranged on the table, with John standing proudly next to them. There it was again, the feeling like she'd missed a step as she saw him.

'What's this?' Jessica asked, walking into the room. But she thought she already knew.

'Nowruz Pirouz,' he said, handing her a mug of fragrant black tea.

'What?' She blinked, trying to take it in.

'In case you missed it, it's the vernal equinox. Not for us obviously. But back on Earth. And here,' he indicated the table, 'we have a Haft-sin table. Most of it is freeze dried I'm afraid, but I checked with your grandma and she said it was all still ok.' He grinned.

'We have freeze dried apple, garlic,' he pointed to small foil packages. 'Sumac, vinegar, saffron. I had Lucca grow some wheatgrass. Look!' He held up a small pot of green fronds. 'Some chocolate coins, that I am fairly sure you are obliged to share with the crew. And your grandmother sent this in my care.' He took her hand and placed in her palm a tiny delicately painted egg. It was light as a feather, made of a thin metal. How much work had John put into this surprise? How many people in NARESA had he conspired with? When had he spoken with her grandmother?

'John, I...' A lump formed in her throat. The faint smell of cardamom from the tea brought back a hundred memories. She could hear the voices of her mother and her grandmother. The cool feel of fresh new books and notebooks, New Year gifts from her mother. 'You did this all for me?' She stared at him.

'I had a little help.' He shrugged his shoulders. 'I know how important it is to you. And I figured you'd probably lost track of the days.'

Jessica swallowed and pressed one hand to her lips, the tiny egg still clenched in the other. He had remembered, he had planned all this just for her. Warm tears pricked at her eyes. For the first time since launch she was overcome by a feeling of homesickness.

'I'm sorry. I didn't mean to upset you.' John looked worried.

'You didn't, not one bit.' She reached over and gave him a hug, catching her breath as he squeezed her back. 'This is gorgeous.' She pulled away and looked into his hazel eyes. 'I'm just a little overwhelmed.'

'I know Nowruz is a time for family. You must miss them.'

'Yeah, I do. But it's a time for friends too.' She pulled away from John and picked up one of the gold chocolate coins.

'Nowruz Pirouz, John.' She said softly, looking up at his kind face. Could John, the person who always seemed to know what she was thinking, could possibly guess the conflicting feelings that had been tormenting her for the last few months?

Later that evening the Haft-sin table was replaced with poker chips and cards.

'I'm in.' May said.

'In.' Lucca followed.

'In.' Val tossed a chip in the centre.

Jessica barely registered the voices, or the poker chips that clattered into the middle of the galley table, as she studied her tablet.

'Jessica? You in?' John's voice made her look up.

'Hmmm?' John's voice distracted her as she tried to plan the things they had to do the next day. 'We've um...' she looked down at her tablet again, trying to concentrate. Why did her heart have to betray her like that when he spoke? She had a job to do. 'We've got to make sure the HEPA filters get cleaned tomorrow, guys. And we have that video to record for the science festivals in the afternoon.' There was a collective groan from around the table.

'Jessica! Put it away.' Lucca said leaning back in his chair.

'It's our night off.' John moaned.

'Give me that.' May snatched the tablet out of Jessica's hands and tucked it away in a locker behind her chair. 'It's Poker Night. Time to have a drink and relax.'

Each of the crew had a small glass of liquor, individually brewed for each of them to their own taste by a distillery in Germany, with enough shipped with them for a monthly treat. It had been great publicity for the brewery in the build-up to the launch. It wasn't hugely alcoholic but there was something symbolic in it for them. It helped them switch off from the relentless work of maintaining the ship, and to feel a bit more connected to their usual lives. Jessica took a sip of her drink. Pink grapefruit flavoured, slightly bitter and citrusy; it warmed her throat and her limbs relaxed. She needed to try hard to unwind on nights off.

'Alright, alright, I'm focused now.' She lifted up the corners of her cards to remind herself of her hand. A pair of fives. An ok start. 'I'm in.' She tossed a couple of chips into the centre.

'Raise you five.' John pushed forward a small pile of the ultra-thin, ultra-light, specially made poker chips in front of him and leaned back against his chair, arms behind his head.

Jessica loved poker. You had to play the people as well as the cards. She watched them, not just for the physical tells, like the way Lucca always cleared his throat when he was pleased with his hand, or May's impatience to bet when she had good cards, but the behaviours across the games. It wasn't just that she was good at poker. Jessica had studied this crew, analysed them more than they probably realised. It was her job to look after them all and ensure the safety and success of the mission. She knew what made them tick, could usually sense when they weren't ok, and she knew how to handle it. She usually won because she knew them inside and out.

Two hours later her instincts were being put to the test. Jessica and John were in a standoff. The rest of the crew had folded and were watching the final showdown.

Jessica held three tens, a middling hand. *Play the man not the hand.* He had been serious this round. So unusually serious she was convinced it was bluff. John feigned indifference on good hands. That was his tell, to act like he didn't care. But tonight he was studying her carefully, watching her as she studied her cards.

They played only for chips and chores on the ship. Work was the only currency they had. Winner of the game got to delegate one of their activities to the person or people who they beat with their winning hand. Jessica didn't mind doing the extra work, but John would be insufferable if he won.

'Your bid, Jessica.' He held her gaze.

It was the end of the evening, they couldn't play much longer. There was no benefit to saving her chips. It was all in or nothing. *Here goes.*

'All in.' She pushed her chips into the centre.

'Alright.' He said slowly, pushing his remaining chips towards hers. 'What have you got?'

He hadn't taken his eyes off her. Why did it feel like she was about to reveal more than her hand? Jessica hesitated. Before fanning the cards out in front of her.

'Three tens.' She announced.

John's face remained serious as he lay down his cards.

'Straight,' he said.

For a moment they just looked at one another. John bit his bottom lip and a jolt of electricity shot through her.

Seconds later John's face cracked into a wide grin. He leapt out of his chair and cheered.

'Finally, the great Commander is vanquished,' he cried pointing at her.

Jessica put her head into her arms and groaned, as the rest of the crew burst into laughter.

'Ah, smell that recycled, winning air.' John took a deep breath. 'And look at all my lovely winning chips. I'm going to make a little Jessica pile.' He started stacking the chips.

'Urgh, I knew you'd be insufferable,' she grimaced at him.

'Aww, I'm so sad that you have to clean the bathroom tomorrow.'

'I'd do it every day for a month if it would stop you being like this.' She smiled at him in spite of herself. Even after all this time there was a boyish charm about him.

They called it a night and the five of them cleared away like a well-oiled machine. Everyone always had a job on the ship, and even a night off still meant routine activities. May and Lucca returned the empty drink and food packaging to the kitchen area then left to get ready for bed. Valentina went to send an end of day report to Mission Control. Jessica collected up the cards and poker chips, while John tidied up the rest of the galley.

'I still can't believe you won,' Jessica said, shaking her head.

'I know,' John grinned at her, 'and you went in big. You were pretty confident in that last hand.'

'I thought I had you.' She lined up the chips in their box.

'Now who has a good poker face?' John smiled.

'You didn't have a good poker face. You had a straight.' She grinned at him.

'You're just mad because I saw through your three tens.' John retorted, as he tucked a chair under the table.

'More likely you saw my cards.' Talking to him was so easy. Even after months in a confined space together, she wanted to spend time with him.

'I'm hurt that you think I'd stoop that low.' He clutched at his heart. 'Besides, I don't need to look at your cards, I can just look at you.'

'What do you mean?' She slid the poker set into an overhead locker and turned back to look at him. His words rang around her head and she tried to decipher their meaning. He was leaning against the table, an amused smile playing around his lips. The air hummed with tension. Her stomach fluttered; through fear or excitement, she couldn't tell.

'I can read you, even if no one else can.' He said. His words were slow and deliberate.

'No, you can't. You can barely read the back of a cereal packet.' She tried to keep the tone light, afraid of where the conversation might lead.

'Of course I can read you.' He laughed. 'Maybe the others fall for the Commander Poker Face thing, but not me.'

'Give me an example.' said Jessica. She was facing him, arms folded.

'Reveal your "tells" to you? No way I'm not that stupid.'

'I don't have any tells.' Her eyes narrowed, arms still crossed.

'Everyone has a tell, Jessica. Even you. You just need to watch closely enough.' His voice was quieter now.

Jessica's face burned. She glanced around the small galley. They were alone. The others had probably all gone to bed. '

Go on then, prove it.' It was a dangerous request. What was she expecting him to say? What did she want him to say?

'I don't need to prove anything,' he laughed at her. 'Man, you really hate not being in control, don't you?'

'What do you mean?' She drew herself up to her full height, which was still no match for his.

'I mean there's no poker face now.' He was still leaning against the table. 'You're all agitated. I can tell, no matter how hard you try and hide it. You stand up straighter, like you're steeling yourself for a fight. And you get all irritated with your hair and brush it out of your face.' He laughed again as she lowered her hand down from her hair and wedged it under her opposite arm.

'That doesn't make you good at reading me.' Why was she determined to prove him wrong? 'It's easy to see if someone is agitated.' She continued, 'When you get cross, you rub your chin, and put your hand over your mouth as if you're trying to stop yourself saying something.' She paused and contemplated him. 'And when you're trying not to laugh at me you bite the inside of your bottom lip. You're doing it now.'

'I never claimed to be difficult to read. You know me, Jessica, I'm an open book. Whereas you,' He walked towards her. 'You try so hard to keep a lid on everything, you don't realise that it's written across your face, for those who look hard enough.'

'Like what?' The words came out as a whisper.

'Like when you're scared, and you're trying to hold it together for everyone.' He was no longer laughing. 'Almost nothing on your face gives that away. But I can see it in your eyes.' He stared directly into them now, the penetrating stare boring into her as if he were trying to read her mind. She swallowed, uncertain about what was happening. What did it mean that he could read her so clearly in this way, that he'd studied her? Her heartbeat pulsed in her ear.

He took her hand in his. She glanced down at that familiar hand, with its bitten down nails, and skin roughened from constant activity. The hand that had helped her make bread, the hand that had physically supported her on training missions, the hand that had kept them safe on this journey. He stroked his thumb across her palm. Heat radiated through her body and she caught her breath. She squeezed his fingers almost involuntarily.

A thousand thoughts danced around her head. She was flooded by feelings she had been holding at bay for months.

'There's another look,' his voice was low. 'It's the look you have when you're happy about something, but you're trying not to show it. Your lips are pressed tightly together. You're trying to suppress a smile, but can I see it faintly at the corners of your mouth. You'd only notice it if you looked closely enough.' He paused looking straight into her eyes again. His words were soft and languorous. 'It's the look you had when they announced you as Commander of this crew. It's the look you have when you get dealt a good hand in poker,' he reached up and brushed a lock of hair away from her face, 'It's the look you're giving me right now.'

His words were almost drowned out by the thumping in her chest. A lump in her throat stopped her from speaking. Not that she could trust herself to say the right thing. She wasn't sure what was going on, and she wasn't sure how she felt, except that she couldn't imagine being in any other spot with any other person at any other time. She looked down and saw that her hand was still in John's; she hadn't noticed. It was like his hand was just an extension of hers.

'John...' she whispered, unsure what else to say. She studied his face, the crease of his brow, the set of his jaw. His eyes, darker than usual in the dim light, stared wolfishly into hers. The hairs on her arms stood on end. Did he want her as much as she wanted him?

'Jessica...' Her name echoed in the back of his throat. Everything melted away; sights and sounds disappeared. The two of them were the only things that existed. He leaned in towards her. Her lips parted slightly under his hot breath. His lips grazed hers.

'Oh God, John....' She pulled away. This was wrong, they shouldn't be doing this.

'Sorry,' said John immediately. 'I'm sorry. I-'

'No, it's just...' *Just what?*

'No, my fault, I overstepped the mark. I'm sorry, I... I think I've read this all wrong,' he ran his hands through his hair and frowned.

'No, you haven't,' she whispered, 'You haven't.'

'Wait... so you do... this isn't just...?' She could see him searching for the right words.

'I don't know.' She squeezed her eyes shut, trying to still her whirring mind.

She did know. She knew that her heart skipped when she saw him for the first time each day. She knew that his ridiculously inappropriate sense of humour made her smile even when she tried to be indignant. She knew that he made her feel like she could do anything. She knew that when she thought something had happened to him on the spacewalk it felt like the bottom had dropped out of her world. She knew that it was against the rules for them to give in to this. She knew that it could risk the mission.

'Jessica.' Her eyes snapped open as he said her name. She had never seen this earnest look on his face before.

'You know there's something going on here Jessica. You must know how I feel about you?'

'How? How do you feel about me?' She needed to hear it, but at the same time, the thought terrified her.

'When I look at you, it's not like anyone else I've ever looked at.' He paused. words swam around her head.

'Please, don't say any more.' She pulled away. Her stomach swirled. Thoughts raced through her mind. 'There's a good reason why they don't let people do this on mission.'

'Fuck the mission, this is bigger than the mission, how I feel about you, this is bigger than anything'.

'I can't fuck the mission. I'm the one in charge here. It's my responsibility. We're crewmates, and I'm the Commander. If someone finds out I'll lose my job. And it's not just the job, it's the ethics of it, the balance of power, the distraction, the risk...' The reasons weren't for him, they were for her. She needed to remind herself why they were straying into dangerous territory.

'Just tell me, Jessica, tell me you feel the same, tell me there's something between us.'

She was silent for a minute, then the words just fell out of her mouth before she had even considered them. 'I'm scared that if I say it I won't be able to control it,' she closed her eyes as she spoke.

He let out a laugh and shook his head. 'That's one thing I love about you. You think that even for one second you can control this. You can't.'

She looked him in the eye. 'We have to control it, John.'

There was a noise and they both froze. May came back into the galley.

'Hey, I thought everyone had gone to bed,' she said.

'Yeah, we just had to talk about the filter cleaning tomorrow.' Jessica said at the same time as John said 'I dropped the poker chips, we were just clearing them up.'

May raised her eyebrows. 'Ok, well, goodnight.'

'Night,' they chorused.

When May had left John turned to her with a smile. 'That was close.'

'Too close,' Jessica wasn't smiling. 'We have to forget about this conversation.'

'We can't just forget about it.'

'We have to.' She needed space to think, 'I'm going to bed.' She turned away, his confused and dispirited expression etched on her brain. She wanted nothing more than to hug him right now, to run her hands through his thick hair, to kiss him and tell him it would be ok, that they would be ok. But she couldn't promise they would be.

Chapter Twenty
Countdown to first Mars walk: 3 months

John

'Shit!' John slapped his palm against his forehead. 'Shit, shit, shit.' He'd been trying to input data for the last half an hour but the numbers swam in front of his eyes. Even when he could focus on them he couldn't seem to type them correctly. It was like his brain was struggling to communicate with his body. And it wasn't just this task either. For the last few days everything that he touched seemed to go wrong.

And now a task that was scheduled to take him fifteen minutes had taken twice that long, and he wasn't even finished. The rigid NARESA schedule was starting to chafe at him, and he struggled to keep to it. There was no space to think. He leaned his forehead into his hands and closed his eyes.

It had been three days since they had played poker. Three days since he and Jessica had almost kissed. And three days since he had realised just how deeply in love with her he was. He couldn't stop thinking about her, those coffee coloured eyes looking up at him, the feel of her skin, her lips grazing his.

It wasn't the right thing to do; he knew that. It went against all the rules of being on a crew together. Not that John cared about the rules, but he cared about Jessica, and she cared about the rules. And, despite appearances, he took safety on the mission seriously. They were all responsible for each other's lives on board the ship. Though with the way he was handling this current research project, being with Jessica might be less distracting than not being with her and thinking about her all the time.

They hadn't spoken about it since, hadn't had a chance to be alone together. How much of that was by Jessica's design he wasn't sure. Even if she wasn't avoiding him, it was almost impossible to find privacy in the confines of the ship. Every time he turned around someone was within three feet of him. The only privacy on board was in the medical room, that was May's domain, and their own cabins. To be caught going in one of their rooms together would raise too many questions. He loosened his collar; even his flight suit was making him feel claustrophobic.

Jessica was acting almost as if nothing had happened. The only clue that she even remembered the conversation was that she avoided eye contact with him. It was as if shutters had come down for her, and he found himself on the wrong side. He just wanted to know how she was feeling. If anything else had upset her, he would have been the one she would have come to. Only this time he was the one who caused it. The thought that he was causing her pain, and that he couldn't fix it for her made him even more annoyed at himself.

Resuming his task, but only succeeding in deleting a row of data, he swore under his breath and left the desk.

'Get it together, man,' he muttered to himself as he left the room.

He would go to the gym for a run. He wasn't scheduled for exercise till later, but Concordia was depositing its payload on Mars that afternoon. The outcome would determine the next step of their own journey and he wanted to observe the event. *Screw the schedule*; he headed towards the gym. He needed something mindless to do that didn't require any thought processes. Not to give him more time to think about Jessica, he told himself, but something he wasn't at risk of messing up when she unwittingly entered his mind.

Hitting the speed button on the treadmill he began to sprint. The lean muscles in his legs screamed as he pushed them harder, his mind concentrating on just keeping his body moving.

He had accomplished fifteen minutes of not thinking about Jessica when she appeared in person by the side of his treadmill.

Her long brown hair was pulled back into a sensible ponytail. He'd never met anyone else who literally 'let their hair down' when they relaxed, but hers was always a barometer of the mood that she was in. Today she was serious. He'd always thought she was beautiful, but something had shifted since that night. There was something magical in finding out that the person you loved might feel the same way about you. Or did she? Had she just said she did to make him feel better? She was still an enigma, even to him. He knew ten percent of what he wanted to know about her. What he wanted to know right now was how she really felt about him.

'Hi,' she said, as he slowed down the treadmill to a walk. He was conscious of the sweat pouring from him and wiped his forehead with the back of his arm.

'Hi,' he replied, trying to catch his breath.

'Sorry, do you need some space?' She bit her bottom lip.

'Never from you.' He meant it wholeheartedly.

A faint smile appeared on her serious face.

'Are you ok?' she asked.

Was he? Could he spend the next year feeling like this? Wanting to be with her? Not knowing for sure if she wanted to be with him? Each time he saw her, every cell in his body was drawn toward her like a magnet.

'I'm fine.' He'd burdened her with enough of his feelings for now. 'Are you ok?'

She just nodded. John stopped the treadmill and turned to face her.

'Talk to me, Jessica.'

She shook her head, a slight frown on her face.

'Why not? It's me. It's us. Tell me how you're feeling.' There was silence for a minute, then a noise from the galley next door.

'Not here.' Jessica said in a low voice. She motioned for John to follow her. She led him to the other side of the ship down the left corridor.

He hardly ever came down here. Apart from the medical rooms there was a storeroom that was rarely accessed.

'What are we doing?' John whispered to Jessica.

'No one else ever comes down this far,' she replied in a low voice.

He knew why. This was the room they never spoke about, the room they hoped never to have to use.

He'd once read something in one of the few history books he'd picked up. Sailors in the eighteenth century didn't learn to swim because they thought it might tempt fate and make it more likely they'd go overboard. This room provoked the same feeling in the crew and they never talked about it. He tried to rid his mind of morbid thoughts, and then remembered why they were here.

'Jessica.' He faced her in the dim light of the end of the corridor. 'The other night. Did you mean it? Do you feel the same as me?'

'Of course I feel the same,' she said, her voice barely audible.

'Jessica...' his fingers grazed her face, lifting her chin. He needed to see it in her eyes. She looked up at him from under thick, dark lashes, and put her hand over his.

'I love you, Jessica. I'm not sure I can ever stop. But I'll try if you want me to.'

She shook her head again. 'I don't want you to stop,' she was whispering again.

Waves swelled in his chest at her words.

'But nothing's changed. We still can't be together. Not right now. You know that, right?'

The waves inside him crashed. It didn't have to be that way. No one needed to know. They were alone now, and all he wanted to do was take her in his arms and kiss her. But even if he didn't agree with her, he wouldn't let her down. He wouldn't let her do something she might regret.

'I'll do whatever you think is right.' He forced the words out.

'You're a distraction, a gorgeous distraction, but I can't afford to be distracted. When people are distracted, they make mistakes.' She swallowed before continuing. 'Almost everyone I've loved has left me and it's been my fault. And that day when you had the water in your helmet I thought it was happening again. I couldn't bear it if you...' She paused. 'Just don't go anywhere.'

'Jessica,' he didn't know what to say. He just wanted to scoop her up and protect her from the world.

She reached her hand out for his, and he clasped hers. It was small and slender, engulfed by his own. They both squeezed tight. The air held their heavy breaths.

'I'm not going anywhere,' he said, 'Trust me.' She gave an almost imperceptible nod.

'Jessica, can you just...' he paused.

'What?' her eyes searched his face.

'I just need reminding of how you feel every now and then. I can deal with all of it. As long as I know.'

'I will, I promise.' She nodded with a smile. 'John?' Her eyes were wide. He felt he might fall into them.

'Yes?' Her hand was still in his. He stroked it with his thumb.

'It's not never,' she whispered. 'It's just not now.'

Chapter Twenty-One
Countdown to first Mars walk: 3 months

John

The Concordia was identical to the Harmonia in every way, except instead of the descent vehicle to land a crew onto the Martian surface, the Concordia was carrying a payload of supplies. Part of the payload was the biosphere that the Harmonia crew would construct to live in for their thirty day stay on the planet.

Concordia's delivery was a crucial part of the success of the ongoing mission. If there was a problem with the payload the Harmonia might have to be aborted and they would have to fly by the planet instead. Everything they'd been working towards for years, all the meticulous planning, could be dashed in a thirteen-minute journey to Mars's surface.

There were no shouts of jubilation or vigorous handshaking among the crew, like in the movies. The Harmonia crew calmly watched the feed of payload touching down safely, from the bridge. There were just smiles of relief and shaky laughter as they received confirmation that they could continue on with the rest of their mission. The biosphere and most of the supplies they needed for their month long stay on Mars were now waiting for them on the red planet. John imagined the celebrations back at Mission Control and NARESA HQ as one of the hundreds of things that had to go right for this to be a successful mission went as planned. They felt the weight of the world watching them. It was a pressure the Harmonia crew were largely protected from, as their connection to the outside world was filtered through Mission Control.

'Alright everyone, back to work. We're landing on Mars.' Jessica said. They all exchanged broad grins. They were another step closer. While the rest of the crew returned to their tasks John tapped a few buttons on his tablet, taking his time for the rest of the crew to leave, wanting just a few more minutes alone with Jessica.

'Hey,' she turned her chair towards him, a timid smile on her face. Each time he looked at her it was like seeing her for the first time.

'Hey,' he said. 'Good result.'

'Yeah.' She glanced up at him. He wished he could see what was going on in her head.

'They'll be picking the first person soon,' he said.

The first person to walk on Mars. The member of the crew whose name would be immortalised for the entirety of human existence. NARESA had decided that it would be best to select the first person to walk on Mars closer to the landing. The probability of the Harmonia actually touching down depended on the Concordia successfully delivering its payload, which it had now done. There was now almost nothing that could get in the way of them attempting to land on Mars.

'Do you know how the rest of the crew feel about it?' she asked. 'You know, the first person to take the first step?'

'They think it'll be you. We all do.' John said with an obvious smile.

She shook her head. 'It could be any of us.'

'Yeah, but it'll be you. And we'll all be incredibly happy for you.' He leaned forward in his chair and took her hand, wanting just to be connected to her in any way. Jessica glanced to where they were entwined.

'We shouldn't keep doing this,' she said in a low voice, but she was still smiling.

'I know,' he whispered, but he didn't let go. He traced his thumb across the back of her hand as if trying to memorise its contours.

He heard her sharp intake of breath, and watched her chest rise and fall. She looked at him and bit her lip, not moving as he continued to stroke her hand.

'I have to go,' she said. He didn't know if a minute had passed, or an hour.

He nodded and gently let go of her hand. But as she left the bridge she turned back to him. A smile radiated across her face and as he drank it in it warmed his body.

***

Three times each day NARESA sent The Harmonia a package of data. The lag in communication could be up to ten minutes at this stage of the journey, so live conversations were impossible. The data package contained daily schedule updates, technical reports, messages and videos from friends, family and fans, and sometimes media reports about the mission.

A week after Concordia had successfully delivered its payload, and with six weeks till landing, the crew were expecting an announcement about who would be the first of them to set foot on Mars,

Halfway through the day John and the crew received a message on their wrist comms from Jessica.

'It's here.'

'I can't believe they made us wait this long, it's ridiculous.' May said as John joined them all in the galley and they sat at the table.

'They had their reasons.' Jessica said as she brought up the video on the screen overlooking them. 'It was to stop us being distracted by it, so we could concentrate on the mission.'

May rolled her eyes 'Urgh, you're such a company woman Jessica. It's like living with Pollyanna.'

Jessica responded with a mock scowl.

'I'm with May,' John said. 'It's like they had some Machiavellian plot to turn us all against each other. Lord of the Flies in Space. But thankfully we all love Jessica so much that we won't stone her to death when they pick her.' He gave her a squeeze then stopped himself, unsure whether that was ok, whether he'd be giving them away. *I'd hug her even as a friend*, he reassured himself.

Jessica pressed play and Hans Vogel's face appeared larger than life in front of them.

'Good afternoon Harmonia crew. I trust you are well.' He started with some updates from the ground.

'Oh, come on Hans,' May muttered, 'I love you dearly, but please get on with it.'

'And now, it is my pleasure to announce that the first person to step foot on Mars will be Commander Jessica Gabriel, and she will be accompanied on the first sortie by Valentina Kareva.'

John's heart swelled with pride; she had done it. He was never in any doubt that Jessica would be chosen. She was the most capable, smart, hard working person he knew. May, Lucca, and John all cheered with heartfelt delight, missing the end of Hans's recorded message as they gathered around Jessica and Valentina, hugging them. Valentina smiled graciously. She wouldn't be the first, but there would only be two of them on that first mission, and she would be part of that momentous event.

Jessica's lips were pressed together, a hint of a smile at the corners. She was trying to play it cool, he knew, not to impress them, but because she didn't want to make a big deal out of it. It meant the world to her, he knew it did, but she didn't want to make everyone else feel bad.

Lucca and May were excitedly chatting away. He loved this crew. Each one of them would have loved to have been selected to be the first person on Mars. This was the pinnacle of what they had all been working towards for years, but they were all so genuinely happy for Jessica and Valentina.

He wondered if in the elation of the moment he could get close to her, just as a friend, a crewmate. The rest of the group were distracted by the announcement. He turned towards Jessica and pulled her in for a hug.

'I'm so proud of you,' he murmured into her hair.

'Oh, there's nothing to be proud of...'

'Jessica,' he gazed down at her and spoke softly, 'Will you realise now how amazing you are? Do you see how far you've come?'

She nodded, looking up at him with her brown eyes.

'This is it, Jessica. You made it. Everyone will know who you are now if they didn't before.' He couldn't keep the smile from his face, but she was quiet, biting pensively at her bottom lip.

'Hey, don't look so serious. Enjoy it. This will be the biggest moment of your life.'

'I know.'

He wondered if she truly did know, if she had any idea what it would be like for everyone to recognise her, to want to hear about her experience. She'd be in history books. Everything she did now would be through the prism of being the first person on another planet. He knew she wasn't doing it for the fame or the glory. She had a sincere desire to just be the best she could be, and she had done it. He wanted to protect her from it all, to wrap her up and shield her from the frenzy that would envelop them all but focus on Jessica when they returned to Earth.

He pulled her back towards him and tried to convey all that through his touch. *I'll look after you*, he wanted to tell her. She'd hate it if she knew he was thinking like that. He lowered his lips onto her forehead, and kissed it gently, relishing every moment of being in physical contact with her.

'It's you.' He whispered, so only she could hear. He could feel her intake of breath, and a deep sigh as she exhaled into his chest where her head was buried, then she looked up at him and he knew she felt the same.

Chapter Twenty-Two
Countdown to first Mars walk: one day

Jessica

The sun cast a blue hue in the dusty twilight of Mars. Instead of the blue sky changing into yellows and pinks as on Earth, the very fine dust particles made the opposite happen on Mars, and in the thick atmosphere of the Martian horizon, the setting sun was haloed in blue light. Through the panoramic view from the observation deck, the sun looked both comfortingly familiar and wrong at the same time, like seeing a person you know in a dream but they have a stranger's face. It was smaller than the sun she had known for thirty-six years.

The stars that would appear in the sky after sunset would, however, look exactly the same, proving that while they had come many millions of human miles to get to the surface of Mars, in the grand scheme of the universe they had simply crossed a road. The Aneris capsule, that had detached from the Harmonia, and safely landed on the surface of Mars that afternoon, was a speck of dust in the vastness of the universe. The five crew members were waiting in the Aneris, preparing for the first walk early the next morning.

Mountains lined the horizons and large boulders cast long shadows. It was taking a while for her eyes to adjust to the view. For the past eight months, everything in her vision had been within the confines of the Harmonia, or the stars in the vastness of space, with nothing in between. Her eyes ached with the novelty, but she couldn't stop drinking it all in. The view from the observation deck was beguiling. In the depths of space, they were under a blanket of stars. But here on Mars a new sky stretched out through the window above her.

She would be the eyes for millions of people tomorrow. As she set foot on the Martian surface, it wouldn't just be the weight of her surface EVA suit she would be carrying, she would carry with her the hopes of the human race. It might be five years, it might be a hundred years, but other people would come to Mars, and they might live here. She was the one who was breaking the ground, laying the foundation for whatever the future looked like. She would be the First.

In a hundred years' time Mars might be unrecognisable from the uncharted planet she could see before her. For better or worse, it started with Jessica tomorrow.

She felt a presence behind her and knew instinctively that it was John.

'Soon all this will be yours.' He said, gesturing at the landscape around them.

As usual, it felt like he had been reading her mind.

'Do you know what a "sooner" is?' She was still looking outside as she spoke.

'Yeah, I learned about them in American History class. Weren't they people who hid on unclaimed land before the US Government released it so they could stake their claim before anyone else?'

'Yep. And tomorrow I will plant a flag on the surface.' She turned to him as she spoke.

'You think we're staking our claim?' He asked her.

'Of course we are.' She indicated out of the window with her hand. 'That's exactly what we are doing, John. We're pioneers into a new world.'

'Are we the "sooners" or are you worried about encountering settlers already here?' She ignored his teasing.

'I just think it's important that we ask ourselves what we are doing here, and make sure it's the right thing.' Jessica sighed.

'Bit late for that now,' John replied. 'Shouldn't you have asked yourself that question a couple of years ago?'

'That's the thing though John, I don't think you can truly answer it until you are here, looking out at all this. This is an abstraction for everyone else. It's real for us.'

'Are you ok, Jessica?' His voice was full of concern. She knew she sounded confusing. That was the problem with thinking out loud.

'Don't worry, I'm fine.' She turned to him and smiled. 'It's just a big deal. Today I'm just Jessica Gabriel. Tomorrow I'll be Jessica Gabriel, the first person on another planet. Everything changes tomorrow. For me. For you. For the whole world.'

'For me? Don't worry about me.' He grinned at her and leaned against the window. 'I'm always going to be the fifth person. A footnote. I'll be lucky if they get my name right. "Also on the mission, James Eden."'

She nudged him and giggled, 'Don't be ridiculous.'

She was quiet again, her mind racing. She thought she had prepared for this, but now she was here it seemed so real.

'Whatever happens from now on I'm going to be the first person to have walked on Mars. We're going to have to live with that.'

'"We" are?' John raised an eyebrow.

'Yes, *we* are.'

She watched as a slow smile lit up his face. She knew he understood what she was saying. She wanted to be with him, when the time was right. She was staking her claim in advance. But she needed to know he could handle what was ahead of them.

'You know,' she looked at him. 'Most of the Apollo astronauts ended up divorced?' She tried to make her voice lighter than she felt.

He tilted his head at her.

'What are you worried about?'

'We don't know what the future holds John. This might not work out. I don't want to make promises I can't keep.'

He laughed at her. 'You really hate not being in control, don't you?'

She didn't reply. They both knew he was right.

'Babe,' he kissed her on the forehead, then held her tight 'You don't have to worry about anything, we'll make it work.'

She heard him breathe deeply and bury his face in her hair.

'I want to be with you so much Jessica.' He said with a muffled moan.

'John... not now. We can't.' She wanted it too. Wanted him. But they couldn't. She had to do the right thing.

'But we don't have to wait any more. Tomorrow you walk on Mars, and you've achieved what you wanted. There's nothing else to lose.'

'John, we're still crewmates,' she pulled away from him. 'We're still on mission, I'm still the Commander. It breaks every single rule—'

'Screw the rules.' His voice was still low so as not to be overheard, but his frustration was evident.

'I don't get to screw the rules, John. Maybe you do but I don't.' She could feel the heat rise in her cheeks.

'What's that supposed to mean?'

'You get to be Mr Maverick and everything still works out for you. I have to work my arse off and be squeaky clean. It's not enough that people still think my job should be done by a man, and I have to prove myself even more than you because I'm a woman. But because you're John Eden...' The words fell out in frustration, but as soon as she said it she knew she had made a mistake.

'Because I'm John Eden what?' His eyes narrowed.

'Nothing.' If only she could take it back.

'No, it's not nothing. Say what you were going to say.'

'No, Look, I'm sorry. I don't know why I said it. It's not what I think.'

'It's what everyone else thinks,' his voice was flat.

'No one here thinks it, John, you know that.'

He sighed. 'It's fine.'

It wasn't fine, she knew it wasn't, no matter what he said. Her favourite person in the world and she had said the thing that she knew upset him the most. She was meant to be the person he could trust. It was just easier. Easier to push him away.

'I know what you are trying to do,' he said, reading her mind again. He put his hand under her chin and lifted her face so he could see into her eyes. 'It doesn't change anything. It doesn't change how I feel.'

She opened and closed her mouth, trying to will the right words to come out, but nothing did. Why did it have to be this hard? She tried to blink away the tears that threatened to spill.

'It's a big day. Emotions are bound to run high. For all of us.' He reached up and brushed the hair away from her face. 'I'm so proud of you.' His voice was softer now, warmer. 'Look where you are.'

He turned her around to look out of the window. She gazed out at the view, allowing herself to take it all in. The enormity of it all enveloped her like a heavy blanket. Her limbs, which had been light and carefree in the microgravity of space, felt leaden. She sank a little, as if only just noticing the weight of her body.

John wrapped his arms around her, taking her weight against him, holding her tight. She let herself be held up by him. He made her feel safe. She had spent so long holding everyone else up, and she was exhausted. Tomorrow all their hard work would come to fruition. The mission. She pulled away. For a moment she had forgotten where they were, she allowed herself to relax into John's arms. Anyone could have seen them. Jessica pulled away.

'We shouldn't be doing this,' she said.

'Why not?'

'You know why, John. Why do we keep having the same conversation again and again?' She couldn't keep the frustration out of her voice. This wasn't sustainable.

'I guess I keep hoping for a different outcome.' John said with a sigh.

She opened her mouth to speak but she didn't know what to say.

He took her hand again. 'Can we just forget all the crap and just be me and you for five minutes?'

She nodded again, not knowing how to tell him how sorry she was. How she wished things were different, that she was different, more like him. He didn't let arbitrary rules get in the way. He followed his instinct, and he was usually right.

She squeezed his hand, trying to convey with her touch everything she couldn't say at the moment. She closed her eyes as her fingers grounded themselves in his, seeking the comfort she couldn't ask for. Together they turned back to the window and looked out onto the dusty red terrain of the place that would be their home for the next thirty days.

That night, when she got to her cabin she found a note on her bed in John's untidy handwriting.

'I found this on the floor that night. I've decided to put all my money on you.'

Next to the note was a poker chip. She picked it up. *I wonder what the odds on us are?* She thought to herself as she squeezed it tight and smiled.

Chapter Twenty-Three
Day of first Mars walk

John

'It is ridiculous we have to do this so early.' said Val, with half a joke in her sentence. It was five a.m. on the first full Sol of being on Mars. A Sol, or solar Mars day, was almost 40 minutes longer than an Earth day. The crew had been working to Sols for the month prior to landing to acclimatise to the shift in circadian rhythms.

'Val, you know why. It's prime time in Western Europe and lunchtime in the US. Everyone will be watching.' Jessica was pulling on her specially designed spacesuit. They would be working non-stop during their 30 Sols on Mars, and the suits they would wear were designed to be lighter and more flexible than the bulky EVA suits for use in space flight.

'I know why. It is still ridiculous. Yuri Gagarin launched at nine in the morning and everyone stopped and watched such a momentous occasion. We're about to walk on another planet and people will not watch unless they are sitting on their sofa with something to eat?'

'You're about to walk on another planet and this is what you're complaining about, Val?' John shot at the dour Russian. He knew this was her way of deflecting the excitement she was feeling. Both women appeared cool and calm, exactly as he expected them to, but he could see Jessica fumbling with her gloves.

'Here, let me help you.' He stepped into the airlock where they were all watching Jessica and Valentina get ready for their descent onto Mars. He helped Jessica tug her right glove on and secure it.

'Thanks.' She looked up at him, her brown eyes glittering with excitement.

'You know what you're going to say?'

'To a billion people who are watching or listening live? Nah, I thought I'd wing it.' She grinned.

'You've been practising this speech since that first night you saw Mars at the observatory, haven't you?' He grinned at her.

'Well, that "One small step for man..." thing is pretty tough to top. But I hope mine's a bit more inclusive, for all those girls watching thinking it could be them one day.'

'They really are watching you, Jessica,' he was suddenly serious.

'I know,' she said, closing her eyes and breathing deeply. 'You know what I'm most worried about?' She looked at him again.

'What?'

'Falling down the ladder.' He couldn't suppress his laughter. She never stopped surprising him. 'I'm serious John. It'd be just my luck to land on a new planet arse first.'

'Just take it one step at a time.' He gave her a last hug. 'You're amazing,' he whispered in her ear. 'Never forget that.' John stepped back with a smile.

'And you, you big grump,' he said loudly as he turned to Val and gave her a hug that she reluctantly accepted. 'Try and smile for the cameras.'

'No one will see me under my helmet.'

'They'll see this, though.' And he flashed the camera at her as she scowled at him. 'Seriously, good job getting us here, Val.' He smiled at her, and she gave him a glimmer of a smile back.

John stepped aside so May and Lucca could wish them both luck. Preparations complete, Jessica and Valentina were ready to go. John, May, and Lucca left to take their places on the bridge. A fifteen-minute comms lag to Earth meant Lucca was directing the expedition rather than Mission Control.

The wide window on the bridge enabled them to see the surface of Mars, but John's seat was on the opposite side to where Jessica and Valentina would be walking. As they reached the top of the ladder that took them from the airlock to the bridge May turned to John.

'Do you want to sit in my seat for this?' May smiled.

'Why?' John asked.

'You can see out as they descend,' she replied.

'Don't you want to watch them?' John felt guilty at taking the seat, but also knew he really would like to see this historic occasion for Jessica.

'Yeah, but,' she hesitated for a moment. 'I know it would mean a lot to you.'

What did May mean by that? John searched her face for any sign, something that gave away what she was thinking. But she just smiled and gave him a shove.

'Go on.'

John didn't press the matter. Maybe she had somehow picked up that something was going on between him and Jessica, but if he pushed it any further she might ask him directly. He didn't want to lie to her, and Jessica would kill him if he told her the truth.

Jessica would alight from the descent module via a ladder. Her primary role during this first disembarkation was simply to describe what she was seeing to the billions of people across the distant Earth who were waiting to hear from the first humans on another planet. Later that day they would all leave the descent module to set up their habitat for the duration of their stay.

'Opening the airlock.' As Jessica's voice came over the radio the hairs on John's arm stood up. They were the first humans on another planet.

The crew listened in silent anticipation as Jessica opened the external door. They were viewing footage from Jessica's suit camera and an external camera mounted on the capsule. Jessica stood at the top of the steps that led down to the surface of Mars. John looked out of the portal but he wouldn't see Jessica until she'd reached the surface.

'The door is open,' she narrated, 'and I can see it, I can see Mars. I can see for miles around. There's a mountain range to the North, it stretches a couple of hundred kilometres. To the South West, there's a large but shallow crater, about five hundred metres in diameter, well done for missing that Valentina.'

John smiled listening to her. It was her job to detail what she saw. Scientists down on the ground would be hanging on her every word. But he just wanted to know how she felt about what she saw.

'From up here, the surface looks like a fine dust, though there are larger rocks scattered about. There's a light wind blowing across the surface. It just looks...' he could imagine the look on her face as she searched for the perfect words. '...it looks like burnished gold. The sky is the colour of sandstone, but there is a faint blue tinge to it around the sun. My suit is holding steady at twenty-one degrees, but this colour, it makes me feel much warmer.'

'Commander Gabriel, is the ladder in place?' Lucca asked.

'Affirmative, I can confirm the ladder is in place. It reaches the surface, and looks to be nestled about two centimetres into the top layer of the surface.'

'Are you ready to descend?' asked Lucca.

'Confirm, I am ready to descend. How are the pictures looking?'

'Just beautiful. Your suit cam is streaming fine and we've got you on the capsule cam too.' Lucca glanced quickly at all of the screens they had showing all of the different camera angles.

'Copy that. I'm descending now.' Her suit camera captured her taking slow and steady steps down the ladder, the top of which was about eight foot from the ground. John smiled to himself imagining her concentrating hard on not falling.

'We can see you coming down Commander.'

She stepped her right foot on the surface, and then slowly lowered her left foot down. There was silence in the capsule, and John held his breath. This was her moment.

'As we take another step in the journey of humankind, we bring the courage of those that came before us, and the hopes of those that will come after.' said Jessica in a voice that would echo through the ages.

They all cheered. John, Lucca and May hugged, and Lucca was wiping his eyes.

'You did it, Commander,' Lucca said through his tears.

'We all did it. I can't wait for you guys to come out here. Kareva, it's your turn now.' said Jessica. John could hear the relief in her voice that she hadn't stumbled on her words.

They watched as Valentina made her way down the ladder. As she reached the bottom they heard her say 'Oy daaa' which basically was Russian for 'wow'. Valentina was the most pragmatic person John knew, and he had never seen her awed by anything so far. He was pleased to hear that after their multimillion mile journey Mars had finally impressed her. Like Jessica, as she reached the surface she gave a short speech, this time in her native Russian. She would be a national hero when she returned to her country.

The schedule for the excursion permitted the pioneers a few minutes to take it all in, before starting with data collection. Their stay on Mars was to last thirty Sols, but extreme weather or technical problems could force them to abort the mission and leave early. If this happened NARESA didn't want it to be a wasted trip. Almost every minute of their stay was already scheduled.

John watched Jessica break out into a run, like a child who had broken free of their parent's hand. Running was an essential part of their everyday routine on the ship to help them maintain muscle mass and physical condition. But the treadmill was no substitute for having the run of an entire planet.

Jessica and Valentina stayed on the surface for an hour before returning to the capsule. Lucca stayed at the console to confirm the data transfers, while May and John went to assist them back in. John helped Jessica remove her helmet. Her eyes were sparkling as her face appeared, her skin glistening with sweat from the exertion and weight of the spacesuit.

'Oh John, that was amazing! It's so beautiful and desolate out there. It really does feel like another planet. Nothing like Arizona. Was that ok? Did I do alright? How did it sound? Did I get good enough pictures? What's the response like?' Jessica was very animated.

'Woah, slow down. And stand still! I'm trying to undo your comms cap.' As he removed the cap her long brown hair spilled out. She looked radiant, beaming widely and giddy with excitement.

'You're making this really difficult you know.' He said with a smile. 'Look, Valentina is done already.'

'We'll meet you back upstairs.' May said to them both as she and an already de-suited Valentina left the airlock.

They hung up Jessica's suit and helmet and turned to face each other. Jessica was still glowing, infectious happiness radiating from her.

'God, I'm so proud of you. The first human being to walk on another planet. The girl from the observatory,' he told her.

'I didn't do anything special. Just took some steps and ran around, and now I'm going to be a celebrity, whether I like it or not.' She shrugged and laughed.

'You and I both know that's not true. Look at everything you did to get here. Those words Jessica, beautiful.' John smiled with pride.

'I couldn't have done it without you.'

'Of course you could.' John smiled.

'It just felt so amazing. I'm not even sure I could describe how it felt. To be the first person to step on another planet. To go where no one else has been. That tiny red dot in the sky you showed me all those years ago. And we're here. I can't wait till you go out later today.'

'It's going to be amazing.' He couldn't wait.

'To just be able to run and know you aren't going to see anyone else.'

'I saw you running out of the window. You looked so free.' He smiled at her.

'Out of the window?' Jessica frowned.

'Yeah, May let me sit in her seat so I could get a good look.' It had seemed like such a small thing at the time, but he had a sudden sense that Jessica thought it a much bigger deal.

'Why would she do that?' Jessica's tone had completely changed.

'I don't know. Perhaps she just thought it was a nice thing.' He shouldn't have mentioned it.

'But why you? What was she thinking?' Jessica demanded.

'I don't know Jessica. I didn't question it.' That wasn't quite true. He hadn't wanted to question it.

'Do you think she knows about us?' She cut straight to her concern.

'What though? There is no us right now.' He could feel himself tense. She needed to get some perspective. This woman had just been the first person to walk on Mars and here she was getting upset because he had switched seats with a colleague.

'You know what I mean,' she huffed.

'No, I don't actually. There's nothing going on between us right now, something you have made patently clear. So, I don't know what you think she knows.'

Her face clouded over in confusion. 'Stop twisting things. You know how important this is.'

'Yes, I know exactly what's important to you.' His tone was cold now, he couldn't help it. 'Which is why there is nothing going on. So, tell me, what is it that you're worried about May finding out?'

'Nothing. It's fine.' She tried to brush past him but he was in the way of the small doorway. He felt sick. The emotional highs and lows were like the undulations of a rollercoaster.

'Jessica,' he looked her squarely in the eyes. 'If there is nothing going on between us, what are you so worried about?'

He watched her. The face that just now had been so alive, so happy, was now frowning. Her eyes were darting anxiously over his face. Her chest rose and fell with heavy breaths. He hated himself in that moment for pushing her, for being the one who had turned her from so happy to so, what was it? Sad? Anxious? Angry? He just wanted to reach out and tell her it didn't matter. It was ok. She had done a wonderful thing today, and he would always, always be there to support her.

'I'm worried she'll figure out I'm in love with you.'

Her words hit him in the chest. All at once the world appeared brighter again. He forgot where he was and what they were here to do. He forgot that they had just made history. He took her face in his hands and kissed her. She responded instantly, her soft lips parting, his tongue met hers. Everything melted away and all that existed in the world was this woman who he loved and who loved him back.

He slipped a hand around her back, pulling her close to him, the other hand threaded through her hair. It was although they were in a vacuum, with nothing else around them, so close that he couldn't tell if he felt his own heart beating or hers. As he moved his hand slowly down the curve of her back the soft moan that she let out shuddered through her body and his.

A voice over the radio broke the spell, 'Commander? Eden? You ok down there?'

They jumped apart, both panting, trying to catch their breath. Jessica gulped and pressed the comms button on her headset. 'Yeah, sorry Lucca, we're just coming back up.'

'Hurry up, we want to celebrate!'

'Ok.' She muted her speaker.

They both looked at each other, nervously laughing, each of them still breathing heavily.

'Do you think they were watching?' Jessica said, glancing up at the camera.

'No,' said John, even though he had no idea. 'We weren't in the sightline anyway.'

That seemed to satisfy her. If May suspected as John thought she did, he knew she would have made sure they weren't watching. He didn't care right now anyway. His lips were burning, and his body was aching for this woman.

'We'd better go,' she said.

'Yeah.' Neither of them moved.

'Wait!' she started digging into the pockets of the trousers she had been wearing under her suit. 'Here. It's been on Mars.'

She took his hand and placed something in it. He looked down. It was the poker chip he had left in her room the night she was selected to be the first person on Mars.

He leaned in and kissed her again, softly this time, savouring the taste of her. He pulled back after a brief moment, not wanting to push things, not wanting anything to spoil this moment. She loved him, and right now that was all he cared about. Not even the thought of stepping on a new planet could compare at this moment. He looked at her and shook his head slightly, still unable to believe she felt the same way about him.

'What?' She looked at him, her eyebrows raised. 'Are you laughing at me? I always think you're mocking me when you shake your head like that.'

'Not even close. I was just thinking... Everyone will remember this day for a different reason to me.'

'Oh John,' she reached up and stroked his cheek.

'And I was thinking something else.'

'What?' she didn't take her eyes off him.

'That I love you too.'

***

When John stepped out of the capsule on to the surface of Mars himself later that day the thoughts of Jessica that had been consuming him temporarily vanished. He was the last of the crew to step off the ladder from the capsule, the fifth person to step foot on Mars. He didn't care. Relative order didn't matter now they were all here. He looked all around him. The rust coloured surface stretched out as far as his eyes could see. The sky was like nothing he had ever seen before, a warm yellow. It was surreal, as though he were on a film set. John had spent his entire life being part of a famous space family, but as he stood on Mars, it was as if the great weight of expectation was being lifted with every minute.

The five crew members set up the temporary biosphere, the living and working quarters where they would live for the next Martian month. It would protect them from the increased radiation that they faced away from Earth, and from the extremes of temperature on the planet. It was fully sealed and pressurised so they didn't have to wear spacesuits while inside.

The days seemed to pass without pause. As it did on the Harmonia, routine became the backbone of their time on Mars. The day time was spent exploring the Mars surface, on foot or using the SAMSON rover, deposited on the planet during a previous uncrewed mission, or conducting essential maintenance. The early evenings were taken up with experiments and data entry. There was little time to relax in the biosphere at the end of the evening, before a critical night's sleep, to be ready for the next day.

John felt a satisfaction in the tiredness in his body at the end of every Sol. With the more constant physical exercise compared to the last nine months onboard the Harmonia – still orbiting the planet above them, waiting for their return launch – all the crew were exhausted. But he was grateful for every day he spent on the planet.

They had been so focused on their work, and John had been so determined to make the most of the time on Mars, that he and Jessica had spent little time alone together. He avoided thinking about the future, about life beyond Mars. He was mostly successful at keeping his mind on the job, but every now and then he would catch sight of her, frowning over data on her tablet, or sweeping Martian dust off the solar panels, and his stomach would somersault like it did when they launched in a rocket.

One evening, on Sol twenty-six they both found themselves the last ones awake in the living area.

'I can't believe it's nearly over,' John said.

'I know,' Jessica replied. 'It feels like it's gone so quickly. Would you stay if you could?'

He rubbed his chin as he considered her question. Would he stay? What did he have outside of this job? He struggled to think. Up here he could start afresh, he could be a pioneer of a new colony. It would be hard work, but it would be the start of something so much bigger. He could do anything with Jessica by his side.

'I'd seriously think about it. It would depend a lot on who I was stuck here with,' he grinned. 'What about you?'

'I don't know,' she said. 'There's so much I'd miss. I can't imagine not seeing anything green again, or hearing the sea. Only being able to live on things you grow yourself. I'm not sure I would want to.' She was reflective for a moment. 'Anyone who did stay here would have to repopulate to create a new colony.'

'I could help you with that.' He said with a wink.

She laughed at him.

'Seriously though,' she continued, 'you'd have to think about the ethics of bringing a child into this hostile environment, wouldn't you?'

'No more hostile than on Earth you could argue.'

'You know what I mean, physically hostile. Imagine a child not being able to breathe fresh air, to run around in shorts and a t-shirt. Not learning to ride a bike, no jumping in puddles with wellies.'

She was looking into the distance as she spoke. A question played on his mind. He thought carefully before asking her, but it felt important for him to know. 'Do you want to have children?'

She appeared to break free of her thought and turned back to him.

'Oh. I don't know. I mean, you know I probably won't be able to have children after this. I don't know what they say to you guys, but they had the talk with us women. They don't know what the radiation will do to our reproductive system. But, it's unlikely.'

He hadn't known that. 'But did you want to?'

She replied simply, 'I wanted this more.' John wondered if that were still true. Had it been worth the sacrifice?

John had a feeling that whatever future he had with Jessica, almost all ways would be her ways. But that was one of the things he loved about her, and he knew that however long he had to wait, it would be worth it.

He pulled back his sleeping bag later that night and found a note sticking out from just under his pillow. He smiled to himself as he read the meticulous handwriting. It just said:

'It's not never.'

Chapter Twenty-Four
Countdown until re-entry: 3 months

Jessica

A persistent ringing woke Jessica up from a deep sleep. Her eyes were heavy and she felt faintly sick. Through the fog of sleep, she remembered she had taken one of May's sleeping pills last night. The return to the Harmonia craft had been accompanied by a return of her insomnia.

She pushed up her eye mask and squinted at the blinking and beeping screen in front of her. She stabbed the screen and it stopped. The sound still echoed in her ears as she took a deep breath to try and wake herself up. Peering at the screen through half closed eyes she read 'Urgent Transmission for All Crew'. There was a video link attached.

It was 2.07 a.m. They'd never been woken in the middle of the night before. Drowsiness draining away almost instantly, she hurried to wake the rest of the crew. Only Valentina was wide awake as soon as Jessica disturbed her. The others protested sleepily.

Jessica was first to the galley, waiting for the others to play the video on the large screen. She sat, alternately drumming her fingers then brushing stray strands of hair out of her face. What could be so important that Mission Control would disturb them in the night? Though the spacecraft was never silent, there were no warning alarms going off. If something were wrong wouldn't the crew be the first to notice?

She didn't have to wait long for the rest of them to join her, questioning looks on their faces. When they had all sat down she pressed play. Tom, their most frequent CAPCOM, appeared on the screen looking grave. His blue eyes had lost their usual spark and were ringed by dark circles.

'Morning Harmonia crew. Sorry to disturb you so early. We've got some bad news and there is no easy way to say this so

I'm just going to come out with it. The Concordia re-entry vehicle Aries, which was due to land late last night, broke up as it entered the Earth's atmosphere. We are not expecting to find any survivors.' Tom's voice broke slightly on the last few words.

'As you can imagine everyone here is devastated at the loss of Rachel, Josef, Kaspar, Paloma, and Oliva and I'm sure you will be too.' The faces of her colleague flashed into Jessica's head. She could barely take in what Tom was saying.

'You are probably also wondering whether this has any implications for the Harmonia and the Aries capsule.'

He took a deep breath. 'We don't know yet. We are still in the process of recovering the craft and crash investigation will start immediately. We will keep you continually updated with our findings. Please be extra vigilant on all your routine checks and let us know if you find anything unusual. I'll be back in touch soon.' He paused, and they all watched on the large screen as he leaned his head into his hand, his fingertips supporting his furrowed forehead.

'Guys,' the initial formality had gone, 'I'm really sorry.' Then he disappeared and they were left with a blank screen.

Nobody spoke. They just stared at each other, their tired brains taking time to process the information.

It felt like the blood had drained from Jessica's body; she couldn't move. 'Broken up'. The words sounded so benign like it was a china cup that had fallen to the floor. The re-entry vehicle, identical to the one that was to take them home, had been torn apart as it hit the Earth's atmosphere. There would be no survivors. Maybe not even bodies to recover. Five families devastated. Their colleagues. Their friends.

She looked at each of her crewmates in turn. They all wore the same blank, uncomprehending look. The feeling flooded back into her body, her nerves tingling on the ends of her fingers and feet. *Get it together Jessica* she told herself. *It's your job to hold it together for them*. But she couldn't get the faces of the Concordia crew out of her head. Rachel, their Commander, her counterpart, one of her closest friends. She thought of Lilli and Max. They would know by now. How would they explain it to a young girl?

She imagined the spacecraft speeding towards the invisible line that separated the Earth's atmosphere from space. Re-entry was one of the most dangerous parts of space flight. What would it have felt like for them? How soon would they have known? And how long would they have waited for the inevitable? Did the control panel light up with warnings? Did they see the outside of the craft start to twist and warp in the heat? She shook her head trying to rid herself of the thoughts. She had so many questions, though she wasn't even sure she wanted to know the answer to any of them. She looked around at her crewmates. How long before the sadness about their colleagues gave way to the same fears she had about the implications for them? *I've got to keep us going,* she told herself. She couldn't let them see her scared.

Slowly, one by one, the crew unfroze and came back to life.

'I'm going to make us all coffee,' May said getting up. 'It's going to be a long day.'

Valentina reached for her tablet and started typing furiously. 'Jessica, we are going to need to see the NARESA reports as soon as they are submitted.'

Lucca just squeezed his eyes shut, and wiped away tears with his finger and thumb. John put his head in his hand, the same position as Tom, and just breathed the word 'Fuck' with a massive exhale of breath.

Through her shock and grief, Jessica couldn't help but suppress a smile. She knew these people, she could have predicted each of their reactions to this news. May, pragmatic, wanting to look after people; Valentina practical, immediately searching for answers; Lucca, the one most likely to get emotional; and John, never afraid to show how he felt and say what everyone else was thinking.

He turned to face her; his eyes were heavy with pain, his jaw slack in disbelief. It hit her too, like an ice-cold wave washing over her, making her shiver. Her arms ached to reach out for him, but she no longer knew where the lines were, wasn't sure that it wouldn't betray them. Did this accident change the rules? Whatever was going on between them, he was still her best friend. It was only natural for them to want to comfort one another.

She put her hand on his forearm and squeezed. His hand twitched to catch hers, then stopped, clenching into a fist instead. This small sequence of gestures, unnoticed by the others, added to the weight in her chest. She took a deep breath, trying to dislodge it. She didn't have time to get emotional. Her training kicked in. She needed to keep them busy, and the ship still had to function. She expected an updated schedule from Mission Control imminently but in the meantime, she rattled off some routine checks for them to make, and they all drifted off to start them. None of them knew what the crash investigation would turn up, and she knew all of them would be scouring the spacecraft for hints of their fate.

The ship was quiet for the whole day. The hum of instruments, usually drowned out by conversation, reverberated around Jessica's head. There was little further information for them about the accident. It might be weeks before the cause was finally established. NARESA confirmed that teams were working round the clock to understand the implications for Harmonia. They still had three months till they were due back on Earth, but repairs or adjustments might need to be undertaken.

They had all mentally prepared themselves for an unsuccessful outcome. They all knew the risks involved, and the number of things that had to go right for them to return safely. But Jessica was sure that when any of them imagined dying on the mission it would be a quick escalation of events. They hadn't been prepared by any of their training for a long period of waiting, knowing that the odds weren't on their side.

Valentina pored over the technical reports that immediately began coming in from NARESA. Jessica's head swam as Valentina tried to explain one of the reports to her later that evening. Jessica had the basic engineering and physics knowledge required of every astronaut, but it wasn't her strength, and the technical documents showing fuel cells and heat shields were overwhelming at times.

'What are you doing, Val? You need to get some rest.'

Valentina launched into an explanation of oxygen residues on fragments of the outer layer of the capsule found on the ground.

'Val?' She tried to interrupt her.

'Val.' Valentina carried on talking, oblivious to Jessica's interjection.

'Valentina!'

'What?' She seemed to suddenly realise Jessica was there.

'Val,' she said, softening her voice, trying to stay calm. 'There are teams of hundreds of experts down there looking into this, trying to get us home safely. Why don't you leave it to them for a bit?'

'None of them know this ship like I do.'

'I know.' Jessica regarded her bold pilot, her Second in Command, who she would trust with her life in any situation. 'But it's going to take more than just reading technical reports to get us through this.'

'I don't know what you mean.'

'Sure, we need to understand the technical details. And we've got people working on that, with your help. But if we are going to survive the next few months – I mean mentally survive,' who knew whether the other sort of survival was in their control? 'we have to deal with our feelings about it. If we spend our energy trying to suppress those feelings we are not going to be doing our best job, and God knows, this is the time when we have to be at the top of our game.'

Valentina was quiet. Jessica forced herself to stay quiet too. She knew if she just gave them enough space, her team would talk. When Valentina spoke, her voice was determined.

'I am not scared, you know.' It wasn't a question.

'I do know.' And she believed her. Valentina was the most fearless person she knew.

'I am just sad.' The emotion made her Russian accent thicker.

'Sad?'

'About the people. Our friends who died, and their families. All of you. Especially Lucca and his children.' She paused and Jessica thought of the haunted look on Lucca's face earlier.

Valentina continued, 'Whether we live or die, this accident will change everything. It will change the programme, the whole of NARESA. The future of our work is at risk. No, I am not scared. But I am sad.' As Jessica looked at her she could see her face was pale, her eyes tinged with pink.

There was nothing Jessica could say; nothing that could provide any comfort or reassurance. She just took Valentina's hand and squeezed it. Valentina squeezed back.

The quiet admission of sadness from her strong, stoical pilot was almost worse than finding May sobbing in the medical room earlier that afternoon. Jessica had pulled her into a hug and just held her as her shoulders shook with emotion. There was no point in telling anyone it would all be ok because she had no idea whether or not it would be.

She had no words or comfort either for Lucca, whom she found in the greenhouse, tending to rows of herbs, salad leaves, and grains. She had no idea what he was going through. He had a wife and children anticipating his safe return, and he had to live with the knowledge that might not happen, that he might never see them again. Unsure what else to do, Jessica worked silently side by side with him, hoping that he understood that she was there for him if he needed it.

It was only John who she avoided being alone with that day. She wasn't even sure why. It was a time when they needed each other the most. She wanted more than anything to feel the security of his arms, but something was stopping her. He found her in the galley late that night when everyone else had gone to bed.

'You're avoiding me, Jessica.' He said walking towards her. She was leaning against the galley wall drinking a cup of coffee. It was later. She had been up since 2 a.m. but she knew if she closed her eyes she wouldn't sleep.

'I'm not.' She knew he would see through her protest.

'I know why.'

'Do you?' she sighed. 'Because I'm not even sure I do.' She couldn't even look at him.

'Yeah. I think you're trying to hold it together for everyone. And you're doing a great job you really are.' Taking the coffee cup and putting it on the table, he took her hands in his.

'But you know that I can see past that. I know you. I know you are feeling out of control, and a sense of responsibility to everyone. But you don't have to hold it together for me. I'm the one you tell.'

Jessica could feel her eyes start to sting. She blinked hard, trying to dispel the tears that were threatening to fall. The lump in her throat stopped her from speaking. The thoughts in her head were incessant. This was her crew, it was her job to look after them, and she wasn't sure if she could keep them safe. She had no idea what could be wrong with the ship or if they could fix it, even with all the smartest people in the world working on it. And she felt let down, by this spacecraft, by all the people whose job it was to keep her safe, and by science, previously her security blanket, now something that might be the end of them all. She started to shake, unable to contain everything inside anymore.

'Hey,' John wrapped his arms tightly around her, so she was pressed into his chest, and she could no longer hold it in. The tears spilled out, soaking his jumpsuit. His strong grip couldn't contain her shaking, but he stroked his hand gently up and down her back. Her head swam with images and thoughts; John's face when she told him that they couldn't be together, the Concordia re-entry vehicle as it broke up over the ocean, Lucca's sobs as he recorded a video for his wife. Her body was drained yet heavy against John's embrace.

She buried her face in his neck and let his familiar smell calm her down. Her breathing slowed, and the tears stopped falling. As if sensing the slowdown in her emotions John released her and took her face in his hands. 'Hey,' he said again, his eyes searching her face. She refused to look into his eyes, but she didn't try to break free. She hated him seeing her like this, unable to control herself, weak and emotional.

'Jessica? Jessica, look at me.' He brushed the hair out of her face.

She turned her face towards him. His expression was full of concern. She squeezed her eyes shut tight and her face screwed up with pain as tears once again ran in rivulets down her face. He wiped each of her cheeks with his thumbs.

'You're doing such a great job, Jessica,' he said, his voice barely above a whisper. 'I'm so proud of you.'

'I'm scared.' The quiet words fell out of her mouth without her realising.

John nodded, 'I'm scared too.'

'Really?' She looked up at him. She could see in his eyes that he meant it.

'Yes, of course I am. It's completely understandable. But you know what?' He took each of her hands in his and squeezed them. 'There is no one else I would rather have in charge of this crew than you.'

His words started to soothe her. The lump in her throat had disappeared. She felt lighter, as if in her tears she had shed some of the weight that had been holding her down. He was the person she loved most in the world and he had faith in her.

She thought that hearing that he too was scared would make her feel worse. He was strong and usually fearless. But it made her feel less alone; like it was ok to feel afraid. Why hadn't she realised this before? She had been so focused on everything that was wrong with getting close to John, she had overlooked the ways in which it would make everything better.

Right now anything could happen, they might not make it home; yet she had been pushing John away. At this moment she couldn't think of a single good reason why they shouldn't be together. She glanced down at his hands in hers, how right it looked, how right it felt. Without thinking, without analysing whether it was right or wrong, she tilted her head towards him and pressed her lips against his. They were as soft and full as she remembered. He released her hands and threaded his arms through hers, his hands spread across her back, pulling her body closer into his. A warmth suffused through her, releasing the tension as it did so. She reached her arms up and pushed her fingers through his hair.

Their kissing became more fervent; her lips parted and he began to explore her mouth, pushing his tongue against hers. His hands were no longer just holding her up. He ran them urgently along her body, feeling his way, charting her contours. Her skin tingled at his touch. There was nothing else in the world but the two of them. John broke away from kissing her lips and buried himself in her neck. Jessica lifted her head up. His breath was hot on her skin as he covered her in featherlight kisses. She let out a soft moan, and waves of desire rippled through her body. Spurred on by her response John's kisses became firmer and hungrier.

Jessica dug her fingernails into the thick fabric of his jumpsuit and pulled him closer to her. She didn't want a single space between her body and John's. He pressed against her sending pulses through her like electricity.

'Jessica,' he groaned softly, the words tickling her ears.

As if both startled by the sudden break in the silence they pulled apart, each of them breathless. Jessica stared into John's eyes. They were bright with desire but suddenly narrowed with concern.

'Are you ok, sweetheart?' he whispered, still panting.

She nodded silently. This time there was no confusion, no guilt. She didn't want to hide how she felt any longer.

'I love you.' It came out in a whisper of a breath, barely audible above the background noise of the spacecraft.

He broke into a smile and pulled her into him again, her head resting against his chest. 'I love you too,' he whispered back, kissing the top of her head. 'More than you will ever know.' They stood in each other's arms, and for the first time since they had learned about the Concordia accident she felt safe.

After a few minutes, John pulled away. 'Listen, you need to go to bed. It's been a long day, and it'll be another one tomorrow. I'll finish up here.'

She didn't want to go, didn't want to stop. She wanted to stay in his arms until it was all over. With John, she could achieve anything. With John, there was a hope that this was all going to be ok. And now he was the one stopping, encouraging her to go. Had he changed his mind about her?

He must have registered her disappointment because he took her face in his hands again.

'Jessica, I want nothing more than to stay here with you, but I know you well enough to know that if we don't stop now we'll do something that you might regret later. And I don't ever want to be something you regret.'

She nodded, unable to speak.

He brushed the hair from her eyes. 'Promise me you are ok?'

'I promise. Thank you. For everything.' She squeezed his hand, not wanting to let it go, even as she turned to leave.

He grasped her fingers again. 'I'm here for you Jessica. I'm not going anywhere, trust me.'

Chapter Twenty-Five
Countdown to re-entry: 3 months

Jessica

Jessica slept more deeply that night than she had in weeks. Though the Concordia accident still weighed heavy on her mind, and the implications for the Harmonia crew were no clearer, she no longer felt like she was carrying the burden alone.

Jessica stretched as she pulled herself out of bed. The tension of the previous day had dissipated. The future was uncertain, but she could face anything with John by her side. She had finally let him in and she didn't want to let him go. She opened her drawer to pull out a sweatshirt. Nestled on top was a rumpled note.

'I'm always here x'

She smiled to herself, tracing her fingers along his words. His writing always looked like his brain was working faster than his pen.

She picked up a thick notebook from her desk. Tucked between the well-thumbed pages were more scraps of paper with the same scratchy handwriting, each one a tangible reminder that there was someone in her life thinking of her when she wasn't there. She slipped the latest note between the pages, and tucked the book away.

Her heart gave a little jump as she entered the galley, John was sitting at the table drinking coffee, scanning through his tablet. He glanced up and flashed her a grin. A barrier had melted in her, allowing all the feelings she had been holding at bay to wash over her. Now she had let them in, the world felt different. Everything appeared sharper, she was more aware of her surroundings, the ground was firmer underneath her feet.

'Hey you.' Even his voice was like a warm blanket around her.

'Hey you.'

She sat down next to him at the table. He put his hand under the table and reached out for hers. They held just the tip of each other's fingers. There was still a tacit agreement that whatever was happening between them, the rest of the crew couldn't find out. At the sounds of the others approaching they pulled apart. Jessica jumped up to get some coffee.

'Any news?' Lucca said by way of greeting. Jessica wondered if it would be like this every day from now on, the usual good morning had been replaced by this question. Every morning wondering if NARESA had discovered the source of the crash overnight? Until then they would all struggle to move on.

She passed each of them a coffee. 'There are some reports that came in overnight, but nothing conclusive yet.'

'I just want some goddamn answers,' Lucca's fist banged down on the table, making them all jump. 'They've got us here on a... a suicide mission.'

They all sat in stunned silence. Though Lucca was certainly the most emotional out of all of them, they had never seen him display aggression before.

'Lucca, I know you're frustrated.' Jessica said, her voice measured. 'It's just going to take some time.'

'Time, Jessica? Time is the one thing we might not have.' he got up from the table and walked out.

The lightness that had elevated her body since she woke up evaporated. She stood up to go after him, but she felt a weight on her arm. It was John.

'I'll go,' he said.

He came and found her half an hour later on the zero-gravity observation deck where she was floating, leaning her head against the window so she could see Mars. No longer the vast red sphere that they could see a few weeks ago, but a shrinking copper circle, like a penny in the sky. The inertia of zero gravity meant each movement continued until it was stopped and John had to physically stop himself by grasping onto hand and footholds.

'Feels like a lifetime ago that we were on Mars, don't you think?' Jessica said, not taking her eyes away from the window.

'Yeah.'

'How's Lucca?' she turned to face him.

He shrugged. 'As good as can be expected. He feels bad for shouting at you though.'

'I don't care about that.' They had to stick together. It would do no good to get hung up on trivial things.

'I do. It's not fair of him to turn on you like that. And it doesn't do us any good to lose it with each other.'

'He's scared, John. And he's got a whole lot more to lose than the rest of us.' She paused, 'You didn't say that to him, did you? About turning on me.'

'No, of course not. I was a good friend and I listened. I am worried about you though.' He slipped one hand around her waist, the other still holding himself steady. She flinched and peered over his shoulder.

'It's ok, everyone's busy.'

She relaxed and turned towards him. He let go of the handhold and enveloped her with both of his arms. They both bobbed in the air as if they were in the ocean once again. Lightness returned to her body. She could face anything with John's support. One hand rested on his chest and one on his upper arm. He was lean but solid underneath her touch. She already knew how he looked under his flight suit. Between years of intensive training and physical testing, and the close proximity of living on Harmonia, they had all seen each other almost naked. But she wanted to know what his skin felt like against hers, the feel of his fingers dancing along her body. As if reading her mind, he lightly touched the back of her neck and pulled her face towards him. His kiss was gentler and slower than it had been the night before, less urgent and more calming. She didn't want it to stop, but what would happen if one of the crew saw them?

She gently pulled away and leaned her forehead against his. 'You make the world easier to face,' she whispered. She felt his forehead lift in a smile.

'That's all I want to do for you, Jessica,' he whispered back.

'How are you feeling about everything?' Her eyes searched his face, trying to read his expression.

'I can get through anything with you.' His voice was husky with emotion.

'John, you don't have to say that just to make me feel better.'

'It's true. Jessica.' He placed a hand on her cheek. 'I've never felt like this before. I can't even describe it.' As he spoke she turned her head against his hand and pressed her lips against his palm.

John sighed. 'I just love you,' he said. 'That's all there is to it.'

His words sent a pulse of electricity through her body. She had never been loved in this way before, never had someone offer themselves up so unconditionally. As the pulse hit her stomach a thousand thoughts rang around her head, then as John leaned in and kissed her again they all disappeared and her body burned.

A message pinged on John's wrist monitor and they pulled apart.

'We should stop,' John whispered.

Jessica nodded, not trusting herself to say anything.

'That was Val,' he said, checking the message. 'I'd better go.'

Jessica simply nodded again. John kissed her on the forehead and squeezed her hand, his fingertips brushing hers as he walked away.

These snatched moments became her salvation over the next few days. Time alone on the ship was rare so they found themselves constructing reasons to do tasks together, just to be in each other's company. They developed rituals and secret codes that helped them communicate in a space where there was little privacy and comms were monitored. They would take it in turns pressing the poker chip into each other's hands when they wanted to remind one another they were thinking of them. She would find notes from John in her pockets. They messaged each other on their wrist comms. The code '1114' meant meet in the empty corridor at the back of the ship. In these moments they would kiss urgently, their bodies pressed tight against each other, until time or a disturbance forced them to part, panting and flushed. After these interludes, Jessica would feel a heightened awareness of the sensations in her whole body, the fizzle of the nerve endings in her skin. When they parted her arms felt bereft, her lips numb, her body empty.

Sometimes they would simply talk, whispering to each other, their eyes scanning each other's face.

'I'd do anything for you, Jessica, you know that, right?'

'I know,' she said.

'We'll get through this.' He clasped her hand.

She sighed at his words. They were like a tonic, washing away the fear and sense of responsibility that clung to her.

'John...' She struggled to tell him how she felt, almost afraid of putting it into words. She couldn't articulate her feelings in the way that he could. She couldn't tell him how much she needed him, and how at the same time she was terrified of needing him. What if she couldn't live up to everything he saw in her? It had all been so much easier when she didn't have anyone else to worry about in this way, easier when she could just focus on her job. She wasn't sure if she wanted easy anymore. She wanted this, she wanted him.

'I love you.' The whispered words were all she could manage, trying to convey just how much she did with a deep kiss. She hoped it was enough.

***

A few days later they were in the greenhouse together. Each of the crew were scheduled to do the daily maintenance of plant samples. There were hundreds of seedlings, each at different stages of growth, and each being given a specific mix of chemicals to see which would give future astronauts the best chance of growing food on long missions.

John and Jessica had taken half of the specimens each, and were carefully adding drops of different chemicals to water, then administering it to that batch of seedlings, before making up the next mixture and proceeding with the next match.

They worked on the same bench facing each other, not speaking, but occasionally catching each other's eye with a smile.

In the companionable silence Jessica's found herself thinking about everything that had got them here. She thought about the first time that they had met in class, when John had taken her to the observatory. The first time they looked through the telescope...

'Jessica!' John shouted across that desk. 'That's the control sample.'

Jessica looked down at the plants. She had continued to use the mix of water and fifteen percent nitrogen, thirty percent phosphorous, and fifteen percent potassium onto the entire group of control specimens. They should have just received water.

'Fuck. Fuck!' Her heart was beating wildly.

John took her hand. 'It's fine Jessica, it's ok.'

She shook him off. 'It's not fine John. I've messed up this whole control sample.'

'Jessica. Don't worry. It's not important.'

'Of course it's important. Everything is important up here. And what if it were something life threatening? What if I put us in danger? And all because I'm too bloody distracted.' She paced up and down the small space.

'We're all distracted, Jessica. We're all just waiting-'

'No!' She cut him off, stopping to face him again. 'Distracted by you.'

'Oh.'

'My head is just too full. I'm not concentrating.' She raked her fingers through her hair.

'I'm sorry,' he said, his brow furrowed, his eyes alight with concern.

'It's not you,' she sighed. 'It's me. I'm the one getting distracted. I'm the one who should know better. This is exactly what I was worried about. I was wrong to let it get this far.'

Her stomach twisted. How could she have let this happen? She had selfishly let her feelings get in the way of doing her job. And as much as she wanted to be with John, it was her job to protect them all and get them home safely. If that was even possible now.

'Jessica, I'll do whatever you want. We'll cool it. I'll give you space, whatever you need.'

She could see the panic in his eyes. She looked away. The thought of hurting him made her body ache. But it was for the best, just until they got back. If they got back. There was too much at stake. She needed a clear head.

'I just don't think that's enough. We already tried to cool it. Look how well that worked?'

'What are you saying?'

'I don't know,' she pulled away from him again, screwed her eyes shut and pressed her fingers into them.

'Jessica. We'll do what you said before. Forget about this till we get back. It's not now. You were right. I'm sorry.'

She just shook her head, unable to find the words.

'Jessica...' his eyes flickered across her face, searching desperately for clues.

She squeezed her eyes shut again, trying to block out his hurt face. 'John, I can't... I don't... This isn't going to work.'

Chapter Twenty-Six
Countdown to re-entry: 3 months

John

His stomach lurched. He felt sick. He looked at her, trying to understand what she was thinking. He didn't know what to say, terrified that anything he did say would make things worse.

'Don't... don't do this. Please don't do this.' He felt like he was walking on the edge of a cliff, his world falling away below him.

'I shouldn't have let things get this far.' Her voice had become emotionless. 'I'm sorry John.'

He stared at her, frozen to the spot, a chill spread through his body.

There was a movement behind him. 'Jessica!' It was Valentina. 'Jessica, the report has come through. They know what brought down the Aries.'

John locked eyes with Jessica. He tried to swallow down his feelings. They had to focus now. He would show her; he would prove to her that their feelings didn't have to get in the way of getting them back home safely.

***

It had been a week since the NARESA report had come through. It showed a problem with the heat shield of the re-entry capsule Aries, a problem replicated on their own re-entry capsule Aneris.

The Harmonia continued with its usual hum of life support machines. For the first time ever, John questioned the wisdom of human beings exploring beyond their natural realm, optimistically venturing into environments that would instantly kill them at first contact without all of the technology they had invented to keep them alive.

He wasn't afraid of dying. They all knew what they were signing up for. They were doing something that was bigger than the five of them. But for that reason, if they didn't make it, it wouldn't just be the deaths of five people. It could be the death of the programme. The mission had brought such joy and unity to billions of people, it would inspire the next generation of scientists and explorers. To end it with another tragedy on top of the Concordia would undo everything they had been working for, everything that the people worked for since before he was even born.

President Nixon had a speech prepared in case the Apollo 11 crew were stranded on the moon. John wondered if someone right now was writing a speech about them, perhaps had already written one, commiserating their families on their deaths, praising them as heroes. What would they say about John? What had he achieved with his life beyond this current mission? They couldn't describe him as a loving husband, devoted father, beloved brother. Who would truly miss him? The person he loved most was on board with him, and when he thought about what was ahead, it was that fact that hit him in the solar plexus. He wasn't worried about his safety, he was worried about Jessica's. The thought that something might happen to her made him feel physically sick. He'd do whatever it took to protect her, and his crewmates, which is why he had no problem volunteering to make the repairs.

'John, why should it be you?' Valentina was frowning at him. 'You are not the only capable engineer here you know?'

'Val, you know I think you're a hundred times more capable than me.'

'Then why you?' She leaned on the galley table.

'Because I know this part. I worked with the team that helped design it. Anything else Val, but trust me on this one.'

'John's right.' Jessica weighed in. 'He's the one who should do it. And I'm going with him.'

There was uproar the minute the words left her lips.

'Why you?'

'You're not an engineer, Jessica.'

'No, absolutely not.' This last one was John. 'I can do this on my own.' He didn't want her putting herself at risk.

'No, you can't, you need backup.' Jessica was determined.

'Then it should be me.' Valentina pressed.

'No.' Jessica raised her voice, something she rarely did. 'John can make most of the repairs on his own, and if he needs another pair of hands I can manage perfectly well under his direction. But he is not going out there alone, and as Commander, it is my job to go with him,' there were protests again, 'and *as Commander* she raised her voice again 'my decision is final.'

They were all silent. She ran a democratic ship, but at times like this her word was law, that's how this worked. John could see the steel in her eyes, the set of her jaw, and knew there was no further argument.

'Now,' she continued, 'The only way to access the Aneris from the outside is through hatch two. It's a long way and it's going to take a lot of planning. Here's how it's going to work...'

Chapter Twenty-Seven
Countdown to re-entry: 2 months

John

'Can you hold this?' John handed Jessica the drill. Inky blackness yawned around them as they hovered, closely tethered to the underside of the ship.

'Got it.' Her voice came through the radio into his ear as she grasped the drill in her heavily gloved hand.

He looked up briefly and gazed along the length of the ship. The hatch they had left from was three quarters of the way down the ship and on the other side. It had taken them over fifty minutes to get into position. It was longer than they had anticipated, navigating their way along the craft using handrails and footholds, through the array of solar panels, while carrying the tools they would need for the repair.

He was hot and exhausted. They had been out for seven hours. Every muscle ached from holding himself steady while trying to concentrate on the repair. The Harmonia tumbled at thirty thousand kilometres per hour towards an Earth that still looked like a star to the naked eye.

He glanced up at Jessica, but couldn't see her face through the visor, only his own reflection. 'You doing ok?' He asked her.

'I'm fine.' She was tense, he could tell. They had both been on high alert for hours. 'How are you?'

'Hotter than hell, and my nose is itching.'

She laughed, and for a moment he allowed himself a break in concentration as he closed his eyes and let the sound of her voice wash over him. The intense planning of the past week that had been essential in anticipation of this EVA meant that they hadn't been able to talk any further about what was going on between them. John longed for the moment when they had finished this spacewalk and could find a private space just to collapse into each other's embrace. He would kiss her on the forehead and tell her she didn't have to worry anymore, he wouldn't put her under any pressure, he would wait and let her finish her job on the Harmonia. And if he was really lucky she might agree to be with him when they returned to Earth. He wanted to go with her to her warm, welcoming apartment and never leave.

'EVA2, how's it looking?' The call came to John from Lucca inside the Harmonia, who was overseeing this space walk.

'I just need to put the panel back in place and seal it shut. Another twenty minutes, I really need to give the bond a few minutes to set before I put the cover on and we'll be on our way back.'

'Copy that EVA2, don't leave it much longer than that. You need enough oxygen for the journey back. Can you skip the drying time?'

'Negative, Harmonia. I need to know it's done right. Jessica and I could also use a break before starting back, we'll use that time.'

'How long have we got, Harmonia?' Jessica asked.

'You've got around two hours at the current levels, so you know, try not to exert yourself or breathe too hard.' Assessing the oxygen levels was an inexact science. It could be affected by levels of exertion or simply how much the astronaut talked.

'Yeah, thanks for the tip.' She turned back to John. 'Are we going to get it done?'

'Of course. Hand me that back.'

She passed him the drill.

'We can come back and finish it off another day John. I don't want us taking any more risks than we have to.'

'Another EVA is a whole new set of risks. Trust me, Jessica, I'll get it done.'

'Alright, I'll let you concentrate.'

'It's fine, I can multitask.'

'No, I'll stop talking.'

He turned to face her, though they couldn't see each other's faces through their visors. 'Don't ever stop talking to me, Jessica.'

'I won't.' said Jessica. He could hear the smile in her voice.

'Ok, bond is on, Harmonia, could you time us at ten minutes please and give us a call? We're going to go off comms until then.'

Jessica's head turned slightly toward him as he mentioned them going off comms.

'Roger that, off comms and timing you at ten minutes, talk in ten.'

His in-helmet display registered that comms to Harmonia had dropped. He and Jessica were on a private channel.

'Are you off comms, Jessica?'

'Yes,' she said, with a curious tone. 'I assume the comms drop is to save oxygen?'

'Not one bit,' said John, 'I thought we deserved some private time. Come on, sit with me.' He leaned back and hopped up to sit on top of the capsule, their various tethers holding them in place.

'Surely there's something else we should be doing while we're waiting?'

'Look, we can't do anything for the next ten minutes. Just sit with me, you never just sit.'

'Nor do you.' Jessica retorted.

'Then it'll be a novelty for both of us. See? Not a bad view, right?' said John.

He turned the transparency of his visor down to twenty percent. The gold reflection was designed to protect them from the direct light of the sun, but it was behind them at this moment.

'Can you see me?' he said, turning towards Jessica.

'Yes.'

'I want to see you.' She adjusted her visor. John could see her brown eyes looking at him.

They were both perched awkwardly in their spacesuits on the curve of the capsule. The charcoal expanse of space stretched infinitely around them in every direction. The stars in the sky didn't look bigger. In the grand scheme of the universe, they were no closer to any of them than they would have been on Earth. Outside of the Earth's atmosphere, they didn't twinkle, they just shone a steady light. A sense of calm settled over him that he couldn't remember ever feeling before. All the things he had been worried about for the past few weeks had left his head.

'It's so strange,' he wanted to explain the sensation to Jessica. 'We're sitting on the edge of a spacecraft, hurtling through space at thirty thousand kilometres per hour, trying to fix a thing that we don't know whether or not it's going to kill us in a few weeks' time when we try to return to Earth, and I have never felt so at peace.'

'I know what you mean. Look at it out there. It's just so much bigger than us. We're not even a drop in the ocean compared to this universe. Not even a grain of sand. It all just pales into insignificance, doesn't it?'

They both stared out into space in companionable silence. He didn't need to talk, he was happy just to be with Jessica. But at the same time, he wanted to make the most of this moment when they were undisturbed. He wanted to tell her everything that was going through his head and his body.

'Do you know,' he began, 'this is the most alone we've been in over a year. No one listening in. No one able to walk in on us. Just you, me, and millions of miles of space.'

'That's very profound, John,' Jessica teased.

'Wait, I can do better than that...' He thought for a moment, 'Um, ok. A billion trillion stars out there and not one shines as brightly as your eyes.'

She burst out laughing. He loved that he could make her laugh like that.

'Hey,' he said with mock indignation. 'That was my best line.'

'I'd hate to hear your worst.'

'There's still time.' He paused. 'Jessica, I don't even know how to begin to describe how I feel about you. None of the words I can think of are anywhere near enough.'

'I haven't made it easy for you John, I'm sorry.' Her face crumpled under her helmet.

'You don't ever have to say sorry to me Jessica.' He put a gloved handed over hers.

'I know I've pushed you away.'

'You've been worried about the mission, I know.' He wanted her to know he understood, he didn't blame her.

'I don't think it was just the mission.' She was hesitant as she spoke.

He forced himself to stay quiet, to give her space to talk. It was typical of Jessica to stifle her feelings for as long as she could, though unable to hide that something was wrong. He would search for every clue to try and understand, but in the end, it would be just a matter of waiting for her to be ready to talk.

'I was scared.' She looked straight ahead as she said it.

'Scared?' He remembered sitting next to her on Cocoa Beach telling her he had been scared at the Harmonia launch.

'Scared that if I let you in, if I gave into it you'd realise I wasn't enough for you, and you'd leave. You know, like.' She hesitated.

'Like your dad did?' He said, wanting desperately to hold her.

'Yes,' she said in a small voice.

'Oh, Jessica. If you only knew... if you could just see inside my head how I feel about you...' Now he was the one struggling to articulate himself.

'I need to tell you,' she said as he went quiet. 'It doesn't matter whether you had worked on the heat shield or not, you're the person I wanted out here with me.'

'Really?' He still couldn't quite believe it.

'Of course.' She sounded surprised.

'Why?' He wanted to know, wanted to hear her tell him.

'I trust you more than anyone else in the world, John. You're smart, you're the best at what you do, and you're the bravest person I know.'

'You want me out here because I'm good at my job?' He knew he sounded petulant. He just wanted to hear how she felt about him.

'It's more than that, John, you know that.' Her low voice sent a tremor through his body.

'Tell me what it is?' He pressed.

She was quiet for a few minutes. Had he pushed her too far?

'Every time I see you my heart does a little leap. Every time, even after all these years. When you hold me, I feel light. Like all my worries are just seeping away, and I never want you to let me go. But when you do, the smell of you stays on my skin and I can imagine you are still there.' Her voice was soft, so far from her usual authoritative tone.

'Jessica...'

'It's more than that though,' she hadn't finished. I can't think of anyone else I'd rather spend seven hours in the middle of space with, and I still want to go back and spend the night talking to you. I could spend the rest of my life talking to you and never get bored.'

'Jessica...' He began again. She had articulated exactly how he felt. 'I could spend the rest of my life talking to you too.'

'Then let's do it,' she said.

'Do what?'

'Spend the rest of our lives talking to one another. When this is over let's spend the rest of our lives together.' She looked him clearly in the eyes as she said it.

'Are you really serious?' Warmth flooded through him. He couldn't believe what she was saying. It was the thing he wanted most in the world.

'John, have you ever known me to be anything other than serious about anything?' She looked at him sincerely.

'I love you Jessica,' It felt so good to say those words. 'And I will spend the rest of my life making sure you know how much.'

'I love you too John.' Her words poured into him, spreading warmth throughout his body.

She took his hand in hers and, through their thick gloves, they grasped each other tightly. They couldn't feel the contact, but they knew it was there. As they looked out into the vast expanse of space John tried to etch this moment in his mind. He wanted to remember this feeling for the rest of his life.

'EVA, this is Harmonia, that's ten minutes.'

'Thank you, Harmonia.' John replied. He knew their time must be nearly up, but they had said everything important that they wanted to say.

'John, you're not on comms!' Jessica laughed, releasing his hand with a playful push. He had forgotten to switch channels.

'Oh crap!' John said, laughing then composing himself, and in his most serious and deep CAPCOM voice said 'Thank you, Harmonia, copy that.'

John and Jessica giggled together. It was so natural. They could have been sitting on a wall at home. He loved that they could go from serious to giggling like guilty teenagers in seconds. No one had ever provoked such a range of emotions in him.

'I am a professional astronaut, I promise!' he said as he reached into his toolbelt for the final piece of covering to fix onto the cracked area of the heat shield.

'How long John?' said Jessica, slipping back in Commander mode. She was impatient again. He didn't care. They had forever.

'I'm doing this right, Jessica.' His voice was patient. 'There will be a time in a few weeks where we will all be sitting in this thing, holding hands, hoping I did a good job.'

'Understood,' said Jessica.

He knew that 'understood'. It usually meant 'I don't agree, but I'm going to allow you to carry on,' and he sensed the return of her unease. He didn't waver. It was important to get it right.

Every minute that passed felt like ten and the pressure was on to get back in before they got too low on oxygen.

'Ok, done' John turned to Jessica to give the thumbs up as he packed away the last of his tools.

'Ok, Harmonia, we're coming back to you'

'Copy that, at current O2 levels you have ninety minutes to get back in, journey out there took fifty-five, plenty of time, take care'.

'Thank you, Harmonia, John and I are moving back in.' Jessica turned to John. 'Let's go'.

They made their way along the exterior of the Harmonia, one step at a time, searching for footholds and handrails, detaching and reattaching the tether. John looked over Jessica's head towards the hatch that would get them safely back inside; it didn't seem to be getting closer. He cursed their slow progress. EVAs and the training he had done underwater had always tested his patience.

The route loomed steeply ahead as if they were climbing a skyscraper one step at a time, although in space there was no up or down. They had been out here for hours; their bodies exhausted. What he was feeling was normal. They must be making progress, but he felt like he was on a treadmill, his body moving but not going anywhere. His head was cloudy and his chest heavy.

'Jessica,' said John, chewing on the words. His tongue felt like it was expanding, like it might block his airway. 'I need to stop for a minute.'

'Are you ok, John?' without waiting for an answer Jessica spoke into her headset 'Harmonia, we're just going to take a few minutes, halting progress.'

'Copy that. Would you like an O2 readout?'

'Negative, just give us a few minutes.' She turned to face him.

Distantly he wondered why she had refused the O2 readout; it was a standard procedure. The thought slipped away as quickly as it came.

'I'm fine, just need to catch my breath.' The weight pressed harder. John felt like he couldn't fill his lungs. White dots danced in front of his eyes.

'John, just breathe, breathe slowly.'

Her words made John's chest feel tighter. 'I don't know what's happening.' Was he running out of oxygen already? He thought they had more time.

'It's OK, John, just breathe.' She dimmed the display on her visor again so that John could see her. She looked calmly at him.

'We're so far away, Jessica,' he struggled to get the words out.

'John, this is totally fine, you're fine. You just need to concentrate on your breathing.'

Chapter Twenty-Eight

Countdown to re-entry: 2 months

Jessica

'Jessica, this is Harmonia, we are only speaking to you, John's heart rate is high.' Lucca's voice in her ear was concerned. Jessica forced down the panic that was rising. She needed to be calm for John. She had never seen him like this before. It had been a gruelling EVA. They were both exhausted.

'John, how are you doing?' Jessica knew that making him speak would disrupt his breathing pattern, but it was essential to test his awareness.

'I'm ok, I'm sorry, I just lost focus there for a second. I'm good, let's go.'

Jessica hesitated but John motioned forward. 'Come on let's go'.

'Why don't you go ahead of me.' She asked.

'So you can keep an eye on me? I'm fine Jessica, swapping positions is not what we need right now.'

Jessica moved along the handrail, her foot reaching out for the next foothold. Suppressing her unease at not being able to see him, she tried to sense John's progress behind her. He was right, changing positions would waste valuable time and resources, as would trying to persuade him. The sooner they got back in the better.

'O2 check, Harmonia.' Jessica called over the radio.

'Copy that, Commander. Jessica forty-two minutes, John, thirty-three minutes. We have you twenty minutes out, so keep this pace please.'

There was silence. This was the first time Harmonia had called their O2 levels separately. Jessica wondered if John had noticed.

'I didn't panic, Jessica.' John spoke in her ear.

'It doesn't matter, save your oxygen.' Jessica replied without looking back.

The pair stopped to unclip the tether they were attached to, and move the clip to a holding further along.

'EVA, this is Harmonia,' the loud and serious blast from the radio pierced the silence. The three words sounded ominous.

'Go ahead, Harmonia,' said Jessica.

'We've detected a solar flare that will reach Harmonia in approximately eighteen minutes.'

'Jesus....' Jessica paused waiting for a response.

'Can we withstand it in our suits, Harmonia?' John asked.

'It's right on the limit EVA, stand by.'

They were quiet for a few seconds.

'Awaiting instruction, Harmonia,' Jessica reminded them, though she knew that they would be racing through possibilities.

'Just keep going, John.' Jessica pressed. They had no other choice.

Chapter Twenty-Nine
Countdown to re-entry: 2 months

John

'Harmonia, instruction please!' He choked out the request, his breath shallow again. His dry tongue stuck to the roof of his mouth; the muscles at the back of his head tightened; he could feel the pulse of his blood in his ears. His skin tingled as it dawned on him how exposed he was, they both were. At the mercy of elements that their bodies weren't built to withstand, with only a spacesuit and a rapidly emptying oxygen tank to keep them alive. He almost laughed to himself as he thought about the folly of their mission. What human hubris it was to think they could take on space. They really were cowboys, trying to conquer the Wild West. What did Jessica call them? "Sooners". Staking their claim before they had a right to. Was the Universe exacting her revenge?

More seconds passed that seemed like hours as he and Jessica edged along the ship, waiting for further instruction.

'EVA this is Harmonia.' The radio crackled again through the silence, and in the short burst John could hear discussions still going on in the background.

'Go ahead, Harmonia'. Jessica replied.

'OK, we've calculated that the solar flare is sufficient for all of us to move into the shielded area, and we're calculating that the impact will be outside the recommended margins for the suits, but you don't have enough oxygen to have much of a delay.'

'So, what do we do, Harmonia? We're just standing here!' John shouted. Jessica reached out and put her hand onto John's arm. It didn't help. His breath felt short, his heart was beating in his ears.

'Ok EVA, we have some instructions. You are about ten minutes from the solar panel field, we think that if you can get behind a panel, it should offer enough protection for you. We think it's a short flare, under five minutes.'

'What about the oxygen and timings?' asked Jessica. Her voice remained calm and matter of fact, as if they weren't in imminent danger. Why wasn't she more worried? Didn't she understand what was going on?

'We have you roughly ten minutes from the panels,' Lucca's voice came in his ear again. 'You might have to stay there for ten minutes till it's over, then it should be under ten back.'

'That's not a lot of time, can we have an O2 check?' said Jessica.

'EVA, we have Jessica on thirty-nine minutes of O2 left, and John on twenty-nine minutes.'

'Ok, Harmonia, we're moving towards the panels,' Jessica continued moving and John followed without speaking.

His movements became automatic, honed through years of training. He tried to think through the fog that was threatening to take over his mind. What were the numbers? Twenty-nine minutes of oxygen left. Ten minutes to the panels. Solar flare starting about five minutes after that. Five minutes till it passed if they were lucky. Nine minutes of oxygen left. Lucca said it was under ten back.

He let the numbers swim around his head. It would be close. There would be oxygen in his helmet for a few minutes even when the tank was empty. He had once pushed his luck with the fuel in his car before they all became electric. How far could he go when the fuel display read '1 mile'? The nearest petrol station was three and a half miles away. As the fuel display had changed to zero he had willed the car to keep running on fumes. A quarter of a mile away the car had given up, and John had walked the final distance. Would his tank give him the extra two miles?

The four solar panels that powered Harmonia were ten foot wide and set a few feet away from the shuttle. They could shield under a single panel. Jessica had remained quiet since the last instruction. Was she just conserving oxygen or did she not know what to say?

Jessica arrived at the panel first and climbed underneath. John followed her. They tethered themselves to the panel supports, gently floating under its protection.

'Come here.' Jessica pulled John towards her. She had always seemed so much smaller than him, though the bulky spacesuits evened them out a bit. But in this moment her strength engulfed him.

They floated together between the shuttle and the panel. He could feel Jessica's arms through the suit, wrapped around his waist. His arms rested around her shoulders. John could hear the occasional knock of their helmet bubbles as they shifted in each other's arms. Jessica momentarily let go of John to press the control panel on her forearm, and her visor cleared so he could see her face; it was taught, and her eyes were wide.

'Babe,' he swallowed hard, but he didn't know what else to say. He had adjusted his visor to ninety percent so they were looking directly at each other. Still no words.

Their eyes met in understanding. It was the two of them from here, and it always would be.

'It'll always be you, Jessica.' There was nothing else he could stay.

'John, I'm sorry. It's my fault you're here. This is all my fault. I'm sorry.' The last words were a whisper. She was struggling to hold back tears.

'Jessica, no, don't say that. It's going to be ok. We're going to be ok.'

'OK, EVA, flare has passed, you're clear to proceed, hurry!' The words crackled in his ear, and they were both alert again.

Chapter Thirty
Countdown to re-entry: 2 months

Jessica

'Let's go' Jessica didn't wait for a response. 'Harmonia, this is Jessica,' she pressed a button and spoke quietly into a private channel. 'O2 checks every minute, just to me.'

'Copy that, Commander'.

Jessica looked to her side every few steps to make sure John was following her. She could see the entry hatch, but it seemed like miles away.

'O2 check, Jessica nine minutes, John two.'

'How many minutes out are we?' she fired back. Jessica and John were both completely focused on unpinning their tether and climbing up the ship.

There was a pause before Lucca's voice crackled in her ear. 'Just keep going.'

All she could see was the expanse of the ship ahead of her. Why was it taking them so long? She just wanted to get John back in the craft safely.

'This is Harmonia, Jessica five minutes, John one. Valentina is suiting up to come and help you.'

'Jessica, I must be running close to empty, we've still got so far to go,' said John.

'John, we're nearly there. They're coming to help us' Her stomach lurched but there was no time for fear right now. She looked back at John. He had stopped.

'Jessica, don't wait for me,' John's voice was growing quieter.

'This is Harmonia, Jessica four minutes, John is out.'

Chapter Thirty-One

Countdown to re-entry: 2 months

John

He was surprised that it didn't feel different yet. The alarm from his suit was pounding in his ears, telling him that he was out of oxygen. But it didn't feel how he thought it would. He could hear Jessica speaking in his ear, but it was muffled like he was underwater.

He could see the hatch open behind Jessica. Another member of the crew came out. He should be able to tell who it was, each one of the crew moved differently, and had different markings on their suits, but he couldn't tell for some reason. His head felt light, the way it had done earlier, but he didn't feel the same sense of panic as before. The beeping of his suit alarm was growing more distant.

'Jessica, I'm done.' He wasn't sure if he had said the words out loud.

She turned to face him 'They're on their way John, keep with me, stay with me.'

'It's ok,' he told her. He needed her to know it was ok. He was ok. It was just his eyes felt heavy; he was tired. 'I just need to sleep.' He tried to form the words, 'But it's you, Jessica. You're it for me.'

Chapter Thirty-Two
Countdown to re-entry: 2 months

Jessica

'Harmonia, John is unconscious.' She had stopped moving towards the hatch and was facing John.

'John? Can you hear me?' Jessica could see his eyes were closed and he wasn't responding.

'This is Harmonia, Jessica one minute, John zero'.

'Jessica, this is Valentina, I'm nearly with you, I have the winch cord with me. Tie yourself to John as close as you can.'

Jessica faced John, again with their helmet bubbles touching. She connected the belt of his suit to hers with a carabiner. She wrapped her arms around his waist, and for the first time ever he didn't grasp her in return. She choked back a sob as she held his unresponsive body. There was still time. He would be ok.

She felt a shunt as Valentina came up behind her and connected herself to Jessica.

'OK, I have them both, pull us in.' Jessica could hear Valentina speaking. Her body lurched and she tightened her grip on John.

'John, stay with me please, stay with me please,' Jessica begged, her head light, her eyes swimming with tears. 'I'm so proud of you John. We're all proud of you.' Everything around her started to fade away. She forced her eyes to stay open, focusing on John. The spaceship passed by in the reflection of his visor as they were winched towards the hatch.

Jessica's arms were heavy, her grip on John started to loosen. Everything was slow and muffled as if she were underwater, and when the words came they sounded far away.

'This is Harmonia, Jessica zero, John zero.'

Chapter Thirty-Three
Countdown to re-entry: 2 months

Jessica

'Jessica, can you hear me?'

'John? John? Speak to me, John?'

'Extremities are blue.'

'What're the O2 sats?'

'Seventy-nine.'

'That's not good.'

It was cold, so cold.

'Are you getting a pulse?'

'I can't feel anything.'

'Jessica, can you open your eyes?'

'John, sweetie, can you hear me? I'm putting this mask on you to try and help you breathe.'

'Are the sats going up?'

'No, still dropping.'

Disembodied voices drifted around. Faces blurred in and out of focus.

'What's the GCS?'

'Jessica, I'm just going to shine this light into your eyes.'

Too bright.

'GCS nine. I'm getting some response.'

'Ok, keep on with the oxygen.'

A mask. Limbs being lifted.

'No, sweetie, you've got to keep the mask on, it's going to help you.'

'Lucca? GCS.'

'I'm not getting any response.'

'Alright, start CPR.'

The voices pause.

'Nothing's happening.'

'Keep going.'

There is the sound of heavy breathing.

'Come on, come on, don't do this. We've got a spacecraft to fly. We need you.'

The light was still too bright. There were hurried movements.

'Lucca, I don't think it's working.'

'It will, we can do this.'

A pause again, only the sound of gas in a mask. It is cold but tasteless.

'Lucca. It's too late.'

'Come on, one, two, three. Come on, breathe.'

'Lucca...'

'Come on. May, can't we just use more oxygen?'

'It's too late Lucca. Lucca, you have to stop.'

'No, no. Come on, come on breathe. One, two, three...'

'Lucca, stop! Lucca, we've done everything we can.'

'You're a doctor May, isn't there anything else you can do?'

'You know there isn't.' There was a long silence.

'I'm going to call it.'

'No!'

'John Eden, time of death, six thirty-seven p.m.'

Everything stood still. There was no more movement.

Chapter Thirty-Four
Eight years earlier

Jessica

Jessica reached through the water of the neutral buoyancy pool to the handrail of the practice frame. She blinked a few times, exhausted through lack of sleep and exertion. Her eyes closed for a fraction of a second too long, and she missed the hold. Foot slipping, she floated backwards into the water, away from the frame.

'Damn it!' she screwed up her eyes in frustration, and she tried to right herself in the bulky EVA suit.

'Gabriel,' a voice crackled sharply through her headset 'Back to the surface. Now.'

She lumbered her way over to the steps of the pool, her spacesuit restricting the movement of her limbs, the water resisting her body. One awkward step followed another. Surfacing from the pool she came face to face with a squat, broad-shouldered, bald-headed man. Commander Daniels was their instructor at the Neutral Buoyancy Laboratory, NASA Texas. One of the other trainees, who had been observing the exercise on video by the pool, helped remove her helmet.

'What the hell happened, Gabriel?' He began yelling as soon as she emerged from under the helmet. 'That was a rookie mistake, and you, young lady, are no longer a rookie.' His bushy moustache bobbed up and down as he spat the words out. Her cheeks burned at being called 'young lady'. They had only been out in Texas for a month, but already she had felt the full military influence within NASA. She longed for the European politeness of NARESA HQ.

'I'm sorry, Commander. I just slipped.' It was such a stupid mistake. She hated admitting it.

'Just slipped? Honey, you slip in space and you die. You understand that?' Spittle gathered at the corners of his mouth.

'I'm tired. We've been down there for five hours.' It was unlike Jessica to talk back to an instructor, but Commander Daniels's patronising tone and ill humour brought out a rare streak of defiance.

'Oh, you're tired? We're all fucking tired, honey. I've been tired for thirty-five years! You want to get into space? You better work on that stamina. Now dry off and I don't want to see you back here till you can stay the course.' He pointed to the suit room door.

'Yes, sir.' She walked with all the dignity she could manage in the spacesuit to the suit room. Inhaling deeply through her nose she walked past the group of students observing from the video bay, determined not to catch anyone's gaze, especially John's. The last thing she wanted right now was anyone's sympathy.

Standing in the middle of the suit room, hit with the realisation it was going to be almost impossible to get out of her suit without any help, Jessica willed herself not to cry. Out of the pool, she ached more than ever. Twisting one of her gloves with the other heavily gloved hand, she heard a noise at the door. *Please, not John.*

'Hey.' It was May.

'Don't.' She shook her head without looking her in the eye. 'Just don't say anything.'

'I wasn't going to,' she said, her voice neutral. 'I just figured you'd need some help getting out of your suit.' True to her word she helped Jessica get out of the suit without saying anything else.

'Thanks,' Jessica said, hoping May knew without her saying just how grateful she was for her calm and practical support.

'No problem. Go and get some rest.' She headed back to the poolside. 'Hey, don't forget we're all going to Chuck's for chicken and fries this evening.'

'I think I'll give it a miss.' She sank down onto the bench. 'I'm not in the mood.'

'Don't let him get to you, Jessica.'

Jessica grimaced. 'I won't. I just need some space tonight.'

'Ok. Catch you soon.' May returned to the session.

Later that night she put on her running gear and ran the five miles back to the Lab. Breathless and sweating, she scanned her key card, praying that it would let her in at this time of night. The door opened with a satisfactory beep and a click. She made her way through the empty corridors back to the observation bay beside the pool, where she found the video recording of the session earlier.

Discomforting thoughts streamed through her head as she switched the recording on. *What if I'm not cut out for this?* She ran her hand through her hair. What if she didn't graduate from the programme? Everyone would know that she had failed: her grandmother, Hans, the rest of the trainees. She couldn't bear to let them down. *I can't afford to make another mistake.*

An hour later Jessica was disturbed by a noise. She looked around. The video screen was giving off a ghostly glow in the absence of any overhead lights. She had sat in the dark not wanting to alert anyone to her presence. She heard another noise and the hairs on the back of her neck prickled.

'Please tell me you're at least watching porn.'

Jessica jumped out of her seat. 'Jesus Christ, John! What are you doing sneaking up on me like that?' Her heart beat like a drum in her ear. 'You scared the crap out of me.'

'I can tell.' He grinned.

'How did you know I was here?'

'Because, *honey*,' He mimicked Commander Daniels, 'you are just too predictable. You weren't at Chuck's so I tried your apartment. You weren't there, and I know you don't have any other sort of life outside of this job...' he shrugged. 'So, I assumed you must be here. Your car wasn't outside, but I asked the security guard at the gate and he confirmed he'd seen a crazy lady in neon running gear, and I knew it must be you.'

Jessica tried not to smile, her lips pressed together. It wouldn't do for John to think she thought he was funny.

'You're watching the video from earlier aren't you?'

She didn't respond, avoiding his gaze.

'Jessica...' He walked into the observation bay.

'I just need to see what went wrong. Then I can do it better next time.'

'You made a mistake, that's all. You won't make the same one again. And you were right when you told Daniels you were tired. We've been working twelve hour days for the past few weeks.'

'I don't want to fail this training John. I can't fail.' She pulled at her bottom lip.

'Well, firstly none of us wants to fail. We all want this as much as you. Secondly, you are one of the smartest people in this programme.'

Jessica snorted in disbelief. Sure, she was a quick learner, but there were people on the programme with phenomenal brains and a much better grasp of all the mechanics of space flight than she had.

'Well, you're certainly the most dedicated and determined. And the nerdiest.' He grinned, but she remained impassive. 'C'mon Jessica, you don't have to do this. You are the last person who needs to worry.'

'I don't need you to come and rescue me, John.'

He frowned. 'I'm not trying to rescue you. I'm your friend and I've come to, um...'

'...rescue me?' She raised one eyebrow.

'No, that's not what I was going to say. I've come to... to cheer you up and suggest an alternative venue. That's totally different to rescuing.' The grin was back. He grabbed her hand and attempted to pull her up from the seat. 'Come on. I've got the car. There's a beer and some disgustingly greasy fried chicken waiting for you at Chuck's.'

Jessica groaned but left her seat. John pulled her to him by the waist and kissed the top of her head. 'Good girl.'

Jessica elbowed him in the ribs. 'And you can stop patronising me,' she admonished him, but she was smiling now. The tension in her body melted away. There was something about John that never failed to make her feel like life was going to be ok.

Chapter Thirty-Five
Countdown to re-entry: 2 months

Jessica

Numbers swam in front of Jessica's face as she tried to input data into her tablet. Her shoulders were hunched, eyes heavy with lack of sleep. Every time she closed them she saw his face and was jolted back to reality. It had been over two weeks, and each day she woke and remembered what had happened. The memory would crash over her like a wave, the feeling of suffocation so real she struggled to catch her breath. Each day she waited for it to pass, waited until her breathing returned to normal, and the panic subsided before leaving her cabin to join the rest of the crew for breakfast. Not that she felt like eating. It was as though her stomach contained a balloon, making it feel both full and hollow at the same time. She forced down enough food to stop the rest of the crew from noticing, trying to suppress the nausea that followed.

There was no longer laughter at the rundown each morning. Jessica just tried to get through the instructions for the day without looking at John's empty seat. There was a space on board that wasn't just a physical gap. She hadn't realised how much John had held them together as a group, how he had kept up morale on the long, relentless and identical days. Now he was gone there was a void. She rattled through the tasks as if the less time they spent as a team the less they would notice his absence. After the meetings, she would retreat back into her solitude. She didn't want to talk, didn't want to have to make decisions.

Giving up her task, she left the lab. Without thinking about where she was going she wandered along the corridor, past the medical rooms to the back of the ship. The corridor where she and John would meet, and whisper to one another, and kiss. The kissing. Oh, her body ached for him. She rested her forehead against one of the doors and pressed her palms against it. It was the locked room she had told John not to ask about. Now he was in there. The empty shell of the man she loved. It was her fault; he was here on the ship because of her. And he had been out making the repair because of her. She tried to swallow the lump that was heavy in her throat.

Her wrist monitor flashed with a message from May:

'Can you come to the med room as soon as you are free?'

Jessica took a deep breath to compose herself before heading along the corridor.

'How are you doing?' May asked as Jessica entered the room a few minutes later.

'Oh, you know, fine, considering everything. Honestly, you don't have to worry about me.' She tried to smile at her.

'But I am worried about you. And so are Mission Control. They've asked me to talk to you. They've sent me the readout from your bio implant.' She looked down at her tablet, reading from the screen. 'Your blood pressure is higher than normal. Your cortisol levels are up, your white blood cell counts are low.' She looked up at Jessica, a serious expression on her face. 'You're stressed and you're not eating.'

'We're all stressed, May. And I am eating. Just, you know, not loads. I'm not hungry.' She shrugged.

'Are you sleeping?' May's eyes narrowed with concern.

'You know I'm not a great sleeper at the best of times. And, well,' she sighed, 'this isn't the best of times.'

'Jessica, you have to look after yourself. You have a responsibility to.'

'Oh, do I?' Jessica sat up straighter, blood rushed to her face.

'Yes, you do. You have a responsibility to the programme. You are up here, in charge of this crew. You need to be on your game so we can get home safely.'

'Yeah, well maybe I'm tired of the responsibility. Tired of being public property. And tired of Mission Control knowing every bloody thing about me, sometimes even before I know it.' She jabbed at the tablet May was holding, showing her medical results. Her thoughts were still incoherent, a mist descending on her brain. But she could feel anger boiling up inside of her.

'Jessica...' May leaned forward and tried to place a hand on Jessica's.

'You know what May?' She snatched her hand away. 'It's just so completely ironic that Mission Control can monitor everything about us, when we go to the toilet, what we eat, what's going on in our bodies. All this stuff to try and keep us healthy on the mission, but for all their technology and checking up on us, they can't stop us dying when we hit the Earth's atmosphere if the repairs we made don't work. Yes, sure I'm a little bit stressed and tired and you'll throw some pills at me, but they're going to be fuck all use in a few weeks when we try and get home!' Her voice was louder than it had ever been on the ship. She couldn't control herself any longer. She no longer had the energy.

'Jessica...' May tried again, but Jessica bristled at her placatory tone.

'Don't you think it should be "Commander" Dr Wu? Seeing as I am the one with all the responsibility to everyone. I'm the one whose job it is to get us home safely!' She was being unreasonable now. She had never demanded deference to her position. Not only that, but May was one of her best friends. Her only best friend now that John and Rachel were both gone.

'Jessica!' May's voice was raised in return. 'We're all scared, and we all miss him.'

Jessica stared at her friend. The volume of May's exclamation took her by surprise. She was normally so calm.

'I know you are struggling,' May continued. 'But it's hard for us too. And it's not about you being Commander, or having responsibility,' her voice softened again. 'It's about being part of this team. This ship can only function when we work together. You tell us that all the time. And you're not functioning properly.' She avoided Jessica's eyes as she said the last sentence.

'Look,' May spoke again, 'I know it's hard for you. I know why it's harder for you than the rest of us.'

Jessica's head snapped up. What did May know? Had the crew guessed that her grief was about more than losing a crew member and a friend? Did they know that the bottom had dropped out of her world? That she might never be happy again? Did they know that she wasn't even sure if she cared whether she made it through re-entry?

'You were out there with him. But it wasn't your fault. There was nothing you could have done.'

Jessica was quiet for a moment. That wasn't quite true though, was it? There was a memory, one she hadn't been able to get rid of for the past couple of weeks.

'May, if only you knew. There were things I could have done differently.' She swallowed. 'I couldn't protect John. How am I going to protect the rest of you?'

'It wasn't your fault, Jessica,' she repeated.

'It was,' Jessica whispered, almost inaudibly. 'It's my fault he was even here.'

Chapter Thirty-Six
Two years earlier

Jessica

There were folders marked CONFIDENTIAL spread across the meeting room table, sheets of paper spilling out of them. Jessica was pouring over recent medical reports of the Harmonia crew. Hans Vogel, and Dr Cathryn Roberts, the NARESA chief psychologist were discussing psychological risk factors of each member. Also at the meeting was the NARESA flight surgeon Dr Raphael Cardin. This was one of the regular meetings they would have, now that the crew had been selected, to discuss how to get the best from the crew, and to manage the delicate dynamic of the five of them in close quarters for eighteen months.

Jessica studied one of the documents and frowned. 'Dr Cardin? What's this read out here?' she pointed to a line on a medical report.

'That is a slightly raised heart rate, what's known as tachycardia.' He spoke perfect English but with the rapid cadence of a French accent. 'But we are satisfied it is within an acceptable limit. And in the context—'

'Context?'

'There are no other underlying health issues. Mike Sanders is in excellent health. Sometimes these things just happen due to other factors.'

'What sort of factors?' Jessica asked.

'Strenuous exercise, anxiety, stress...'

'Well, space travel is a nice relaxing occupation, so I'm sure things will be fine.'

'Commander Gabriel...'

'No, really, it's like a trip to the Maldives.' She leaned back in her chair and waved her hand flippantly.

'Jessica? What is the problem?' Hans broke off his conversation with the psychologist.

'I'm worried about these numbers,' she handed him the report, pointing at a row of data.

'I've seen them. It's fine. It's within an acceptable margin.' He waved his hand dismissively.

'Acceptable margin?' Jessica inclined her head.

'Yes.' He replied slowly. 'We talked about it during the selection process and agreed that it wasn't something that was a cause for concern.'

Jessica turned to the flight surgeon. 'Dr Cardin, what sort of things can tachycardia lead to?'

'Often there are no symptoms other than a raised heart rate.'

'But what could happen?'

The doctor turned to Hans questioningly. Hans merely shrugged in return which the doctor took as permission to answer the question.

'The patient may suffer from dizziness, headaches, anxiety. But Commander Gabriel, these numbers, though higher than usual, are still within NARESA's acceptable limit.'

'Isn't fainting a symptom of tachycardia?'

'Yes, it can be.'

'And what's the worst-case scenario?'

'I've reviewed the full medical file and I am satisfied that in this case there is nothing to be concerned about. He is otherwise healthy and has shown no symptoms -'

'What's the worst-case scenario, Doctor?' Jessica was pushing hard, but this was her job. This is what they had chosen her to do.

Dr Cardin sighed and replied slowly this time. 'In very rare cases, tachycardia can lead to a heart attack.'

Jessica leaned back in her seat and puffed out her cheeks.

'Am I the only one who's worried about this?' she asked.

'Jessica, we've already discussed this.' Hans said patiently.

'Not with me. And I'm the one who might be a hundred million miles away with an ill, or worse, dead crew member.'

Hans sighed and put his fingers to his mouth thoughtfully.

'Ok Commander Gabriel, what do you suggest?'

'Swap him out.'

'You think we should deselect him?'

It would be awful. The end of Mike's career as he knew it. But with so much unknown and out of their control, Jessica wanted to minimise every risk that she could.

'You know how much respect I have for Mike.' She leaned forward, her hands flat on the desk. 'He is one of the best engineers I know, and he is great for the team. But we'd be foolish to take this risk when we don't have to. I don't want to take it. It's not fair on the rest of the crew, nor on him. If something went wrong there'd be very little we could do.'

'Who's backup engineer for Harmonia?' Dr Roberts asked.

'John Eden.' Hans replied, picking up John's folder and starting to flick through it. 'You want John on your crew?' He glanced sideways at Jessica.

'Yes, I do.'

'Is this personal Jessica?'

'What do you mean?' Her face was impassive but a slight tinge of pink appeared at the top of her cheeks.

'I don't like to get involved in people's private lives, but I know you and John are very close.'

She sat forward in her chair. 'That has absolutely nothing to do with this. Yes, we're friends. But we're all close, Hans. We're in this bubble,' she waved her hands around trying to explain what it was like. Hans knew. He'd been one of them. He knew it was a necessarily small world they lived in. So few people understood the absolute commitment it took to be an astronaut. It was a way of life. One that left little room for outsiders, which meant that they built close relationships within themselves.

'That's what it's like Hans,' she continued. 'A bubble. But that has nothing to do with this decision. You should know me better than that. John is one of the most talented and knowledgeable engineers in the pool. Plus, he is a team player, he gets on with everyone. He would have been my first choice.' She was aware that she was speaking very rapidly, and she sounded defensive. Nothing was more important to her than the success of this mission. She thought Hans knew that about her. She didn't like the insinuation she was anything other than professional.

'You are right that Mr Eden is very good at his job.' He leafed through John's file, though experience had taught Jessica Hans had greater insight to any of his team than was contained in these reports. 'And yes, I can see he is an asset to the team. But he also has a certain... disregard for the rules, don't you think?'

'He follows the ones that count Hans,' she replied quietly. 'He's just not a military guy like Mike. But that doesn't make him any less good at his job. In fact, we need someone who can think like John out there, where we're going to be on our own and going to have to improvise if something goes wrong.'

Hans appeared thoughtful.

'You must have rated him enough to put him on backup, Hans.' Jessica persisted.

Hans sighed again. 'Ok, let's look through his file...'

An hour later, after much debate, they had decided; Mike was to be grounded for medical reasons, and John was to be promoted to prime crew for Harmonia. They ultimately all agreed it was the best decision, but Jessica had pushed them hard.

It wasn't personal, she knew it wasn't. It was the right choice. She didn't want to take an avoidable risk with a member of her crew not at full fitness. She was sad for Mike, of course she was, he was a friend as well as a colleague. She had volunteered to be the one to tell him, it was her job to do that. He was going to be devastated, and probably angry at their decision. But she was right to support John for prime crew, he was the right choice. This was going to change both their lives.

Chapter Thirty-Seven
Countdown to re-entry: 2 months

Jessica

Jessica sat by herself on the observation deck later that day, her feet hooked under a rail to steady herself in the microgravity of the nose of the ship. The Harmonia continued her steady course back towards Earth, the continuous speed imperceptible to her occupants.

The crew had been avoiding Jessica since her outburst at May. She suspected they were giving her space, unsure how to handle her like this. She leaned her head against the window and stared out into the blackness beyond. It was a vast empty space, with almost nothing between their spacecraft, and the Earth five million miles away. She'd never felt so alone.

The spacecraft hummed and whirred around her as the systems that kept them alive continued to function routinely in the background. Outside of the craft it would be silent, with sound unable to travel in the vacuum of space. But it was a mistake to imagine that space didn't have sounds just because humans couldn't hear them. Various probes had recorded radio waves from planets that scientists had converted into soundwaves. The sounds were eerie and otherworldly, the whistle of the planet Saturn, the glacial creak of Jupiter, and the slow drumming heartbeat of Earth as jets of plasma hit its magnetic field. What sounds was her body making, undetectable to the naked ear? Did her limbs creak as they unfolded themselves from the shape of John? Did her heart beat slowly and indecisively, unsure whether to carry on? Was there a whistle through the cells of her skin as they stayed exposed and untouched by John's hands?

Her mind flashed back to the day in Hans's office, her insistence that John be on the prime crew. He wouldn't have been on board if it wasn't for her intervention. He would be back on Earth, angry at being left, envious at the crew being up here, but at least he'd be alive. Whatever she had told Hans, she had let her feelings get in the way. She had selfishly wanted John with her on the mission, and now he was gone forever. But she had also wanted to make him happy by promoting him to prime crew. Falling in love with John had happened without her realising it. If she had realised, would she have tried to stop it? Would she have been able to?

She had left herself open, vulnerable, she should have controlled herself. She clenched her fists and pressed them into her face, anger bubbling up inside her. She should have known better. It was her fault that everyone she had loved had left her; first her father, her mother dying, and now John. Both of them had died because of her, because of what she had asked them to do.

Her shoulders began to shake. Hot, salty tears pooled below her eyes. They didn't fall in microgravity, the droplets simply clustered together till she wiped them away with her sleeve. She bit down on her fist to stifle the wail that threatened to escape. A low guttural moan echoed around the cabin. It flowed through her body till she could have been weeping from every pore. She cried so hard that she could barely breathe.

She didn't know how long she had been sitting there before the tears ceased to flow. The anger that she had been feeling started to ebb away as if all it had needed was releasing. She felt calmer than she had in a long time. She leaned her head against the window again. Something caught the corner of her eye. She twisted her head but she still couldn't see it properly, she couldn't be sure... She shifted to the other side of the window. Yes, there it was. Standing out against the eternal darkness of space, shining in the reflection of the sun's rays, tiny, but unmistakably planet Earth. She laughed out loud in disbelief. She had almost forgotten that it actually existed.

The thoughts of home, with its trees, and fresh running water, and blue skies, had all seemed like a world away. It was all real again. But the real world was now a world without John. She'd been afraid to think of it, unsure whether she wanted it.

She put her hand up to the window and tried to touch the Earth. With one finger she could blot out the whole planet. But it wasn't gone, and it never had been. Just because she couldn't see the Earth, it didn't mean it wasn't there. Just because she couldn't see John, it didn't mean he wasn't there. She could hear his voice telling her, 'Wherever you are Jessica, don't forget you are loved more than anyone could ever be loved. Nothing can ever change that.' She closed her eyes, and she could feel a warmth coursing through her body. An energy pulsed in her muscles that she hadn't felt since John died. She opened her eyes again and stared again at the glowing planet Earth. 'Guys...' she said softly into the silence. 'Guys? You have to see this,' louder now and more purposeful.

She pushed herself towards the door and headed back through the spacecraft calling for the rest of the crew. 'Guys? Guys! Come here. Val? Lucca? May? Come on!' Her words echoed urgently through the craft. She could have called them on comms, but her body just propelled her forward. She met them at the entrance to the capsule as each of them came rushing to find her.

'What's wrong?' May's voice was full of concern. 'Jessica, are you ok?'

'I'm great,' she smiled for the first time in weeks. 'Come with me.' She grabbed May by the wrist and called to the other two over her shoulder. 'Come on!'

They followed her along the passageway to the deck where microgravity forced each of them into the air.

Jessica directed them to the front of the enormous observation window. 'Look at that,' she said triumphantly. Each of them squinted out, and she watched their faces as it dawned on each of them what they were seeing. Valentina's face relaxed into a smile, May grinned, and Lucca burst into noisy tears. Home was within sight. They started hugging one another in mid-air and chatting loudly about what they were looking forward to back on Earth. It was although for a few minutes they could forget that they weren't yet sure if they were going to make it; for a few minutes they forgot that one of them hadn't.

Jessica contemplated them all. Each one of them had been brave enough to volunteer for this mission. They had trained hard, and worked as a team. They had risked their lives for scientific endeavour, the benefits of which they would be unlikely to see in their lifetimes. And even now, as they were about to face their biggest risk, one which they may not survive, they were here, talking and laughing, supporting each other.

'Hey, team,' they pulled apart and fell silent, even now, automatically responsive to her command. 'I'm... I'm really sorry, I haven't been on my game these past few weeks. I haven't been there for you like I should have been. I'm just... I'm sorry.'

May grabbed her hand. 'It's ok, Jessica. We understand why.'

'It doesn't matter why.' She looked earnestly at them. 'It's my job. My responsibility. I'm going to do better now I promise.'

'Jessica. It is ok not to be perfect all the time.' Valentina spoke quietly.

Jessica was silent. Valentina rarely offered psychological insights, but when she did they hit the mark like a precision missile.

Jessica turned to Lucca. His eyes were bloodshot and his face drawn. Jessica wondered whether he had been eating properly too. She should have been looking out for him. He gave her a brief smile then pulled her into a floating hug.

'He was like a brother to me,' he said, his accent thick with emotion. 'And I know how much he meant to you.' She wondered if he did know how much. She dismissed the worry, none of it mattered now.

'Lucca,' she pulled away and looked him in the eyes. 'We're going to do everything we can to get you home safely to your family.'

He nodded mutely.

'So,' Jessica said, trying to inject some brightness into her voice. 'What's the first thing we're all going to request to eat when we get back?'

Jessica quietly left the three of them talking excitedly about ice cream, and lasagne, making her way to the sleeping quarters. But it wasn't her own she was heading for. She hadn't been in John's room since he'd died. Everything looked untouched as she opened the door. Pulling open one of the drawers, she rifled through until she found what she was looking for. It was one of John's NARESA sweatshirts, navy with the NARESA logo on the breast. She pulled it over her head. It was soft and well worn. She stretched the neck of the sweatshirt up to her face and breathed in heavily. The heady scent filled her lungs; the faint aroma of coffee, the sweet essence of the oil John used as he worked around the spacecraft, the lingering smell of his skin. A thousand memories of John flooded her brain, running in the sunlit park together, cooking at her apartment, sitting on the edge of the Aneris capsule. The air left her body and she felt like her lungs might collapse under the weight of her grief. Steadying herself on the wall of the cabin she took a deep gasping breath.

You can do this, she told herself. *You have to do this for him, don't give up, don't let John down.* She steeled herself to go back to the crew, to be the Commander they needed, show them that she was here for them, ready to get them home. She took another breath of the soft cotton sweatshirt, and she wore it for the rest of the mission.

Chapter Thirty-Eight
Day of re-entry

Jessica

It was the last run-down meeting of the mission. They had spent the week preparing the re-entry module Aneris for undocking. They gathered up rock samples, evidence from all the various experiments they had been running, and all the equipment they would need for the three hour ride home. The Harmonia craft would remain in orbit, waiting for work to upgrade it and prepare it for another mission. Or would it just be mothballed? Jessica wondered. Either way, there had been a lot of work for them to do in the last week. It kept them distracted from thinking about the journey they were about to make. All the checks suggested that the heat shield was now fixed, but they wouldn't know for sure until it was too late to do anything about it.

Jessica had to force herself to eat breakfast. She needed the energy to get through the intense day, but her throat was dry and her stomach churned. The rest of the crew looked like they were forcing theirs down too. Jessica wondered if they felt the same sense of unease, a leaden feeling in their stomachs. Her arms were heavy as she pushed her hair back from her face.

'Look, there's a video here from mission control.' she said with a lightness she didn't feel. She pressed a button and it appeared on the big screen. It was Tom on his final CAPCOM shift.

'Hi, Harmonia crew,' he said 'We're all so proud of you and looking forward to getting you home safely. There are a few people here waiting to say a few words to you.' He panned the camera around and they saw members of each of their families. They were sitting in the large, comfortable family room at Cape Canaveral. Specially assigned liaisons were with them, people from the space programme whose job it was to support them while their family member was on mission. Big TV screens in the background of the room would, if they were lucky, show the live stream of the retrieval of the Aneris capsule. The crew would be stretchered out, and airlifted to the nearest military hospital for check-ups and quarantine before their families could see them.

Each family came to the camera in turn. Jessica recognised Valentina's parents and her sister. They spoke in guttural Russian. Though she could understand most of what they said she tried to tune it out, focusing instead on Valentina, who remained almost stoical, apart from a slight frown as she pressed her lips together, fists clenched under the table.

May's family were next, her father a bespectacled man with short grey hair, and her mother, petite with the same bobbed black hair as May.

'May, honey, we are so excited to have you back home.' Her mother spoke warmly, and May broke into a smile. 'We miss you so much. We're thinking of you. It's going to be a tough journey but we know you're ready for it and we're all ready for you here.' She told May how much they loved her and said goodbye. Mrs Wu did all the speaking, while Mr Wu stood mutely behind her, looking wan and lost. Jessica gave May's hand a squeeze as the camera transferred to Lucca's wife and two sons. Giovanna was beautiful, with curly dark brown hair and big brown eyes, but her olive skin looked pale, and her eyes had a haunted look. She spoke in rapid Italian, squeezing her boys as they spoke. The boys waved at the camera and said hello to their papa. It was clear from their excited faces that they had no idea about what had been going on. Lucca wept openly as he listened to their words. Jessica squeezed his arm, at a loss for any other way to reassure him.

'Jessie?' Only her grandmother called her that. Jessica's heart leapt. She had missed her so much; for years it had just been the two of them. At that moment she ached for a mother's touch; a tight embrace that told her everything would be ok, and even if it wasn't, she would be right beside her. Her grandmother looked drawn; her brows furrowed as she spoke. She was so unconsciously expressive, as her mother had been. 'I'm thinking of you all the time,' Her grandmother's voice, her accent still noticeable after all these years, was so familiar and soothing. 'You have done such a good job Jessie Joon, I am so proud of you. I will be here when you get back. And I will make you my *bamieh*.' As Jessica swallowed back the tears she could taste the fragrant Persian donuts that her grandmother had made her as a child. 'I love you *joonam*. Be safe.'

Jessica breathed deeply to stem the tide of emotion that was threatening to overcome her. She had to remind herself that all these people were a few hundred kilometres below them, waiting for them, unsure what would happen in the next few hours. She had to keep it together today, every task they had to execute was crucial.

Just as she was pulling herself together another person appeared on the screen.

'Hello Harmonia crew,' Jessica could recognise that English-American accented voice anywhere. 'I know losing my grandson must have been a shock for you. It was a shock for all of us. But exploration is not without risk, as you are all no doubt feeling acutely now. You have done a great thing, and you will be remembered for it well beyond your lifetimes. But we very much anticipate you being here in a short space of time so we can all celebrate your great achievement. And while we mourn for John, he died doing what he loved, with people he respected, and also loved.' Jessica felt Elizabeth's eyes boring into her own. 'He would have been encouraging you all to have hope and faith in yourselves, and in the people who have been supporting you for these past few years. You are pioneers, and in the true pioneer spirit, I know you will be brave. And we too will try and be brave as we await your safe return.'

The screen went black, and there was a sudden silence, though the faces and voices reverberated like echoes inside her head. For a moment she was no longer on the spacecraft, she was back on Earth, warm fresh air on her skin, listening to the sounds of everyday terrestrial life. She was mentally disconnecting from the Harmonia. For the first time in years, home was within her reach.

She was jolted back to the present by a squeeze of her hand. It was May.

'You ok?' she whispered.

'Yeah, fine.' But May just looked at her.

Jessica reached her hand up to brush away her hair and realised her face was damp. There were tears pooling on her cheeks in a way she had not realised and could not control. She was desperate to get her crew to safety, or what she had left of it. She had let John down, she couldn't protect him. Even if they returned safely, there would be a hole in her life where he once was. She wiped her face on her sleeve. She stood up, gave each of the crew a hug, and then said simply 'Let's get to work.'

***

Jessica looked at the thick leaf of checklists in her hand, pressing and depressing switches as she read down the list. They had simulated this hundreds of times, but the movements still felt awkward in their bulky spacesuits. Every surface of the tiny capsule was covered with controls or cargo. The Harmonia, which had felt cramped and claustrophobic at times now seemed vast in comparison. There was barely an inch to spare between her and Valentina who sat next to her, strapped into her chair. Each of the chairs was individually moulded to their bodies to minimise the impact of the brutal re-entry process. Jessica tried not to think of the John-shaped chair that sat empty behind her. They had shared out the tasks that would have been his, and NARESA had forced them to spend a difficult few days in the previous week simulating this in the capsule, so they would be ready for the real thing.

There was a constant stream of technical chatter between mission control and the crew in their capsule, as they went through each process. Tom was CAPCOM for their journey home. She imagined him sitting at the console in Mission Control, chewing on his fingernails and raking his hands through his black hair. Would he guide them to safety or would his be the last voice they heard? Either way, it was out of his hands. In a strange disembodied way, Jessica felt sorry for Tom. He would have very little control over the outcome, all they could do was hope that the repairs that John had made would protect them.

'Aneris, you are go for undocking from Harmonia.' His crackly voice sounded over the mic.

'Copy that Control.' Jessica responded.

Valentina flicked a switch and there was a series of loud clunks as bolts on top of the capsule decoupled itself from the main spacecraft. With each clunk the capsule shuddered, but Jessica and the rest of the crew didn't even flinch. They were trained to expect every noise so they could tell when something wasn't functioning normally. Besides, the ride was going to get far bumpier than this in a couple of hours.

Two hours later they were orbiting just a few hundred metres above the Earth's atmosphere. They were tantalisingly close to home. The vivid blue ocean glowed through the tiny portal in the side of the capsule. Jessica found the sight almost calming as if she were standing beside the ocean on a beach.

'Preparing for deorbit burn.' The voice of CAPCOM jolted her back to the control panel.

'Ready for deorbit burn.' Valentina spoke back. The front thrusters would fire and slow them down so they could make their descent through the atmosphere.

'We are go for deorbit burn.' Valentina pressed the button that ignited the thrusters. The capsule jolted and they were thrown back into their seats.

More than any other carefully planned manoeuvre, timing was crucial at this stage. The burn of the thrusters was precisely calculated to ensure they entered the Earth's atmosphere at exactly the right angle. Too steep and they would overheat and burn up on re-entry. Too shallow and they would bounce off the Earth's atmosphere back into space like a stone skimming off the surface of the sea. An image of John at the beach flashed into her mind. Her stomach twisted and she screwed up her eyes against the unbidden memory and focused on the task at hand.

Next to Jessica, Valentina concentrated on the thrusters, watching for them to automatically switch off, prepared to manually step in should the mechanics fail.

'Aneris, this is Mission Control, you are looking great. Preparing for atmospheric re-entry in twenty-three minutes.'

In around twenty-five minutes they would find out whether the repairs to the heat shield had been successful. Less than half an hour and they would know, one way or another.

They continued their last circumnavigation of the Earth before making their descent. There was no time to think as they continued through their checklists detailing the series of actions they each had to methodically take to get themselves home safely. Instrument lights flashed in front of them. The minutes passed like seconds.

'You are go for re-entry. Preparing for radio blackout in ninety seconds.' They would be uncontactable as they passed through the Earth's atmosphere.

'Expect to regain signal after three minutes. Aneris,' Tom paused 'good luck. We're waiting for you all.'

This was it. This was the beginning of the end of their journey. Jessica closed her eyes and allowed herself a few seconds to think of life back on Earth, her grandmother, her neat little apartment with its soft bed, pink cherry blossoms against cerulean skies, the smell of summer rain. She opened her eyes again to the array of instruments reading out their every move.

The capsule began to spin and judder more furiously than it had ever done as they hurtled towards the Earth. Jessica held her breath and gritted her teeth as she listened to the crunches and groans as the outside of the capsule grew hot. The calming blue ocean in the portal had been replaced with white hot flames, blazing at the edge of the capsule.

'You're still looking good Aneris. Sixty seconds to radio blackout.'

'Copy that.' Jessica checked the instrument panel, going through the motions she had practised hundreds of times. When they hit the comms blackout they would be on their own for three minutes, Valentina piloting them through the atmosphere, and they would find out whether the repairs John had made had worked.

Jessica started to feel the pressure of gravity on her body. It became harder to lift their arms. The pressurised flight suit didn't stop her feeling the tightness in her chest.

'Forty-five seconds to radio blackout.' Tom advised them.

A few seconds later Tom spoke again, this time his voice sounded concerned.

'This is Mission Control, we're getting anomalous biometric readouts on Captain Kareva. Has she lost consciousness?'

Jessica peered awkwardly at her pilot. 'Val? Val? Valentina?' Jessica could see her head slumped, her body pressed back into her seat under the extreme pressure.

'That's affirmative Control. Looks like she's passed out under the Gs.' Jessica hoped that was all it was. She would be operating on her own for this final part of the journey.

'Are you prepared to take over Commander Gabriel. We're going to lose comms soon. Do you copy?'

Jessica grabbed Valentina's checklist. They had practised this hundreds of times. She knew what to do, but the instructions swam in front of her eyes as sweat poured down her face. The air outside roared around them as the capsule soared through.

I don't know if I can do this. She squeezed her eyes shut and tried to breathe as her insides constricted, and her head rolled around as she battled against the G force. The temperature was almost unbearable. Was this it? Was this the moment when the Concordia capsule broke apart? There was a crunch and the capsule juddered harder. Jessica gasped, struggling to catch her breath.

'Aneris, do you copy?' Tom's voice spoke into her ear.

'I copy, Control.' Jessica replied, her voice hoarse.

'Jessica, you can do this.' His was firm but reassuring 'you've done this a hundred times. It's just like back in the sims. You can do it.'

She was so tired, she could barely move. For a second she was weightless again, in the safe arms of John, a million miles from Earth, and not yet encumbered by the fear for survival. There was a grinding of metal as the capsule buckled in the heat. Jessica suddenly felt the full weight of her body and the 5Gs forcing her back in her seat.

'Commander Gabriel? Jessica, you can do this. Jessica? Do you copy? We're about to lose you. Aneris...' There was just static. They were completely on their own for the next crucial minutes.

'Commander?' It was Lucca's voice in her ear now. She pictured Lucca's children waving to their papa on the camera, May and Valentina's parents, Elizabeth Eden. Her grandmother.

'It's ok Lucca, I'm on it.' Her voice strained under the force. 'Let's get this thing home.'

Chapter Thirty-Nine
Re-entry

Tom

'Aneris, this is Mission Control, do you read me?'

Silence.

'Aneris, this is Mission Control, do you read me?'

Tom stood over his console, his hand rubbing the back of his neck. Hans Vogel sat stoically in the chair next to him. Tom paced the same square of carpet that he had been standing on for the last three hours. Hans was resolutely still.

Another voice spoke into Tom's earpiece. 'We are at four minutes fifty seconds radio blackout,' reported one of the flight team.

'Hans, they were meant to be back in range nearly two minutes ago.'

'I know,' he said in a low voice. His face was taut. 'Search and Rescue, this is Mission Control, do you have sight of Aneris, yet?' he demanded in a louder voice.

'Mission Control, this is S&R,' Helicopter propellers thumped in the background. 'Negative sighting of Aneris.'

'Copy. Standing by for any reports.'

'Aneris this is Mission Control, come in, Aneris?' Tom pinched the bridge of his nose with finger and thumb. 'Come on, Jessica,' he muttered to himself.

'We are at five minutes forty-five seconds radio blackout.'

'Aneris,' Tom continued, 'this is Mission Control, do you read this, Aneris? Come in, Aneris.'

The entire room was silent. Every member of the flight team watched their screen, willing for a signal to return. Observers at the back stared up at the empty sky on the big screen.

'Aneris...' Tom began again, wondering if it was pointless.

There was a crackle of static. Tom held his breath. More crackling.

'Mission Control, this is Aneris, we read you.'

It was Jessica.

Tom released his breath and relief washed over him. He laughed shakily as her voice came over the radio again.

'Hope you've arranged a soft landing for us.'

Chapter Forty
Re-entry

Jessica

Jessica dimly registered the cheers in the background. 'We made it,' she whispered to herself. There was stillness for the first time since leaving the surface of Mars, her body now just a passenger of Earth, instead of falling through space.

She turned awkwardly to Valentina, who turned to her with an enormous smile on her face.

'We did it,' Jessica said to her. They clasped hands again. *You did it John,* she thought.

'You kids ok in the back there?' she called to May and Lucca, but all she could hear in response was shaky laughter.

They stayed reclining in their seats, listening to the sounds of the helicopters that had come to retrieve them. Adrenaline still charged through Jessica's body and blood pulsed in her ears. They would be stretchered out and quarantined for two weeks where they would be grilled by medics and researchers, and no doubt the press. And they would see their families, even if they couldn't touch them.

Jessica sighed and closed her eyes as the sound of propellers drew closer.

They were home. They had survived. They had been to another planet, the first humans ever to have done so. She had achieved her dream, and the world could be her oyster from now on. But there was a pain inside her that was nothing to do with the impact with the Earth. She had left a part of herself in space that she hadn't expected. The relief of making it home alive gave way to a feeling of emptiness. One of her crew had not returned. They had survived because John had fixed the heat shield. He had protected her, but she had failed to protect him. And in doing so she had lost the most important person in the world to her. The person who had filled her life with joy, and who had loved her for who she was. There would forever be a void in her life, but she could no longer just fill it with work like she once would have done.

She was jolted back to reality by a scrape of metal. The capsule lock opened revealing a patch of clear turquoise sky. Shakily she reached up and unclipped her visor. The smell of scorched earth and hot metal filled the capsule. A face in a hazmat suit appeared smiling widely through her visor. 'I hear you guys need a ride home.'

Jessica smiled, 'I think we do.'

The NARESA recovery crew employee turned to her colleagues and said 'They're all good in here, we're going to take the crew out, get them to the transport. Then we'll start on the freight, then we'll take the body last.' Jessica's heart lurched at her words. The recovery crew were just doing their job but she wished she hadn't heard that.

Not wanting to be heard, even in a whisper, Jessica said to herself '*You're home, John*'.

Chapter Forty-One
2 months after re-entry

Jessica

'We are here today not to mourn, but to celebrate the life of John Eden, who sadly lost his life while working in the service of his country, and on behalf of all of us, so we could understand a world so far from ours, and imagine a future beyond our planet. John died doing what he loved most...'

Jessica stood on the dais in the grounds of NARESA HQ, alongside the Harmonia crew. It was two months since they had returned to Earth. Thousands of people had come to the memorial service. World leaders and representatives of NARESA stood on the raised platform. The US President had flown to Germany to deliver a speech and was standing at the lectern, eulogising about a man she barely knew. By her side stood Elizabeth, looking small and pale, stoically surveying the crowd. *He would have hated all this fuss.* Next to Elizabeth stood Ingrid, tall and beautiful as ever. Though she and John had not been together when John died, the press had seized upon their previous relationship and she was being immortalised as the grieving girlfriend, a role that she had assured Jessica, in one of the few brief conversations they had had since her return, that she wasn't encouraging.

Jessica looked to the ground as another layer of sadness enveloped her. No one had known how much she and John meant to each other. In the weeks since she had returned she had been trying desperately to keep a lid on the overwhelming sense of grief that threatened to engulf her. People had congratulated her on her return for her achievement in being the first person on Mars, while at the same time commiserating her for the loss of her crew member. Jessica had lost the sense of how much grief it was 'appropriate' to display. No one knew the hole he had left in her life, and it made no sense to tell them now.

As the service wrapped up Jessica itched to escape. She slipped through the crowd of people. Since the return from Mars, and even before, someone from the NARESA public relations team guided her every move but for once she wasn't being escorted anywhere. Not knowing in which direction to travel, she headed for the first door she could see.

Inside the building, Jessica found herself in a situation she rarely found herself in during the day since her return from Mars; she was alone. A grey corridor stretched ahead of her, with identically framed photograph portraits on the walls. Directly in front of her was an old looking picture of a man, the brass plaque below it read 'Alexei Leonov, First Space Walk'. Jessica walked slowly along the corridor. It felt strange not to be subject to a rigorous schedule. She walked past a few more pictures and again stopped in front of 'Valentina Tereshkova, the first woman in space'. Jessica smiled, thinking of her own Valentina, who had returned briefly back to Russia where she had stoically tolerated a parade through Moscow in her honour before returning to NARESA to do what she loved best, flying.

Jessica started to walk again, her footsteps echoing along the empty corridor. Jessica stopped once more in front of the most well-known portrait in that collection 'Neil Armstrong, first human on the moon'. The portrait was a photograph she had seen a thousand times before, in textbooks, on documentaries and in history books. Armstrong was in his white space suit, holding his glass helmet at waist height, with a picture of the moon in the background. Jessica stepped back to take it in, and brushed against the portrait that was hanging directly opposite Neil Armstrong.

She turned to see something that made a thousand realisations hit home all at once. The plaque underneath the portrait read 'Jessica Gabriel, first human to walk on another planet'. She gazed upwards, taking in her official portrait, Jessica in her Mars surface suit, a broad smile on her face. Every other person who would ever view this picture would imagine it was joy at having been named the commander of the mission, but

Jessica knew the truth. She could remember the day of the photo clearly.

They had gone to the studio as a team, all wearing their Mars surface suits. Each of them had taken their turn in front of the camera, Jessica was last, sitting on the chair against a starry background. As she looked into the camera lens, she could see John over the photographer's shoulder. He had found a wig from somewhere in the depths of the studio and was wearing it pouting behind the photographer. Jessica had burst into laughter. The bemused photographer had said 'We want happy Jessica, but not hysterical.'

As Jessica glared at John his face became deadpan, but he was still wearing the wig, and she tried desperately to suppress her laughter. That smile, the smile for John, was the one that would stare back at people for generations to come.

A wave of enormity and grief flowed through her, and she momentarily lost control. She slid down the wall in front of her portrait and sat there, with her head in her knees, underneath the portrait of Neil Armstrong. Not quite crying, but also not far from it.

'Jessica?'

She looked up. It was Hans, staring down at her, his clear eyes full of concern. Any other time she would have leapt up, dusted herself off, embarrassed to be seen in such a state. But she was exhausted, she couldn't find the energy to move. With her mission complete she didn't have to pretend anymore; she no longer needed to be on her best behaviour. She rested her forehead back on her arms.

'It's quite the hall of fame isn't it?' Hans had sat down on the floor next to her. He was looking up at the portraits all around them. 'It must feel like quite a lot of pressure? But you deserve to be up there.'

Jessica remained silent, staring at the floor.

'I keep telling you Jessica, it wasn't your fault.'

'I was the Commander,' she croaked. 'I was in charge. It was my job to keep him safe.'

'You didn't do anything wrong.' His voice was gentle. 'No one blames you,' he said more firmly. 'No one at NARESA thinks you are to blame. Nor does anyone in John's family. Elizabeth Eden made that very clear.' He smiled wryly at her.

'If only I had done something differently. Planned better, anticipated the flares, kept John calmer. Bought him in sooner.' These were the thoughts that plagued her night and day.

'Jessica, the Commission found no evidence that you did anything wrong. You know that.' She looked up at him. Yes, her name was cleared. But there were institutional criticisms; NARESA itself had come under fire, particularly in the media. 'Without doubt, there are changes we have to make as an institution to make us fit for the future.' Hans said, reading her mind. 'I want you to be part of that future. Because I know you did everything right.'

'I was the one who persuaded you to put John on the crew.' A thousand commissions could clear her name. But that fact would always be true. John was on the mission at her insistence. Jessica screwed her eyes shut, and tried to suppress the sob rising in her chest.

Hans sighed. 'Jessica, I, and I alone, am responsible for crew selection. Yes, I take data from other sources, doctors, psychologists, trusted colleagues.' He emphasised the last two words and smiled at her as she lifted her head. 'But I didn't need persuading. John was the right person for the job. I know it was the right decision because you are sitting here next to me, safe and alive, because of John's expertise.'

'You know Jessica,' he looked up and down the corridor of portraits. 'I have seen dozens of men and women come through these halls, on the way into space. Most of them are either running towards something or running away from something. I wonder which it is for you?'

She looked down at her hands, trying to process his words. Obviously she was running towards something. It had always been about the dream to go to Mars. That had been what had driven her for so long.

Hans continued. 'Being an astronaut is an excellent profession to go into if you are afraid of committing to someone.'

'What?' She turned to him.

'The hours, the commitment, the long absences. All very good excuses to avoid being in a long-term relationship.'

'Why would you think I was avoiding that?' she demanded. He was wrong. He didn't know her as well as he thought.

'It's a natural response when you think that everyone you love will leave you, and you believe it is your fault.'

The words felt like a blow to her chest. That wasn't how it was. This wasn't some sort of psychodrama she had constructed in her head. People *had* left her. First her dad, then her mum, now John. And her mother and John had been in situations she had put them in. Of course it was her fault.

'It really wasn't Jessica.' How did he know what she was thinking? 'Not your mother, not John, and I am certain not your father.'

'How do you know?' she choked, 'Even I don't know why my father left me.'

'I know it was nothing you did. I am a father myself, as you know, and I can promise you that it was nothing you did. I would be proud to have a daughter like you.' He placed a hand over hers, an uncharacteristic show of affection.

'How do you know all this anyway?' she muttered.

'I know how to read psychologists' reports.' He replied gently. 'Do you think I would have given you one of the most important jobs in space exploration since Armstrong landed on the moon, perhaps the most important ever, without really knowing you?' He raised an eyebrow at her. 'You have to learn you are not responsible for other people's actions. You cannot control everything and everyone.'

She frowned at the floor as his words sank in.

'How ironic then, that you should be running away from getting close to someone on Earth, but then should find connection so deeply while on the way to another planet.' His tone was casual.

Jessica turned to look at him. He smiled at her rather sadly. 'I am truly sorry for your loss.' He knew about her and John. She could see it in his eyes. But they weren't admonishing, they were sympathetic.

'I'm sorry,' she whispered.

'You didn't do anything wrong.' She wanted so much to believe him.

'But Jessica,' he spoke more firmly now. 'It's time to stop running.' He got up from the floor. 'And I know you think that everyone you love leaves you, but there are plenty of people still here who care about you very deeply.' He gestured to a window, where outside people would still be around for John's memorial. 'Perhaps you should let them in.' With that, he walked down the corridor, back towards his office.

Chapter Forty-Two
3 months after re-entry

Jessica

A month after the memorial Jessica was back in England. Elizabeth had summoned Jessica to the home where she had retired.

Being in Elizabeth's house would have been a dream a few years ago. Elizabeth Eden would always be a hero to Jessica, even though in space royalty, First Person on Mars outranked First Female Commander. Jessica was still struggling with her new-found status, the media events, the autographs. Today though, Elizabeth, the house, the mementoes, all just remind her of John.

'How are you feeling about what happened to John?' Elizabeth was never one to mince her words. Jessica had grown used to answering questions about John, but his grandmother's directness was disarming, and she sensed she couldn't get the truth past her.

'To be honest, I'm struggling.' Jessica replied.

'Struggling?'

'Yes, I'm able to answer all of the usual questions I'm asked, about the mission, what went wrong, how John saved us. But I miss him, I didn't know how much I'd miss him.' Jessica looked away, she wouldn't let herself cry in front of Elizabeth, her idol.

'Jessica, I know.' Elizabeth smiled and put her hand on Jessica's shoulder, an intimate gesture for Elizabeth whom Jessica had never even seen hug her grandson.

'I can see it in your eyes Jessica, I know the look that you gave each other. I've been in love too you know. Even to the most practised, it's hard to hide when you're in love.'

Jessica tensed. What had John told her?

'I don't know what you're talking about.' She made one last ditch effort to deny it.

'Follow me dear.'

Jessica followed Elizabeth through the hallway to a brightly lit, smartly decorated living room. Two stiff looking sofas faced one another. A screen was hung on the wall between them.

'Take a seat Jessica.' she gestured to one of the sofas. Jessica sat down whilst Elizabeth walked over to the curtains and pulled them almost together so that the room became darker.

'I haven't been looking forward to this,' Elizabeth said, sitting down next to her.

'What is it? What's wrong?' Jessica put her hands on top of the older woman's.

Elizabeth turned to face Jessica and even in the darkness Jessica could see tears glistening in her eyes.

'I'm sure you remember filling out all of the pre-flight paperwork, and I know it was a prerequisite of all astronauts to complete a will.'

'Yes of course.' Where was this going?

'Well, you may remember supplying somewhere for NARESA to send your video diaries should anything happen to you.'

'Yes, I do remember that, ' Jessica replied.

'Well,' said Elizabeth, 'The default was that the diaries would go to your next of kin unless you supplied a different name. John's next of kin was his mother, but they weren't close, and he decided that I should get the diaries.'

Elizabeth reached out to the table in front of them and picked up a remote control.

Jessica could hardly breathe. Was she about to see John's video diaries?

'I don't think I should see these.' She put her hand on Elizabeth's wrist. 'These were the only things we had, the only place we could talk to ourselves, he may not have wanted us to watch these.'

'Oh Jessica, darling, he really did.' Elizabeth said.

She pressed a button on the remote control and the room filled with light as the TV lit up. Jessica blinked at the sudden brightness.

John's face appeared on the screen taking Jessica by surprise.

'Wait!' she cried, putting her hand on Elizabeth's wrist again. Elizabeth paused. John's face remained on the screen frozen in place. 'Wait,' she said more quietly. 'I just need a minute.' It wasn't the first time she had seen John on the screen since his death. The TV channels had repeatedly shown reels of John's pre-launch TV appearances. Each one had made her catch her breath. But this would be the first time she had seen recent videos of him, videos recorded since she had realised she was in love with him.

She took a deep breath. 'Ok.'

'Hi Grandma,' John's voice pierced the silence. The hairs on Jessica's arm stood up. She put her hand over her mouth as his familiar face filled the screen.

'So, if you're watching this Grandma, you're either watching it with me, because I've decided for whatever reason to show this to you, or, you're watching it because things haven't gone well. Let's assume it's the latter, as there is no conceivable way I'm going to watch myself pouring my heart out in front of you. That sounds like a really terrible way to spend an afternoon.' John said. He was dressed in his blue jumpsuit, in his room onboard Harmonia.

Jessica reached for Elizabeth's hand. It was soft and thin. She felt Elizabeth's fingers slowly curl around her own.

Jessica felt like a hole was opening in her stomach.

'So, Grandma, I imagine you're wondering why I put you down as the person who should get these diaries, well, it's because I knew you'd understand, I knew you'd be ok with this. You were right, Grandma, I'm in love with Jessica. I think you knew that before I did.'

Jessica felt a squeeze of her hand. She looked at Elizabeth, who was smiling knowingly.

'Um, well. These diaries are for her. I needed her to know how I really feel, in case I couldn't tell her.'

Jessica's head was swimming, her hands shaking. Seeing him on the screen, talking about her, it was overwhelming.

'Ok, Grandma, everything from here on in is for Jessica, so I'm afraid you're going to have to turn off. You know how much I love you, and that was easy to say because you're never going to watch this, I'm not going to die, no-one is ever going to hear me say these words except me, but anyway, leave the room please.'

Elizabeth released Jessica's hand, reached down and pressed pause on the remote. John's image froze on the screen once again.

'I haven't listened past here.'

'But don't you want to watch?' Jessica wasn't sure she could do this on her own.

'No dear, this is between you and him. He's insistent.' She smiled wryly.

Elizabeth stood up slowly and walked towards the door. 'I'll be in the room next door if you need me.' This time it was her voice that quivered. Watching this must have been painful for her too.

With Elizabeth out of the room, Jessica turned dazedly to face John again, frozen in time on the screen. The room was dark, John appeared as large as life on the screen. She could almost imagine they were sitting opposite each other.

Steeling herself, Jessica pressed play on the remote. John was just sitting there, looking straight into the camera, directly at Jessica.

'Come on, Grandma, leave the room!' said John with a smile.

Jessica laughed at John expecting his grandmother to be reluctant to leave.

They both sat there in silence looking at each other, Jessica smiling in spite of her sadness.

'Sweetheart, it should just be you and me now.'

Jessica straightened her back and took a deep breath, trying to be ready for whatever John was about to say.

'So, this is day one hundred and four onboard and this is the first time I'm actually recording anything in here. I'm sure you and the others do this, but I've been saying 'Hey everyone, I'm going to record my diary' and just sitting in here, alone, thinking about my day, thinking about you.'

Jessica's heart leapt as she imagined him.

'But, you know, May can be pretty insistent sometimes, so I thought I'd give it a try. What have I been doing in those times on my own in here? Thinking about you, thinking about us, wondering about the future, what will be happening one year from now? Is this something that is just going to fade away?'

'No,' Jessica whispered involuntarily. What was she doing? He couldn't hear her.

'I want you to know, Jessica, you know me and words...' He rubbed his hand over his mouth and chin. She remembered the light scratch of his stubble as he pressed his lips to hers.

'It's just, you've changed me, I feel like a completely different person when I'm around you, full of enthusiasm, full of life, full of love. I really hate being so restricted with you. You know what? I don't care that I'm on my way to Mars, I don't care that I'm going to be one of the first people to walk on Mars. When someone like me meets someone like you, all of this is pointless. You're the one Jessica, and I want you to know that.'

Jessica caught her breath and burst into tears. Seeing his face, hearing his voice, listening to those words. How had she not noticed it earlier? How could he be feeling all that, yet come out of that room and act normally around everyone? She tried to think back to times when he had seemed low. Was that when he had been recording a message like this?

John appeared to gather himself and simply said 'Ok, I'll record something better next time.' Jessica shook her head and smiled through the tears as John leaned forward to press the stop button. The screen faded to black then up again. John was sitting in exactly the same position, but the date at the bottom of the screen indicated that it was two days later.

'We were laughing so much today, sweetheart. We were filming a video for social media on the observation deck. You and Val and May were all dancing in zero gravity. You were singing, and bumping into each other, your hair was all wild. Even Val was getting in the swing of things. You were doubled over with laughter; you could barely catch your breath. It was so joyful. I love that you take almost everything seriously. But every now and then you take me by absolute surprise. When you laugh... I could just watch it forever.'

Jessica remembered that day. How her stomach had ached from laughing. How she had looked over at John wiping away tears of laughter. He always made her laugh, even when she was trying not to. He would wink at her or grin and wouldn't be able to help smiling. Though no one thought he was funnier than he himself did. She laughed to herself thinking about how he would giggle at his own jokes.

'I didn't think I could ever feel like this,' John continued. 'You know, I'm on the first human mission to Mars, and it's nothing in comparison to what's happening in my mind, in my heart with you. Jeez, I know that sounds sappy, sorry Jessica. It's what you've done to me.' He looked up from under his thick eyelashes and grinned sheepishly. 'There are probably millions of people on Earth who would swap positions with me right now. But I'm thinking of an ordinary couple, who have been working all day, and they're just getting home. No one knows who they are and they're sitting together now, drinking a beer, looking up at us. They're together, and no-one cares. How come they get to be together and we don't?' John's eyes looked glazed and he put his hand up to his face, with his thumb and forefinger pinching the bridge of his nose, his eyes screwed shut. He reached forward with his other hand to stop the recording.

The next video started, and this time it was John just talking about his day. Jessica closed her eyes. She wanted to imagine he was there in the room with her, sharing his day, unable to keep still as usual.

Another day. John in his NARESA sweatshirt; the one in a drawer in her apartment. The smell of him was fading, replaced over time by her own. But he had worn it, it had been against his skin, and it was the closest thing she had to him.

'I watched you step out onto the surface of Mars today, making history. You blow me away. I'm so proud of everything you've achieved, everything your mum would have wanted for you. And I feel proud that I might have played even a tiny part in that. Taking you to the observatory that night. It changed both our lives forever. I knew then, I knew you were someone special. I never told you this but I wanted to ask you out. But you know, Charlie... and I had to leave before I could pluck up the courage.'

'I'm sorry, John.' She whispered, her eyes closing again.

'It's ok,' he continued. 'We were both young then. I definitely wouldn't have been good enough for you then. I don't even think I am now, but I'm trying. And if something had happened between us then? Well, I would have been a distraction for you. You needed to focus to get where you are now. I can't regret anything. Our choices have brought us here, and even though we're not properly together in that way, I get to be with you every day.'

There was a pause and Jessica opened her eyes to see a new video on the screen. This John looked pale and drawn.

'Um, I'm not sure where to start. So, the Concordia re-entry vehicle crashed and our friends on board died. So yeah, that's pretty shit.' She listened to him try and process out loud the tragedy that had happened.

'We are up here, no idea if we are going to get home safely, or whether we're going die like our friends. Whatever it is that has gone wrong is probably going to be down to me to fix, so no pressure or anything.' He gave a wry smile. 'Oh, and I think I'm in love with my Commander. Wait, no that's wrong... I *know* I'm in love with my Commander.'

Jessica felt her heart skip at his words.

'I think she loves me back. I don't know, you'll have to ask her. I mean, we haven't done anything wrong. I don't really know what your rules are. Is declaring our love a violation? That's all it is. Ok, a kiss, there might have been a kiss. Just one. Well, one kissing incident, probably there were several kisses. I didn't count. But it was just one time. Will it happen again? I don't know. We've all got bigger things to worry about don't you think? Like whether we're going to live or die. So, you're gonna let us off that one, right?'

Jessica laughed at him.

'I'll look after her. That's the most important thing. I'll look after them all, of course: May, Val, Lucca. But she's it for me. So, believe me, it's in my interest to get her back safely. I'll look after you, Jessica.'

His words rang through her ears and surged through her body, numbing the pain that she felt.

Another video. This one was dated the night before John died.

'Tomorrow we fix the heat shield. You and me, Jessica. I just think we can do anything together, you and I. I told you recently that I was scared. Almost nothing scares me Jessica, but thinking that I couldn't protect you? That terrifies me. I know what to do, and I know I can do it. I just don't know if it's enough to get us home safely.'

'It was enough, John, you did everything right,' she said.

'But you know what?' he continued 'Any one of us can make that repair, you know that. We're all trained enough to do it. It's not complex. But you trusted me to do it. You said you'd trust me with your life, and that's what you are doing.'

Tears streamed down her face.

John spoke again. 'You know how much I worried about not deserving to be here. That I was only here because of my family name. I was a bit of a dick about it I know...' He laughed to himself. 'I struggled to believe in myself. But you did, Jessica. You believed in me. Hans told me how much you pushed for me to be on this mission.'

'I needed you there, John,' she told the screen.

'God, I love you for that. And you know what? If I can get the ship back safely, if I can fix it, I'll know then. If everyone gets back, I will have earned my place.'

'We did get back. You did it. It was because of you we got back. We all came back except you,' she sobbed.

'But you know me Jessica, I'm an optimist. I'm pretty sure it'll all be ok.' He smiled. 'Trust me.'

Epilogue
Ten years later

Jessica

The once damp and rusty walls of the Eden Observatory are now no longer open to the elements. They are covered with shelves of books dedicated to the study of space. Serious looking tomes on astrophysics, astronomy, and aeronautics are stacked side by side. The room is no longer cold, no longer smells of the air outside. Instead it is scented with the smell of paper and ink and book binding glue. Gentle spring sunshine shines through the glass skylight in the domed ceiling where a high-powered telescope once peered into the night sky.

The telescope donated by Elizabeth has been upgraded and moved out of the city observatory to a rural spot where there is no faint amber glow from urban lights. The top floor of the observatory is now a grand reading room with a high curved ceiling and polished wooden tables dotted with reading lamps.

On the floor below is another library room, this one more relaxed, with more shelves of books, comfortable chairs, and even a children's area for parents studying while raising young children. Tiny brightly coloured tables are covered in crayons and colouring pages of space scenes. A child-sized bookshelf contains books to keep children happy while their parents scan the larger bookshelves for titles that will help them write essays and dissertations.

Dozens of people are milling around the circular room, holding glasses of champagne. Administrators and academics from the University, the City Mayor, other UK space scientists, and of course Elizabeth Eden, frail now, but as mettlesome as ever. They are all here to celebrate the opening of the new library. Jessica smiles and presses hands with people keen to meet her. Ten years has done little to dim her celebrity, and has been insufficient for her to get used to it. It is warm and airless in the room and Jessica feels her chest tighten. Her eighteen-month spell of living in a hermetically sealed environment has left her with a craving for fresh air whenever possible. Even now she spends as much of her time outside as possible, tending her garden, or walking in the German forests. She wonders if she can slip out unnoticed.

The old stone steps that she had climbed with John remain unchanged as they curl around the walls. Jessica pushes her way out of the door into the watery spring sun and gulps down fresh air, her lungs expanding gratefully.

The sign in front of the building reads John Eden Library. It had been Elizabeth's idea, a fitting way, she said, to memorialise her grandson. He is a hero of their time. Children learn about John in science lessons. Space aficionados read his biography, authorised for release by his family. In death he has finally surpassed the fame of his father and grandmother.

In front of the new library is a small cherry tree. It is young, its trunk still narrow, delicate branches weighed down with rosy blooms. A light breeze lifts some of the petals from their stems, and they flutter down like confetti on to the white stone plaque nestled by the roots.

John Eden

23.08.2004 – 28.03.2039

"To some this may look like a sunset.
But it's a new dawn."
– Commander Chris Hadfield

It is ten years to the day since John died on the Harmonia. The grief no longer pulses through her but sits like a dull ache that she only notices when she is quiet and still, which is rarely. In the beginning, she thought about him every minute of every day. Now, there are days, weeks that go by without her thinking of him. She cannot talk to anyone, cannot ask anyone if this is normal. Not Lucca, who called her today from back home in Italy with his family, as he does every year on the anniversary of John's death. Nor May, back in Cologne, appointed as Flight Surgeon for NARESA's next generation of astronauts. Even if she wanted to, she cannot ask Valentina, who is currently on her second journey to Mars. They understand her grief at losing a crew member and her best friend. But they don't know that she lost her soulmate that day onboard the ship.

Sitting on the ground she traces John's name with her fingers as lightly as they traced the features of his face, hundreds of kilometres above the Earth.

John, she says his name in her head. *I hope I've made you proud. I hope I've done enough.*

She closes her eyes and sees his face, remembering the look he gave her when he thought she was being ridiculous. His brows furrowed, his eyes quizzical, then a shake of his head and a wide smile. She knows she didn't need to do anything for him. He loved her for who she was.

I didn't fly again John. I hope you're not disappointed. I just couldn't do it. But you helped me realise that there are more important things than that.

Tears fall down her cheeks, but they don't sting as they used to in the beginning. They are warm and laced with happy memories. She sits quietly for a few minutes

'Hey,' a hand touches her lightly on the back. She turns and smiles at the dark-haired man who has squatted down next to her. 'You ok?' His blue eyes gaze kindly into hers.

'I'm fine,' she says, and she means it.

'You want a hand up?'

'Please,' she reaches out her hand and he helps her to her feet. Jessica stands next to her husband Tom, solemnly staring down at the stone.

'That's a lovely quote,' he says. Did you choose it?'

'Yes, Elizabeth asked me to.' She frowned thoughtfully. 'You don't mind, do you?'

'Of course not. I know how much you loved him.' There was such an artless openness to his face that she knows he is genuine. She is grateful she doesn't need to hide her feelings from Tom anymore, that he understands.

He had been brave enough to have the conversation with her early in their relationship. He had told her that he had known, they had all known.

'Tom...' She wants to reassure him.

'You don't have to say anything. Not today.'

'I love you,' she tells him, and it is true. She hugs him tight and buries her face in his chest. He holds her and kisses the top of her head.

She feels protected in his arms. Tom, the man who guided her safely down to Earth, who was there for so many days during their mission, patiently supporting her in the background. Theirs is not the vivid, overwhelming love that she had for John. It is a steady and safe love. He makes her feel grounded and happy. Her grandmother died not long after she returned to Earth and for a while, she felt she had no one. Alone in a sea of strangers, months of touring, of interviews, of photographs with a fake smile. Tom saw through it all, and quietly stood beside her, until after a few years she realised how much she missed him in the moments he wasn't around.

'Give me one more minute?' she asks him.

'Of course, take as long as you need. I'll meet you inside.' He is respectful to the last.

She turns back to the memorial. A light breeze lifts more petals from the cherry tree and they settle on her shoulder.

You've changed me more than you will ever know, John. You saved me in so many ways, you really have . No-one can ever take away what we had. I'll never forget it. Jessica suspects she will be missed and must return inside. She enters the ground floor room. There are people in here too, mingling among the new books, families with children noisily playing in the colourful area near the window. She smiles reassuringly at Tom whose concerned eyes follow her as she moves around the room. A little girl with brown hair falling over her serious face is concentrating on a picture she is colouring. Jessica perches on a tiny seat next to her.

'What are you doing, sweetheart?' She asks gently.

'Colouring in some planets.' She answers solemnly. She has written her name in oversized letters at the bottom of the page, Rosana; Jessica's mother's name.

'This one is Mars,' the little girl explains patiently. 'You've been there haven't you Mama? What colour is it?'

'Hmmm,' Jessica selects an orange crayon. 'We call it the red planet but really it's a dark, dark orange. Try this one.'

'Can we come here every day Mama?' She asks, looking up from her colouring. 'They have biscuits.'

Jessica laughs. Her daughter has inherited her sweet tooth and will do anything for a biscuit.

'I'm afraid we can't, darling. We have to go back home soon.' Back to Cologne, to NARESA HQ where she now teaches other young astronaut trainees. 'And they won't have biscuits here all the time. Today is a very special day.'

The little girl continues with her picture, kicking her short legs under the table, unconcerned by travel details, as only four year olds can be.

A little boy, with his father's black hair and blue eyes, toddles over to Jessica and crawls into her lap clutching a book.

'You want me to read you a book, Teddy?' She lifts him onto her knee. 'Ok, what have we got here then?' She reads the familiar title with a lurch of her stomach. The Astronaut Who Stayed In Space. On the cover is a picture of a smiling man in a spacesuit, floating among golden stars in an indigo sky.

'That's your book Mama,' Rosana says matter of factly.

'You're right sweetie, it is.' She had written and published when Rosana was a baby. It was a book about discovery and loss; a book that she wrote for her daughter to encourage her to be curious and take risks.

Tom sits down to join his little family and Jessica opens the book to read to her son, though she doesn't need to read the words on the page to remember what they say. While still reading aloud her eyes lift from the page and drift through the window to the cherry blossom tree outside.

I'm ok, John. Trust me.

THE END